THE
APHRODITE

THE CLOAK OF APHRODITE

Kendal Grahame

This book is a work of fiction.
In real life, make sure you practise safe sex.

First published in 1994 by
Nexus
332 Ladbroke Grove
London W10 5AH

Copyright © Kendal Grahame 1994

Typeset by TW Typesetting, Plymouth, Devon
Printed and bound by
Cox & Wyman Ltd, Reading, Berks

ISBN 0 352 32954 8

THE CLOAK OF APHRODITE

CHAPTER ONE

Medea sat cross-legged on the rich, marble floor of the massive palace bedroom, savouring the coolness of the smooth stone against her naked buttocks, relaxing in the gentle morning breeze that wafted through the open portal near her bed. She drew her legs up within the embrace of her arms, pressing her thighs against her sumptuous breasts and resting her head on her knees, and gazed at the supine form of Jason, her lover and husband.

He lay on top of the silken sheets, his bronzed, naked flesh glistening with fresh sweat, deep in sleep, recovering from their night of passion. She licked her lips as she viewed his perfection; the smoothness of his skin, the firm, powerful muscles of his body, his handsome face framed by a dark, thinly-trimmed beard, and his long, thick manhood that rested, incongruously harmless and flaccid across his stomach.

She felt the familiar twinge between her legs as she gazed at his penis, remembering its wonderful size when aroused and the way it had penetrated and pleasured her over and over again during the previous hours.

They had made love many times during the long, Aegean nights aboard the *Argo* as they returned from her home at Colchis, bearing the legendary Golden Fleece in triumph. Many times the sounds of her orgasmic shrieks would echo across the stillness of the water, the only other sound being the incessant rhythm of the oars cutting through the sea as the brave Argonauts drove the mighty vessel home towards the shores of Iolcus. Such nights were the stuff of dreams!

The days too had been filled with arousal for the beautiful

1

young Queen, as she savoured the perfect nakedness of the powerful oarsmen rowing in sensuous unison, their straining bodies symphonies of muscular definition, their manhoods, not always entirely flaccid in her presence, promising future erotic pleasures.

King Pelias would not be able to refuse Jason his rightful place on the throne now and she would be Queen, able to command anyone she chose to soothe her newly awakened, but now near-insatiable, lust.

Medea rose from the floor and walked slowly around the large room, touching the opulence of the hanging drapes, marvelling in her ownership of such wondrous treasures. She pressed her nakedness against the heavy, silken curtain, drawing the material between her legs, possessing it like a lover. In truth, as a King's daughter she was used to wealth, but nothing to measure with the vast riches that were now, so very nearly within her grasp.

A large, black guard stood watching her, just as he had all night, apparently unmoved by her nudity in the same way as he had remained unaffected by the sight of her energetic couplings with her husband throughout the night. She walked over and stood in front of the huge man, staring straight into his eyes, willing him to respond to her beauty, knowing, with an almost perverse sense of satisfaction, that if he did she could order his immediate execution.

She breathed deeply, forcing out her large, firm breasts, the hardening nipples just touching the ebony flesh of his massive chest. No response. Undaunted, Medea smiled and licked her lips suggestively and ran the palm of her hand softly over his crotch, happily discovering that her attentions were, at last having some effect on this stone-faced slave.

Feeling his erection hardening quickly to her touch, she knelt before him and removed his phallus from within the simple loin-cloth which was his entire clothing, and rubbed the thick, black stem roughly, demanding reaction. She opened her mouth widely and took him inside, her tongue playfully circling the bulbous head, one hand rubbing the

2

gnarled stiffness steadily, the other cradling his heavy balls. She moved her head backwards and forwards, her long, flame-red hair brushing against his thighs as she suckled on the mighty organ like a baby at a breast, tasting his saltiness as his excitement became more and more distinct.

Without letting him fall from her mouth, she glanced up at his face, amused at his wide-eyed expression that seemed to assimilate both terror and lust, knowing that he was completely within her power. She bit into his hard, erect flesh, hearing him suppress a groan of pain, and gripped his scrotum cruelly, her wet lips still encircling the base of his penis. His hips began to move in response. She sucked harder, drawing in her cheeks to afford him the greatest pleasure of contact within her mouth, swallowing hard as though trying to devour him.

She looked again at his face, seeing that he was sweating profusely, his eyes closed. She should certainly have him killed for his impertinence!

Suddenly, there were sounds from behind her. She quickly pulled her hungry mouth from the large, throbbing stalk and looked fearfully at where Jason was beginning to stir from his sleep. She scurried over to his side as he slowly opened his eyes, his first vision of the morning being the face of his lovely wife; his second the superb, unsated erection of the slave.

Jason sat up, his face betraying a fearful anger.

'What is this? What do I find in my own bedroom?'

'He was in this way when I awoke,' lied the beautiful Medea, attempting to calm her husband with a gentle stroke of her hand to his brow, the palm still damp with the unfortunate slave's genital sweat. He has been watching your wondrous performance throughout the night, seeing how well you fucked me, and it has been too much for him.'

'But he is a slave, it is not permitted to even look at one so high and pure as the future Queen of Iolcus, let alone to lust for her!'

'Truly, my husband you are right,' said Medea, a mischievous grin beginning to play across her face, 'but I fear that *you* were the object of his desires!'

Jason jumped to his feet furiously.

'What?' he roared. 'He lusts after my backside rather than the divine beauty of my wife?' He stood in front of the trembling slave, glaring into his face. 'Is this true, slave? Speak!'

The guard shook violently, his eyes filled with terror, unable to utter a sound. Despite his panic, his erection remained solid and upright, the creams of his lust glistening at the end of the black phallus. Suddenly he uttered a deep, guttural moan of terror and he was lost, the sperm jetting from within his body, soaking the thighs and groin of his master. Jason's face became twisted in anger and he drew back his hand and slapped the slave ferociously across the head, sending him reeling to the floor. 'Guards! Guards!' he cried, kicking the prostrate figure squarely in the gut.

There were the sounds of clattering swords and rushing feet as a small group of soldiers rushed into the room from their posts at its door. Seeing the trembling figure on the floor and assuming an assassination attempt had been made, they grabbed hold of him and dragged him from the room before a cry of innocent protestation could be heard, much to Medea's relief.

'Take him away,' barked Jason, 'have him thrown into the deepest of the dungeons of Pelias for the pervert he is!'

The soldiers obeyed, collecting up the remnants of the unfortunate slave's clothing from the exquisite marble floor. Medea stood behind her husband, her arms wrapped around his fine physique, her hands stroking his groin sensuously, wiping the jism from his hard flesh.

'Ah, my husband,' she breathed. 'You are so powerful, so decisive!'

Jason turned to her, pressing himself firmly against her. She knew he would feel the wetness of her arousal, causing him no doubt to wonder at the apparent suddenness of her excitement. 'See how I respond to you, my love,' she sighed quickly, her arms slipping smoothly around his waist and her hands caressing his strong buttocks. 'See, I need you now!'

4

Jason stood back slightly from her, allowing his erection to rise between their naked bodies. Another servant took the place of the slave at the doorway, watching the movements of his mistress and master with advised impassiveness. Medea looked over her shoulder at him, then turned back to Jason, bending her body so that her face was level with his crotch, her legs purposely kept straight in order to afford the newcomer a view of the most perfect and luscious bottom in all of the Greek kingdoms.

She took Jason's firmness within her eager mouth, determined this time not to lose the fluids of love, the very cream of Eros himself. She sucked gently at her beloved pleaser, tasting her own scents on his skin, the memories of their wild bout of the previous night filling her mind with unbridled lust. She rubbed the lower part of his thick stem with both hands, her mouth only able to take half of his fearsome length before she choked on its joyous intrusion. His hips began to thrust involuntarily towards her face, in the same way the hapless slave had allowed himself to do just moments previously. She suckled harder, allowing one hand to wander round to his buttocks, tracing a line between them with her fingertips. As her delicate touch met the tight sphincter of his anus he groaned, and Medea tasted the sweetness of his juices as they filled her mouth, his hardness throbbing between her suckling lips. She swallowed quickly as he pumped more and more into her, relishing the taste of every drop, knowing that this was just the beginning.

Soon, he had no more to give and he drew back from her, his manhood drooping slightly, its lust sated for the moment. Medea kissed and licked around the wet flesh of his length, her fingers still probing at his bottom, her other hand caressing his fine thighs, tracing the outline of his powerful muscles.

After just a few minutes of this exquisite treatment his erection began to rise again, ready to give her the pleasure she so desperately needed. She stroked and licked at the monster until it stood proudly upwards, the veins prominent, the head purple with desire. Gripping him by his

5

stiffness, she led him back to the bed noticing, to her pleasure, that the watching slave now possessed a massive erection, peeking uncontrollably from the tiny loin-cloth around his slim hips. She promised herself that she would have sport with this one, maybe later. She would possibly even allow him the full pleasure of her temple of delights, before having him put to death.

She knelt on the bed, pressing her face against a pillow, her back arched, her bottom presented to her lover in a most erotic fashion. Jason wasted no time. He crouched between her heels, gazing in adoration at her perfect rear, the wetness of her waiting pussy and the invitation of the other puckered hole no doubt filling him with lust. She felt the warmth of his kiss against her anus, the dampness of his tongue sliding over the tight orifice, the probing of his thumbs as they parted the outer lips of her sex, his mouth suckling at them, ensuring her readiness.

Then he was standing at the edge of the bed, his hands resting on her bottom, his stiff erection pointing directly at the target of her cunt, ready to impale her.

'Take me, my husband,' she cried, with genuine passion and eagerness for what was about to happen. 'Fill me again with your monster cock; split my tiny sex open with your pounding thrusts!'

She felt Jason push into her. Despite his size her hot sheath accommodated the full length in one sensuous movement of their bodies. 'Oh, Jason, my love,' she cried, 'it is so big, and yet it slithers inside me like a wild eel!'

'It is the tight, wetness of your perfect cunt,' grunted her lover, his thrusts becoming faster and more urgent, 'that causes me so much pleasure; I must fill you at every opportunity!'

She felt him grip her buttocks firmly as he hammered into her, his groin slapping noisily against her bottom, sending tremors throughout her body. 'By all the Gods of Olympus,' she shouted, 'I am coming, I am coming!'

'Come then, my love,' Jason called out. 'Sate and release yourself upon my thrusting shaft!'

Medea squealed and raised her bottom slightly, stiffening her legs to afford him total access to her burning hole. She felt her juices flooding from her, easing his fierce penetration, the sensations of orgasm tearing at her very soul. 'Yes!' she cried. 'Yes! Do it as hard as you can! Fuck me! Fuck me! Fuck me!'

Jason obeyed willingly, his movements now ferocious in their intensity, his wife's buttocks rippling from the slapping of his thighs. The explosion of feeling between Medea's legs made her cry out in ecstatic pain, her teeth biting into her hand, drawing blood. Her lover roared with lust and she felt him expand within her ravaged sheath, the tip of his phallus prodding against the very entrance to her womb as he filled her with his seed. She arched her back and pushed her buttocks out further to meet the final pounding of his hips as he emptied himself within her body, the juices of Eros and Aphrodite mixing to seal their mutual bliss.

The two lovers lay, side by side across the silken sheets covering the bed, the coolness of the morning beginning to give way to the heat of the day, sweat glistening on their sated bodies. Medea's thoughts returned to more earthy things; they must meet that day with Pelias, the pretender King of Iolcus and Jason's uncle, and they must demand that he return the throne to her husband, as was promised before the search for the Fleece of Phrixus.

She rose from the bed and walked to a small table in the corner of the room and sat before a large mirror of pure silver framed in solid gold. She took up a comb carved from the shell of a giant oyster, and as she ran the blunted prongs through her long, fiery tresses, she marvelled at her own reflection, happy in the perfection of her beauty, and with the knowledge that her looks could capture and control someone as inordinately powerful as Jason.

She angled the mirror to reveal her entire body, the upward curve of her large breasts, the arrogantly upturned nipples, still erect from the effects of her lovemaking, her narrow waist, and the wide, receptive hips that seemed made to welcome a lover's thrusting thighs. She stood and turned sideways, smiling proudly as her gaze took in the sight of her large, firm buttocks and long, shapely legs. Once Queen, she would have any man she wanted; none would be able to refuse. Jason would continue to serve her, of course, but her needs far exceeded the strength of just one human being, and soon she would have the power to sate her salacious appetite in any way she chose.

Medea walked slowly from the room, enjoying the lustful gaze of the soldiers as their eyes feasted upon the sight of her nakedness. Her sex-lips were still conspicuously red and puffy from her recent adventure with her husband. She stood at the side of a large, square bath, sunken into the marble floor, and tested the temperature with her toe before stepping into the milk-white and heavily perfumed water. She relaxed in its warmth, closing her eyes and gently caressing herself between the legs as she planned the things that she would say to the King at their meeting.

Two beautiful, black slave-maidens stripped and joined their mistress in the bath, soaping their hands and using them to wash her all over, their expert fondling and fluttering fingers bringing her quickly back to the point of arousal. Jason joined her in the bath and two more young girls slipped into the sultry warmth with him. Their hands quickly roamed over his firm body, massaging and soaping him, concentrating more than Medea might have liked on the erection that quickly showed itself from beneath the murky water.

Jason seemed unperturbed by their actions. 'Pelias is a devious and evil man,' he said, ignoring the gentle rubbing of two soft hands on his penis. 'We must take care. He will not give up his kingdom lightly.'

'*Your* kingdom,' corrected Medea, relaxing again to the insistent probing of her maids' fingers at her pussy-lips. 'Don't forget that you were born to rule Iolcus. Remember also that he murdered your father, Aeson. You owe him nothing, save his death!'

'You must also remember that my father willed my obedience to Pelias; I had no choice in searching for the Fleece at his command, and nor will I be able to refuse any other tasks he chooses to impose upon me.'

Medea stretched out her leg under the water and pressed her toes against Jason's testicles, feeling the rhythmic caresses of the maids as they bathed his long phallus. 'I will charm the old man with my looks and sensuousness. He will be ours to command when I have aroused him.'

'Not so,' said Jason, laughing. Medea withdrew her foot angrily.

'You doubt that I could do it?'

'Not at all, if he were a fit man,' said Jason, standing, his erection jutting forward ridiculously as he stepped out of the bath, 'but word has it that he has lost his desire for sex; he has no need of such pleasures.'

'I don't believe it,' said Medea, climbing out of the perfumed warmth of the water, joining her husband at the side of the bath, and casually taking his penis gently in her hand. 'He was always notorious for his virility! Why, was it not he who impaled the thirty virgins of Daphne in just one night?' She rubbed firmly though nonchalantly at his stiff manhood, whilst Jason dried his upper body on warm linen provided by one of the hand-maidens.

'That was the work of a much younger and stronger man,' he said, happily responding to Medea's phallic stimulation. 'Now I doubt if he could raise it for Daphne herself!'

'If I cannot seduce him,' said his wife, 'then we must kill him, for I fear he will break his promise to hand over the throne!'

Jason closed his eyes and stiffened his buttocks under Medea's gentle touch. Realising his moment was near, she moved her hand quickly up and down his long staff, releasing his seed over the dense waters of the bath. He took a second to recover, then spoke, his breathing stilted from his efforts. 'I will not murder my uncle, whatever he has done.'

Medea broke from him angrily. 'Oh, you're pathetic,' she shouted. 'Sometimes I think you would prefer to spend your time on these mindless adventures, rather than rule the country that is rightfully yours!'

Jason just shrugged, proving her point. She stormed

from the room, grabbing some robes from a slave, returning almost immediately, throwing the clothing roughly to the floor, anger tearing at her expression.

'I tell you, Jason,' she yelled, in a piercing voice that echoed around the walls of the bathroom, 'if you go on another quest, you go without me!'

'So be it, my love,' said Jason, slipping a fine robe about his body. 'So be it.'

Medea looked furiously into his eyes, realising what was happening. 'You're planning something . . . you knew all along that he was going to send you off again . . . didn't you?'

Jason nodded, more in relief that his secret was out than in apology. 'Pelias will explain; come, we will be late.' He put on one of his sandals, but before he could reach for the other, Medea grabbed it and threw it through one of the windows. They heard it splash into the distant sea below.

'You cannot go before your King wearing just one sandal!' she cried, triumphantly. Jason grinned.

'If one sandal I have, then one sandal I shall wear! Now come, woman, your King awaits you!'

Medea followed her limping husband obediently, her mind filled with anger at both him and Pelias. She meant what she had said; if Jason was to embark on yet another journey she would set forth on her own odyssey, her own voyage of discovery, and discover wonders that her husband had not even imagined.

The throne-room of Pelias was a dim and sober place. The old King lay on a large couch, naked save for a ludicrously large crown perched on top of his balding head. He was surrounded by at least six beautiful young girls of many races, all naked like him, some caressing his wizened body half-heartedly, some resting from their unpleasant labours, their eyes glazed with boredom. He sat up as he saw Jason and Medea enter.

'Always one sandal!' he cried, pointing the finger of a claw-like hand in accusation. 'He always comes before me wearing just one sandal!'

10

Medea smiled to herself knowing, as did her husband, of the oracle's prophecy that Pelias would meet his successor and that he would be dressed in such a way. Jason was clearly taunting the old man, and she had unwittingly encouraged the joke by throwing his other sandal into the sea.

'Pelias, you know why I am here,' said Jason, his voice booming out across the cavernous room. 'I claim my rightful place to the throne of Iolcus!'

'Yes, yes,' said Pelias, struggling to sit erect, pushing to one side a lovely young blonde nymphet who had been desperately sucking on his unresponsive sex. 'All in good time. First, I need just one more service.'

'No more services, Pelias,' said Medea, haughtily. 'Jason has done enough in bringing you the Fleece.'

'What would you have me do?' said Jason, ignoring his wife's oration. Pelias smiled, a grin with more than a hint of evil.

'You do well to remember your father's wishes,' he said, glaring at the furious woman. 'However, the task I set before you is dangerous, and I wonder if you are quite the man for the job.'

Medea cast her eyes up to the heavens. Jason was surely not so stupid as to fall for this?

'I am more than able to tackle anything you ask of me, Pelias!' announced her stupid husband, his machismo offended. The King grinned.

'What do you see before you, Jason?' he said.

'I see an old man, naked amongst many lovely young girls, also undressed and eager to please their master.'

'Indeed, and you are right! But what you also see is the drooping, useless appendage that would at one time be readily and permanently upstanding, constantly servicing these young wenches until they could take no more!'

'Certainly, your reputation would have it that way,' said Jason, glancing at the pathetic gristle that hung limply from the King's bushy crotch.

'I have been struck by a mysterious malady; the desire is within me, but I cannot raise the strength. I desperately

11

long for my superb length to rise, to fill these virgins' eyes with terror and lust, but it is not to be!' The old man sat back, exhausted by his speech.

'What can I do?' said Jason, his eyes beginning to savour the delightful view of the surfeit of nakedness about him, his interest obvious to Medea from the movement at the front of his flowing robes.

'Travellers have told of a wondrous garment, a cloak that once graced the shoulders of Aphrodite herself, that has the power to rejuvenate a mortal's sexual prowess.'

'I have heard of such a garment,' said Medea, her eyes misting with memories of her past sorceries. 'It is truly a most powerful prize!'

'Indeed it is,' continued the King, stiffening his buttocks in a desperate attempt to coax his manhood into responding to the feather-light touch of two oriental girls of infinite beauty and innocence as they licked at his insensitive penis, 'and I hear that it now lies in the Temple at Paphos.'

'Your need is clear,' said Jason, 'and my quest is set before me.'

'My Lord,' called Medea, firmly, 'if, as it would appear my husband is willing to undertake this task on your behalf, may I ask a favour too?'

'Ask.'

'I wish to undertake a challenge of my own. I would like to arrange a great games to be held on Jason's return, in celebration of his acceptance of the throne of Iolcus. I, too will commission the building of a great ship, one with oars so well tooled that they can be operated by a crew of women, and I will embark upon an odyssey to the lands of Lesbos, Circe and Scylla to Rhodes and to Crete, to search for the greatest athletes in the known world, and to seek that ultimate athlete, the great Heracles himself!'

Jason and Pelias listened in silence to Medea's speech, the former looking to the King to refuse to support such a fantastic idea. The old man obviously saw things differently, his smile slowly becoming a broad grin as he saw a way to rid himself once and for all of the meddlesome witch as well as her handsome, but not too bright husband.

'You have my blessing for your quest,' he said, regally. 'I will arrange for the games to take place in three years' time, and will instruct my craftsmen-builders to erect a giant stadium for the event. If, however Jason fails to return with the Cloak of Aphrodite or, for that matter you, Medea, fail to deliver the mighty Heracles to the games, then the agreement ends and the kingdom remains mine.'

'But Heracles has chosen to exile himself on Crete,' complained Jason. 'He will not be easily persuaded to return.'

'Then your lovely wife must use all her powers of persuasion,' said the old man, leering suggestively at Medea. 'I am sure that she has it in her to succeed.'

Medea smiled in gratitude for the compliment and with the memory of Heracles' fine physique, the thought of seducing him into compliance thrilling her. 'I will do my best,' she said, meekly.

'Then those are my terms!' Pelias lay back, his crown falling ludicrously to one side on his head as he caught hold of the lithe body of an ebony-coloured waif and forced her face towards his groin.

Jason and Medea bowed in agreement, and turned to leave the throne-room.

Outside the palace, they stood for a moment as their eyes became accustomed to the strong sunlight after the gloominess of Pelias' abode. 'Your odyssey is doomed from the start,' said Jason, stroking Medea tenderly on the cheek. 'Heracles swore that he would never leave the shores of Crete following the death of his squire, Hylas, for which he blamed himself. He has sworn a sacred oath.'

Medea took hold of Jason's hand and put it over her breast, thrilling as his fingers cupped the large mound automatically. 'I shall tempt him, and if I fail I shall bewitch him. Either way he will return with me to Iolcus!'

'Tempt him?' said Jason, with some surprise. 'You would be unfaithful?'

Medea grinned and squeezed her husband's buttock gently. 'I have sworn no oath of fidelity, and I release you from yours, for the duration of our quests. Three years is a long time, and we are both slaves to the temptations of Eros.'

'If you are certain . . .' said Jason, clearly both shocked and delighted at his wife's attitude.

'I am certain,' she said, kissing him lightly on the cheek, 'although I still demand faith in your love. Your heart is mine, and mine alone!'

'Agreed,' said her husband, strongly.

They parted, Jason to seek the remaining Argonauts to persuade them to join him on his latest adventure, Medea to find her crew of strong, brave women to embark on an odyssey into certain danger.

Over the next weeks, the sounds of industry echoed throughout the city. Most of the inhabitants were employed in the building of the two great vessels that were to traverse the seas and encounter many adventures. The sons of the boat-builder Argus had been blessed with their late father's skills, and *Argo the Second* took shape quickly, as strong and as powerful as the magical ship that had taken Jason to Colchis.

Medea had meanwhile been fortunate to commission Ancaeus, a skilled craftsman who had been one of the pilots on the original *Argo* to build her vessel; smaller, faster than her husband's ship, but just as resilient to the vagaries of the God Poseidon.

Her search for a worthy crew was not so successful, however. The boat was nearing completion and she had only three women volunteers whom she felt she could trust on the arduous journey that lay ahead; Iole, a tall, alabaster-skinned beauty from the North and a virgin of just seventeen years, and the olive-skinned sisters Electra and Nana, who had shown their strength of character by killing their mother when they discovered her infidelity.

Medea was beginning to regret the rashness of her idea when she chanced to be visited by a small, hunchbacked old woman one evening as she toiled at the poorly-drawn charts given to her by her husband.

'I hear you are looking for a crew,' said the hag, her voice cracked with age.

Medea hardly looked up from her studies. 'What of it?' she said, rudely.

'I can help you. I have many followers who would serve you well.'

'You, old woman,' said Medea, incredulously, 'how would you know such a group?'

'I am Madeleine, Queen of the Island of Tipos.'

'The land of wanton women? But you cannot be; Madeleine is beautiful, young, she . . .'

Before Medea could complete her sentence the woman threw off her cloak, her action somehow causing a blinding flash, the room filling with white, sweetly scented smoke. Gradually, the mist cleared and Medea found herself looking into the eyes of the most devastatingly beautiful female she could have ever imagined, the lovely face enhanced by the most perfect of smiles. She stood, a good six feet in height, over two inches taller than Medea herself, her long, nut-brown hair cascading over her bare shoulders, her powerful but erotically feminine body swathed in black hide from her magnificent breasts to the level of her crotch, the garment short enough to reveal the sensuous curl of a wisp of pubic hair. Her long legs were wrapped in the cross straps of her sandals, the leather tied in rough knots at the tops of her thighs. The whole outfit, though clearly serviceable, was one of blatant eroticism, instilling in Medea thoughts of lust that she had not thought possible before.

'Do you believe me now?' said Madeleine, still smiling broadly.

'You are beautiful,' sighed Medea, lustfully, 'truly beautiful.'

'And so are you, Medea. I have watched you being fucked by that delightful husband of yours, and how I have envied you.'

'How did you watch us? How did I not know?'

'I have many skills; like you, Medea, I am a witch. Unlike you, my powers are increased and enhanced by sexual adventures. I can draw strength even from just hearing the cries of orgasmic lust.'

'Why have you come to Iolcus? Surely there is as much sex to be had on Tipos? It is fabled as a land of never-ending pleasure.'

15

'And so it was,' said Madeleine, sitting on a small chair
the slant of which caused her legs to open involuntarily,
revealing the pinkness of her sex to Medea's eager gaze,
'until it was attacked by a tribe of harridans escaping from
Lesbos, women of amazing strength who raped the wanton
women of Tipos in ways they did not enjoy, and killed all
the males on the island, thus making it a hell for us.'

'Why the disguise?'

'When the remaining women in my tribe escaped the
clutches of these evil ones we killed their Queen, and they
have vowed to search for us and take their revenge. So you
see, in joining you we will both be serving your cause and
escaping the terror that has dogged us for so long.'

'How many of you are there?'

'Forty, including myself. More than enough to crew
your vessel.'

'I already have three other volunteers.'

'I know,' said Madeleine, shifting in her seat, her legs
parting even more to enhance the view that was thrilling
Medea, 'Iole, Electra and Nana; strong, fine women.'

'You are well known for your insatiable sexual appe-
tites,' said Medea, trying not to stare at the obviously
dampening slit that was being flagrantly displayed before
her, 'and yet you say all the men of Tipos were killed. You
must be very frustrated.'

'We take solace in each other's tongues. Have you ever
tasted the sweetness of another woman's cunt?'

Madeleine sat back, raising and opening her legs wide,
dipping the fingers of one hand between her sex lips invit-
ingly.

'Never,' said Medea, nevertheless falling to her knees
obediently before the offered prize, her nostrils taking in
the musty, erotic scent as she moved her face nearer and
nearer to the open mouth of Madeleine's pussy.

'Taste me, Medea, taste my juices, my nectar, as you
would eat the ambrosia offered to you by Jason . . . and all
the others.' Medea stopped short and looked up at
Madeleine's lovely face, realising from her expression that
she must know of her many infidelities.

16

'How long have you been spying on me?' she said, the thought of being watched whilst indulging in sexual excess giving her much pleasure.

'Only a few nights, since the *Argo* returned from its great quest,' said Madeleine, pulling at the open lips of her sex in preparation for the yearned for touch of Medea's tongue, 'but already I have seen four, or is it five, fine erections other than that of your husband enter your wicked body!'

Medea smiled and turned back resignedly to the hairy softness so close to her mouth. She pushed out her long tongue nervously, the tip touching Madeleine's wet slit, and pushed it inside, like a small cock. The taste pleased and excited her and she pressed her mouth greedily against the wet sex-lips, sucking gently. There was a groan and her lover pushed her hips forward on the chair, taking more of her tongue inside her erotic warmth, her heels resting on Medea's back.

'Oh, Medea, your tongue is so long! Lick the top, where you know you would like to be suckled.' Medea obeyed, allowing the tip of her tongue to flick gently over the hard bud of Madeleine's clitoris. 'Oh, sweet Zeus, it flutters like the wings of an insect! I fear I will come and scream so loud your neighbours will think a murder has been committed here!'

Medea pulled her face reluctantly away from the sweet honeypot between Madeleine's legs. 'Let them think what they will,' she said, 'I want you to come!' With that she dived her head back to its soft cushion, her mouth quickly tasting again the delicious flavour of cunt, her tongue lapping swiftly over the bud, causing Madeleine to buck her hips upward as she approached her urgent release.

The scream that emitted from between Madeleine's clenched teeth was indeed deafening. For a moment, Medea thought her lover had died whilst in the throes of ecstasy and she drew her head away, only to have Madeleine clutch her hair roughly and ram her face back to her saturated mound. She licked again, this time allowing the flatness of her tongue to rasp heavily against the full length of her lover's wide open lips, drinking in more of the sweet nectar as Madeleine finally relaxed.

The Queen of Tipos lay back panting heavily, Medea still kneeling between her legs, kissing her pussy gently. Finally, Madeleine sat up, easing her lover's head from its heavenly pillow.

'And now, my love,' she said, tenderly holding Medea's face in her hands, 'now it is your turn.'

She stood up and, catching the hem of her leather garment in her hands pulled it swiftly over her head, revealing her body in all its splendour. She spread the hide on the cold floor and lay back on it, prone.

'Take off that fine robe and squat across my face, my darling, and I will give you the best sensation you have ever known.'

Medea did as instructed, anxious to experience the first-ever touch of a woman's tongue to her aching cunt. As she undressed, she gazed at the wondrous body of her lover, the long, long legs, the flatness of her stomach, the wet, matted hair between her thighs. Although flat on her back, Madeleine's breasts still pushed upwards, the nipples dark and erect, much longer than her own.

As ordered, she squatted over the beautiful woman's face, lowering her bottom slowly down until she felt the wet, lapping tongue of her lover fluttering sensuously over her pussy. She closed her eyes as the sensation of expert cunnilingus took hold of her, delivered in a way that only another woman understands. She began to sob with the sheer pleasure of the moment, her whole being captive to the incessantly probing and flicking tongue, her orgasm immediately near.

'Oh, dear Queen of Tipos, you are taking me over the edge already!' Madeleine replied by increasing the speed of the fluttering against Medea's clitoris, making her squeal with pleasure as she came.

Collapsing on Madeleine's soft body, Medea buried her head between the erotic embrace of her thighs, drinking in again the scent of sex. There was a slight draught as a breeze seemed to play across her bottom, but she ignored it, happy to rest on her exotic cushion, breathing deeply in sated bliss.

She felt a gentle prodding at the lips of her sex, and as she opened to the intrusion she realised that it was not, as she expected, Madeleine's fingers or tongue, but something far bigger, and very familiar. She raised her head up from the warmth of her lover's thighs and looked back over her shoulder, seeing to her delight the naked form of Jason behind her, feeling his wonderful length enter her easily.

'I came to tell you that my ship is ready, and that I will be leaving tomorrow at first light,' he said, pumping steadily into her. 'Then I saw your perfect bottom upturned and demanding attention and I felt that I must take it . . . a marvellous way to say our farewells, don't you agree?'

'Yes, my husband,' said Medea, turning back to face Madeleine's crotch, 'and when you have sated me, perhaps you will pleasure my dear new friend.'

'Indeed I will,' said Jason, his strokes becoming harder. 'In fact I feel her lapping hungrily at my balls now; I am certain that she will be more than willing!'

Medea climbed from on top of Madeleine and sat back to watch as Jason busily serviced the beautiful woman, this first shared infidelity somehow blessed by the mutual experience. She thrilled as she witnessed her husband's long stalk sliding effortlessly into the soaked sheath that she herself had prepared with her darting tongue, and decided to join them in their copulative embrace.

She squatted again over Madeleine's lovely face, her friend's tongue immediately lapping over the folds of her pussy, causing her to gasp with pleasure. She gripped Jason tightly, pressing her mouth to his, feeling the rhythm of his thrusts into the receptive cunt of their mutual lover beneath them.

'If the Gods permit me to spend eternity with them on Olympus,' she panted, 'then this is how I would wish to spend it!'

'Your friend has the hottest sheath I have ever plundered,' responded Jason, the pace of his movements increasing, 'the memory of this night will stay with me for the rest of my life!'

The three lovers enjoyed each other for most of the night, until Jason had to leave in order to prepare for departure. Madeleine reluctantly stood back and allowed the husband and wife to share their bodies for the last time, enviously watching their loving embrace before they parted, for years and, quite possibly, for ever.

CHAPTER TWO

Despite his exhausting sexual bout with Medea and Madeleine, Jason could not sleep, the promise of the second quest filling his mind with excitement. Paphos lay many miles to the South East of Iolcus, a journey of infinite danger, rarely attempted by any others than the most experienced sailors or avaricious of merchants.

It was, of course, the very prospect of adventure that thrilled him; he was easily bored, and the short time he had been home had already made him restless and more than willing to accept Pelias' challenge. Whilst he acknowledged that the throne of Iolcus belonged rightfully to him, the thought of ruling from a great palace filled him with despair and he wondered if, in truth, he would ever return to claim it as his right. Only the pleasures offered by the lovely Medea would persuade him, although they were indeed exquisite.

He sat, naked on a low bench in front of the fire, staring absently into the dying embers, one hand nonchalantly stroking his penis, still a little sore from the exertions of the night. Truly, the warrior Madeleine and his insatiable wife had given him a wondrous send-off! He thought again of Madeleine's superb breasts, far larger and firmer than any that had been pressed against his muscular torso before; of her full mouth, and the way her lips suckled on his iron-hard length as Medea paid oral homage to his anus. He felt himself stiffening, and shook his head as though to rid his mind of carnal thoughts, determined to concentrate on the quest ahead.

He closed his eyes and thought of Hera, the Goddess

21

who had guided him on his journey to Colchis. Would she serve him again?

The fire cracked, the sound causing him to snap his eyes open. The flames became higher, fierce and hot, burning the flesh of his legs, but he sat, transfixed. Gradually, the face of Hera appeared within the blaze, her eyes filled with compassion for her favourite mortal.

'I have been thinking of you, Jason,' she said, smiling.

'And I, you,' he said. 'Will you be with me on my journey to Paphos?'

'Alas, beloved mortal I cannot support this quest,' she said, sadly, 'for it is your intention to steal from a Goddess, a most ill-advised ambition. Aphrodite and I rarely agree on anything, and she will be furious if I help you to take her cloak. As it is, the future decrees that she and I will clash, and the result shall be a great war; I cannot tempt the Fates further.'

'Then I shall succeed alone,' said Jason, defiantly. 'But tell me, sweet Goddess, why have you come to me this night?'

'Whilst I cannot help you directly in your design,' Hera breathed, her voice filled with emotion, 'I can guide you safely to within one day's sailing from Paphos. This I will do if, with the help of your brave Argonauts, you perform a simple, and not unpleasurable task for me.'

'You must know, beloved Hera, that I would lay down my life for you.'

'That has been a temptation to me ever since I first enjoyed the sight of the perfection of your body, Jason, to bring your soul to Olympus and love you for eternity; but it is not to be. No, your future lies elsewhere.'

'What do you want of me, then?'

'I wish you to make a slight detour in your voyage, to call at the island of Lemnos, the inhabitants of which are in dire need of your help. I cannot say any more; your reception by the people of this wretched land will signify whether or not they are worthy of your succour.'

'The mystery excites me, Hera, I shall do your bidding.'

The image within the flames smiled, and began to fade.

22

'Thank you, Jason. And now, my sweet mortal, lie on your bed, and I will caress you into sleep.'

Jason obeyed, the lovely face of the Goddess disappearing into the embers. He lay back on his cot and immediately felt the gentle touch of Hera's fingertips across his naked skin, though he saw nothing. Her caresses were everywhere: over his brow, his firm jawline, his neck and chest. They followed down to his stomach and groin, at the same time tantalisingly wafting along his legs like a dozen pairs of soothing hands, eventually meeting together at his now erect penis, drawing it upwards from his body, until he felt the unmistakeable sensation of wetness as an invisible mouth seemed to close over the thick, bulbous end. The unseen fingertips playfully danced over his hardened flesh, tickling, stimulating and arousing.

The ghostly massage continued with delicate urgency, his cock thickening and lengthening to incredible hardness, the perceived touch of many nymphets coaxing him to early orgasm. He groaned and stiffened his buttocks, the soft wetness of the invisible mouth drawing his fluids from deep within his body until, with a massive gasp of relief his seed was released, vanishing down the magical throat of his unearthly lover.

Jason slept well for the next two hours, until awakened by the sounds of activity outside his room. He felt strangely refreshed, despite the short duration of his slumber and leapt from his bed, eager to begin his new adventure.

He flung open the door, to be met by the sight of an old man and a divinely lovely girl of barely eighteen years of age, both dressed in the long, dusty cloaks of travellers.

'Who are you?' he demanded, totally oblivious of the fact that he stood naked before these two strangers.

'I am Creon, of Corinth,' said the old man. 'I have heard of your impending voyage, and wish to ask a great favour. Your King, Pelias suggested that you may be willing to help me.'

Jason stepped back and bade them enter, noticing for the first time the way the young girl's eyes seemed transfixed by the sight of his drooping manhood. He made no attempt to cover his nakedness, considerably enjoying her obvious interest.

He stood before the now cool hearth and indicated that they should sit on the bench before him. 'What is this favour, so important that it brings you to my door at the crack of dawn?'

'We came here so early to be sure of catching you before you set off.' The old man looked tired, and greatly troubled. 'The favour I ask is simple; I wish you to allow my daughter, Glaucis, to travel with you as far as Icaria, where she is to meet her future husband.'

Jason shook his head. The girl was truly lovely, as delicate a virgin flower as anything he could have desired, but the idea was ridiculous. 'I'm sorry,' he said, 'but it is impossible. Only one woman sails with the Argonauts, Atalanta of Calydon, and she is a great hunter and warrior. Your daughter is too frail, too gentle; the only thing she has in common with Atalanta is probably her virginity!'

Glaucis raised her head, angrily. 'It is true, sir, that I am a virgin,' she said, haughtily, 'that I have never tasted the scent of a man or felt him penetrate my young body; but what of it? I am a skilled map-reader and seer; you may find my worth invaluable.'

'You know the charts of the Aegean Sea?' said Jason, his objections failing steadily the longer he looked into the bright, blue eyes of the fair-haired maiden.

'Intimately,' said Glaucis, her eyes fixed on his.

'Then you will take her?' said Creon, a little too anxiously.

'I will take her,' said Jason, holding out his hand. The old man stood and shook it vigorously.

'You will not be sorry,' he said. 'She has been a good daughter to me, and now she is to become a woman. I thank you, sir!' Something deep inside Jason was telling him to be cautious, to be wary of the old man's apparent delight in handing over the trust of his daughter to a stranger who was about to embark on a long and dangerous journey, but he was already falling under the spell of her innocence.

24

Jason led her father to the door. 'Your daughter will remain with me now, and I will let her see what charts I have. She will be in safe hands.' Creon smiled, somewhat knowingly and left.

Jason closed the door and turned to Glaucis, who had removed her cloak and stood before him wearing a short robe of thin, white material, which did little to conceal her small, almost boyish charms. She was, indeed a most beautiful child, and Jason felt he must don a loin-cloth quickly before his appreciation of her innocent sexuality became too obvious.

'So, you are a virgin,' he said, wrapping the material around his waist. 'How do you feel about the notion that you will be spending days, weeks, even months at sea with fifty lusty sailors, all keen to impale you at any moment?'

'Sir, I have held myself pure these seventeen years, I will give the pleasures of what lies between my legs to none other than the one I love.' She looked down at his groin. Jason followed her gaze, noticing that his hardening penis was protruding from the inadequate covering of cloth. 'I will, however, give some form of relief, should the strain become too much.'

The words were softly spoken, the sensuousness of her tone erotic in the extreme. Jason felt himself hardening fully, her gaze unmoved by the sight. 'In what way will you provide this relief?' he said, his voice a little shaky.

Glaucis said nothing, but dropped to her knees in front of him, taking hold of his thick stalk in one of her tiny hands. It looked huge within her grasp, the fingers unable to meet around its swollen girth. She moved her hand up and down the full length gently, drawing the loose skin back and forth expertly. 'I was shown how to do this by a very wise woman in Corinth,' she said, now using both hands to pump his already throbbing phallus, her face inches away from the end. 'She taught me that if I did this well enough, men would allow me to keep the treasure of virginity as long as it suited me.'

Her erotic caress was heavenly, comparable only to the sensational release given to him by Hera, just hours previously. He pushed his hips forward, anxious to allow the

25

thick, pouted lips of her tiny mouth to swallow him but she backed away, increasing the pace of her stimulation at just the correct rate until, with a muted roar, he came, his fluids spurting forth past the young girl's shoulder, to land on the floor behind.

Once she was sure that he had no more to give, Glaucis released her grip of his drooping penis and stood, smiling sweetly with an innocuous innocence that he found irresistible. He bent his head and kissed her lightly on the brow. 'I do not think you will have any problems, Glaucis, although I fear that your skills will be much in demand.'

'Thank you, my Lord,' she said, humbly. 'And now, may I view the charts?'

Argo the Second ploughed slowly through the warm Mediterranean waters, heading towards the first night of the journey. All but three of the original Argonauts who had returned with the fleece had volunteered to join Jason on his latest quest, along with four newcomers; strong, young men from the boat-yards of Argus, who had tired of watching the results of their labours sail away to great adventures, and who now sought to fulfil ambitions and fantasies themselves.

There had been some rumblings, some dissension amongst the crew when Jason had introduced Glaucis, but Atalanta had taken her under her wing, threatening a firm and well-aimed kick to the genitals of any who dared to interfere with their delicate passenger. The men respected and feared Atalanta, famously still a virgin despite being nearly thirty years of age and of amazonian beauty, and many desired to be the one to deflower her.

Some had tried, of course, but all had failed. She would offer herself as a prize to any who could beat her in a race, but none could come even close to matching her fleetness of foot. Defeated, some expounded that she held the desires preferred by the women of Lesbos, though none would say such a thing to her face.

The first day of the journey was singularly uneventful, the familiar landmarks around Iolcus gradually slipping away

26

into the distance as the great vessel headed into the un-known. Jason and Glaucis spent the day poring over the inadequate charts and talking of adventure, both past and present. At times, he became concerned that he was falling deeper and deeper under the spell of the young virgin, her fresh innocence intoxicating him, the desire to possess her flesh growing stronger with each hour.

The darkness of night came quickly and still they la-boured, Jason concentrating all the harder in an attempt to avoid looking into the sweet face of Glaucis, for fear that his lust would take over his reason, and he would split her hymen there and then with his almost permanently erect phallus.

Glaucis recognised his torment as the moon rose and they were about to part in order to rest. Once more she drew his seed from him with her gentle and erotic caress, this time, to his great joy, kissing his spent manhood, just once and very lightly, as though in promise of things to come.

The morning came and with it a silence. The wind had dropped completely, and there were no sea-birds to be seen or heard. A slight mist hung over the glass-like water as the *Argo* cut its swathe through the shimmering surface, adding to the uneasy atmosphere.

Jason was looking out to sea from the prow; Glaucis stood at the stern of the vessel, feasting her eyes on the rows of naked male-flesh as they strained at their oars.

Atalanta joined him at his look-out point. 'She is very beautiful, Jason,' she said, resting her hands on the rail and peering out to sea.

He turned and looked at the amazon woman, resplen-dent in her nakedness, save for a thick strip of tough hide which crossed her body from shoulder to waist, dividing her magnificent breasts, their thrust high, as though in greeting to her leader.

'She may be young, innocent and a virgin,' the powerful woman continued, 'but she is very wise. Listen to her coun-cil, Jason, but beware her wiles. She may want you for herself.'

'She is betrothed to one of Icaria,' said Jason, almost wistfully. 'You can have no fear of her turning my head.'

'It is not your head I worry about,' said Atalanta, reaching forward and gripping his long penis. 'Your needs are those of any man, perhaps even stronger.'

Jason grinned, the memories of the wondrous touch of Glaucis' small hand causing him to stiffen slightly in her grasp. Atalanta breathed harder, rubbing him firmly.

'Race with me, Jason,' she said, her thumb sliding over the damp end of his rising erection. 'I may let you win!'

'Perhaps one day,' he said, tugging her hand reluctantly from his cock. 'But remember, if I take the tissue of your maidenhead there will be a queue of lusty sailors ready to follow, and you will be powerless to resist!'

Atalanta smiled and walked away, Jason savouring the sight of her firm, gently-curved buttocks that moved provocatively with her gait.

'Perhaps, one day,' he thought.

A cry from atop the solitary mast broke his fantasy. 'Ship! I see a ship!' Jason peered into the mist, his eyes at last detecting the shape of a vessel ahead of them. They closed in, rapidly, throwing restraining ropes onto the decks, a small boarding party climbing onto the large wooden hulk.

It was a merchant ship of a type commonly seen around the shores of Greece, but its wood was rotten, the paint long faded, the sails tattered. There was no sign of life.

Jason clambered aboard the vessel to be met by Castor, who had led the boarding party. 'It's a dead ship, Jason,' he said, 'long deserted.'

Jason looked around, a sense of foreboding annoyingly playing across his mind. 'There is something here,' he said. 'I feel it.'

'But there is nothing,' protested Castor. 'The ropes are rotted to dust. There will be no prize within this hulk.'

'Search below!' commanded Jason, 'and do not return to the *Argo* until you have combed every part of the vessel.' He grabbed hold of a rope and swung himself back to his ship, joining Glaucis at the stern.

'I feel it too,' she said. 'There is something aboard that vessel.'

They waited for nearly an hour until Castor suddenly appeared, white faced at the railing of the hulk. 'Jason!' he called, 'Jason, you were right. You'd better come aboard!'

Once again he climbed up onto the rotting deck, to be led by Castor down into the bowels of the ship, the stench unbearable. They joined the other members of the boarding-party, who were standing by a large cage. Expecting to be greeted with the sight of a fearsome beast, Jason braced himself and pushed through the men, peering into the darkness through the stout, rusting bars of the prison. His eyes slowly opened in surprise.

Standing, seemingly terrified at the back of the cage was a woman, naked save for a thick-linked chain around her neck and another around her waist. Her long, black hair was caked in dirt, as was her face, nonetheless lovely for that. Her large eyes blazed widely, the pupils remarkably piercing in their intensity, fixing on Jason as though recognising his leadership.

He looked at her for a moment, feeling himself becoming drained under the ferocity of her stare, but assuming that the dreadful smell of the decaying room was causing him to feel faint. He broke her gaze, and walked quickly out into the sunlight. He ordered the men to release the woman, clean her up and bring her to him.

Waiting in the relative safety of his cabin, Jason pondered over the fate of his guest. How had she survived for so long? What had she eaten? Why had the crew of the merchant vessel abandoned her to a slow, agonising death of starvation?

There was a knock at the door and Glaucis entered, holding the hand of the woman who timidly followed her into the room. She was dressed now in a simple robe around her waist, her firm breasts bare, the two chains still intact.

'We could not break the links,' said Glaucis, 'they are made of a material strange to us.'

29

'No matter,' said Jason, helping the woman to a seat opposite his. Glaucis sat next to him, holding on to his arm a little nervously. The woman stared at her, and Jason noticed that Glaucis seemed to be uncomfortably held in her gaze, as though being hypnotised. The stranger's eyes certainly had incredible depth, their colour almost amber, cat-like in their shape.

Glaucis suddenly stood up. 'I must go,' she said, hurrying to the door, 'you will probably be able to discover more about our guest if I leave you alone.' She left the room rapidly, the woman watching until the door was firmly closed behind her, before she turned back to Jason.

'Thank you for freeing me,' she said. Jason eyed her suspiciously. There was no smile, no warmth in her gratitude and yet, somehow, her very coldness generated a feeling of intense sexual desire within him that he couldn't control.

'What are you called, and why were you caged so?'

The woman relaxed back on the chair, her large breasts rocking gently with her movement. 'I am Syphis, of Tanea. I was taken prisoner by the evil pirates who had stolen the vessel, to be used by them as their will commanded. They abused me for many weeks until, thank Zeus, they were taken by a poisonous malady which drove them all mad, and they all cast themselves into the sea, to drown in agony.

'I have waited in these chains since, eating the flesh of rats and drinking their blood. It has been many weeks since my body bathed in the warmth of the sun, hence my strange pallor.'

Jason regarded her, curiously. Her colouring was certainly unusual, a slight tinge of green seemed to mix with the whiteness of her flawless skin. He looked again at her unsmiling face, and into her eyes. He felt a stirring in his loins, his penis stiffening as though it had a mind of its own. 'You are very beautiful, Syphis,' he said, his voice faltering under the hypnotic power of her stare.

She knelt before him, reaching under his loin-cloth with her hand and clasping his thickening erection. 'Let me

30

show my gratitude to you for rescuing me,' she said, gently rubbing the stem up and down.

'There is no need,' he said, although he dearly wanted her to continue. 'You have been abused so much by others, you surely can't want . . .'

'I *do* want, Jason,' said Syphis, kissing the end of his stalk tenderly. 'I want to be loved, not raped.'

'But someone may enter,' he said, lying back and relaxing under her expert touch.

'Nobody will enter,' she said firmly, and he knew, somehow, that it was so.

Syphis stood up and tore off the material that shrouded her lower body, revealing herself naked again to his lecherous eyes. The chains around her neck and waist seemed to add to her erotic availability and Jason caught hold of them, dragging her to him in order to force her mouth against his. Her thin tongue darted around his mouth, searching, tasting as it played against his, her hands tugging away his loin-cloth and grabbing again at his erection.

They fell onto the bed, Syphis squirming like an eel over his body until her wet pussy was pressed against his face, and her tongue began to lick around the bush of hair between his legs. Jason parted the sweet-smelling, hairless lips with his fingers and suckled hungrily at the flesh of her warm cunt, driving his tongue inside her as far as it would go. She wriggled herself against him, rubbing the bud of her clitoris against the hardness of his chin as he drank from her heavenly chalice, the wetness soaking his face.

Syphis raised her head from his groin and started to moan, a long, guttural cry that seemed to come from the ether around them, rather than her throat. She sat down firmly on his face, her sex-lips smothering his mouth, his nose buried inside the cleft of her buttocks. He began to worry that she would stop him breathing, the powerful grip of her thighs about his head being far more than he could fight, but suddenly she squealed loudly as she reached the pinnacle of her orgasm and raised herself slightly, allowing him to gasp gratefully for air.

He thought she would climb from him, her lust temporarily

31

sated, but instead she lowered her cunt back to his mouth, her movements clearly indicating that she wanted more. This time, however, he felt her close her mouth around his aching erection, swallowing him down the back of her throat, taking the full length so that her lips pressed wetly against his bushy pubic mound, one hand cupping his heavy scrotum, the other playfully fingering between his buttocks.

The sensation of being taken so completely inside a woman's mouth nearly caused him to come there and then, but he managed to control himself, albeit with extreme difficulty. He concentrated his attention once more on licking her sweet outer lips, running his tongue around and between them, up to her tiny, puckered anus then back along the wet, open slit to her engorged clitoris, drawing it gently between his teeth whilst flicking at it with the tip of his tongue. All the time, she suckled at his stiffness, drawing it in and out of her accommodating mouth, hardly seeming to take a breath.

He began to wonder how many of her captors had experienced the pleasures she was now giving him, and whether they had been able to stop themselves from sending their juices down the tight, wet sheath of her throat. The flesh of her mouth seemed to undulate, her tongue, despite his size and incredible hardness, able to play round and round his thick stem, sending ecstatic signals to his brain as he continued to eat hungrily at her softness, her wetness soaking his face and hair.

He felt her release his penis from within the warmth of her mouth and she sat up straight, squatting slightly on her heels with her bottom pressed firmly against his face. He parted her buttocks with his thumbs and licked wetly along the crack, pausing occasionally to attempt to probe the tip of his tongue inside the tight sphincter, feeling her shiver in response when he did so. He reached round to caress her sex but found she held her own hand there as she fingered herself, and decided to allow her to continue her self-satisfaction, returning again to the delightful task of analingus.

She began to grind her bottom against his face in the way that she had done before when nearing orgasm, her breathing becoming heavy and stilted, her buttocks shaking as she rubbed furiously at her mound. Once again the cabin was filled with the long, strange cry and then the final shriek of passion as she came, her juices flowing anew to soak his chin and neck as he pushed his tongue over an inch inside her tight arsehole.

After a moment, Syphis climbed from her lover and sat back on the chair, recovering, her legs wide open, the prominent lips of her delightfully hairless cunt looking more inviting than ever. Jason gazed at it, his need strong. Still unsmiling, she climbed back onto the bed and squatted over his groin, taking his stiffness in her hands and directing the swollen head to its target. She allowed just the end inside her, gripping him tightly with her vaginal muscles, her eyes once more capturing his in a fixed stare.

Jason felt his penis throb and knew that some of his juices had entered her. He began to push upwards, the extra lubrication making it difficult for her to resist entry despite her vice-like grip of his stalk within her sheath, and gradually he eased the full length deep inside her, their mounds pressed together in total unison.

Syphis sat motionless and impassive, impaled on the huge stalk, waiting for him to make the next move. Jason wasn't going to disappoint her. He gripped her buttocks firmly and raised her up so that just the tip of his phallus lay within her, then pulled her resolutely down onto his crotch, her buttocks slapping against his thighs as he drove his staff deep into her body again. He repeated the action, willing her to respond, but she just hung above him for a moment then fell down onto his mighty tool, absorbing him within her tightness without her expression changing in the slightest.

He rammed her quickly up and down onto his lap, using her body as he might his own hand, her large breasts bouncing steadily in time to his rhythm. He found her lack of response most disconcerting.

He pulled her from him, his manhood flopping noisily onto his stomach and threw her onto her back, diving between her legs and thrusting his stabbing spear back into

33

her hot sheath. He licked at her neck and ear, pawing at her breasts and pumping into her with an amazing ferocity, the point of their unison making obscene, wet sounds. Syphis lay still, her arms resting by her sides, her eyes staring at the ceiling.

Furiously, Jason pulled from her again and turned her over onto her stomach, pulling at her thighs and pushing her knees under her so that her bottom was presented to him. She had enjoyed it when he had used his tongue in her tight, little hole; perhaps this was the secret of her arousal.

He wet his finger liberally with the copious juices flowing from her sex and deftly inserted it into her anus, moving it round and round to ease the tightness. She moaned slightly, as welcome a sound to his ears at that moment as the playing of Orpheus on his lyre. He pushed a second finger delicately inside her, feeling the muscles of the sphincter relax to his incessant probing, meanwhile using his other hand to wet the massive length of his sex with more of her juices.

Slowly, he removed his fingers and pressed the thick head of his erection to her hole, parting her buttocks with his thumbs, opening the sweet sphincter in preparation for his ultimate intrusion. At first her body resisted his attempts at this unconventional entry, then the muscles seemed to suddenly relax as though giving way to the inevitable, and he slid inside, deep within her, hearing her groan with obvious pleasure.

Jason began to thrust in and out of her steadily, her bottom accepting more of his superb length with each intrusion. At last, his pubic mound pressed against her buttocks, he held himself still, fully inside her, cupping her pendulous breasts, squeezing her erect nipples between his fingers.

'Oh, my Lord, you have discovered the way to please me best,' she cried, 'hammer into me with whatever force you desire. My body is yours to ravage as you choose.'

He pumped in and out of her triumphantly, the tightness causing him a little pain, but her cries of arousal more than compensating for his minor discomfort. 'Yes, oh yes,' she sobbed, 'your wonderful cock feels so large inside my tight hole! You are making me come . . . join me in this wonderful release, fill me with your cream!'

The tightness of her anus relaxed completely, and Jason was able to thrust wildly into her, his fine manhood stretching to an even greater size as he neared orgasm. He heard her begin the now familiar moans of her climax and fucked her even harder, closing his eyes and gritting his teeth as the jism shot from his lust-racked body deep into her bowel, her cries of ecstasy echoing around the entire ship.

They relaxed, recovering from their shared release, Syphis gently washing Jason's flaccid manhood with a lightly-soaped cloth. He felt himself responding to her delicate touch, wondering if he had the strength for more when she bent down and kissed him lightly on the tip of his rising stalk and, looking into his eyes and smiling for the first time since they had met, she spoke.

'There is one more pleasure I have to offer you, Jason, one more experience that is so beautiful you will wish the feelings to be your last.'

She bent down again, taking hold of his stiffening erection in her soft hand, and took it once more into her mouth. Jason watched her at work for a moment, then lay back his head and closed his eyes, to savour the sensations.

He felt her sucking gently on his now rigid prick, her tongue lapping greedily round and round the stem. Incredibly, it felt as though her tongue had circled his member three, maybe four times, the excitement created by her oral expertise being so acute. He felt her draw back her head, until his penis left the warm wetness of her mouth, but *her tongue remained circled around it!* Jason sat bolt upright, looking down in wonder at the sight that met his eyes. Syphis looked up at him, her eyes fully amber in colour and slitted like those of a snake, her tongue thinly wrapping itself many times around his erection, the tip slithering under his buttocks and into his anus. He was

35

at once horrified and wildly aroused, the sensations he was feeling totally indescribable.

There was a loud hammering at the door. 'Jason, Jason!' It was the voice of Glaucis, sobbing in panic. 'Jason,' she shouted, 'you are in danger! I know who Syphis is! She is evil, you must escape!'

Jason looked back at the woman who restrained him so vulnerably. He tried to pull away, but the grip of the rasping tongue held him firmly. Syphis pulled her head back slightly, drawing her tongue from within his anus, grinning in uncontrollable madness as it snaked over his stomach, then his chest towards his neck, whilst still encircling his now drooping manhood, holding him powerless.

The ever-growing appendage curved relentlessly around his throat, and began to tighten its grip. Jason tugged in terror at the demonic extremity, but the more he struggled the tighter she squeezed his genitals and neck. He roared in pain, kicking out with his feet, but to no avail.

There was a resounding crash as the door burst open under the combined strength of two of the Argonauts. Glaucis dashed in and, without a moment's hesitation raised a dagger and sliced the writhing tongue from the demon's mouth. Syphis fell back, screaming in agony, the detached flesh quickly withering and falling back from Jason's body. Two hard but well-aimed thrusts from the swords of the crew-members finished the job of sending Syphis back to Hades, her broken body quickly dragged from the cabin and thrown into the water as food for the creatures of the sea.

Jason sat on his blood-soaked bed, his expression one of total bemusement. 'How did you know?' he asked of Glaucis, who was endeavouring to clean up the cabin.

'I knew something was wrong when she forced me to leave you alone, with nothing more than a look from those evil eyes. Castor and I returned to the hulk and, after much searching we found the remains of human flesh near her cage. She must have seduced and killed the entire crew, one by one, and eaten them in order to stay alive. They knew her power, that's why they caged and chained her, but she had a greater strength than iron bars, the ability to arouse human lust!

'Castor and I returned to the *Argo*, hopefully in time to stop her evil, but when we heard your cries of orgasm we felt that we had been too late. Thanks to Zeus and Hera, we were not.'

Jason cradled Glaucis' head in his hands, his body still trembling from his experiences. 'Thanks to *you*, Glaucis,' he said, softly. 'I have been remarkably stupid and we have only just entered the second day of our journey. I nearly paid for my idiocy with my life. You have already proven your worth, and I shall be grateful through all eternity. From now on, I will seek and be guided by your council, as my personal oracle.'

'My Lord, Jason, I will serve you in any way I can,' she said, her eyes betraying more emotion than pure respect.

He rose from the bed and grabbed a cloth to girdle his bruised lower body. 'Now, I must wash, then convince my Argonauts that they have a leader worthy of their deference, for I feel I may have fallen somewhat in their esteem, succumbing as I did to such simple trickery!' He walked out into the brightening sunlight, feeling sated, shaky and more than a little foolish.

CHAPTER THREE

Medea awoke slowly from her short sleep, the coolness of the morning breeze playing gently across her nakedness. She felt the weight of Madeleine's head resting on her groin and remembered affectionately how she had drifted off into unconsciousness as her new lover's tongue had soothingly licked at the ravaged lips of her pussy.

She stroked the sleeping woman's hair lovingly, running her hand down, across the smooth, tanned skin of her back, her fingers touching the firm, sumptuous globes of her bottom and between, the tips lightly caressing the tight sphincter of her anus.

Madeleine stirred and raised her head wearily, focusing slowly on the beauty of Medea's countenance. 'Good morning, my love,' she said, dryly, 'how do you feel?'

'Very, very good,' said Medea, still fondling Madeleine's bottom, 'you are truly a wondrous lover, and your tongue is like a wild serpent, tasting and exploring every part of my cunt.'

Madeleine smiled and licked her lips. 'I will take a glass of water, to ease my parched throat, then I will lick you again, until you flood my mouth with your sweet come.'

Medea shook her head, pulling herself up from the floor. 'No, my treasure, we must hurry to the shore. Our vessel is ready for naming, and to receive the blessings of Poseidon.'

'Very well,' said Madeleine, her disappointment obvious, 'but afterwards, perhaps . . .'

'Then,' said Medea, laughing, 'you must take me to meet the Women of Tipos, the wanton, prick-denied harlots who are to steer our vessel to Crete!'

38

'You will not find them so denied,' grinned the beautiful Madeleine, dressing herself in her hide bodice and drawing up the long, leather straps of her sandals. 'They and the Argonauts will have entertained each other, much as we did throughout the night. I fear, therefore, knowing the insatiable nature of Tipos women that Jason will be finding his crew are not so ready to pull on the heavy oars for some hours!'

Medea laughed, pulling a short robe of translucent, white silk over her superb body, happy in the knowledge that her charms would be fully and erotically displayed to the many, lusty sailors she would meet on her way to the shore.

She also worried that her concupiscent desires would become too great on the long quest and wondered if perhaps the choice of an all-female crew had been wise.

She mused that Jason too had only the company of his own sex on his journey, save for the virgin Glaucis who was, in any event, betrothed and thus unavailable to him, and the amazon Atalanta, who would never allow her hymen to be split by any mere mortal. She knew that he too would suffer from the same yearnings of deprivation, and somehow this feeling of shared denial made her more at ease.

She squatted over a small pot in the corner of the room and began to pee, her back turned to her friend. Almost immediately and to her great delight she felt Madeleine's hand slip between her legs and cup her sex, her flow running noisily through the playful fingers as they fluttered against her labia, pulling and prodding at the soaked lips. She sighed with the pleasure of this new sensation, resting her head back against the other woman's shoulder.

'Ah, sweet Medea,' said Madeleine, her fingers now rubbing with a circular motion as the flow of urine became a trickle, 'I will teach you so many things on our journey. We will have much to occupy ourselves with during the long, cool Aegean nights!'

'We must go to the docks,' insisted Medea with a sudden surge of resolve, firmly, albeit reluctantly pulling the wet fingers from between her legs. 'Come, we must wash and hurry there, or we will miss our own ceremony!'

Madeleine smiled and crouched over the same pot, seductively pulling apart her pussy-lips as her yellow liquid flowed copiously into the container. 'Run your hand under my outpourings, sweet Medea, and you will feel its heat and lust for its taste.'

Medea sighed and reached out and gripped the crouching woman's hairy sex, the torrent of piss flowing warmly over her hand. An unexplainable and uncontrollable feeling of salaciousness gripped her and she felt herself involuntarily squeezing the soaked and pulsating lips, the desire to dive between Madeleine's legs and drink from her fountain almost overwhelming.

She shook her head in mock anger, and pulled her dripping hand away from its heavenly clasp. 'Madeleine,' she said, determinedly, 'I will wait for you outside, in the street!' She quickly rinsed her hands and face in the bowl provided and made a pretence of storming out of the room, pausing to look back, however, with a grin at the stooping figure. 'Don't be long about it!' she commanded, stepping out into the warmth of the morning sunshine.

The boat-builder, Ancaeus stood proudly at the walkway to the mighty craft, smiling as Medea and Madeleine approached. He held his hand out in greeting, grinning broadly.

'She is complete, down to the last oar,' he announced, his voice full of dignity, 'the finest vessel to sail from these shores since the *Argo* itself!'

Medea clasped his hand, warmly. 'You have done well, Ancaeus,' she said, 'and in such a short time!' She walked past the beaming craftsman, and strode up the long plank to the vessel's deck. She had supervised the building, of course, but to see the ship, *her* ship fully fitted and ready to sail filled her with an indescribable joy.

'And here is your crew!' shouted Madeleine, as a large group of strong, young women approached the anchorage.

40

One by one they walked onto the boat, each gripping the hand of Medea in respectful greeting, before seating themselves at the oars of the mighty vessel. Medea turned to Madeleine, the trace of a tear showing itself in the corner of her eye.

'This was your idea,' she said, her voice choked with emotion, 'to have the brave women of Tipos here to greet me; this is why you tried to delay me!'

'Not the only reason,' said Madeleine, coyly, 'and besides, you wouldn't be stopped.'

Medea smiled and turned back to look at the ship, the women now ready to take her command. 'Ancaeus,' she called out, 'unveil the name we agreed, and I will dedicate this vessel to the service of Zeus!'

The boat-builder grinned and tugged away a large cloth that covered the prow of the ship, revealing the fine lettering beneath, proclaiming the inscription, 'PHALLICIS'. Medea smiled as she saw that Madeleine saw the humour of the name, its erotic connotations intentional. Then, breathing deeply and closing her eyes, she held her arms out to the skies, the assembled company joining her in reverent prayer.

'Oh, mighty Zeus,' she called, 'we, the humble crew of the fair ship *Phallicis* dedicate ourselves to you, and beg your protection and succour throughout the great adventure that faces us. In return, we offer our unfailing devotion to you, and remain ready to do your bidding at all times.'

Medea opened her eyes, slowly. There was no movement in the heavens, no sign from the Gods. For a moment, there was nothing but a terrible silence. Suddenly, Ancaeus pointed up to the sail, shouting excitedly.

'See, the Gods are with you! See!'

All heads turned to look upwards. The heavy, canvas sail, which until now had hung lifeless against the solid oak mast, was fluttering quite strongly in a freshening, offshore breeze. 'See,' repeated Ancaeus, agitatedly, 'Zeus has blessed your journey! Why, you may not even have to row from the harbour!'

Medea smiled. She was cynical enough to appreciate the happy coincidence of the rising wind but, nevertheless, its message seemed to be well received by the crew, who were piously offering thanks to the invisible deity that had seemingly responded to their prayers. For herself, she reasoned that the strength of her own powers, coupled with those of Madeleine would be needed to guide and protect them on their adventure, and that the Gods probably had far better things to do than worry about the progress of one, insignificant vessel.

'Come, then,' she called to Ancaeus, 'the storerooms are filled, the water loaded; we will take your advice, and that of Zeus and set forth this very instant!'

There was a loud cheer from the assembled throng and Ancaeus ran to the stern of the ship, taking the tiller, ready to guide it through the narrow entrance of the harbour. The women of Tipos gripped the oars and began to row in expert unison, the mighty craft shuddering into motion with remarkable ease, the sail catching the breeze as it pulled away from the shore.

Madeleine joined Medea at the prow, resting her hand proudly on her shoulder. 'Our adventure begins,' she said, emotionally, 'the quest to find the strongest, and with luck the most handsome athletes in all the Greek Kingdoms, and to fill the empty seats of this craft with their powerful, naked bodies!'

Medea looked into her friend's eyes, her expression one of humour. 'It seems, dear Madeleine, from the look on your face, the need to find our first contenders is most urgent.'

Madeleine smiled, and let her hand fall surreptitiously to Medea's bottom. 'Not *so* urgent, sweet lover,' she breathed, 'not *so* urgent!'

For three days and three nights the vessel *Phallicis* ploughed through the smooth waters of the Aegean, its sharp prow cutting through the swell in an almost erotic fashion, the wake bearing witness to the passage of the craft, like the tremors that follow orgasm. Their first destination, the Island of Scyros was still over a day's journey away and the wind had all but ceased, the women of Tipos having to strain constantly at the oars to maintain progress.

Medea enjoyed watching them at their labours, their bodies naked save for small, protective loin-cloths of soft leather, their sweat-soaked skin heavily tanned from the unyielding assault of God Apollo. Her nights were spent in the gentle arms of Madeleine, their mutual caresses and her sensuous self-discoveries highly enjoyable, but serving only to heighten her lust for male contact, her memories of Jason and his fine erection becoming worryingly indistinct.

She stood at the prow of the vessel, staring vacantly into the distance, her thoughts many miles away. She blinked against the glare of the newly-risen sun, wondering what great adventures her husband was already confronting, what marvels he was encountering. Madeleine came and stood beside her, slipping her arm affectionately around her friend's waist.

'Are you missing your husband, sweet Medea?' she said, matching her gaze towards the horizon.

Medea nodded. 'I miss his warmth, his words of love,' she said, 'but mostly, if I were to speak honestly, I miss his wonderful cock.'

'Or, perhaps any cock?' said Madeleine, knowingly. 'Remember, I have seen you perform with servants and slaves; I have watched the rapture on your face as they impaled your body, and your head hardly seemed to be filled with thoughts of Jason at those times!'

A seabird dived to the waters ahead of them, deftly pecking up some unfortunate sea-creature in its beak and flying off before the ship could crush it. Medea watched its movements absently.

'I am certain that you are right,' she said, 'but I have yet to be filled by a larger phallus than that of my husband, nor one more expertly wielded!'

'Indeed, Jason is a truly wondrous lover,' said Madeleine, her eyes sparkling with the memory, 'tell me, was he the first to enter your marvellous body?'

43

Medea nodded. 'It seems so long ago, when I opened my legs in terror and waited for him to rupture my hymen.' Her voice became soft as she gazed into the distance of the past.

'Tell me,' said Madeleine, eagerly, 'tell me in detail of your deflowering; it will help to ease your lust.'

Medea looked into her friend's eyes and smiled. 'It will probably make me feel worse,' she said, 'but I will relate the story of my loss of innocence, if only to give you pleasure, for I think, in truth, that is your purpose.'

Madeleine grinned and sat on an upturned barrel, her eyes wide with anticipation. 'Don't spare any detail,' she said, licking her lips, 'and speak in the language of a sailor; you know such talk soaks me!'

'It was on the Island of Macris, in the kingdom of Drepane,' began Medea, 'just a few weeks before the *Argo* finally returned to Iolcus, bearing the Fleece of Phrixus. The Colchians, from whom the prize had been stolen, caught up with the *Argo* and demanded of the ruler of that fair land, King Alcinous, that he force Jason to return the Fleece.

'Alcinous was a wise man, and realising that the Argonauts would not take kindly to being ordered to surrender their prize, insisted that under ancient laws Jason had the right to retain the Fleece if he had taken my virginity, as heir to the throne of Colchis. If not, then I was to return, with the Phrixian trophy to my homeland.

'Until that time I had not considered myself worthy of Jason, let alone offered my body to him, but gladly agreed when the terms were put to me, my desire to lay with him being so great.

'The word of Jason or myself was not to be sufficient; the Colchians demanded that they witness my deflowering, to be sure of the pact. The idea of many eyes feasting on my submission both thrilled and horrified me, my emotions becoming somewhat calmed by Jason's offer of marriage.

'The ceremony was held in the cave of Macris, followed by a sumptuous banquet. All indulged heavily except my

44

new husband and myself, both of us feeling somewhat nervous of what was to come.

'At last, the time arrived. The Golden Fleece itself was laid across the bridal couch, and a throng of drunken, naked men sat or stood around this heavenly "stage", awaiting our performance. I was led, nude save for a simple garland of flowers around my head to the couch, even the hairs from my sex shaven to signify total submission.'

'Hairs from your what?' insisted Madeleine, leaning forward.

'From my cunt, Madeleine, from my cunt,' said Medea, in an exasperated tone, 'now, may I continue?' Madeleine nodded, satisfied for the moment.

'The men whistled and cheered, applauding wildly, as I lay on the warmth of the Fleece. Immediately the soft hair touched my back my trembling stopped, and my body was at once aroused, the lips of my pussy opening wetly to the leering gaze of this most appreciative of audiences. I could feel my juices flowing, a trickle coursing from my gash to run between my buttocks, soaking my bottom.

'I looked around me, seeing a sea of nakedness, and many fine erections looking as though they were ready to impale me in turn. The magic of the Fleece was working well; I *wanted* them, every one! Had it not been for the arrival of my husband, I am certain that I would have leapt upon the nearest male-flesh and demanded that he fuck me, there and then!

'Jason stood before me, naked with his stalk hard and proudly erect, its length quite superb and terrifying. He moved towards me and I closed my eyes, expecting the monster to impale me immediately, my buttocks clenched in anticipation. Instead, to my delight I felt the warm wetness of his tongue as it slid over my hairless and vulnerable sex-lips, his mouth all but devouring the puffy flesh. I felt his tongue slide between the virgin lips of my sodden hole, causing me to writhe about in ecstasy on my sacred bed, lifting my hips into the air and pushing my cunt hard against his feasting face.

45

'He withdrew his long tongue from inside me and, raising my legs and parting them widely to afford the onlookers a better view, he allowed the tip to flutter over my erect clitoris. I stiffened my buttocks and groin, willing him to continue his wet caress until I felt the unmistakeable rise to orgasm begin to take hold of me, my body becoming lost on its inexorable journey.

'I had experienced many comes at the touch of my own fingers, but this was so very different. The incessant flicking of my lover's wet tongue at my bud, the cheers and ribald comments of the onlookers, the magical driving-force that seemed to emanate from the Fleece, all this combined to afford me the most shattering climax it would be possible to imagine.

'I screamed and bucked my body up and down, the men applauding loudly as the force of my hips thrusting in the air knocked Jason from the bed, leaving me to grab frantically at myself, rubbing my clit until the sensations began to subside.

'I remember sobbing as I lay back on the wet bed, Jason kneeling by my side, his look one of both desire and tenderness, his huge erection superbly hard, pressed against his stomach, the head covering his navel.

'My body was so racked with lust and love, his monster phallus held no fears for me anymore. I lay still, opening my legs as wide as I could, drawing them back so my knees touched the hardness of my nipples. There was another loud cheer as Jason assumed his position, holding the purple-headed staff in his hand, guiding it to its target. I felt the thick, bulbous knob touch my wet sex-lips, feeling them open to its welcome intrusion, admitting the entire plum-sized end into my virgin body. He pushed forward with a gentleness I had not anticipated and I felt him touch the resistance of my hymen. Suddenly, and so very easily the barrier gave way, the only discomfort being a slight pain as his wonderful cock eased its passage into my tight sheath.

'Jason pumped in and out of me carefully, gradually easing more and more of his penis inside my aching cunt, until every inch of his magnificent stalk was held in my wet grasp. I stiffened and relaxed the muscles of my pussy in the ways taught to me by the old women of the court, hearing him groan and feeling his manhood throb in response to my actions. I ran my hands over his strong back, narrow waist and iron-hard buttocks, kissing and licking his firm chest as he began to pump steadily into me.

'The pace and urgency of his movements increased, his thrusting in time with the rhythmic chant of our coarse audience, the hard end of his staff hitting against the very entrance to my womb, sending waves and tremors of pleasure throughout my body. He raised my legs and rested them onto his shoulders, fucking me almost vertically, the expression on his face proving that his mind was lost to the lust of the moment, his body totally in the control of Eros.

'I responded as best as I could to his heavy shafting, pushing my bottom upwards to meet his incessant thrusts until I saw him grit his teeth and clamp his eyes tightly shut, and I knew he was about to empty his seed within me. The assembled throng cheered and stamped as he roared with the force of his orgasm, the speed and power of his fucking knocking the very breath from my small body. I managed to force my hand between us and fingered my clitoris furiously, determined to finish with him on this, our first fuck and, with the most deafening of cries I came, the pulsating of his cock inside me helping to carry me into the oblivion of perfect orgasm.

'We lay motionless for a short while, and I could feel the racing of his heartbeat reverberating through my chest, matched by my own. The tenderness within my womb increased and I sensed the gentle throbbing of his cock inside me, less and less, until he had no more to give.

'After a moment he pulled from me and turned to face the men, his wet and drooping phallus bearing the final and insurmountable proof that I was no longer a virgin. There were more cheers, then handshakes, back-slapping and accolades for my husband as the men began to leave the cave and afford us our privacy, whilst I lay within the dampness of my marriage-bed virtually ignored save for the odd, lustful glance.

'I am sure that, because my introduction to the delights of Eros and Aphrodite was so public my subsequent promiscuity can be explained and forgiven for, whilst Jason is as perfect a lover as can be, I can never resist the temptation of taking others, as you well know.'

Madeleine drew a long, deep breath. 'A wonderful story,' she said, genuinely, 'and yet, you did not indulge your desires with any others of the surfeit of male nakedness that surrounded you?'

'Indeed not, though it was more out of respect for my husband than lack of desire, I can assure you! But now, Madeleine, I have related my tale of lost honour, now you must tell me your story!'

'Gladly,' said Madeleine, her eyes fired with lust. 'Like yours, the account of my loss of innocence is one of ceremony, the deflowering of the Queen of Tipos being a most significant and public event but, unlike in your tale, my favours were not to be restricted to just one lover.

'As you know, the people of Tipos are renowned for their love of all things erotic, savouring and sharing all the many delights of Aphrodite, learning and experimenting, teaching and, above all, enjoying.

'Monogamous relationships are unknown to our people; in fact, such a concept would be frowned upon. Clothing is spartan, and impromptu couplings are a common sight in the streets and market-places, passers-by often joining in with such a display should the mood permit.

'The deflowering of Kings and Queens of Tipos is a very special event, the reason for much rejoicing and celebration across the land. My time came on my sixteenth birthday, an event for which I had been well-prepared.

'Throughout my puberty I had been instructed in the ways of self-pleasure and, consequently the arts of pleasuring others. I learned to pick up the lightest of objects using just the muscles of my vaginal lips, the many and varied ways of self-stimulation, the erogenous pleasure-areas of both men and women, and so many other marvellous

48

treasures that my mind filled with wonder at the delights that were to come.

'A week before the ceremony I was locked in a great room with a dozen women who prepared me, making sure that I had absorbed all my teaching, and that I was truly worthy of being the Queen of the most promiscuous race on Earth.

'On the day before my birthday my body was oiled and laid on a bed of ripe fruits, the juices soaking my body, lubricating me, as the hand-maidens introduced appropriately-shaped food-items into my virginal orifices.'

Medea stopped her friend's tale with a movement of her hand. 'Madeleine, you chided me for speaking in such riddles,' she said, smiling, 'now tell me, whatever do you mean?'

'I'm sorry, you are right,' continued Madeleine, 'the women gently eased bananas and long, slim pears into my cunt, and smaller objects, such as oiled peppers into my anus, to teach me the pleasures of intrusion. Their touch was tender and soothing and, thanks to them, any fears I may have held concerning penetration were dismissed.

'I slept well that night, and awoke refreshed and eager to lose my innocence. I was dressed in a simple layer of sheer silk, my nakedness clearly visible through the diaphanous material. Even at that age, my breasts were close to the immense size they are today, far out of proportion to the rest of my body, and I remember feeling a little self-conscious about them, knowing that my nakedness was about to be viewed by a host of people.

'I was blindfolded, then led out into another room, where I could hear the sounds of people breathing, their numbers obviously great. Many hands touched me as I was led by the arm amongst them, some grabbing and pulling at the silks, gradually baring my body entirely. My cunt was soaked by this time, my need for sexual relief greater than it had ever been before, or indeed since.

'Whoever was leading me made me stop and, taking my hands in hers stretched my arms out in front of me, guiding my fingers until they touched the reclining body of a man, who appeared to be lying on a couch or table of some description. My point of contact with this person was his upper body, and I ran my hands delicately but excitedly over his fine chest, feeling the power and strength of his hairless pectoral muscles and the firmness of his flat stomach.

'I moved both my hands downwards, anxious to discover whether his nakedness was as complete as mine, until my fingers touched the coarse fur of his pubic area. I ran them through the curled hair, breathing in the strong, male-scent that arose from his genitals, wondering why I hadn't yet touched his penis. I pushed my hand down further, until I was able to circle the base of his stalk, which I now discovered was being held in some way vertically from his body. I rubbed my hand gradually upwards, as I had been taught, testing the length, delighted with its superb dimensions.

'The tip seemed huge, almost half as wide again as his stem, the knob spongy and slightly damp. I found that this delightful phallus was held erect by two, soft-skinned hands bearing a clear female perfume, the owner of which seemed to be presenting the monster for my attention. I added my other hand to our erotic grip, leaned my head forward and managed to steer my face towards the end, pushing out my tongue and making my first oral contact with the sex-organ of a man.

'His taste was strong and highly arousing. I opened my mouth and took as much of him within me as I could, suckling on the thick, hard flesh whilst both I and my unknown companion rubbed his cock firmly up and down. I felt him throb within my lips and tasted the saltiness of a slight emission against my tongue, swallowing his juice hungrily.

'I would have been quite content to continue in this manner for hours, but others had different ideas. I was pulled from my pleasurable labours still blindfolded and raised bodily into the air by two obviously exceptionally tall and strong men, one of my legs held by each, their grip firm around my thighs and calves. Despite my eyes being covered, I could sense myself being slowly lowered, fully expecting that I was being plunged onto the waiting phallus of my secret lover. Instead, I felt my lower regions being immersed in a sort of thick, warm oil, with the slithering of small, eel-like creatures wriggling against my most intimate parts causing me the most erotic of sensations. I squirmed my buttocks within the living ooze, my pussy becoming alive with feeling, and sharply sensitive.

'After a few moments of this extraordinarily stimulating experience I was raised again by the thighs, my legs this time drawn almost painfully apart, then gently lowered once more. This time I did feel the touch of what had to be the thick, bulbous end of my mystery-lover's cock pressing against the slippery wetness of my cunt. I managed to rest my feet on the table on either side of his body and held myself still with just the tip of him parting my lips, aroused but anxious. I lowered myself cautiously, scarcely daring to breath until I felt my labia close around the ridge, holding him inside.

'There was no pain; just exquisite pleasure. The action of the strange fluids in which I had been bathed was to ease the penetration of the monster phallus remarkably, so much so that our pubic bones quickly met, his magnificent erection buried deep within my deflowered sheath.

'I felt about my lover's body and, discovering he was firmly bound I surmised that it would be necessary for me to make all the required movements in order to achieve satisfaction. I began to raise and lower my pelvis, thrusting my sex against him, absorbing the full length with each downward push. My excitement was compounded by the fact that, though the room was filled with silence I was aware that there were many eyes enjoying the sight of my naked, rutting body.

'I bounced up and down rapidly on my unseen stallion, thrilling at the depth of his penetration, until I felt him throbbing within me, his stifled groans telling me that I had accepted my first gift of male lust juices. I pumped my body wildly up and down on his, willing him to give more, until he fell limply from within me.

51

'Almost immediately, I was raised again by my strong companions and carried a small distance, then lowered once more onto another firm stalk, slightly smaller than the first, but no less satisfying. I began my dance of delight again, this time feeling the beginning of my own orgasm building within my loins. I fell forward over the stranger's body and found his mouth with my own, kissing him with the passion of long-time lovers, my hips bucking up and down as I fucked myself with a frenzy of crazed lust.

'Someone raised my head from my greedy kiss, and I felt my mouth being offered the warm, soft-tipped hardness of another splendid erection. I parted my lips willingly, allowing the thick prick into my mouth, suckling greedily on it like a child at its mother's breast. Then, the delightful invasion of my body became complete as a third staff slid effortlessly into my well-lubricated bottom.

'At last, there was a cheer from those who had gathered to witness the ceremony as the three superbly developed men plunged their manhoods in and out of my orifices until, as though at a pre-arranged signal they orgasmed in unison within me. I swallowed heavily, whilst using the muscles of my nether regions to grip the thrusting flesh that was impaling me. The feeling of having so much cock inside me at once was too much, and the come I desperately wanted tore through my body with the force of a thunderbolt, causing me to cry out in the way to which you, my darling Medea have become accustomed.

'This was not the end of my initiation, however. For the next two, maybe three hours I remained blindfolded, constantly being carried from one couch of pleasure to another, until I had been fucked by more men than I could count.

'Eventually, when my exhaustion became too severe, the blindfold was removed. I blinked and looked around the room, seeing it filled with naked men and women, some indulging in copulation, all grinning at me. Only they would know who had deflowered me, which is, or rather *was* the custom of our people.'

Medea looked into Madeleine's eyes and smiled. 'You

must miss those days very much,' she said, sympathetically. Her friend's eyes glazed slightly with tears.

'I do,' she said, sadly, 'I do.'

Medea leant forward and kissed her on the lips. 'Come, dear Madeleine,' she said, taking her by the hand, 'let us lie together until we sight Scyros, for your tale has filled me with a need that only your warm, fluttering tongue can satisfy.'

The sombre cliffs of Scyros loomed large and forbidding against the backdrop of a quickly darkening sky, the air filled with an eerie silence as the *Phallicis* drifted gently towards the only visible area of beach. The sudden shout of an un-named and unearthly creature echoed from within the thickly-wooded tract that framed the grey sand; otherwise, there was no sign of life.

'This place must be accursed,' said Madeleine, 'I have heard many stories of the island, but I never thought that the Gods would one day bring me to its shores.'

'We must find water, and fresh fruits,' counselled Medea, her expression also betraying her unease. 'We have no choice but to land here.'

The virgin Iole appeared behind them, gazing at the dreary landscape through her hypnotic, steel-blue eyes. 'The fall of these rocks reminds me of my home,' she said, wistfully, 'a land of mystery, but also of wonder. You should not be deterred by appearances.'

Medea looked at the youngster, enviously savouring the sight of the tall girl's slim, lithe body, her long, near-white hair cascading over her slender shoulders and down her back to touch the small, round globes of her bottom, naked save for a thin strip of leather. Her skin was almost pure white, freckled by the sun, her breasts small but firm, tipped with tiny rose-coloured nipples, erect in the cooling breeze of the evening. She held herself with regal poise, her beautiful, fresh face still bathed in the innocence of childhood, her body possessed by a subtle sexuality that seemed to be yearning to be explored.

Iole appeared strangely out of place in the company of

53

the women of the *Phallicis*, her tender frailty at odds with the strength and resilience needed to steer the mighty vessel on its long journey through the waters of the Aegean and Mediterranean seas. She'd certainly pulled her weight though; not once wincing under the strain of powering the heavy oars, her delicateness of form belying her fortitude and strength.

'You clearly love the land of your birth,' said Madeleine, inquisitively, 'why ever did you leave your home? Surely not solely for the promise of this fine adventure!'

Iole smiled, a little sadly. 'I have a destiny, a fate that I must greet,' she said, facing out again towards the darkening shore. 'I must prove myself as a woman of courage and guile, to become worthy of Heracles himself!'

Medea looked shocked. 'Your future lies with Heracles? How do you know this?'

Iole turned to her and smiled, almost with an air of resignation. 'I had the most frightening, but nevertheless erotic dream,' she said. 'I will see Heracles kill those dear to him, then he will take me as his lover, and impale me with his magnificent staff daily and with such force that I will be powerless to resist, until the God Thanatos, sweet death himself, takes that fine warrior to his bosom.'

'But, surely you need not submit to this?'

'My people believe in the power of the dream,' said Iole, firmly, 'my fate is sealed.'

Madeleine caught Medea's bemused expression and shrugged, turning to watch as the roped boulder was lowered to anchor the *Phallicis* in the shallow water and a small boat was lowered into the gently lapping waves.

'Come with me, Iole,' commanded Medea, clambering over the rail, 'and Electra and Nana. Let us see what adventure awaits us on this dismal island!'

The olive-skinned sisters joined Iole and their leader in the boat and took up the oars, rowing the vessel quickly towards the shore. Once the craft was safely beached the four women began to walk towards the wooded thicket, their hands cautiously resting on the hilts of their sheathed knives, their eyes and ears sharp for the slightest movement. The undergrowth quickly became almost

impassable, the daggers now being used to gouge a painfully slow trail through the twisted stems and branches,
their path leading them steadily upwards.

At last, the thicket began to ease and they found themselves walking between the sheer sides of a rift in the
strained rock of the cliff, shaped as though carved by the
axe of a giant in a fit of fury. The silence hung over them
like a shroud, along with the darkness of the sudden night.

For the first time since embarking on their quest, Medea
felt afraid. Madeleine was right; there was an aura of evil
about the place, she could feel it, smell it, *taste* it. It occur-
red to her to return to the *Phallicis*, but their need for
provisions, especially water was great. She had to continue.

Suddenly, there was a sound. The women stopped short
in their tracks and listened hard. At first, the silence returned maddeningly, then there came the distinct cry of a
man in pain. Medea bade the others to be silent and led
the way in the direction of the shout, her heart thumping
noisily against her chest.

They came to another small gap in the rock and eased
themselves through, taking comfort and cover behind a
large bush. The moon had risen now, the Goddess Artemis
unfolding her cloak in all her glory, casting the sharp
brightness of her eerie light on the scene before them.

Medea gasped at the sight that greeted her eyes. Approxi-
mately twenty men sat or lay in the small clearing in front
of them, chained to each other and to the rocks by thick
links of iron. Each of them was as black as night itself, their
ebony skin shining almost blue in the playful light, their
muscular bodies flawless in their athletic perfection.

'What sport we can have with these,' whispered Electra
to Nana. 'Let us hope their manhoods are as powerful as
their bodies!' Medea hushed for them to be quiet, although
similar thoughts were playing across her own mind.
Crouching low, she led the other women around the back
of the group of unfortunate prisoners until they hid behind
one of their number who was somewhat isolated from the
rest.

Medea pushed her hand round his neck quickly and

clasped his mouth, the point of her knife pressing against his throat. 'Say nothing, friend,' she hissed, 'we mean you no harm.'

Gradually she relaxed her grip on the slave's mouth. 'Tell us, friend, why are you all chained so?'

The prisoner turned and looked at them, his eyes darting with fear. 'You must leave!' he said, his voice trembling, 'you are in great danger!'

'There are many of us, and we will only leave when we have released you from these shackles,' said Medea, tugging hopelessly at the rusty metal around the man's ankle, 'what must we do?'

'The keys to our chains are held by the evil Rapis, our captor. He is very powerful and quite mad. He must be vanquished or, at least distracted. He . . .

The man stopped short, his eyes staring at Iole. 'What is it? What have you seen?' said Medea, anxiously.

'You have the way to both distract, and probably vanquish Rapis here, in the form of this beautiful child, but only if she is a virgin.' He grabbed hold of Iole by the shoulders, gripping her painfully. 'You are untouched; I pray you are untouched!'

Iole nodded, pulling herself from the man's grip. 'What must I do?' she said, quietly.

The slave smiled, his teeth shining white against his sweat-covered, black face. 'No man, however powerful, can defeat Rapis,' he began, solemnly, 'but it is said that the spell cast by a white-haired virgin when she impales herself upon his mighty phallus will conquer the evil, and bring him to subjugation. Our liberty is in the hands of this sweet innocent!'

'Are there any dangers?' said Medea, gripping the man's arm.

'Only if he suspects that she doesn't find him sexually attractive. This is the problem, as you will discover. Rapis is the most repulsive of men!'

There was a sudden crash of breaking undergrowth at the far end of the clearing. A large, shadowy figure stood silhouetted against the moonlight, one hand clutching a

56

fearsomely long whip. 'I hear the sounds of conversation!' shouted the newcomer, in a dark, growling voice. 'You know you may not speak! Silence!'

With a mighty swing of his arm, he brought the whip slicing through the air to strike the supine form of one of the slaves, his cry of pain echoing around the steep walls of the cliffs.

'This is he, this is Rapis,' said their informant, shuffling quietly away from them, 'please help us if you can, but take great care!'

Medea turned to look at Iole, seeing that she had already begun to rise from the shelter of the hiding-place. 'Iole!' she hissed, 'be careful!'

'This is my destiny,' said the virgin, walking out into the moonlight, 'Zeus will protect me!'

She stood in the centre of the clearing, waiting like a condemned person for the arrival of the executioner. The chained prisoners saw her first and began to sit up, their eyes feasting on her delectable form. Rapis swung round when he sensed her presence and stood, open-mouthed as he saw her. Medea closed her eyes in horror. The evil jailer stood a full seven feet in height, his body naked but as hairy as a bear, his face twisted with his evil, the cold eyes, bulbous nose and wide, drooling mouth only just visible within the thick, matted hair of his beard.

'Who are you, child?' he said, stepping forward and holding out a massive hand, preparing to touch the frail form before him. Iole stood her ground, breathing heavily, her small breasts rising and falling sensuously.

'I have come to offer you my hymen, my Lord,' she said, her voice shaking with terror.

'Have you, now,' said the giant, running his hand down her back and cupping both of her tiny buttocks at once in his firm grip, 'but surely, you must find me repulsive?'

Iole took a deep breath, wincing under the pressure of his fingers digging into the soft globes of her bottom. 'Not so, my Lord,' she said, 'you are truly a giant man, a wondrous stud, with a manhood that will rise and fill and stretch my tight sheath so that no other can satisfy me.'

Medea saw the young girl glance at the big man's crotch, noticing that it was, indeed rising to assume the most magnificent proportions.

'Look at the size of that,' hissed Nana, her hand snaking under her loin-cloth to fondle herself between her legs, 'she is so tiny; he will kill her.'

'Better that we take him,' whispered her sister, her eyes filled with lust, 'we are more experienced at controlling the thrusts of such a stallion!'

'You know it must be a virgin,' said Medea, angrily, 'and we are many years too late as far as you two are concerned.' The others grinned, and the three women settled to watch the deflowering of their colleague, fearful for her survival but aroused by the event.

Rapis now stood with his erection proudly standing aloft, soaring like a great weapon from the thick bush of his genital hair. Iole gripped hold of his staff, her eyes closed against the unpleasant sight of his face and began to rub the skin of his cock gently up and down, whilst the giant caught hold of the flimsy leather garment covering her virginal treasures and ripped it away from her body, drawing it to his face and sniffing the delicate aroma of her sex on the damp material.

He threw the cloth onto the ground and grabbed Iole hard between her legs, causing her to cry out in pain. 'Oh, my Lord,' she sobbed, 'take care. Remember that I am a virgin, and that I need you to introduce me gently to the wonders of Aphrodite. Once my treasures are plundered, then you may have me as you will!'

Rapis grunted and softened his grip, allowing his fingers to rub against the swollen lips of her sex. In the sharpness of the moonlight Medea could see everything; the gnarled, groping fingers, the long, heavily veined tool that would shortly plunge into the small form of the fair virgin, the expression of lust that was transforming Iole's face from innocent beauty to wanton harlot.

'By Zeus, she's really enjoying it,' said Electra, the movements of her fingers between her legs increasing in pace. Medea hushed her.

'Rapis may not be so gentle with us, should he discover our hiding place!' she cautioned, this time allowing her own hand to trail down to her wet sex.

Iole had now knelt in front of the giant, her eyes still tightly closed, both hands rubbing firmly at his stem. Gradually she pulled the end of the monster stalk to her lips and took it in, the large knob filling her mouth completely. The beast leant back, his hands on his waist, stiffening his buttocks as he savoured the oral caress of his inexperienced lover.

'Ah, such a mouth, it craves to be fucked!' he cried, tossing his hairy head back, 'see, slaves how this virgin sucks me! I cannot be so repulsive that one so beautiful pays such homage to my weapon!'

Something in what he said made him stop her. He pulled her roughly by the shoulders to her feet, and stared into her face. 'Open your eyes!' he roared, 'open them and gaze at me! Tell me of the ugliness you see, so that I may let my whip taste the plumpness of your pretty little arse!'

Iole opened her eyes slowly. 'No, my Lord,' she said, her voice clear and confident, 'I cannot say that, for I see only the face of a strong and handsome man who is about to split my maidenhead and plunge into me! Please, my Lord, my sheath is soaked and ready for you; please fuck me now!'

She struggled from his grip and turned her back to him, bending over and grasping her heels, her legs slightly bent, her backside presented to him in abject vulnerability.

'By the Gods, I know this must be a trick, but I cannot resist such a divine offering! I pray that you will turn and find me repulsive before I spend my seed, otherwise my powers will be lost forever.'

Iole turned her head and looked over her shoulder at Rapis' face. 'No, my Lord, it need not be so! You are the handsome lover I have yearned for all my young life. Take me! Fuck my virginal cunt with your giant cock!'

The beast was shaking visibly with lust, one hand resting on the delicate back of the lovely blonde, the other holding

59

his stiff manhood and directing it towards its target. 'Trick or not, I cannot resist the sight of such a perfect arse, knowing that I am to be the first to impale those sweet, succulent lips!'

He moved his hips forward until the thick head of his prick touched her delicate, petal-like labia. Medea bit into the back of her hand, nervously. 'He'll never get into her,' said Nana, 'he is so large and she, so tiny.' Iole opened her legs a little more and pushed her bottom back further, as though coaxing his entry to her body. Rapis pushed forward again, gripping her buttocks with both hands, the head of his giant cock disappearing within the folds of the young girl's soaking pussy.

Iole raised her head and cried out as the massive man split her virginity, his staff slipping deeper and deeper into her sex. 'Oh, yes,' she cried, 'I am being fucked at last, and by such a handsome man!'

Rapis began to pound heavily into her, lifting her body completely with each thrust, ramming as much of his engorged cock into her as possible. 'See, slaves,' he cried out, triumphantly, 'all these years you and others have mocked my ugliness, and now you watch me as I fuck the most beautiful virgin in all of the world, and *with her consent*, because she finds me so handsome!' Iole fell to her knees, her lover kneeling with her, still deep inside her, pumping furiously.

'Oh, yes, my Lord, fuck me harder, fill me with your wondrous seed!' The speed of the big man's thrusts was fierce, the small form of the young girl shuddering under the wild onslaught. Medea looked around her, seeing that all twenty of the watching slaves were massively erect, bearing the promise of joys to come. She returned her gaze to the performance in the centre of the clearing, marvelling at the way Iole was able to withstand the incessant assault of the giant phallus within her tiny hole.

Suddenly, Rapis held himself still, his hands high in the air. 'I come, my seed shoots within this delicate child's body, and with it the curse is broken!' He began to pump

60

again with ferocious speed, emptying himself inside Iole's accommodating sheath until he was spent, and he fell to one side of her kneeling body, exhausted.

Medea, Electra and Nana walked nervously from their hiding place and stood before the unlikely lovers. Iole now lay on her back, her sex-lips reddened from the onslaught, the whiteness of her skin flawed with the marks of scratches obtained in passion. 'The slaves are free, and so is Rapis,' she said, panting heavily.

Medea looked at the supine form of the giant man and watched in astonishment as the unsightly hair fell away from his body, revealing the firm, muscular physique of a young adonis, the face transformed into one of strength and magnificence.

'He was cursed by Poseidon,' said one of the slaves, standing as the shackles fell away from their limbs, 'when he sailed through the Bosphorus single handed, a feat never before achieved by mortal man. The beauty of both his body and his mind were changed to what you saw, and only the genuine adoration of a virgin and the gift of her hymen could release him. Now we are all free, and it is thanks to this brave young girl!'

The other men cheered as they were able to shake away the restraining chains and gathered around the four women, Medea noticing happily that many of their erections remained stiff and proud.

'Tomorrow,' she announced, 'you will begin to build a ship to take you from these shores to Iolcus, where you will help to prepare for the games that are to be held to celebrate the return of Jason. When he awakes, Rapis will lead you with all the strength and wisdom that has now been returned to him.

'Tonight, however, the women of the *Phallicis* have much need for those fine stalks that thrust so magnificently from between your legs. For one more night you are slaves, but not to evil, but rather to Eros, and you will perform for us in ways you have yet to imagine!' She caught hold of two of the men by their erections. 'You will service me now,' she continued, 'for I have a great desire to orgasm, then we will return to the ship and fuck all night, and I swear that the waves that we will create will lash the very shores of Iolcis itself!'

CHAPTER FOUR

Jason stood at the tiller of the *Argo*, guiding the vessel's path through the rising swell. The sail was full, the breeze constant and cool, allowing the exhausted crew some well-earned rest. Atalanta stood at the prow, peering into the semi-darkness of the moonlit night, shafts of silver illuminating the perfection of her tall, strong body, resplendent in its near-nakedness. Between them the Argonauts slept, still at their oars, the slumber of near collapse.

The days had slipped into weeks, the sea maddeningly calm until today when, at last a strong Westerly had sprung up, heading directly, as though by some sort of divine intervention in the direction of Lemnos. Perhaps, Jason mused, the Goddess Hera had had a quiet word with the powerful deity Zephyrus and urged him to send the breeze, despite her declaration that she wouldn't be able to offer him specific help. But no, such thoughts were close to blasphemous, and he certainly couldn't afford to offend the Gods.

He quickly dismissed the ideas from his mind and concentrated his gaze instead on the delightful figure of Atalanta. With her back to him she looked decidedly erotic, her long, black hair cascading down her smooth back to her perfectly formed bottom, the ends lying suggestively between the pert cheeks, caressing the secrets within.

Jason thought of her offer; to race with him, hopefully to be the first to catch her and claim the sweet prize of her virginity, to lie between those firm, long legs and sink his cock deep inside her willing body, to teach her the pleasures of Eros. The long days and nights of abstinence were beginning to have a profound effect on him despite the regular and expert ministrations from the lovely Glaucis, and he was finding his thoughts drifting more and more into the realms of the carnal.

Glaucis would gladly ease his torment almost nightly, but of late this seemed to make things worse rather than better. The delicate caress of her tiny fingers made him ache to enter her, to thrust his stiff weapon deep inside her virginal body or to have her take the swollen end into her lovely mouth, to suckle, to swallow.

Occasionally she would put her face close to his cock and he would arch his back and push himself forward as her hands moved rhythmically up and down along the hard shaft, willing her to open her sweet mouth and take him inside. But always she would move her head back, not out of revulsion but of innocence, as though the idea of sucking on him never entered her mind.

And the kiss! Every time, on each occasion that she had eased the strain of his frustration and drawn his seed from him she would lean forward and lightly kiss his softening manhood, just once before bathing it with a cool, damp towel. She would smile, the full, pouted lips parted slightly, the eyes shining with youthful purity and he would ache, oh, how he would ache.

Atalanta began to stretch, raising her arms high above her head and standing on the balls of her feet. Jason watched in awe as she stiffened her legs and buttocks, opening her raised arms wide as though in prayer to some invisible deity and then relaxed, peering once more into the darkness.

He wondered if she would really object if he simply walked over to her, pulled her to him and fucked her, there and then. But no, this was not the way it was to be, she had made that abundantly clear. But one day, he would race with her.

He turned his attentions instead to thoughts of Medea. Had she taken other lovers yet? He knew full well of his wife's desires and needs; he was no fool, the string of young men visiting her bed during his supposed absences was well reported and he enjoyed the thought, fantasising about the pleasures she was likely to have experienced. He took pleasure in his spouse's joy, but also enjoyed the games of deceit and infidelity himself.

Jason allowed his thoughts to drift back in time to the night of his wedding, the taking of the virgin Medea in the cave of Macris. His free hand trailed to his crotch as he recalled the sight of his young wife lying naked on the fleece, her legs open, her hairless cunt presented to him as if a prize, the lips visibly wet and puffy with excitement.

His fingers circled the rising stiffness of his cock as he remembered the sheer eroticism of the moment, the sight of many men watching in anticipation, and the total submission on the face of this exceptionally beautiful young woman.

He rubbed himself slowly as he remembered the taste of her sweet virgin pussy, the incredible wetness inside her as he probed with his tongue to her hymen, the way she writhed as he licked, and the way she had screamed when she came against his face.

He closed his eyes as he remembered the best part of all, when her delicious cunt had accepted him fully, his cock never longer, never harder than when it first slid deep into her delicate body. And oh, such a body; how he needed it now!

Jason was suddenly aware that he was not alone. Snapping his eyes open he looked behind him, seeing Glaucis standing on the step below, her eyes transfixed by the sight of the now fully erect phallus he still held in his grasp. He looked down foolishly, then struggled to cover himself with the sparse material of his loin-cloth.

'Your needs are truly great, my Lord,' she said, softly, reaching out and stroking his now receding penis through the coarse cloth with the backs of her fingers, 'do I not please you enough?'

'Your caresses are both welcome and satisfying,' he replied, 'my mind was elsewhere, my thoughts carnal in the extreme, and not for innocent ears such as yours.'

Glaucis reached under his loin-cloth and gripped him, coaxing him back to full erection. 'Come to the cabin, Jason, I will take care of you.'

'No,' he said, reluctantly, 'I cannot leave the tiller. Please; I'll be fine.'

'Then I will do it here,' she said, kneeling before him. He wanted to stop her, but couldn't. Gently, almost casually she rubbed the long, thick stem with her small hand, the fingers curled partly round the firm sex-flesh, drawing the loose skin up and down. Jason closed his eyes and gave himself completely to her erotic massage, relaxing his body to the pleasures of her delicate touch.

'It is so very big, my Lord,' she said, softly, 'I have wondered, many times, what it would feel like . . . inside.'

He opened his eyes and looked down at the kneeling form. Glaucis gazed up at him, the innocence in her expression as she held onto his stiffness exceedingly inappropriate. 'I would dearly love to show you, to slip every inch inside your tiny body.'

'But I am betrothed.'

'And I am an honourable man,' he said sharply, pulling her hand from him swiftly. Glaucis stood up, looking shocked.

'You do not want me to give you pleasure?' Her pained expression caused his anger and frustration to soften. He bent over and kissed her lightly on the top of her head.

'I am fine,' he lied, 'please, leave me now. Go to bed.' Glaucis did as asked, walking slowly from him, reluctantly, like a scolded child. He watched her until she disappeared below deck, the ache returning.

'How are you going to stop yourself from fucking her?' It was Atalanta who stood before him now, her long hair blowing rebelliously across her face. 'It is many weeks before we reach Icaria. You are strong, Jason, but even you will crack under the strain of the lust you feel for that child.'

'You speak wise words, as ever, but I have to be strong. It is not permitted. I have sworn an oath to deliver her safe and intact to her future husband, though I must confess

66

that the thought of some other man being the first to sink his hard shaft between those delicate thighs pains me terribly.'

'Who would ever know if you took her? She would not admit it, for fear of losing her future throne in Icaria.' She was teasing him and he knew it, but it was difficult to argue with the logic of her words.

'*I* would know! I would sate myself, rip the child's hymen then regret it for the rest of my days.'

'It is not merely lust you feel for Glaucis, is it?'

Jason looked unnerved. 'Nonsense!' he retorted. 'I lust for what I cannot have. Nothing more.'

'Let me finish what she started,' said Atalanta, reaching inside his loin-cloth. He jumped with surprise as her strong fingers circled the base of his cock.

'You, Atalanta? You can't, you must not . . .'

She began to rub him vigorously. 'My virgin hole remains a treasure for he who beats me in a fair race, and I pray that one day it will be you, Jason. But this is something else, this is something that I am permitted to do. Like Glaucis, I have eased the pressures of abstinence amongst many of the Argonauts.'

She pulled his stalk into the cool night air and pumped her hand furiously up and down, coaxing it once again into a proud and stiff erection. The roughness of her palm contrasted strongly with the delicate, almost wispy touch of Glaucis. 'Steady, not so hard!' he cried. 'I fear you'll tear my fine manhood from my body!'

Atalanta slowed her movements down slightly, her grip still firm and demanding. 'I am no delicate flower, coaxing your seed from within your body,' she said, huskily, 'I am a demanding woman; you will give your lust to me!'

She knelt before him and began to pull hard at his aching cock with both of her hands. Despite the pain, he began to feel incredible pleasure in her insistent, violent masturbation and felt his release coming mercifully near. She seemed to sense it too, rubbing his tortured flesh ever harder and at a furious rate, her whole body shaking with the effort, her breasts bouncing against his thighs. Jason

67

began to breathe heavily, his buttocks stiffening, his legs trembling.

Suddenly, and without a hint of tenderness or forethought Atalanta clamped her thick lips around the end of his cock, drawing the head deep into her mouth. With a roar he came, sending torrents of sperm to the back of her throat, relishing the sight of her swallowing every last drop. She suckled on him until his tenderness meant that he could stand it no more and he had to reluctantly force her head away. Then she stood before him, wiping her mouth on the back of her hand.

She smiled, coquettishly, waiting for him to speak. Jason couldn't say a word. After a moment, she kissed him lightly on the forehead and walked away, to return to her post at the prow of the ship.

From the door to the cabin Glaucis watched, a small tear in her eye.

It was Atalanta that first spotted the small open boat through the haze of the mid-afternoon sunshine. As they neared the bobbing craft it became clear that it was occupied, though whether the lone occupant was alive or dead it was impossible to tell.

The Argonauts rowed quickly in the direction of the boat and soon they were upon it. Jason dived into the warm water and swam to the craft, grabbing its shallow side and lifting himself into the vessel. Inside lay a man, old and thin, his eyes tightly closed. Jason leant towards him, pressing his ear close to the man's face.

'Is he alive?' shouted Glaucis from the deck above.

'Just barely! Come, send down ropes and get someone to help me with him'

Two of the crew dived into the water and swam to the boat's side, pushing against it to force it towards the hull of the *Argo*. Ropes were lowered and gradually the old man was raised onto the deck of the large vessel, the struggle waking him from his unconsciousness. His eyes darted, looking in abject terror at the faces of his rescuers.

'Who are you,' he said, his voice hoarse and dry, 'where am I?'

Glaucis poured cool water onto the man's lips. He drank, choking slightly, grabbing at the bowl with wizened hands.

'See how he gulps down the water,' said Glaucis, her concern for the old man apparent as she ran her hand gently over his forehead, 'he must have been at sea for many days. His skin feels like leather.'

'Please, you must tell me,' the stranger continued when his thirst had been abated, 'are you of this world, or have I travelled to the land of Hades?'

'You are aboard the ship *Argo*, headed for Lemnos.' Jason spoke with pride, but the old man became agitated, his expression startled.

'No, no,' he said, vainly attempting to stand, 'I cannot return there, I cannot take any more!'

'What do you mean?' said Jason, allowing him to clutch his arm as he rose from the deck, 'what is there in Lemnos that you fear so?'

The old man took another sip of water from the refilled bowl offered to him by Glaucis. 'My name is Thoas, King of Lemnos, and the last surviving male on the island. The womenfolk are the Cabeiri, strong and wilful, and very demanding.'

'What happened to the men?' asked Atalanta.

'Dead, all dead,' said Thoas, shaking his head, 'over a year ago. Only I was allowed to live, to be used by over a thousand women. I cannot return; I have no strength left. They will kill me with their rampant demands.'

'Then this is the task set us by Hera,' said Jason, gazing regally into the distance. 'We must visit the island, and repopulate the Cabeiri!'

There was a loud cheer from the assembled throng of Argonauts. Jason grinned. What an opportunity! At last there would be relief from his frustrations, and what relief it would be!

'Take care,' said Thoas, sitting on an upturned barrel, his spindly legs barely up to the task of holding him erect for more than a moment. 'The women have desires, needs that even your brave crew may find difficult to fulfil.'

Jason shook his head. 'Not my brave Argonauts. You can be sure that when we leave the shores of Lemnos not a single pussy will remain un-stretched!'

Atalanta and Glaucis caught each other's glance and frowned at their leader's crudeness but chose to remain silent. Thoas laughed, his grin causing the salt coating the burnt skin of his face to crack. 'Perhaps you will be the saviours of my people, maybe it is fate that has brought you to this place.'

'But how did you come to be adrift in this boat?' asked Jason. 'You could have died in this heat.'

'Better to drift into the arms of death than spend another night in the grip of so many insatiable females.'

'I cannot say that I agree with you,' laughed Jason.

'You are young, strong and powerful. I am old, hardly capable of carnal thought, let alone action. There is no greater torture, believe me.'

Jason shook his head. 'Apart from the possibility of dying from sheer pleasure, is there any other danger that we should be aware of?'

'Beware Hypsipyle, the Queen, my daughter,' croaked Thoas, 'she is the most beautiful of all, and the most demanding. It will take quite a man to please her.'

He looked into Jason's face, his eyes glinting. Glaucis saw the look and knew the intent. She also knew that Jason would accept the challenge to couple with the Queen of Lemnos, to prove his manhood to the assembled throng.

'How far to Lemnos?' he barked, after a moment's pleasurable deliberation.

'One day, possibly two,' said Glaucis, 'you will have to wait yet, before you can release yourself on those unfortunate women.'

Jason laughed and turned to address his oarsmen. 'Row, my fine Argonauts, row your hearts out! Let us make it in one!'

Not since their remarkable escape from the jaws of death within the Symplegades, the legendary crashing rocks on their triumphant return with the Golden Fleece had the

Argonauts tugged at the heavy oars with such determination, such force. The mighty vessel tore through the heaving swell of the sea throughout the remainder of the day and most of the night, until the shores of Lemnos were reached as the new dawn began to approach.

Ordering the ship to be put to anchor, Jason peered into the half-light at the gently sloping beach, the darkness of the rim of trees and the mountains silhouetted in the distance. Glaucis came to his side, taking his arm like that of a lover.

'It is said that Lemnos is the most beautiful of the Aegean islands,' she said, softly, her voice warm in the coolness of the morning. Jason looked at her, feeling a pang of regret at his treatment of her the previous night. They hadn't spoken a word to each other throughout the previous day, he preferring to stand at the tiller, shaping the course for Lemnos. Glaucis had remained in the cabin.

'It will be good to set foot on dry land again, to taste fresh water, and feel the sand slipping between our toes.' He spoke tenderly, anxious to placate her.

Atalanta joined them. 'I feel that the sensations you are awaiting have more to do with slipping your fingers into the silky confines of wet, willing pussies,' she said, haughtily.

Glaucis smiled, a little too bravely. 'Indeed,' she said, 'the men have worked up a hunger for women-flesh that quite unnerves me. I will be more relaxed when they are sated!'

Jason turned again to look at the brightening image of the shoreline, squinting his eyes against the glint of the rising sun reflected by the mirror-like surface of the water. 'It has been many weeks since we left the shores of Iolcus. The men have their needs.'

'And you, yours?' said Glaucis, quietly.

Jason sighed. 'And me, mine,' he said, presently.

A cry came from the top of the mast. 'Warriors, warriors, we are attacked!'

Looking in the direction of the frantic man's wave, Jason saw the sight of a hundred, maybe more fearsomely dressed men, their swords drawn, spears at the ready. He turned angrily to Thoas, who was crouching in a corner, his limbs shaking with terror.

'What is this trickery?' he demanded, pulling the old man to his feet, 'you said the men were dead! Who are these, that wait to do battle with us?'

'I spoke the truth,' insisted Thoas, 'there are no men left alive on Lemnos!' He looked at the ever increasing number of armour-clad figures and smiled.

'These, my friend are the women. They wear the armour of their dead husbands in fear of attack. They must think you are pirates! Send one of your number, one who is persuasive and tactful to explain that your mission is one of peace. When they hear that so many lusty adventurers are waiting to impale them on their fine erections their swords and spears will be cast aside.'

Jason called Echion, the scholar to his side. 'Echion, my fine friend, use your skills to calm the nerves of these women. Tell them we mean them no harm.' He smiled and winked at the young man who, nodding in compliance slipped over the side and swam towards the waiting throng.

He watched the brave Argonaut swim towards the waiting throng, anxiously hoping that he hadn't sent a good man to his death. Echion arrived at the beach to be immediately surrounded by armed guards. Then he could be seen no more.

A full hour passed before he returned, climbing exhausted back onto the *Argo*'s deck. His sparse clothing had been torn from him, his thighs and groin marked by numerous, fine scratches. Jason caught his shoulders. 'What is this? Have you failed?'

'No, my Lord,' the young man spluttered, 'all is well, and you are welcome to disembark. But they are like animals! They grabbed my simple cloth from me and tore at my genitals, feeling and grabbing all at once. I feared I may lose my stalk, that it may be torn from my body!'

There was a loud cheer from the oarsmen as they stood up, readying themselves to go ashore. Jason grinned broadly. 'Come, my fine Argonauts! Let us join these love-starved maidens and satisfy their every whim! Let no man return to the *Argo* without great soreness of cock, blistered tongue and roughly scratched body!' He turned to Atalanta and Glaucis. 'I trust we may leave the safety of the *Argo* in your capable hands?'

'Go, Jason,' said Atalanta, 'have your fill. Hera has demanded that you repopulate the island; it is your duty.'

'You are right,' said Jason, with mock sincerity, 'it is my duty!' With that he was over the side, joining the others of his crew in a mad swim towards the beach where already they could see the women throwing aside their heavy garments and rushing headlong into the waves to welcome them, preparing themselves for the joys to come.

Jason pulled himself to his feet as he reached the warming sand of the Lemnian beach, amused at the sight of his fine Argonauts as they ran, naked and rampant amongst the throng of willing females, grabbing wildly at the surfeit of woman-flesh on all sides. He pulled his loin-cloth away from his body and stood, proudly nude, watching the bacchanalian scene developing before him.

'Jason, I have waited for you.'

The voice was strong, but distinctly feminine. Jason looked in the direction of the sound and drew a sharp breath as he saw a figure so lovely, so erotic as to be the stuff of dreams. Exceptionally tall, over two inches taller than Jason himself she stood, bare foot with her legs planted firmly apart, her hands placed resolutely on strong, rounded hips. She wore nothing but gold, fashioned into rings and chains, arranged in ways to accentuate and eroticise her body, to display her charms at their most delectable.

Jason suddenly regretted casting his clothing aside, feeling somewhat foolish as his penis uncontrollably began to rise in response to the sight before him. Her hair was jet black, darker even than Atalanta's, shining almost blue in the strengthening sunlight. Her skin was olive and flawless, a sheen of light seeming to emanate from her very pores. Her breasts, ringed in thick gold were superbly large, raised

73

high by the shackles of chains that supported them from around her neck. Further chains snaked here and there around her lower body; one thin shard of gold slipping between the hairless folds of her prominent pussy, parting the labia which glinted with the wetness of desire.

'I am Hypsipyle, Queen of Lemnos,' she said, her voice husky with lust, 'you are welcome to our island.'

Jason bowed his head in greeting, noticing at once that his erection now stood ridiculously upward, the evidence of his need to impale this vision of erotica wetly visible at the tip. 'I am glad to meet you, my Queen,' he said.

'Clearly,' she laughed, reaching out and catching hold of the huge stalk, 'fuck me now; lose this surge of lust within my hungry body, then we will return to my palace at Myrine, where we will make love with less urgency, and enjoy many pleasures.'

Without allowing him to reply she turned her back to him and, bending her legs slightly she arched her body until her hands were flat on the sand and she looked at him from between her outstretched legs.

'Fuck me, Jason, hard! Spare me no mercy! I need to feel that monster inside me!'

All around him were the sights and sounds of copulation s the Argonauts threw themselves upon woman after woman, the breezeless air scented with sex. Before him was the vision of the perfect female bottom, presented to him like a mare to her stallion. Jason was powerless to resist. He grabbed at the chain which ran between her sex-lips and the cleft of her bottom and pulled it roughly to one side, the action opening up her pussy in preparation for his impending onslaught. Taking his stiff cock in one hand he guided it to the wet entrance and thrust heavily forward, thrilling as the hot, soaked sheath accepted every inch in one, hard movement, the contracting vaginal muscles gripping and almost sucking his invading flesh like a deep, hot mouth.

He held onto the thin chain with his other hand as though riding a wild animal, hammering into the tight confines of her pussy with all the force he could muster, his only desire being to release his pent-up frustration within the divine pleasures of this perfect body.

The Queen groaned heavily with each thundering thrust, digging her hands into the sand for support. 'Yes, yes!' she squealed, 'how I need this! It has been so long, so very long! Harder! Harder, I command it!'

Jason was lost, the sperm already rushing along the thick stem of his penis to enter the lovely woman's body. He roared out, tugging hard at the chain, feeling it bite into the base of his stalk as he came, pumping wildly, feeling no pain, only pleasure. The links rubbed against him roughly, the sensation only heightening the joy of his release.

Hypsipyle fell to the sand, exhausted from his onslaught. Jason knelt at her side quickly, more for fear that his legs might give way than concern for his lover, panting heavily.

'I needed that,' she breathed, 'I needed it quick and hard. It has been so very long, far too long. Now we will return to Myrine, and I will teach you how to pleasure me more.'

Jason rose with her, meekly and in total submission, her spell complete.

A great feast was hurriedly prepared in honour of the arrival of the Argonauts who, one by one wearily trudged into the magnificent hall of the palace at Myrine, their ardour temporarily sated by the orgy at the beach. Jason sat at the head of the table with the Queen, who was now dressed in resplendent, but nevertheless revealing robes of the finest silk. He seemed in awe of her beauty, transfixed by the sheer flawless beauty of her countenance and the sight of her sumptuous breasts, their firm voluptuousness enhanced by the opaque material. She wore her shining black hair high on top of her head, accenting the delicate slope of her long neck and shoulders, her small ears bearing the considerable weight of jewellery of the most opulent design.

The food was good and, above all, fresh to the jaded palates of the adventurers; the drink was strong and plentiful. As the day wore on into the hot afternoon clothing was again cast aside, and couples began mounting each other at will; a second orgy developing quickly. The strong-bodied oarsmen, their erections virtually permanent, rushed from one unclothed nymphet to another, the groans of pleasure and satisfaction echoing around the hall.

Jason watched the scene grinning broadly, happy that his crew were enjoying a well earned reward for their long labours of the previous weeks. Hypsipyle reached into the loose cloth around his groin and caressed his penis to full erection as he watched, casually stroking the firm length whilst all the time gazing at his handsome features.

Jason roared with laughter at the sight of one of his men attempting to force a rather large but phallically shaped item of fruit into the rear of a willing and exceptionally fat female, the drunken laughter from the couple causing them both to fall to the floor in a heap. 'See those idiots,' he chuckled, turning to the Queen, 'see what fools they . . .' He broke off when he caught the power of her gaze, her look serious, her eyes shining with lust and desire.

'I need you again, Jason,' she whispered, her words barely audible above the cacophony, 'but I need you in my way.' She tore her gaze from his and looked lovingly at the firm stalk in her gently moving hand. 'I want this so badly, deep inside me again.'

Jason leant forward and kissed her mouth with a passion reserved for true lovers. He slipped his hand inside the silk of her dress, quickly finding the warm wetness of her sex, his finger sliding inside at his touch. 'Let us teach these rampant devils how to fuck; let us show them what . . .'

'No, Jason, not here. I want you alone, to myself. Come, let us go to my bed-chamber.'

Hypsipyle stood up, still holding Jason by the cock, and led him by it from the table. They walked slowly from the room, down a long corridor to a large door of dark, heavy wood. Releasing her erotic grip, the Queen opened the door and ushered Jason within.

The room was a temple of opulence, the centrepiece of which was a giant bed blanketed in large cushions and drapes. All around, the walls and ceiling were covered with fine, gold framed mirrors, all turned to reflect the image of the bed to which Hypsipyle now led Jason, like a goat to slaughter.

She bade him lie on his back in the centre of the vast expanse of soft pillows and calmly removed the useless strip of cloth from around his loins, throwing it contemptuously to one side. He lay his head back, seeing his reflection repeated a thousand times in the mirrors above him, pleased with the sight of his fine, tanned body and the superb erection resting heavily on his muscular stomach.

He felt his lover tugging at one of his arms and looked towards her, seeing her wrapping a strong strip of leather around his wrist, the other end fixed securely to the edge of the bed. He watched, with increasing curiosity and arousal as she walked around to the other side, repeating her actions with another tether, then again as she moved to the foot of the bed and spread his legs wide, tying them by the ankles tightly.

He tried to move; he could not. 'You need not have tied me so,' he said, grinning, 'I am yours to command, my Queen.'

'Maybe so,' she said, slipping the silk from her smooth body and revealing the delights of her nakedness once again to his hungry gaze, 'but if I am to have my ultimate pleasure you must be restrained.'

Jason began to feel excitedly nervous; the more so when she crawled, cat-like onto him and began to pinch and scratch at his flesh. She bent her head and took his nipple into her mouth and sucked lightly, then bit, hard enough to make him flinch. She then sat on her haunches, the wetness of her pussy touching his thigh, the expression in her eyes one of total lust. Without taking her gaze away she bent forward again and took the other nipple into her mouth. He jumped at the pain of her teeth biting into the tender flesh, but this time enjoyed the sensation.

The Queen straddled his body, the open lips of her labia pressed against the base of his fiercely hard cock like a wet mouth. She continued to bite and nibble at his chest, clawing the flesh, occasionally drawing blood with the sharpness of her fingernails, the exquisite pain filling his head with a craving for more. She moved her thighs back and forth, drawing her soft cunt along the full length of his erection, his response being to move his backside in a vain attempt to penetrate the soft pouting sex-flesh.

'You tease me, my Queen,' he groaned, 'but there is much pleasure in what you do.'

'I have just begun,' she breathed, kissing his mouth lightly, 'I will torment and arouse you so much that, when I finally allow you within my body you will experience a fuck like you will never know again. Every nerve-ending in your body will be alive with lust, your entire consciousness will be in the control of Eros.' With that, she slid her body from him and stood at the side of the large bed, staring lovingly at the prone and helpless figure.

'I must prepare,' she said, mysteriously, 'meanwhile, I have some entertainment for you, to keep you in readiness for what is to come.' She clapped her hands loudly and a door swung open, allowing a boy and a girl, barely sixteen or seventeen years of age to enter. Both were naked, fair of complexion and hair, their faces fresh with innocence and excitement.

The girl was slim, almost thin, with tiny breasts but long, rose-pink nipples. A sparse bush of white-blonde curls covered her sex, the lips already reddened with arousal. The boy was equally small in stature but handsome in the extreme, a young adonis of slim but muscular physique. His small penis was fully erect and coated in a damp, glistening sheen, clear evidence that the young couple had been enjoying each other until summoned by their Queen.

They moved to where Jason lay and stood on either side of him, as Hypsipyle quietly left the room. They regarded the tethered figure for a moment, both seeming to take particular interest in his massive cock, lying in painful erection on his belly. Then, as though receiving a silent instruction, the girl took up an ornate ewer from a small table and poured its contents, a warm, silky oil, over Jason's chest and groin. She allowed it to trickle along the full length of his penis, the sensation causing it to twitch. A small pool of white fluid oozed from the end onto his skin. The girl dipped the tip of her finger into it and then put it suggestively to her mouth, licking it and sucking to the knuckle.

The boy began to massage the oil into Jason's body, the girl following his example. Carefully and smoothly they passed their hands over his torso, pulling gently at the lust-racked flesh. They seemed to be taking particular care to avoid touching his genitals which, he realised was to the good, for the slightest erotic caress would have caused him to explode in orgasm.

Jason closed his eyes and bit into his lower lip, tasting blood as he forced himself away from the orgasm which threatened to burst within his teased body, anxious that he should be able to serve their lovely Queen on her return. He felt the girl slide her body across his and squat over him, in much the same way as her mistress had done moments before, the warm wetness of her pussy touching his engorged cock. He mused that he might enter her but, almost before the thought had crossed his mind he sensed the boy joining them on the bed, kneeling across Jason's legs behind the vulnerably positioned body of the young girl.

She put her face towards Jason's and pressed her lips to his, her tongue seeking out the depths of his mouth. As she did so he felt her press her cunt against the base of his cock and knew instantly from her movements that her lover was inside her. She groaned within their oral embrace as the young man began to thrust in and out of her body, the sensation of feeling their passion so close without being able to participate driving Jason to the edges of insanity.

The thrusting became faster and faster, the rutting of the inexperienced couple quickly heading for its climax. All the time the girl held Jason's kiss, her backside wriggled in response to her fucking, and the hard bud of her clitoris rubbed against his fiercely hard erection. He heard the boy groan, the pumping even faster, the girl at last raising her head from his and crying softly as her own release matched that of her lover.

The movements slowed gradually, much to Jason's relief, and the sated couple fell away from his body, lying momentarily at his sides. Then, without a word they slipped from the bed and were gone, silently from the room.

Jason lay quietly, staring up at his image in the mirrored ceiling. He hadn't dared catch sight of the boy and girl as they fucked each other whilst using his body for their bed; that would have been too much. Happily, his fine erection remained, ready for whatever else the Queen had in store for him.

He didn't have to wait long. The door opened once more and Hypsipyle re-entered. Now she wore a garment of black shining hide decorated with gold and silver chains, which covered all her body save for her superb breasts and the pouting lips of her hairless pussy. Her erect nipples were now pierced with small, golden rings, to which were attached thin chains which trailed from them around the back of her neck. The outer lips of her sex were similarly pierced, two tiny rings on either side of her open slit, delicate, silk-like strands of chain pulling them slightly apart.

In her hand she held a fearsome-looking whip, hide-handled with many strands of thin leather. Jason looked at the implement with a mixture of lust and apprehension, knowing what was to come.

'I trust my servants pleased you with their antics,' she said, slowly and deliberately drawing the strand of the whip between her legs, soaking them with her juices.

'Regally so, my Queen,' he said, his voice hoarse with lust, as he watched the movements of the whip, seeing her work the strands into a ball and push them inside the loose lips of her cunt before slowly withdrawing the wet leather and sensuously stroking it across the palm of her hand. 'Now pray, what further delights do you have in store for me?'

The Queen said nothing, but swished the whip in the air, droplets of her own juices flicking across his oiled body. She trailed the strands across his thighs, up between them to his balls, before pushing them against his anus, as if trying to gain entry. Then she raised the whip high. Jason closed his eyes.

'Watch!' she commanded. Jason snapped his eyes open in obedience. Immediately he did so she brought the whip swishing down on his thighs, the pain sharp but bearable. Another stroke and the thin shards of leather kissed his stomach, just missing the thick length of his engorged penis. Again she whipped him, this time on the other side of his belly, the tip of one sliver of leather just catching the head of his cock, causing him to cry out.

Hypsipyle grinned manically at his response and brought the full force of the whip across the stem of his erection. A lesser man might have lost his ardour at this treatment; Jason was made of sterner stuff, and was far too aroused not to respond as she clearly wished. Again and again she beat him across the genitals, thighs and chest; and as a result, his monstrous cock grew ever more purple with desire.

Suddenly she threw the whip to one side and flung herself across him, grabbing at his penis with both hands. Squatting across him again, but this time with her back to him she sat down hard on his stalk, taking every inch deep inside the soaking sheath of her cunt. She leant forward, holding his ankles with her hands and began to bounce up and down on his groin, affording him a full view of this exquisite penetration and her perfect bottom framed by the thin hide, the four, small pussy rings adding to the eroticism of the image.

The Queen was lost in the arms of total ecstasy now; all that was needed to bring her to the point of orgasm were her own wild movements. Jason watched in awe as she thumped her body up and down, harder and harder, her buttocks slapping against his groin. He wanted to reach out and caress her delightful bottom, to insert his fingers into her forbidden orifice, knowing the pleasure this would give her, but the restraints held his wrists tightly.

With a scream that would have been heard in the very depths of Pluto's underworld she came, her fingers gripping Jason's ankles tightly, the nails digging into his flesh. She hammered her backside against him, grunting like an animal as she sated herself on his hard sex-flesh. Another cry and the force of her assault began to ease, her breathing becoming sharp and stilted.

Her movements slowed gradually, her sighs melting into whimpers and she relaxed in her heavenly position, his long cock still firmly embedded in the warmth of her pussy.

'Oh Jason,' she panted, lying back on his body, her sweat mixing with his own and the lightly perfumed oil that soaked his body, 'I meant to torment you into begging for my favours and instead it was I who raped you!'

'Hardly a rape,' he whispered. 'Had you not leapt upon me at that moment I would have torn myself from these shackles and penetrated you, whatever your objections might have been.'

The Queen moved to his side, his cock slipping out of her to rest again against his belly, still hard and ready. 'There would have been no objections,' she said, slowly, 'and there never will be. Stay with us, Jason, become King of Lemnos.'

'That cannot be, sweet Queen, I have a great quest to perform, a destiny to fulfil.'

Hypsipyle smiled resignedly and slipped from the bed, carefully untying the leather restraints that held her lover's aching limbs. 'I felt you would say that, and I am sad. Nevertheless, you and your fine Argonauts will stay with us for one week, to complete the task set for you by Hera, to repopulate our land.'

Jason sat on the bed, rubbing his wrists, his erection bobbing ridiculously. 'You know of Hera's command?'

'It was our prayers that brought you to us. Each of us was made fertile and ready, your seed is all that is necessary to bring life to this sad island.' She looked at his stalk and grinned. 'I see from the state of your fine prick that there is much seed within you now, which rightfully belongs to me!'

Jason ran his hand softly over the smooth skin of the warrior maiden. 'And how will I please you this time?' he said, tenderly.

The Queen turned and lay on her stomach, bunching a pair of large cushions under her groin so that her bottom was presented to him in a most indecent way. 'Tether me, Jason, and enter me from behind. But whip me first, as hard as I tortured you!'

He tied her quickly with the strips of leather that had so recently held him at her mercy and took up the whip. She looked over her shoulder at him as he positioned himself to beat her, her face a picture of desire, her eyes shining with lust. Raising the flail he ran his free hand over the softness of her pert buttocks, teasing her as she had teased him.

'Flog me, lash me, punish me for the pain I caused you!' Her voice was almost crazed, the wriggling of her body giving display to her obvious yearning.

Jason brought the whip down with a swift, hard stroke, the strips of leather lashing across the perfect globes of her bottom with a stinging crack. She cried out, her hands clawing at the restraining bonds around her wrists. 'Yes, more! Harder! I must be punished!'

Three, maybe four more strokes were delivered with equal force to the quivering, red-lined buttocks before Jason threw the scourge to one side and positioned himself behind her, ready to impale her sweet treasures with his aching length. Parting the cheeks of her bottom with one hand and taking his cock in the other he pressed the thick, bulbous end to the target of her soaked cunt and pushed forward, slipping deep inside the hot sheath once more.

Slowly he began to fuck her with long, deliberate strokes, the sight of her lashed arse and the knowledge that she was tethered and at his command stimulating in the extreme. He watched transfixed as she stiffened the muscles of her upper thighs, and he felt his stalk gripped tightly in her silky pussy, the deliberately sensuous movements of her bottom compounding his joy.

Gradually his pace quickened, and with it her muffled moans of pleasure, her head pressed hard into a cushion. Despite her restraints she managed to arch her back, taking his full length deep inside her, the tip hitting urgently against the entrance to her womb. The sight of her up-turned bottom, the tight sphincter damp with sweat from his belly, seemingly beckoned to him, demanding attention.

Carefully he pushed a finger, well lubricated from her sweet juices, into the welcoming orifice. The Queen groaned loudly, pulling hard at her tethers as she tried to force her arse ever upwards, the steady pumping of his long prick in and out of her soaked pussy matched by the rhythmic movements of her hips.

A second finger entered her anus, both now pushed deep to the knuckle. With his fingertips Jason could feel the movements of his hard cock against the thin wall of membrane that separated the two plundered sheaths.

'Take me there, Jason, enter my tiny hole with your mighty cock! Fuck my bottom! Fuck me as hard as you wish, tear me apart!' Hypsipyle's cries were hoarse and near-hysterical, her lust clearly overpowering her senses. Jason slowly withdrew his engorged shaft from the oozing heat of her cunt, the tight lips drawn out with the superb width, then cautiously pressed the huge end to her puckered anus, pushing forward with tender care, fearing his great size would hurt so delicate a sheath, however willingly offered.

'Yes, Jason, there! Yes! Push in, push in! Spare me no mercy! Hurt me, defile me!'

Her voice was pleading, begging. He pushed forward with great force, hearing her moans of ecstasy and pain as the great shaft slid, inch by searing inch into her arse, stretching, probing.

'More, more!' she yelled, her head pulled back from the cushion, her fingernails digging into the palms of her hands.

'I do not wish to injure you, my Queen,' said Jason, feeling the intense tightness around his shaft lessening slightly.

'You are the first to do this, Jason,' she panted, 'I want the pain of your wonderful invasion of my virgin hole to be with me for ever. Fuck me, harder! Fill me with every inch!'

The muscles of her anus relaxed completely now and Jason felt his full length slide effortlessly into her deepest secrets. He began again to thrust harder and quicker, the sensation of the gripping contact along his entire pained cock drawing him ever closer to his release.

'I cannot hold back any more, sweet Queen,' he cried, the surge of his orgasm beginning to build with his loins. 'I must come, I must fill your sweet bottom with my cream!'

'Yes, Jason,' she shouted, 'do it now! Harder, give me everything, yes, yes!'

Her body began to shudder as her loud squeals heralded her come, matched in timing by Jason's groans of pleasure as he fucked her backside heavily, the sperm jetting from his iron-hard cock deep inside her. He fell across her body still thrusting into her, their moans and sighs of joy echoing around the room, reverberating against the glass of the mirrors.

They lay silent for some time, Jason still embedded inside the Queen's deflowered orifice. He reached over and gently untied the strand of leather around one of her wrists, gasping at the deep red gash her struggles had caused it to make in her flesh. Easing himself from her he untied the remainder of the tethers, stroking the bruised and cut areas with the tips of his fingers.

Gradually, the Queen slipped into exhausted sleep and he lay at her side, caressing her olive-skinned body lovingly until he too entered the realm of Hypnos.

CHAPTER FIVE

The journey on board the *Phallicis* from Scyros to Medea's next destination, the beautiful, wooded and mountainous land known as Arcadia, had been slow and arduous. The Westerly wind that had so aided Jason's passage in *Argo* had forced the Phallician women to do without their sail and, causing them instead to row constantly against the prevailing weather.

Now at last, Arcadia lay before them, a veritable paradise on earth, the very domain of the God of nature, Pan himself.

Their vessel was moored some distance from the shore, the anchor-stone embedded in soft silt. Already, most of the women had waded ashore, anxious to test the firmness of land again, leaving Medea, Madeleine and a handful of others on board. Medea had decided to postpone her own trip to the beach until her crew had tasted its delights, and Madeleine, as ever, remained at her side.

The sun was beginning to lose some of its awesome power, the evening sounds starting to fill the air as the shadows lengthened on the deck above. They lay quietly in the small cot in Medea's cabin, their nakedness bathed in the sweat of love, resting from the labours of pleasure.

'You remember we spoke of the loss of our virginity,' Madeleine said quietly, her fingers playing lazily with the soft folds of puffy flesh between Medea's legs, 'and you told of your wonderful first night with Jason?'

'It seems so long ago,' said Medea, wistfully, 'another time, another age.'

Madeleine turned on her side and rested her head on her

hand, looking at the sublime face of her lover. 'You obviously love him deeply, don't you?'

Medea nodded. 'More than life itself,' she said.

'Then why take other lovers? I mean, I can understand you wishing to lie with me, to ease the pain of frustration and neglect that a long journey inevitably brings, but there were so many in Iolcus alone. Why, I counted five, maybe six . . .'

'There have been many.' Medea put her hand to her forehead, wrinkling up the delicate skin with a look of confusion and self-doubt. 'I have needs, needs so strong that even a wonderful lover such as Jason cannot sate my lust. Before I laid with him I was unaware of the power of these desires, but from the very instant that he impaled me on that regal bed in front of those baying voyeurs my libido became transformed, as though out of control.'

'Would it worry you if Jason discovered your secret?'

'Sometimes I feel he already knows. But is it not just sex? Why not enjoy the pleasures so divinely granted to us by Aphrodite whilst we can? A fuck with an unknown lover, a complete stranger can be just as exciting, indeed *more* exciting than lying with a husband, no matter how much love you feel for him.'

'Indeed, I agree, for such is the wisdom of my people. As I have related before, fidelity amongst the men and women of Tipos was unheard of, almost a sin in itself!'

'And there would be no arguments or jealousies?'

'None.'

'There, then, such is my point.' Medea reached for a silver goblet and drank the remains of some cool wine. 'Jason and I released each other from any vow of fidelity for the duration of our quests and we feel no shackles around us, no unrealistic chains on our emotions.'

'You mean you do not care if he lies in the arms of another, even as we speak?'

No,' said Medea, with little conviction in her tone, 'no, let him enjoy her, as I will enjoy myself with others!'

She grabbed hold of Madeleine's naked body and pressed her own against it, the two women laughing as they hugged closely on the small bed. Their lust recently sated, they tickled and slapped each other, rolling about like children at play.

After a moment or two of this they lay again, side by side, staring at the low, wooden ceiling of the cabin. 'Tell me, Medea,' said Madeleine, 'of your first encounter with another after Jason had relieved you of your virginity.'

There was a short, quiet pause as Medea relived the memory, a faint smile playing across her lips. 'It was on a small island called Skos, two days from the Bosphorus. The *Argo* had anchored to take up supplies of fresh fruit and water and most of the men were in the hills, hunting for meat. I had decided to laze about on the shore, to enjoy the caress of the sun.

'I remember the day being excessively hot, so hot that I had to lie in the shade of some bushes at the edge of the beach. The setting was beautiful, the sky cloudless, the sea calm and azure-blue, lapping sultrily against the near-white sand of the beach. Close to where I lay a small cascade of water fell from the cliffs above, a long stream of sparkling, cool water hitting a shallow pool before running over a bed of pebbles and into the sea.

'My only companion was a young Colchian slave who had joined us on our escape from his homeland with the fleece. We knew him only as Taki; he spoke very little, but was always keen to help the Argonauts, to be of service to them.

'This day, Taki had offered to accompany me, to stand guard against any unknown dangers that may lurk within the thick woods beyond the beach. I told him that it was unnecessary, that I could protect myself, but he insisted.'

'Was he handsome?' asked Madeleine, curling her arm around Medea's waist.

'Very. He was not particularly tall, probably the same height as me, and his hair was blond, unusual for his race. His body was slim and very athletic, and his skin bore a deep, golden tan which emphasised his lithe shape in a most appealing way.

'He stood silently beside me on the beach, plying me

occasionally with cool wine or grapes. He wore nothing but a small leather thong, the thin strip of hide disappearing between his strong buttocks, the pouch concealing other obvious delights. The more wine I drank the more I became interested in whatever secrets were held within that purse of leather, and he caught my gaze a couple of times as I feasted my eyes on the promising bulge.

'I knew I wanted him, but I knew also that I was the wife of Jason and besides, there was no way this grateful slave would betray his new master. I decided to walk to the water's edge, to bathe my feet in the shallows, to perhaps cool my ardour.

'I stood up and walked out of the shade, the sudden feel of the searing heat of the sun striking my back with a vengeance. I was wearing a dress of lightweight, white linen which left most of my back bare but otherwise covered my body, and I had to raise it slightly as I stepped into the gently lapping waves to avoid it becoming wet.

'The water was cool and soothing to my legs, the playful nibbling of tiny fish at my toes a most delightful sensation. I let my dress fall, the hem floating on the surface and I waded further into the welcoming swell. Soon, the water was past my waist and I lay back, letting my feet rise from the sand and floated in the waves. I shouted to my companion, "This is heaven, Taki, come and join me!" and closed my eyes, drifting in the cool embrace of Poseidon.

'Taki was soon at my side, his hand cupping my head, allowing me to float without movement. I opened my eyes and looked at his form, silhouetted against the sun. I couldn't see the expression on his face but he could see mine. I smiled and licked my lips in as suggestive a way as I knew how, then closed my eyes again. Almost immediately I felt the touch of a cautious kiss on my forehead, then another, braver touch of his lips to mine.

'I stood up in the shallow water and pulled him towards me, pressing my body hard against his as I returned his kiss, the deep searching of my tongue within his mouth telling him that I was his, that he was to have me.

'Without a word he led me back to the beach, lying me

on the shaded sand, crouching at my side. He quickly pulled off my wet dress and, for a few moments simply stared at my nakedness, his eyes savouring the sight of my body, knowing with certainty that he was about to fuck me.

'He leant forward and kissed me again, a sweet, delicate embrace, gently arousing in its tenderness. He then spoke, for the first time that afternoon. "What of Jason, my lady?"

'I replied "Jason will never know, come, I want you", or similar words, not being in the mood for conversation. We kissed again, this time with much more passion, his hands roaming over my body, feeling, touching, learning. He pinched each of my nipples in turn, squeezing them hard and causing them to rise to full erection before diving his head down to my breasts, suckling on one, then the other, his hands stroking my belly and back.

'I shifted myself within his embrace, anxious for him to touch the place between my legs, the wetness beginning to run from the opening lips to dampen the sand below my bottom. His gently searching fingers stroked my groin, my thighs, my buttocks but he seemed a little wary about pressing them to my most intimate prize, I . . .'

Madeleine sat up, exasperated. 'Why do you insist on speaking in this way? Intimate prize, indeed. You wanted him to touch your cunt, so say what you mean!'

Medea laughed. 'I am sorry, dear Madeleine, you are right. It's just that it was such a romantic encounter, and crude expressions don't seem somehow fitting. Nevertheless, I will continue in the way I know you prefer.

'He knelt between my legs, kissing and suckling again at my breasts, then moved his head lower and lower, his tongue snaking across my flesh, nearer, nearer. I felt the tip of his tongue touch the newly grown hair above my pussy and raised my legs high in the air, my heels touching the back of his head, drawing him to his target. Still he held back, licking the tops of my thighs and nibbling at my pubic hair, his breath warm against my soaked lips, the closeness of him driving me insane.

'I could stand no more of it. I grabbed his head and forced his mouth to my aching pussy, and shouted "Lick my cunt, lick my cunt!" as I gripped his hair, holding him a prisoner between my thighs. At last I felt his tongue lapping at me, the tip flicking deftly over my hard bud, the combination of his expert technique and my extreme arousal caused by his teasing bringing me to orgasm almost immediately.

'I felt twinges in my buttocks, the sensation of erotic spasms shooting down my legs as his oral caress took me over the edge, and I shuddered and mewed with the pleasure of a most exquisite come.

'As the feelings within me subsided he sat up and gazed at me, smiling as he wiped his mouth on the back of his hand. We were both sweating profusely, the heat almost unbearable. Taki stood up and removed the little thong from his loins, revealing his erection raised in proud anticipation. "It is so hot, Taki," I said, "let me bathe again first." He grinned and held out his hand, helping me to my feet.

'He kissed me lightly on the mouth, letting me share the taste of my arousal, then took me by the arm and led me towards the waterfall. He stepped into the shallow pool and made me follow him, taking hold of me under the gently falling water, the sudden coolness a sharp contrast to the searing heat of the sun. He held me close and we kissed under the soothing shower, the water cascading over our naked bodies, running from us into the pool.

'Although he was about the same height as me his legs were somewhat shorter than mine, the shape of our bodies consequently ideally suited for what was to happen. Taki pushed his hand between my legs, parting the lips of my pussy, then carefully guided his stiff cock within me, his short but thick length quickly inside my burning hole. He gripped my buttocks with both hands and began to move in and out, fucking me gently at first under the cool shower, the water flowing over my body, over my back and my breasts, down between the cheeks of my bottom, trickling sensuously along my legs to the pool below.

'He gripped my legs, first one, then the other, holding me under my thighs, raising me so that my legs were wrapped around his upper body, his thick prick still working

91

steadily in and out of my cunt. He bounced me up and down, using me to satisfy his rising lust, my arms clinging to his neck, my legs now over his shoulders, the only other contact between us being our genitals.

'After a few minutes of this delightfully erotic position he let me down and I turned my back to him, pressing the palms of my hands against the rock wall of the cliff and presenting my bottom to him. He was back inside my pussy in an instant, fucking me hard, the force causing my knees to buckle, the pleasure intense. Over and over his strong groin thwacked against my buttocks, the water spraying around us as he drove himself into me.

'He suddenly withdrew, and I needed to feel him inside me again, immediately. I turned and faced him, grabbing at his stalk with one hand, rubbing my erect clitoris with the other. I almost dragged his hardness back inside me, raising one of my legs over his shoulder, the other remaining on the ground, my pussy stretched wide to accept his wonderful thickness.

'Gradually his pace increased, his fingers gripping my bottom firmly, pulling my hips to his in steady rhythm. Faster and faster he moved, our wet bellies slapping together noisily as he neared his release.

I felt him swell inside me and I was suddenly taken with a desire to taste his seed. I pulled myself from him and fell to my knees in the water, grabbing his strong thighs and clamping my hungry mouth over his stiff tool, drawing his entire length to the back of my throat.

'My timing was perfect. I felt the muscles of his thighs stiffen and sensed the now familiar throbbing of a man's cock against my tongue, this method of release being a favourite of my husband's. I felt the hot sperm jetting into my mouth and swallowed hard, suckling his spurting weapon greedily, until he fell back from me, falling heavily into the pool. We hugged each other tightly under the incessantly cascading shower, kissing with a passion of long-time lovers, bathing in the coolness of the water, my sated lust subsiding with the pounding of my heart.

'Our fuck had been quick and abandoned, but was all

the more satisfying for its suddenness, and for the excitement of my first infidelity.'

Madeleine lay back, her fingers toying with the wet lips of her own pussy. 'Did Taki fuck you again?'

'Twice more, on the beach, but never again when we returned to the *Argo*. It could not be. My need is for variety, the heart-stopping exhilaration of clandestine meetings. I have the love of Jason and he has mine. Sex is something quite separate.'

'I am envious, Medea,' said Madeleine, genuinely. 'Perhaps one day I will find a fine husband who I can cheat on regularly.'

Medea laughed and slapped Madeleine hard on the rump. 'Come, my dear friend, Arcadia awaits!'

As Medea and Madeleine waded ashore they were met by Electra running excitedly from the cover of the thick woodland onto the beach. Her hair was wild and unkempt, her face flushed with exhilaration, her eyes sparkling. She rushed over to them, gripping them by the arms like a child with a special secret to impart.

'We have truly found paradise!' she chattered, 'we need travel no further! All we could ever want is here, on Arcadia!'

'What do you mean?' said Medea, holding onto the excited girl's arm. 'What is so special about this place?'

Electra caught her by the hand and almost dragged her up the beach towards the trees, Madeleine following behind. 'Come on, you'll see!'

Medea decided not to ask anymore questions, not that Electra was in any mood to answer them. They stumbled through the thick bushes and hedged into the relative coolness of the shading woods, the sun occasionally bursting sharply through the canopy of leaves. None of them were dressed for brushing against twigs and rough branches; Electra wore only a small piece of hide around her waist which just preserved her modesty, Medea and Madeleine were clothed in thin linen slips, still wet from their swim and practically transparent.

Mercifully, the trees soon gave way to a sudden clearing,

93

the brightness of the sunlight contrasting vividly with the darkness of the woods. Electra stood still, holding an arm out as if in demonstration. 'See, did I not say we have all we need?'

Medea and Madeleine looked in wonderment at the scene before them. There, in the comfort of the long, dry grass just yards in front of where they stood lay their crew, all happily coupling with at least one athletic, lithe young man, each one no less handsome than another. The groans and sighs of coital bliss filled the air around them, together with the scent of fresh sweat and arousal.

Nana, Electra's lovely sister, knelt on her hands and knees close by, her bottom being steadily penetrated by the long, thick and glistening cock of a black youth of superb physique. Nearby, Iole lay on her back, her legs held high in the air by two fine athletes as a third fucked her heavily, wriggling his backside as he invaded every part of her recently deflowered pussy.

All around them, close on forty young women were being satisfied by at least twice as many fine, handsome men, a sight which brought the heat of lust to Medea's crotch like a shaft of lightning from Mount Olympus itself.

Madeleine walked into the centre of the throng as though in a trance, casually divesting herself of her flimsy garment and letting it fall to the ground. Almost immediately she was joined by three naked young men, their erections hard and ready, and led to an unoccupied corner of the glade. Medea stood for a moment, enjoying the scene, happily recounting her luck. What good fortune, to find so many suitable athletes, first on their visit to Scyros, releasing the black slaves of Rapis and now here, in the paradise called Arcadia.

'You must be Medea, wife of Jason and soon to be Queen of Iolcus.' The voice was deep but warm in tone, coming from behind her. Medea turned quickly, to be faced by a tall and broadly muscular man who appeared to be about thirty-five years of age, his face strong with experience, framed by his lightly-curled, black hair cascading to his shoulders. He grinned as he looked at her, his eyes shining wickedly, as though he was about to play a wild prank on her.

He was naked, his lower body exceptionally hirsute, the torso, by contrast, showing hardly a trace of hair. His penis hung limply, the damply matted curls surrounding it giving evidence of recent copulation with one or more of Medea's crew. She gazed at the long, thick appendage, her mouth becoming dry as it steadily thickened and rose before her, hardening to a size that she would not have dreamt possible; it was as long as her forearm and of even greater girth.

'I am Faunus, the shepherd,' he boomed, proudly, 'this is my domain.'

'Your domain?' queried Medea, trying in vain to ignore his huge phallus, 'you do not speak as a shepherd.'

'My flock is one of fine athletes, such as you see before you.' He waved in the direction of the seething mass of grunting nakedness in the grass.

'How do you come to know my name?'

'I know much about you. News of your quest has travelled to this island and I have waited eagerly, preparing my flock, ordering them to be in readiness to serve you.'

Medea looked at the scene of bacchanalia and laughed. 'They certainly seem well prepared,' she said.

Faunus reached out and took her wrist, putting her hand to his immense cock. Medea curled her fingers around the thick stem, vainly trying to encompass it within her grip. 'Come,' he said, gently, 'let me lead you into the woods and sink my fine staff within your silky purse which I sense is yearning to be stretched and sated.'

'You are so enormous, Faunus, I am not sure that my tiny pussy can accommodate such a monster!'

Faunus simply grinned, his eyes glinting as he led Medea into the trees. He strode purposefully into the thick woods, clutching tightly at her small wrist as though he was concerned that she may escape. Medea found herself stumbling over the bracken and clumps of grass as he almost hauled her along, his phallus waving menacingly from side to side, the erection fierce and incongruously threatening.

'Slow, Faunus, you will have me too exhausted to please you!'

'We are here, sweet Queen,' said her captor, brusquely. 'Now lay on the grass and I will soothe your temperament before taking you completely.'

Medea stripped off her flimsy slip and sank obediently to the ground, relaxing back on the soft, cool grass. Faunus sat at her side, taking up a small set of pipes which seemed to have magically appeared at his side and put the instrument to his lips. A gentle, ethereal note sounded as though from the air around her, sweet and hypnotic, causing her to shiver with delight. She closed her eyes as another long, sweet tone filled her mind, then another, the music without true form but with an unworldly beauty she found irresistible.

Slowly she felt herself falling under the spell of the syrinx, her very soul being willingly drawn within its control. Her sleep was heavy, the dream immediate.

Medea opened her eyes dreamily, finding herself lying on the softest of beds in a darkened but nevertheless obviously grandiose room, the bedroom of a fine palace. She kicked the rich, silk sheets off her bed, the sticky heat of the night becoming increasingly unbearable. The light from the full moon illuminated the great room, casting sharp shadows and creating eerie shapes in the darkened corners. A slight breeze occasionally gently wafted the thin lace curtains in front of the open terrace window.

She was alone again, lying naked and beautiful but feeling unwanted, unneeded. Her husband Jason would be with his men, drinking himself senseless until the morning, endlessly recounting tales of past quests. She tossed her head to one side and slapped the pillow hard with her arm out of frustration. Why had she done it? Why had she married this dreadful man?

She knew why, of course. Her husband was extremely rich, handsome and famous throughout Greece. Although she had had power as a future Queen of Colchis, it was not enough; she had great ambition, and Jason would help her achieve her aspirations.

She hated him; hated the way he pawed her on the rare occasions when he felt so disposed, despised the way he sweated profusely when he mounted her, pumping her with his pathetically small prick, fucking her with the finesse of a baboon.

They'd been married for less than a year now and he'd accepted her distaste for him with little concern, happy to drink the nights away with his friends and simply use her when he wished. For her part, she'd become resigned at a tender age to being his chattel, a cold, loveless marriage with little to cheer her in the long, sultry days she had come to loathe.

Not that she'd remained completely faithful; a brief fling with a rather delicious young servant had helped to sate her desperate lust for a few weeks until Jason had stumbled upon them as they humped happily amongst the tethered horses in the great barn. The poor wretch had been sent packing, lucky to escape with his life.

Since then, nothing. Her only relief now from the endless boredom of the dreary days and long, desolate nights was the gentle, but expert attentions of her fingers and her dreams and fantasies.

Medea rose from her bed and walked to the window. The breeze had picked up slightly and she enjoyed the feeling of its coolness on her naked body, and the way it made her shiver in its embrace. She stepped out onto the terrace and looked into the moonlit scene, the large lawns silver, the trees in the distance dark and mysterious.

She leant against the balcony wall, the sudden coolness of the stone against her thighs and abdomen giving her a strange, almost erotic sensation. She pressed her crotch hard against the unyielding barrier, feeling the familiar wetness begin to slip from her to mix with the light covering of moss on the gnarled brickwork. She ran her hands sensuously over her lithe form, caressing her large, up-turned breasts, pinching her nipples between her thumbs and forefingers, imagining a fantasy lover fondling her body, arousing her before taking her completely.

She ran one hand slowly down, over her flat stomach to

her soft, down-like pubic hair and between her pouted, opening lips, delving all four fingers inside, her thumb finding the hard bud of her clitoris. She tossed her head back as she submitted to the ecstasy she was giving to herself, the ends of her silky, red hair brushing across her firm, pert bottom. Her probing quickly became an anxious, urgent fondling as she felt her orgasm rapidly approaching, arching her back and rubbing furiously at her neglected pussy.

It was then that she saw the stallion. The beast stood passively in the garden below her, seemingly looking at her, watching as she pleasured herself. She stopped and looked back at the magnificent animal, its jet-black coat glinting in the strong moonlight. She'd never seen it before, the only horses in the stables being bay or piebald, much smaller in stature and tamer in manner. This creature was quite different, that was quite apparent. Wild, untamed, its spirit unbroken. Medea suddenly felt a desperate need to sit astride its great back, to feel its strength between her legs, to ride free in the wind.

The horse raised its head and snorted loudly, as though beckoning to her. Medea felt in a trance, hypnotised by the sheer power of the beast. She walked from the terrace, through her bedroom, down the stairs to the great hall. The tiled floor felt cold to her bare feet as she moved quickly to the huge front door, desperate to get to the stallion before it galloped away.

She opened the door carefully so as not to startle the animal, and stepped out into the night. The beast stood motionless, waiting for her. She walked over to it and gently stroked the side of its giant frame, feeling the heat of its body against the palm of her hand. Then, gripping the mane tightly with both hands she expertly launched herself onto the broad back of the creature, her naked legs splayed wide apart over its massiveness.

Immediately, the horse broke into a swift canter, Medea wrapping her arms around its neck, gripping tightly as it headed for the trees. For a brief instant she was afraid, then relaxed as the steady movements of the animal's firm muscles rubbed against her groin, both soothing and exciting her, the wetness of her cunt becoming one with the sweat of the beast.

As the pace increased, she found herself involuntarily matching its movements with her own, rubbing her now highly aroused pussy against the smooth, hard back, returning to her near orgasmic state of a few moments before. Her large breasts bounced heavily as she rode with the animal, her nipples firm and erect in the cool, rushing air.

They were in the trees now, rushing dangerously through the darkness, branches skimming by, leaves brushing against her body, grabbing and scratching like a thousand unseen fingers at her tender flesh. The speed and the danger filled her with a sense of exhilaration, forcing her to gasp for breath as she rode her stallion hard, bringing herself rapidly over the edge.

With a wild cry she came, her shouts echoing against the trees as she rubbed her pussy savagely against the animal's back, gripping the hair of its mane and biting gently into its neck. The strength of her orgasm was so great that she momentarily lost her balance, almost slipping from the back of the horse, hanging on to its firm neck for dear life. She shifted back into place, gripping the animal's girth tightly with her thighs, pressing her tender pubic mound hard against the rigid spine that moved, snake-like beneath her, arousing her soft sex-flesh with its regular motion.

Suddenly the horse pulled to a halt and she was thrown into the darkness, crashing into a soft clump of leaves and moss. Stunned for a moment, she lay on her back, the after-effects of her orgasm and the shock of her fall causing her to become a little giddy. The full-moon shone directly above her, the trees seemingly moving around her, their high branches swaying mockingly.

She took a deep breath and sat up, blinking in the half-light. The horse was nowhere to be seen. She began to feel nervous, even frightened. She hadn't an idea how far they had ridden, or even in what direction. The pleasure and exhilaration of the experience had been all that mattered, now she felt vulnerable and alone, naked and afraid.

It was then that she saw the stranger. At first, she could only make out his shape; tall, muscular and solid, standing less than six feet away. He stepped forward into the shaft of light that streamed from above and she caught her breath. Like her, he was naked, his skin ebony-black and hairless, shining with a light coating of sweat, the muscles defined sharply in the unforgiving moonlight. His body was perfect to her eyes; his chest large and strong, his waist and hips slim, his legs long and powerful. His manhood hung heavily between his muscular thighs, far larger even in its flaccid state than any fully excited erection she'd seen in the past.

She struggled to her feet and stood before him, looking into his gaze, his eyes showing little expression. He towered over her, a menacing figure, but she somehow knew that she was in control, that this was perhaps her fantasy made real.

She used her fingertip to touch his chest lightly, running it playfully between his heavy pectorals, feeling the warm wetness of his sweat. His scent was strong but not unpleasant, very male and extremely arousing to her senses. She ran the finger down his body slowly, her eyes fixing his stare, feeling the firm ridges of his abdominal muscles, his navel, the sparse, wiry hair of his groin. Her hand moved relentlessly down until she gripped his now stiffening cock, feeling it grow thick and long in her grasp. She pulled determinedly at the huge phallus, marvelling at its size, knowing that she was going to have it, that it would sink deep inside her aching body. It stiffened more and more under her caress, until her fingers were unable to encircle it, and still it grew.

She kissed the stranger lightly on the chest and knelt down before him, worshipping his superb, black physique with her mouth. She licked and kissed his firm stomach tenderly, pushing the tip of her tongue into his tiny navel, tasting his saltiness, then moved her face down, her tongue tracing a line of saliva to the base of his cock. He was fully hard now, a stallion's length, massive and demanding, all she could ever want. She ran her tongue wetly along the

100

long side of his stiffness, measuring it in her mind, over the ridge to the peach-sized end that would soon impale her.

She grasped his thick stalk with both hands and gently rubbed it up and down, feeling it throb under her sensuous touch. A small daub of white pre-come appeared from the wide slit in the huge, bulbous end of his prick. Medea bent her head forward and stuck out her tongue, tasting his fluid and licking it sensuously over her lips, a thin sliver of his nectar joining her lips to his sex, like a strand of spider's silk.

She opened her mouth as wide as she could to accommodate his monster phallus, taking him to the back of her throat, sucking greedily on her prize, moving her head swiftly back and forward, exciting and stimulating him between her wetly pouted lips.

She suckled on him as a baby would on a nipple, drawing in her cheeks to coat his thickness with her full mouth, running her tongue round and round the end. She rubbed the exposed stem quickly with one hand, the other cupping his large balls, feeling their weight. His hips began to make involuntary fucking movements, pushing his thick cock to the back of her mouth, and she knew that he was hers to command.

She took him from her mouth, holding his cock erect against his stomach and licked steadily at his plum-sized balls, the tip of her tongue circling them lazily. She drew first one, then the other into her mouth, all the time rubbing his stiff cock with both hands, before running her tongue slowly up the full length of it to the tip, taking it once more between her greedy, sucking lips .

She dug her teeth lightly into his hardness, drawing back along its length to the ridge, then enveloped as much of his length as she could manage with her mouth, feeling it touch the back of her throat. She wanted to take him completely, to swallow his full length down her throat, but his thickness made it impossible.

She pulled her head back, drawing him reluctantly from her oral grasp. Now she wanted him inside her loins, to take her fully and totally.

She lay back on the bracken, opening her legs wide, her

meaning clear. Her lover knelt before her, his long pole jutting from his groin ludicrously, and reached under her bottom with both of his strong hands. She kept her shoulders on the ground as he raised her hips, bringing her cunt to the warm wetness of his mouth. He clamped his thick lips over her full mound, his tongue flicking in and out of her soaked pussy, fluttering against her hard clitoris like a butterfly's wings. She writhed on her bed of dry leaves and twigs, driving her hips into his face, coating him with her juices as he quickly brought her to orgasm with his mouth, smothering him with her lust. He carried on licking at her, tasting her flow, swallowing and relishing her juices.

The fluttering of his tongue concentrated solely on her engorged clitoris now, its post orgasmic tenderness swiftly giving way to arousal once more, taking her back to the oblivion of pleasure. She mewed happily, feeling the tip of his tongue prodding at her sopping wet sex-lips, probing inside. It slithered into her like a writhing eel, searching every crevice, deeper and deeper. His tongue was amazingly long, the oral fucking giving her new sensations as it slithered swiftly in and out.

Finally, he kissed her pussy gently with his full lips, and lowered her bottom carefully to the ground, raising one of her legs high and gripping her ankle firmly with one hand. With his other he gripped his mighty cock, directing it at her waiting opening, pressing the thick end against her greedy sex-lips. Despite his size, she felt him slide into her easily, three or four careful thrusts pushing him in to the hilt. He held himself still for a moment, letting her body get used to the wondrous intrusion, then began to steadily fuck her, making her feel his entire length with each thrust. She felt the sharpness of the broken twigs and bracken scratching at her back as she was pushed over the ground by the force of his strong pumping movements, but she didn't care, every nerve ending joined to unite at the place of ecstasy between her legs.

With the suddenness of a crash of thunder she came again, screaming into the darkness, her legs gripping firmly around his powerful waist, her fingernails digging into his back. She sobbed with the sheer joy of the moment, wanting it never to end. He raised himself on his hands and knees so that she appeared to be suspended from his body, thrusting herself against him, sating her lust. Once again he held still, forcing her to ram herself against him, taking his full length as hard as she could, until her orgasm subsided.

She fell back heavily to the ground, panting, seeing his great cock spring up before her, shining in its black wetness. He lifted her body again as though she were as light as a kitten and turned her over, so that she lay on her stomach. Clutching her hips at the side, he pulled her to a kneeling position, her perfect bottom thrusting out to his eager gaze.

She knelt in this position untouched for a moment, knowing he was savouring the view. Then, without warning, she felt the soft wetness of his tongue licking along her spine, moving with agonising slowness downwards. Every now and then he would draw his tongue back into his mouth to give it more wetness, then it would return, ever on its relentless journey to where she wanted him so badly.

She began to tremble as the tip touched the top of the crack between her buttocks, and slithered slowly down between them. She cried out softly as it touched the virgin sphincter of her anus, probing wetly at the tight little hole, pushing to gain admittance. She felt his thumbs dig into her buttocks, parting them, opening her to his desires and then felt the long tongue slide into the tightness of her arse, moving deftly in and out, his thick, wet lips clamped firmly against her bottom. She reached between her legs to rub herself, needing only the slightest touch to her clitoris to send her over, another shattering orgasm taking hold of her body. She sobbed real tears, the frustrations of her loneliness ebbing away with each spasm, the pleasure intense.

He lay on his back and held the monster erect, waiting for her attention. Still his face showed little emotion, no words were necessary, and none were spoken.

Medea squatted on her heels over his thighs, lowering

herself down to impale her sex once more. Slowly, it slid into her again, the relaxed wetness of her pussy accepting it this time in one movement. She ground her pubic mound against his, gripping his shoulders, and began to ride her stallion. This time, she was the mistress, he would be hers to command. Furiously, she bounced up and down on him, feeling the thick end of his shaft hitting against her cervix, sending waves of erotic pleasure through her tortured mind. She hammered down harder and harder, determined to bring him with her this time. She felt his strong hands grip the softness of her buttocks, pushing at her bottom, forcing her harder and harder to match his upward thrusts. She gritted her teeth, knowing that she was coming yet again, crying out as she felt his finger stray into the tightness of her anus, invading her like another, much smaller prick.

Suddenly, she arched her back and sat hard on him, his cock and finger both as deep inside her as they could go. She screamed as once again the fires of lust tore at her cunt, the spasms of the orgasm shooting through her limbs. She tensed and gripped his stalk firmly with her vaginal muscles, delighted as she felt the tell-tale throbbing as he shot his seed within her aching body. He grabbed her by the waist and rammed her up and down on his tool, using her, almost masturbating with her body, roaring as he emptied inside her, his nostrils flared, snorting like an animal.

When it was over, she closed her eyes and collapsed onto his sweating body, her breathing heavy with exhaustion. Gently, he lowered her to his side, ran his hand over her trembling body, and kissed her lightly on the mouth.

Medea awoke slowly, still lying in the bracken. The brightness of the moonlight had been replaced by the early-morning sun, its warmth not yet strong enough to ease her shivering as she stood naked and looked around her.

Her lover was gone; standing close by, however, was the large, black stallion, waiting to escort her safely back to her home. In the distance, as though carried on the breeze, she heard the light, mellow tones of the pipes, the music of love and erotica. Then she heard laughter, the raucous, wicked chuckle of Faunus coming from all around her.

Medea felt afraid; she had been bewitched, convinced that she was home in Iolcus with Jason, and that she hated him, her desires unfulfilled. She closed her eyes and concentrated bitterly on the truth, the Jason she loved, the pleasures he gave her. The music became louder and louder until only the high notes were played, screeching with an ever more demanding assault on her senses.

She opened her eyes and stared determinedly at the figure of her tormentor, seeing him at last in his true form. His lower body now seemed even more hairy, the feet turned to hooves, the ankles high and bony. The muscles of his hairless chest appeared more prominent and sinewy, his arms thick with power, the hands clawed around the delicate instrument. His face, still handsome bore a devilish grin, his tousled hair unable to conceal small, white horns on top of his head.

Medea clamped her hands firmly over her ears, vainly trying to block out the diabolical sound, realising the truth at last. 'No, Faunus,' she cried, 'you have not captured my will, for I know you now! You are Pan, the mischievous one, the devil of trickery, and I will not succumb!'

Suddenly she was wide awake again in the woods, Pan sitting at her feet playing gently on his pipes, his sated cock lying flaccid along his thigh. His physique was once more that of a human rather than a God, his expression calm. Medea looked hungrily at his superb penis, still large despite its softness and wet from recent copulation. She felt the ache within her loins and knew he had taken her whilst she dreamt of her stallion.

'You did not need to entrance me, to put me under the spell of Hypnos in order to fuck me. I was willing, eager for your fine prick.'

Pan grinned, stroking his cock gently. 'It is just my way,' he said with a tenderness she had not heard before. 'I must have my fun. And you moved so wildly! The dream must have been good.'

Medea smiled and reached forward, taking his stiffening

erection in her hand and rubbing it slowly up and down. Pan lay back on the grass and closed his eyes as she caressed him, his cock hardening more and more with each gentle stroke of her small hand. Soon he was fully stiff, a magnificent weapon of superb proportions, ready once more to enjoy the pleasures of Eros.

She bent her head forward and licked along the side of his cock, tasting her own sex-perfume on his flesh as she ran her tongue wetly over him. Gradually she moved upwards, measuring the immense length with her lapping tongue until she took the huge, bulbous knob into her hungry mouth, suckling on it and drawing it as deep into her mouth as she could manage.

Crouching across him, she felt him squeezing and probing her bottom until, to her delight he pushed a finger inside her anus, sliding it back and forth, his thumb quickly finding the erect bud of her clitoris. Still sucking heavily on his cock, she gripped the stem with both hands and began to rub it rapidly up and down, feeling it throb and tasting the sweet juices of his excitement across her tongue.

Pan slowly withdrew his finger from her, then Medea groaned with joy as two, or possibly three slid effortlessly into her anus. She felt the muscles of her virgin sphincter relax completely as her lover expertly turned and prodded his fingers, his thumb constantly flicking her bud.

Medea pulled her face from his cock and looked lustfully into his eyes. 'I want you to fuck me,' she said, huskily, 'I want you to fuck me there.'

Pan looked genuinely concerned. 'You have a sweet and inviting bottom,' he said, softly, 'but I am large; I fear it will hurt you.'

She gripped his wrist and pulled his fingers from within her, enjoying the pleasurable sensation of his withdrawal and crouched on the grass on her elbows and knees, her bottom presented to him like a prize. 'I *want* it to hurt,' she begged, 'fuck me, fuck my bottom now!'

Pan shrugged and positioned himself behind his willing and beautiful victim, his cock pointing threateningly towards the tiny, vulnerable orifice. She felt him ease his fingers into her again, turning his hand slowly to ensure that she was ready for the ultimate intrusion of her young body, then he withdrew. Medea closed her eyes, resting her face on the ground, and waited to have her arse fucked for the first time.

Pan leant forward and kissed and licked her anus, moistening it with his saliva whilst drawing the wetness from her pussy to soak his penis. Then he was pressed against her, the spongy but hard end of his cock pushing at her tiny, puckered hole, demanding entry.

At first she felt that he was right, that it was too large and that she would not be able to accommodate him. Suddenly, however, as though in reluctant submission, her body allowed him to enter her, the pain sharp as three or four inches impaled her lovely bottom. She groaned with the ache, the immense thickness stretching her, but the exquisite pleasure of the experience quickly took over her senses and she relaxed, giving herself entirely to him.

Steadily, inch by inch he eased more and more of his fine length into her until she felt the warmth of his belly pressed against her buttocks and knew that she had taken him completely. Now he began to fuck her in earnest, gripping the soft flesh of her backside tightly as he pumped in and out of the tight hole.

'Ah, sweet Queen,' he grunted, 'such a perfect arse! I'll warrant that there will be many who will follow me on this path of pleasure!'

'None will fill me so completely,' panted Medea, allowing the fingers of one hand to claw at her pussy, determined to come whilst so erotically impaled. 'Such a big, fine stalk, it stretches me so much!'

'Then you will take two, if needs be. Believe me, once a young girl has savoured the pleasures of anal intrusion she can be satisfied with nothing less!'

He began to pump in and out of her furiously, Medea rubbing her clitoris rapidly in time with his thrusting. The pleasure was, indeed intense, but she felt the need for more, a cock deep inside her cunt, possibly another in her mouth. She began to fall under the spell of her own fantasy, the thought of many, lusty males taking her at once filling her mind. There would never be enough; the more she had, the more she would want.

Pan suddenly roared, his cry snapping her out of her dream as she felt the throbbing of his cock deep inside her bottom, his fingernails clawing at her ravaged buttocks. She thrust her backside back and forth to match his orgasmic movements until, with an equal suddenness she came, her fingers rubbing furiously at her bud, the searing sensation of ultimate pleasure filling her entire consciousness.

Medea fell forward onto her stomach, feeling Pan delicately withdraw his long, softening penis from within her anus. As the still large end left her body she groaned with bliss, happy in her discovery of this new delight.

'Medea! Medea! Come quickly!'

It was Electra's wild and terrified cries that forced Medea from her post-orgasmic trance. She stood up, shakily as the young girl ran into view, her expression filled with horror.

'Oh, Medea, I don't believe it! We are bewitched!'

Medea grabbed the shivering girl by the arms. 'What do you mean? What has happened?'

'There is great trickery here,' sobbed Electra, her voice calming slightly. 'We fell asleep in the arms of many fine lovers, and now, well, you must see!'

Medea looked angrily at Pan, who merely grinned. 'If you have harmed a hair on the head of any of my crew you will regret it.'

'Just a bit of fun,' he said, 'just a bit of fun.'

Electra dragged Medea through the trees and back to the clearing where the orgy had taken place. There were her crew, the heroines of the *Phallicis*, naked and bewildered, surrounded, not by a bevy of handsome and athletic lovers but by a flock of goats.

CHAPTER SIX

Jason lay on his cot watching Glaucis as she busied herself with the many charts spread across the large, oak table in the corner of the cabin. She sang quietly to herself as she studied the maps, her voice as hypnotic to him as those of the Sirens of Capri. He felt the now all too familiar ache within his body, the need to possess this lovely child, to take her completely.

The desire to lay with her, to split her maidenhead with his long shaft was fast becoming an obsession, as was his longing to feel the softness of the full lips of her young mouth around it. She pleasured him nightly with her expert hand, often two or three times, but it was not enough. Time after time he had to summon up all his strength of will to prevent himself losing control, throwing her frail little body to the bed and leaping upon her, raping her mercilessly.

Jason shifted in his cot, his penis becoming uncomfortably hard within the tight confines of his loin-loth. Glaucis looked up from her labours and smiled, her innocent eyes shining in a way that tore at his heart.

'Do you have need for my touch?' she said, walking over and sitting beside him on the bed.

'I have need for much, much more from you, but I also know it can never be.'

Glaucis looked into his eyes, her own reflecting the sadness of his expression. 'You have Atalanta, she serves you well with her mouth,' she said, her voice betraying hidden emotion.

Jason held her small face in his hand. 'Does that trouble you?' he said.

Glaucis pulled away and stood by the map table. 'No, why should it? What you do with her is your own business. I have a fine, strong lover waiting for me in Icaria.'

'Indeed you have,' said Jason, swinging his legs out of the cot and sitting up, 'and the sooner we arrive the better it will be for all of us.'

'I agree,' said Glaucis sharply, hurriedly returning to her work. Jason walked briskly from the room, allowing the door to swing freely in the breeze. A moment later he heard it slam.

He was annoyed with himself, angry that he should let this youngster, no matter how enchanting, affect him in this way. He decided to spend the rest of the day on deck.

'Land! I see land!' The cry came from the sharp-eyed Castor, who was perched high in the sail. Jason followed the direction of his gaze, peering into the shimmering horizon.

'There should be no land for three days yet,' he shouted, 'what is this place?'

Glaucis joined him on deck, clutching one of her charts. 'There is nothing on the map, no island within miles,' she said.

Jason squinted at the chart, his hand resting involuntarily on her shoulder. Glaucis glanced into his eyes and he pulled his arm away. Castor clambered down from the mast and stood at their side. 'There is no island on the chart,' said Jason.

'See for yourself,' said Castor, walking to the rail at the edge of the vessel. 'My eyes never deceive me . . . there!' He pointed into the haze, beckoning Jason to join him.

'I still can't see,' said Jason, 'no wait, yes, you are right! An island! Who knows what mysteries and adventures an uncharted land will hold for us!'

'Take care, Jason,' said Glaucis, touching him lightly on the arm. 'These waters are well traversed by merchants and adventurers. The charts should be accurate. This land may not be all that it seems.'

'Whatever monsters or demons lurk there, I care not. An unexpected opportunity to fill our barrels with clean, cool

110

water and our bellies with fresh food is all that matters.'
Leaping quickly to grasp the tiller, he called out to his
oarsmen, 'Row, Argonauts, let us reach the island before
nightfall!'

The anchor-stone slipped silently into the calm water, the
setting sun casting playful shafts of deep red light across
the rippling surface. From a distance, the island had
looked no more remarkable than any other but here,
moored just yards from its stony beach and in the shadow
of sheer, grey cliffs the place exuded an atmosphere of ma-
levolence.

'I do not like this place,' said Glaucis, gripping Jason's
muscular arm tightly as they surveyed the calm but dis-
quieting setting before them. 'There is something wrong,
something evil. Remember, I can sense these things; I am
rarely wrong.'

'We cannot be scared off because an island looks inhos-
pitable,' said Jason, slipping his arm around her small
shoulders to comfort her. 'We shall wait for morning when
I will take a small group of Argonauts to search for food
and water. You will be safe here.'

'Take weapons and, above all, take great care.' Jason
looked deeply into the young girl's eyes. There was a real
look of concern, and perhaps something more. He felt his
heart tightening within his chest as she held his gaze, his
manhood stiffening at the sight of her perfect innocence.

'Forgive me for losing my temper with you earlier,' he
said, softly.

'Forgive me for tempting you with what I cannot give,
for I surely yearn to.'

Jason kissed her lightly on the tip of her nose, his heart
pounding. 'Let us go to my cabin,' he said, 'and you can
ease my pain with your delicate touch.'

They walked slowly, arms entwined to the cabin door.
Once inside, Jason lay on his cot, his arms behind his head.
Glaucis casually unknotted his loin-cloth, pulling the
rough material from under his body and letting it slip to
the floor. She reached over to a shelf and took up a small

111

bottle of oil, carefully pouring some of its contents onto the palm of her hand.

Jason watched her movements tenderly, his cock stiffening quickly to full erection in anticipation of the pleasures to come. Slowly and deliberately, Glaucis spread the oil over the hard thickness with both hands, adding more fluid from the bottle to lubricate the deft, flowing movements of her sensitive fingers.

Kneeling across his legs, she curled her grip around his swollen shaft and gradually began to slide her hands up and down in a steady, lascivious rhythm, all the time fixing his gaze with her own. Up and down, up and down, the sensuous touch of her tiny hands brought him both delight and despair.

She leant forward and kissed the peach-sized end of his cock very lightly, Jason immediately feeling it throb in response to her touch. Still she stared at him, her tongue running across her upper lip.

Jason wanted to shout out 'suck it, suck it!', to feel her soft mouth enclose his raging stalk. Her pumping became steadily faster, both hands moving together, gripping his iron-hard prick tightly. He could feel the warmth of her breath on the tender flesh of his knob, that perfect mouth only a couple of inches away. He stiffened his buttocks and pushed his hips upward and she held her position, her lips now less than an inch away; so near, so far.

'Suck it, suck it!' he said in his mind, the movements of her hands now rapid as she brought him closer to the sweet release he so desperately needed.

'Do you like that, Jason?' she said sultrily, knowing the answer.

Jason nodded, his eyes closed. 'Suck it, suck it!' his brain raged.

'Look at me, Jason, look at me,' she whispered. Jason opened his eyes and stared into her lovely face, so close to his huge cock. He felt it throb again, a small white trace of fluid appearing from the wide slit. Glaucis looked at it, then returned her entrancing gaze to Jason, smiling sweetly. Then, without warning she pushed out her delicate tongue and licked the sperm from him, taking it lushly into her mouth.

Again she stuck out her tongue and licked the tip of his cock, running her tongue slowly around it, tasting him. She began to open her mouth, still pumping him expertly. She was going to do it! She was going to suck him!

Jason gritted his teeth, then bit heavily into his lower lip, but it was too late. 'No, by Zeus, no!' he cried, but no power on Olympus could halt the inevitable. Despite the pain of his bleeding lip he exploded into orgasm, his mind sending conflicting, searing messages of release and desire, a strong jet of sperm spurting from his stalk, soaking the face of his lovely temptress.

Glaucis continued to rub him up and down with both hands, gradually easing the pressure of her grip and the speed of her movements until his fine cock lay flaccid in her grasp. Jason looked lovingly at her face, her beautiful features and long, blonde hair soaked with his juices, the traces glinting in the half-light of the flickering candle.

'That was very sudden,' she said, wiping the sperm from her face with a small towel, 'was it because I licked you?'

Jason nodded. 'I thought you were about to grant me heaven, to take it inside your sweet mouth.'

'I don't know,' she answered, sitting up on the edge of the bed. 'I thought about it, but I wasn't sure. I don't know if I could.'

'Perhaps another time,' said Jason, more in hope than certainty.

'Perhaps,' said Glaucis, opening the door to leave. 'I need some air, to be alone for a while. You must sleep, Jason, for you will need your wits about you tomorrow.'

She left the cabin, closing the door quietly behind her. Jason lay back on his pillow, his mind racing with thoughts of the young virgin, his cock quickly stiffening again.

It was early morning when Jason waded ashore on the island, the sharp pebbles of the beach digging into the soles of his feet. With him he took the eagle-eyed Castor, a tall, heavily muscled wrestler from Sparta, Echion, blond, slim and lithe, barely eighteen years old, and the brothers Calais and Zetes, renowned as warriors, very dark skinned with long, black curls falling to their shoulders.

The group stood for a moment on the beach, surveying the scene. Jason turned and looked back at the *Argo*, seeing the figure of Glaucis watching from the deck. He turned back to his companions.

'We must tread very carefully,' he said. 'There may be nothing to fear, but Glaucis senses something, and she has been right before.'

The others nodded, no doubt remembering the close call with Syphis. They walked slowly towards the cliffs, looking upward at the climb that lay ahead.

'These cliffs are sheer,' said Castor, 'perhaps there is another way.'

'There is, look!' Echion pointed excitedly to the far edge of the beach. The others looked in the same direction and gasped. At the edge of the beach stood the figure of a young girl, naked save for a jewelled band around her neck, her skin coal-black. Even at this distance they could see that she was lovely, and as they approached her the extent of her charms became more and more apparent.

Still probably a teenager, she held herself with poise and confidence, her superb body displayed with pride. She was tall, possibly six foot, with short, black hair curled tightly to her elegantly shaped head. Her cherubic face beamed in welcome, her large, brown eyes shining, her thick-lipped mouth smiling widely.

Her breasts were magnificent, large, firm globes with almost jet-black and firmly erect nipples set in wide areolae. Her waist was slim, the belly curving sensuously to the thick bush of hair between her long, shapely but muscular legs.

'By all the Gods I must fuck this one,' said Castor as the men's pace quickened.

'Perhaps she will take us all, or maybe there are more like her,' stammered Echion, the front of his wet loin-cloth showing evidence of his long abstinence. They stumbled through the undergrowth, worried that she might disappear.

114

When they were less than ten feet away the girl turned and began to walk away, still smiling over her shoulder. 'By Zeus, look at that fine arse,' uttered Calais, staring at the perfect, rounded buttocks of their temptress. 'I swear I will sink my cock inside it, or die in the attempt!'

The men laughed, hurrying to catch up with the stranger. They followed her through some bushes to a small cave set at the base of the cliff. She disappeared inside, beckoning them to follow. Jason stood his ground for a moment. 'Wait,' he said to the others, 'remember what Glaucis said. We must be cautious.'

Zetes pulled aside the material around his groin, showing his not inconsiderable erection. 'I will be cautious when I have dealt with this!'

Jason grinned and shrugged his shoulders, following the others into the cave.

The sudden darkness of the grotto caused them to move more carefully, their feet slipping on the damp rocks. The air was cool, the only sounds being the steady dripping of water from the roof and the echoes of their own movements. 'Where is she?' whispered Castor, 'I can't see her.'

'She could only go one way,' said Jason. 'Come, she must be close.'

'I can see daylight,' said Echion, 'see, ahead!'

The five brave Argonauts strode quickly in the direction of the shaft of light until they found themselves once more in the open, the hot sun of the morning beating down on their backs. The girl stood just a few feet away, still beckoning silently for them to follow as she walked through the bushes, the vision of her perfect bottom acting like a magnet to their lusts. They followed quickly, seemingly unable to shorten the distance between them until they rounded a large rock and stood in awe of the sight that met their eyes.

The setting was idyllic, a wide clearing by a small, silver waterfall that cascaded into a lake of the deepest blue. Within this perfect scene were thirty, perhaps forty young girls, all of them as black as the richest ebony, some small and lithe, others, like the vision that had welcomed them on the beach, tall and superbly shaped, each of them a dream of pure eroticism.

'Am I dead?' said Echion, his eyes wide with the shock of so much exquisite perfection so close. 'Have the Gods taken me to their hearts?'

'No, you are not dead,' said Castor gruffly as he walked towards the nearest girl who giggled excitedly as she made a grab for his penis, 'but I fear I will be if I don't sink my rod into this pretty child!'

The others followed suit, walking into the midst of the throng of woman-flesh, the scent of feminine arousal strong and incredibly stimulating.

Jason was pulled from the others by at least six pairs of hands, the only sounds made by the women being a gentle mewing or pleasurable sighing as his loin-cloth was tugged from his body, his erection springing into view. He held onto two of them, one in each arm, kissing each in turn firmly on their full mouths. Two more stood behind him, one caressing and nuzzling his neck and shoulders, the other kneeling to lick his buttocks. Before him knelt two more gorgeous youngsters, greedily sharing the taste of his cock as they licked and suckled him, lapping their long tongues over the near-purple end, the rigid stalk and his plum-shaped balls.

He ran his hands down the long, smooth backs of the girls in his arms and cupped their bottoms, allowing his fingers to snake between their superbly rounded buttocks, feeling the heat and wetness of their pussies, the lips open and ready for sex.

Calais was already keeping his promise to himself, his cock embedded deep in the plump bottom of the girl they had seen on the beach. Castor lay with two of the smallest girls, their slight frames dwarfed by his huge bulk as they nibbled excitedly on his erection. Zetes and Echion were nowhere to be seen, lost in the sea of ebony arousal.

One of the two girls who had been busily sucking on Jason's engorged manhood turned her back to him, crouched on her hands and knees, moving her upturned bottom at him provocatively. He lost no time in kneeling behind her, pushing his cock against the yielding softness of her moist cunt, sinking deep within her with remarkable ease. She sighed happily as she took the full length, the lips of her pussy gripping tightly around the base of his shaft, her vaginal muscles making sucking movements as he held himself embedded inside her hot sheath.

One of the girls wriggled under the body of the crouching beauty until Jason felt her lapping greedily at his balls. Another tongue began to work on his anus, probing and prodding against the tight sphincter whilst a fourth girl stood astride the first, her back to Jason and bent forward so that he could pay similar oral homage to her delightful arse.

He licked hungrily at the sweet orifice, fucking heavily into the wriggling form of the young girl below him. He heard Calais roar, and knew that his seed had entered the lovely bottom of his lover, and he also knew that he would soon follow suit. He felt his shaft thicken within the silky purse of the cunt that held him so tightly, the tremors of orgasm building up from the base of his cock, feeling the sudden and surging desire to release himself within her perfect body.

He pressed his face hard against the upturned bottom of the girl bending before him, his tongue rasping against her anus as he came, his furious thrusting movements dislodging the other two suckling mouths from his nether regions. He felt as though his orgasm would last forever as he pumped more and more of his seed deep into her, the ever-increasing wetness of her delightful sheath drawing everything from him.

He fell back, exhausted, collapsing onto a bed of lithe, black bodies, hands roaming and grasping at him, fondling and teasing. To his amazement his stalk remained stiff and proud, quite ready to impale another sweet pussy without a sign of post-orgasmic tenderness.

He didn't have long to wait. Almost before he could recover his breath another ebony beauty, her flawless skin shining with sweat, mounted on top of him, absorbing his rampant prick inside her soaked pussy. As his new lover

117

quickly moved up and down on her heavenly perch another squatted across his face, pressing her pussy against
his mouth, demanding the attention of his tongue. This he
gladly gave her, suckling at the soaked lips with the vo-
raciousness of a starving man. Other tongues, lips and
hands trailed over his body, licking, sucking and caressing
every inch of his flesh as the two women above him used
his body as they chose.

Despite the satisfying violence of his recent orgasm he
felt himself coming again. He wanted to hold back, to
pleasure more of these young enchantresses and tried to
grab the girl who was happily bouncing up and down on
his aching cock, to slow her movements until his crisis past.
It was to no avail. Her pounding, if anything, became faster and more demanding and Jason once more entered the
oblivion of ecstasy, his sperm shooting up into the welcoming sheath of his lover's succulent cunt. Once more his
come lasted far longer than anything he'd experienced before, his cries of joy loud and uncontrollable, muffled
within the silky folds of sex-lips against his mouth.

After a moment he pulled himself to his feet and surveyed the scene around him. Everywhere he could see the
squirming, black bodies of the women, those who were not
satisfying themselves with the sturdy bodies of the Argonauts were pleasuring each other with their fingers and
tongues.

Jason looked down at the bodies of his lovers, their eyes
and smiles wide with anticipation, their legs open, fingers
pulling at their wet pussy-lips, preparing themselves for
him. His penis stood, rock hard, his desire unsated, his
need to fuck still as strong as ever despite two shattering
orgasms.

Castor called over to him, standing in the midst of a
crowd of lovelies clawing at his body. 'What is it with this
place? The more I come, the more I want! I can't lose this
stalk!'

Jason shrugged his shoulders and grinned. 'Whatever
magic this is, let us enjoy it before the spell wears off!' He
dived down again onto the waiting bed of sex-crazed nym-

phets, his cock immediately sinking deep into the eager wetness of yet another pussy.

Jason's first sense as he slowly dragged his mind from the unconsciousness of exhaustion was an incredible ache within his penis and an almost maniacal need for sexual fulfilment. He opened his eyes wearily, the dimness of his surroundings immediately apparent, the sole illumination coming from a solitary, flickering torchlight, the flames casting eerie shadows on the dank walls that faced him.

His next perception was of being restrained, chained by his wrists and ankles to a cold, stone wall, his arms stretched high above his head. He gripped the rusty links and tugged sharply at the tethers, the unyielding metal tightly circling his wrists and digging into the flesh. His legs were splayed apart, painfully so, the restraints around his calves equally resolute. He gritted his teeth, wrenching at the chains until the pain in his wrists became too great to bear and he collapsed against the dripping wall, his heart pounding.

'What place is this?' he cried into the darkness, his voice echoing against the stone.

'You are in great danger, Jason, and I cannot help you.' The voice was gentle and concerned, a voice he knew well.

'Hera? Where are you?'

'I cannot appear before you, Jason. The magic in this place is too powerful. You are prisoners of the Sphyledes, sisters of the Sirens of Capri and protected by Poseidon himself. I am permitted to warn you, and no more.'

'What will become of us? What do these devils want? They seemed so welcoming, so warm to us!'

'And by this simple trickery they have worked their evil and enchanted you. The Sphyledes are insatiable, nymphomaniacs; no mortal man could ever hope to satisfy the myriad of carnal needs of one of them, let alone the numbers who hold you captured now. They are unable to experience the sweet release of orgasm, such is their curse. Their spell holds you in a permanent state of copulative desire; no matter how many times you release your seed within their bodies you will ever be unsated, ever more in need of sex, until . . .

119

'Until what,' said Jason, almost shouting into the ether, 'what is the fate that awaits us?'

'You are all superb athletes, Jason, and will serve the needs of the Sphyledean nymphs for some time but the outcome is predetermined.'

'Hera, tell me, I must know.'

'You will all die, exhausted, your mortal bodies wrecked by the demands of your captors. It may take a month, maybe more, but you will die unless you can escape.'

'Then escape we will!'

'It will not be easy; the Sphyledes are very powerful. I must go, I cannot help you. I am sorry, Jason; I will be thinking of you . . .

The room suddenly seemed colder, the presence of Hera gone. Jason looked about him, his eyes slowly becoming accustomed to the darkness. Here and there were piles of sacking or cloth on the floor; nearby lay a small bucket, possibly containing water, but too far to reach.

There was a groan from the opposite wall. Jason peered into the half-light, at length making out the figure of Castor, chained in a similar way to himself, his huge nakedness coated in sweat.

'Castor,' he hissed, 'it is I, Jason. Are you injured?'

'Nothing ails me, save the need to shag myself into oblivion,' the powerful man muttered, tugging hard at his restraints. 'What has happened here?'

'We are bewitched and in great danger. Hera has told me in a half-dream of the powers of these fine women! We must escape or die in the attempt.'

'Bewitched? Die? These beauties are angels, so perfect that I still keep a fine stalk despite fucking so many!' Castor shook his body so that his aching erection bobbed painfully up and down in the cool air of the dungeon.

'We will *never* lose the desire to fuck, *never* tire of mounting those fine, black nymphs!'

'So, what of it?' Castor looked bemused.

'Ah, Castor, my dear friend,' said Jason, mockingly, 'you are a great wrestler, probably the greatest in the world but, a thinker you are not.'

'I don't understand; surely this place is heaven?'

'We have both already collapsed from exhaustion, and we have been in this place less than a day. The Sphyledes, for that is their name, intend to keep us, to drain us until we are wrecked and of no further use to them, then they will allow us to die.'

'How do you know this?'

'Hera told me, but she cannot help us.'

'Then we are finished!' Castor looked suddenly very worried, his great brow knitting, his eyes staring wildly into the half-light. 'Without our strength, how can we fight our way out of this trap?'

'We still have our brains,' said Jason, looking about him, trying to focus his eyes on the various shapes in the dark room. 'What has become of the others?'

'I last saw Calais and Zetes when all three of us were busily servicing the needs of the most lovely of maidens, so young, so willing! By Zeus, how I wish she were here now! Just one more fuck, Jason, then we will think and plan!'

'Control, Castor, control! What of Echion?'

'I am here,' groaned a weary, muted voice in the darkness. 'I'm afraid I cannot stand. There were so many, and they all wanted so much!'

There was a sudden crash of bolts being pulled across rusting clasps and a heavy door swung open, the light from the outer chamber revealing the full nature of their prison to Jason's eyes. The unmoving shapes on the floor that he had tried to make out in the flickering light cast by the torch now proved to be many skeletal remains of past conquests of the Sphyledes, lying where they had dropped, exhausted. Through the door marched two women, clothed in heavy leather tunics and thongs, each carrying a long spear. They stood at either side of the doorway, allowing a third woman to enter. Jason gasped as he saw her, a sudden feeling of desire burning in his crotch.

Easily six feet tall, she was naked save for black, hide boots that covered her entire legs to her crotch. The leather was neatly cut away at this point to accentuate the shape of her glistening, black pussy-lips and the red, pouting gash

121

between, every trace of hair having been removed. Her hips were broad, her waist narrow and, as she turned to look at the goggle-eyed Castor, Jason was able to savour the sight of the most perfect bottom he had ever dreamed of seeing, jutting pronouncedly with a receptive curve that could make a grown man weep.

Her breasts were mountainous, huge globes of firm woman-flesh, the nipples erect and ready for suckling. Jason's already stiff cock seemed to harden even more, its full length pressing stiffly against his belly.

'I am Michelas, leader of the Sphyledes,' the vision breathed, in a voice as musical as the songs of Orpheus. 'You have pleasured my charges well, and will continue to do so soon. But now it is my turn to enjoy the fine bodies of our guests!'

She walked over to Castor and stroked his chest and stomach with the palm of her hand, grinning broadly. 'See how this one sweats for me already,' she said, her fingers trailing down to grip his splendid erection, 'and how he aches to sink his fine shaft into my wetness, to fill me with the fluids of Eros!'

Michelas rubbed her hand gently but with purpose up and down his length, her eyes fixed on his as Castor strained in vain to stop himself from coming, seemingly forgetting that, in this place it would not be a problem. Suddenly he was lost, a guttural groan coming from his mouth, the jets of sperm shooting out across the stone floor.

As though proud of her achievement, Michelas let go of his throbbing member and walked to Jason, her eyes glinting with lust. Behind her, Echion managed to drag himself to his feet, his small but eager young cock ready to join the fun. She took hold of Jason's penis with both hands, staring happily into his eye as she caressed her stiff prize.

'This is truly a magnificent weapon,' she said, running her tongue over the thick lips of her mouth, 'quite the biggest I have seen for some time. I will take you first.'

Jason coughed, desperately trying to keep control of his mind, even though command of his body was denied him.

'There are five of us,' he said, 'five lusty and experienced lovers. Why not take us all, at the same time? Imagine, five firm cocks entering you, five fine, strong male bodies servicing your every need!'

Michelas looked into his eyes, long and hard, the fingers of one hand absently pulling at the lips of her sex, the other still gripping Jason's erection. Jason waited nervously for an answer, the germ of a plan entering his mind.

She drew a long breath and let go her grip on his tool, putting her fingers to her mouth and tasting his genital scent. 'I feel that would please me greatly,' she said, almost distantly, her eyes closing for a moment as she savoured the thought. 'Five men together, to fuck me until they can fuck no more!'

She stepped back to the door quickly, her decision made. 'Have these three and their sleeping compatriots brought to my bed-chamber in one hour,' she commanded to the nervously bowing guards. 'I will prepare!'

With that the three women were gone, the door slammed behind them, and the room once more plunged into near darkness.

There were a few silent moments as Jason mused over the precarious position they were in. His plan might work; it depended on just how powerful Michelas was.

Echion was the first to speak. 'She may be deadly, but I swear that I have never seen a woman more beautiful. If I die fucking that sweet body I will not complain.'

'Nor I,' said Castor, his prick once more hugely erect. 'Did you see that arse? Such perfection! By all that I believe I pledge that I will sink my shaft between those exquisite buttocks to the hilt!'

The door opened noisily once more and the jaded figures of Calais and Zetes staggered in, both collapsing to the floor as the room became dark again. 'Greetings, fellow heroes!' mocked Jason.

Calais groaned. 'I ache, oh how I ache!'

'I too,' sighed Zetes, leaning back on some sacking, 'yet I cannot stop. Even now, after thirty, no more like forty hard fucks, I yearn for another sweet honeypot to dip my raging stalk into!'

'Oh, no,' moaned Calais, 'don't speak in that way. I thought I'd lost the inclination and now your words have caused me to rise again!'

'You will never lose the desire,' said Jason, 'and, eventually you will end up like the poor wretch you are using as a pillow.'

Zetes sat up and quickly pulled back the sacking, seeing the grinning skull beneath. He and Calais looked around themselves in wide-eyed horror, their eyes becoming accustomed to the dimness, the sight of many victims of the Sphyledes lying about them.

'Jason, what are we to do?' said Calais, immediately realising their predicament.

'We are to be called to the bed-chamber of Michelas, the leader of these vixens, in one hour. There are five of us, strong, lusty men, still strong despite our labours of the past hours. We must fuck like we have never fucked before. We must sate this devil, exhaust her, defeat her. I believe that, if we can make her come then the spell will be broken, the curse lifted. If any in this world can do it, it is five fine Argonauts!'

The hour seemed to pass very quickly, the iron door bursting open and the two guards entering, spears brandished. Jason and Castor were released from their shackles and the five men were ushered out of the dungeon to the long, stone stairway which led to their destiny.

At length, another large door faced them, its ornate, erotic carvings and rich design suggesting that behind it must indeed be the bed-chamber of Michelas. One of the guards beat heavily on the unyielding wood with the handle of her spear. There was a short pause, then the sharp cry of 'Enter!' sounded from within.

The guard turned the great brass ring that unlatched the door and pushed against the heavy oak whilst the other girl motioned to Jason and his colleagues to move forward. They shuffled almost meekly into the room.

Nothing could have prepared them for the sight that met their lustful gaze. Michelas lay on her back on a great bed, totally naked, her long legs bent at the knees and splayed wide. Her lower back and bottom were supported by three cushions, the effect being to raise her groin in arrogant display, her black, hairless pussy-lips parted, the pink gash visibly wet with excitement.

She rested one hand behind her head, the fingers of the other playfully tweaking her long nipples. She smiled, in an almost gentle way, the beauty of her features near-hypnotic in its flawlessness. 'Come to me,' she purred seductively, 'come to my bed, all five brave heroes. This will be the best fuck of my life!'

The men moved as one towards the enchanting vision before them, their manhoods waving menacingly before them, their minds no more on escape. Jason knelt on the soft bed between her long, ebony legs and ran his tongue along the inside of her thigh, the scent of her arousal filling his nostrils as he moved inexorably upward towards her pouting cunt.

Gradually, using all the self control he could muster to stop himself from immediately ramming his hard cock into her gaping pussy he traced the line of her thigh to her buttocks, taking her ankles in his hands and raising her legs high, pushing her knees against her massive breasts. He teased her mercilessly with his tongue, licking around and around her anus and pussy without driving the wet tip into either hole, knowing from her shudders that he was having the desired effect. Still he teased, parting her buttocks with his thumbs, her ankles now held against her ears by Castor and Echion, who knelt on either side of her, their erections being steadily manipulated by her expert hands.

Jason raised his head and gazed at the beauty of the treasures between her widely stretched legs, his lust at last overtaking his will. He leant forward again, breathing deeply through his nose, savouring the strong, feminine aroma, his cock twitching in anticipation. He pushed his tongue forward, his eyes closed until the tip touched her anus, the tight sphincter seeming to relax at his insistent probe. Parting her buttocks more with his thumbs he stiffened his tongue and pushed it forward harder, hearing

125

her groan with pleasure as it slowly entered the warm, taut orifice.

He pressed his lips against her bottom, sucking against her flesh, drawing his tongue in and out of her anus, his nose delving within the soft, wet folds of her cunt. She responded by stiffening her buttocks and thrusting her hips against his face in rhythm with his oral caress.

Jason removed his tongue from her bottom, replacing it immediately with his finger, then two, then three, continuing the fucking movements inside her hole as he slithered his tongue over her pussy-lips to her bolt-hard clitoris. Drawing the bud between his teeth, he nibbled on it gently, flicking the end of it with the tip of his tongue. Her hips began to writhe in response to his ministrations, her groans becoming louder, albeit muffled.

He glanced up at her face, seeing that Castor was squatting over her head, his balls filling her wide mouth, the thick lips sucking on them hungrily. Calais and Zetes now had their manhoods within her steadily pumping grasp, and Echion was contenting himself by suckling on one of her long nipples. Jason went back to his pleasurable task, lapping greedily around the lips of her pussy, his fingers snaking in and out of her tight anus.

Michelas' responsive thrusts became more and more urgent as he drank from her sweet chalice and, for an instant, he felt that she was close to coming and that the spell might be so easily broken. The more he licked however, the more she bucked, but that was all.

Raising himself, Jason aimed his engorged cock at the waiting gash of her pussy and plunged forward, sinking his long shaft completely inside her in one, slow movement. He held still for a moment, feeling the muscles of her hot sheath tighten around him, gripping him and massaging his length. He eased his fingers from within her tight anus and gripped her ankles again, pulling her legs wide as he began to thrust steadily in and out, each time almost pulling his huge cock completely out of her throbbing pussy before plunging it again deeply within her, their pubic mounds grinding together in a subtle, erotic dance.

126

He began to move more urgently now, pounding his thick length in and out of her, the oozing lips of her cunt gripping his shaft snugly. He could feel himself coming already and, knowing the powers of rejuvenation they all possessed, he drove ever harder, hammering at the lithe, black body for all he was worth.

Groaning through gritted teeth he felt his first release, his fluids shooting deep within her trembling body. Quickly he pulled from her and moved to kneel beside her head, motioning to Castor to take over. Castor threw himself on his back, holding his cock erect and pulling Michelas onto him. The beautiful Sphylede needed no further persuasion and squatted over the mighty wrestler's body, lowering her crotch towards his, swiftly absorbing his fine erection within her silky sheath. Calais and Zetes lay on either side of the rutting couple, allowing her to grip their cocks again with her long-fingered hands. Echion positioned himself kneeling by her head, his penis soon deep within her suckling mouth.

Jason took the opportunity that was so erotically presented to him and slid behind her, squatting on either side of Castor's broadly muscled legs. He watched for a moment as Michelas slid up and down on his friend's thick shaft, seeing the lips of her pussy drawn out by his girth, then rested his hand on her bottom, holding her steady as he approached her lovely rear.

He pressed the massively bulbous head of his cock against her anus and pushed hard, feeling the tight sphincter relax and open, accepting his invasion easily. Gradually he eased more and more inside her bottom until his pubic hair rested against her flawless buttocks, feeling the size and shape of Castor's stalk against his own.

Slowly the two men began to pump in and out of her, quickly building up to a steady, almost savage rhythm, the sounds and scents of their multiple copulation tearing at Jason's senses. Echion groaned, losing his seed down Michelas' throat, whilst the brothers Calais and Zetes lay happily on their backs, contentedly allowing their sperm to spread across their thickly-haired chests as she pumped viciously at their weary stalks.

127

Once again, Jason could feel the exquisite, tearing sensation within his groin as his orgasm neared, the flow within his pounding prick unstoppable. He gripped hard onto Michelas' buttocks as his fluids shot deep into her arse, the grip of her sphincter around his massive width causing him to grimace with the perfect pain.

Rapidly again he withdrew, Zetes quickly taking his place. This time Jason presented his erection to her face and she happily took it within her thickly pouted lips, tasting and enjoying her own anal scent. Calais knelt at their side, offering her his engorged shaft which she took in her hand, pulling him towards her until her wide mouth accommodated both large cocks, her tongue lapping quickly from one to the other.

Over and over again the five men switched places, the positions ever more inventive, their movements as measured and fluid as their labours aboard the great ship *Argo*. They worked together as though one entity, their only purpose being to sate this lovely young woman.

As the night wore on each of the five athletes impaled her bottom, pussy and mouth time after time, her reactions and responses growing ever more manic. They were becoming exhausted, but knew that they mustn't, in fact *couldn't* stop until their task was complete.

It was close to dawn that it happened. Jason lay on his back, his cock firmly embedded once more in the sweetest arse he had ever seen, Michelas leaning back so that Echion could enter her ravaged pussy from the front whilst she sucked steadily on Castor's ever rampant erection, her hands once again incessantly pumping the stalks of the reclining brothers Calais and Zetes.

A sound like no other, a mixture of a groan and a cry from Hades itself began to build up within her throat, louder and louder, echoing around the very walls of the chamber. The cry became a scream, Michelas' movements on Jason's groin growing furious and severe, demanding, her downward thrusts on his stiff cock threatening to drive him into the bed.

Harder and harder she pounded, Castor no longer within her mouth, her hands clasped to her head, Echion gripping on to her rutting body, desperate not to be forced from within her orgasming sheath.

'She comes!' shouted Castor, stating the very obvious, 'she comes, we have done it!'

Michelas suddenly thrust herself forward, still impaled on Jason, Echion falling from her body like a leaf from a tree. A second cry began to emanate from deep within her throat and she held herself still, squatting over Jason with just the thick knob of his penis inside her anus. He watched, fascinated as the second orgasm tore through her body, then a third, and a fourth, the tight hole constantly dilating and relaxing around his shaft. The Argonauts had once again achieved the impossible.

Michelas lay quietly on the bed, surrounded by her ever attentive lovers, their sore manhoods now resting limply, the spell broken. Jason stroked the perfection of her body, the black skin coated in a sheen of sweat as she drifted off into a sated sleep.

The door to the bed-chamber swung open; there were no guards. 'Come,' said Jason, 'we are free to go, our work is done here.' The men padded out of the room, through the stone corridors to freedom, and to their next adventure.

CHAPTER SEVEN

The sun burned fiercely over the *Phallicis*, the heat too
great for the labour of rowing, the wind a mere whisper of
the breath of the God Aeolus. Many days and nights had
passed since their landing at Arcadia and the women were
becoming anxious to reach land once more.

Naxos lay close, perhaps only three or four days rowing
from where they now drifted becalmed. The island was well
known as a pleasure-haven, the inhabitants being followers
of the cult of Dionysus, the inventor of wine, and were
known to regularly indulge in the wildest of bacchanalia,
so much so that they were also known as the Bacchants.

The *Phallicis*' lack of progress towards Naxos had
caused much disquiet amongst the crew, their frustrations
leading to many short-tempered arguments and petty
squabbles. The ever increasing heat of the summer had not
helped the situation, and Medea was beginning to find life
aboard the vessel unbearable.

So it was that she found herself this hot afternoon, floating alone on her back in the calmness of the Aegean, her
eyes closed to the glare of the sun, her naked body gently
bathed by the cooling water. She had taken to relaxing in
this way some days previously on the advice of Iole, who
had told her of the soothing properties of the Northern
volcanic springs, and found this similar experience extremely restful. Here, at least, she could be alone with her
thoughts and fantasies, able to dream undisturbed by triv-
ial disagreements.

As ever, her thoughts turned to Jason. She wondered if
he'd been unfaithful to her yet, whether he'd enjoyed the

naked touch of another's body. She mused over what he might say if he knew of the pleasures she'd allowed herself already. She began to think again of Pan, the wicked lord of Arcadia, and his amusing trickery. She remembered his huge stalk, the first time she'd seen one larger than Jason's, and the way that she had let him impale her virgin bottom. Even her husband hadn't asked that of her yet, but she vowed she would demand it of him on their return to Iolcus.

Medea let her hand float across her body until the searching fingers found her soft pussy, delving between the velvety lips. She felt a feather-like tickling sensation against her shoulder, and water splashing a little across her face. She opened her eyes, startled for a moment and looked about her, but saw nothing. Assuming that she had been brushed against by a passing fish she closed her eyes again, her fingers finding their way between her legs once more.

She began to think of Madeleine, and the wonderful love-making that they enjoyed together night after night. She had taught her so much; the pleasures of sharing the joys of another woman's body, how to bring bliss and delight with the touch of her tongue to a sweet-tasting cunt whilst enjoying the same sensations herself. She remembered also how Madeleine would often concentrate her licking to her anus, her fingers probing the tight sphincter, the lapping of her warm tongue and rhythmic penetration of two or three fingers rarely failing to bring her to orgasm.

She found her mind wandering to thoughts of Iole, tall and white-skinned, her shining blonde hair, her frail, delicate body, a virgin until impaled on the massive stalk of Rapis. She wondered what the child's reaction would be if she, her leader were to make approaches to her, to beg to sink her tongue into the tight little honeypot between her long, slim legs. She imagined those same lithe limbs wrapped tightly around her neck, almost tasting the pureness of young sex-lips and the other delicately scented, puckered orifice.

Medea's fingers moved urgently over her clitoris, her breathing becoming heavier. Suddenly there was another touch, like the fluttering of a bird's wings, running along the side of her body, then another, on the other side. She opened her eyes and let herself float upright, treading water, just in time to spot the tail-fin of a large fish disappearing beneath the glassy surface. All around was quiet, save for the rhythmic lapping of the water. She lay back again, her feet floating slowly to the surface, her eyes once more closing to the brightness of the sunlight.

She began to think of the statuesque Atalanta, sole female member of Jason's crew, devastatingly beautiful and, although in her late twenties, still a virgin. Medea knew the legend, of course; that none may touch Atalanta's treasures who could not beat her in a race. Had Jason run with her? A fine athlete such as he would stand a very good chance of winning, and of deflowering the lovely huntress. Had he impaled her with that monster stalk of his?

Or possibly he had conquered the child-like Glaucis, despite her promise of fidelity to her betrothed. Jason was a great seducer; he could easily charm such an innocent waif into his bed.

Medea found these thoughts inordinately arousing, her fingers once more playfully caressing the soft lips of her pussy. She imagined Jason's huge phallus entering Glaucis for the first time, the throbbing monster splitting the tight hymen, causing the tiny blonde nymphet to squeal in pain and pleasure. In her delicious fantasy she saw Atalanta at their side, traces of virgin's blood on her thighs, evidence of her own surrender, her wild eyes filled with lust. She pictured Atalanta directing the pace and depth of Jason's thrusts, her finger deep inside his bottom, in total control.

Medea's body was touched again, this time the contact being more precise, more deliberate, like the gentle stroke of a lover's finger across her thigh. She let her hand trail away from between her legs, her body relaxed, waiting for the next sensation.

The finger returned, ghost-like, soothingly stroking along her inner thigh, tantalisingly moving upward. Medea kept her eyes firmly shut, not wishing to lose the excitement of the mystery. Which member of her crew had come

132

silently to her side, to tease her so? Iole? Madeleine? Perhaps one of the others: it didn't somehow matter.

The finger seemed to move away, only to return higher, just inches from her cunt, fluttering from one thigh to the other. Then there were more fingers touching her; her legs, her bottom, her breasts, slithering and sliding about her body, the sensuous contact with her skin making every nerve-ending alive with erotic sensation.

At last the fingers touched her between her legs, sliding their full length between the oozing lips, each one followed quickly by the next; ripples of quivering, gliding contact, snaking against her erect clitoris, down, inexorably and unfailingly to her anus before seemingly drifting off into the water.

This was not one person; the feelings were too intense, too many fingertips played against her achingly sensitive skin. Medea opened her eyes to see the faces of her temptresses, to beg them to continue, her hands reaching out to return their caresses with her own.

She was alone. The waves of the azure-blue sea lapped gently as before, the sunlight glinting brightly on the ripples. Still the sensations continued, the fingers slipping and slithering against her tortured flesh. Medea peered into the water, once more letting herself float erect, her change of position having little effect on the constant caresses of her unseen lovers.

At first she saw only her reflection, broken by the calmly undulating water. Then she saw a flash of silver, then another, and many more, swift, darting movements of eel-like fish swimming against her nakedness, purposely massaging her flesh with their silky forms.

She brushed them away with her hands, watching fascinated as they returned almost immediately, as if their task of arousing her beyond imagination must be completed. She shivered, not with fear but with lust, the constant, gliding touch of their sleek, darting bodies against her tender flesh making her head swim.

Suddenly she felt her waist grasped firmly, the grip urgent and demanding, and very definitely human. Medea felt herself being turned in the water to face her captor and wriggled in a vain attempt to free herself from the unyielding grasp, her fingers scratching at the very male hands that held her. The surface of the water broke in front of her and she saw him, and ceased her struggles.

Before her, effortlessly floating in the sea despite still holding her slim waist with both of his hands, was possibly the most handsome youth she had ever set eyes upon, his expression warm and smiling, his eyes bright with fun. His darkly-tanned skin was flawless, his thick, black hair cascading wetly over powerful shoulders that floated just above the surface of the water.

'Who are you?' she said, her voice shaking with the mixture of emotions caused by her extreme sexual arousal and the shock of the stranger's sudden appearance. 'Where did you come from?'

The handsome youth's grin broadened as she felt him pull her body against his, feeling him press his powerful chest against her large breasts. She floated helplessly in the water, completely at his mercy, her heart pounding both with concern and excitement.

His expression showed that he meant her no harm, but his silence unnerved her. 'Please,' she said, meekly, 'tell me what you want of me.' She felt him slip one of his hands behind her, touching her bottom, steering her crotch towards his, his grin unbroken, his actions answering her question. Involuntarily, her legs seemed to drift apart in the warm water as she was pulled towards him and her intensely aroused cunt felt the touch of his thick, erect shaft pressed against his belly. She lost control, her mind now totally in the grip of Eros, her body aching to be sated. Their lips met, the kiss of lovers, Medea wrapping her arms around the stranger's neck and her legs around his waist, raising and moving her body until his cock found her burning hole and slid, eel-like within the tight, slippery sheath to the hilt.

He began to move rapidly inside her, his upward thrusts being particularly strong, as though he were standing on a rock rather than floating free. The water splashed about

134

them as they thrashed their bodies together in sudden but necessary urgency, the salt stinging Medea's eyes. Gripping the youth's waist with her knees she hammered her bottom up and down, meeting his superb, driving lunges, her body demanding that he impale her fully each time. They held their kiss throughout, their tongues lapping hungrily around each other's mouths, their bodies rolling round and round in the sea. The tiny fish returned, slithering between her buttocks, some nibbling at the tiny hairs around her anus, others arousing every inch of her skin with their constant touch.

Her orgasm happened suddenly; as unexpected as had been the abrupt appearance of her mystery lover. Medea broke from their kiss and threw her head back, her eyes closed as the sensations began with her loin and quickly spread through her body, the incessant throbbing of the stiff erection held within the velvety tightness of her cunt telling her that he was sharing her joy.

She cried out loudly, her voice carried away by the gentle breeze and threw herself back, her only physical contact with her lover being at the crotch. She slipped momentarily under the water and felt him slipping from her, the emptiness inside her immediate. She struggled to become upright, her head quickly breaking the surface.

For a moment her eyes were dazzled by the sun, then she saw him, swimming powerfully into the distance. She watched him glide through the water, her emotions a mixture of disappointment and total sexual satisfaction, wanting him to return to her, to continue to love her in the warmth of the sea.

The youth turned and looked back, his smile as broad as before. Then he drew away again, swimming with incredible speed until he suddenly plunged beneath the surface, the last sight Medea having of her ethereal lover being the silver flash of his broadly finned tail.

The giant anchor-stone of the *Phallicis* slid almost noiselessly into the glassy waters off the coast of the beautiful island of Naxos. Medea watched its progress absently, her

135

mind still preoccupied with thoughts of her magical encounter three days previously.

Madeleine stood at her side, staring with equal intent at the shimmering surface of the sea, clearly deep in thought. Medea hadn't found it easy to tell her friend about the incident; somehow it had seemed so unreal. Only now had she found the strength to relate her tale.

'The islands of the Cyclades are well known to harbour many mysteries, and many dangers,' said Madeleine, quietly, as though attempting to reassure her friend. Her expression, however was wistful, betraying her envy of Medea's experience.

'There are many legends, but I have heard nothing of such an entity,' said Medea, pensively.

'Perhaps he was one of the children of Poseidon himself!'

Medea smiled, shaking her head. The thought had nevertheless crossed her mind, as had the idea that, if the Gods willed it, she may even become the mother of an immortal.

A large seabird landed suddenly on the deck, close to where they stood, then flew quickly away. Medea snapped her thoughts back to the present. 'They say the people of Naxos live only for pleasure, and that wine was invented by their leader, Dionysus,' she said, anxious to put fantasies of motherhood from her mind.

'Of all the lands in the known world, this is the one I have most longed to visit,' replied Madeleine, gazing at the lushly wooded island, 'the only land to vie with Tipos as a haven of debauchery!'

'I pray that you are right,' said Medea, her mood brightening. 'Come, we must prepare ourselves for whatever lies ahead!'

All but three of the Phallician crew set foot on the white sand of the beach, their excitement and apprehension clear. The frustrations of the long journey were soon to be eased, of this all were convinced.

They followed a well-trodden track leading from the beach into the trees and ascending steeply up the hill, the effort of the climb eased by the welcome shade of the greenery. Soon, however the canopy of leaves broke and they were at the top of the hill, and Medea felt the sea breeze suddenly brushing lightly against her cheeks, caressing her face with its soothing coolness.

She sat with Madeleine on a small rock and looked out to sea, back towards the Phallicia. Already she felt that this was a paradise, a jewel of the Aegean. She breathed deeply, the scented, warm air filling her lungs, the peace and freedom of the moment stimulating her. She wondered if she would ever return home to Iolcus; perhaps she would stay here after the others had left and spend the rest of her days with just the island for company.

'I feel so calm, almost bewitched,' said Madeleine, echoing her own thoughts.

'Remember Arcadia,' cautioned Medea, 'we felt much the same in that land of delights, to our later regret.'

Madeleine grinned, clearly remembering pleasurable encounters. 'This feels different, somehow,' she said, turning to look at the other women, all of whom were absorbing the powerful ambience of their surroundings, 'this place is special.'

'Let us hope you are right. The crew will become impossible to control if they don't discover the pleasures for which they crave soon!'

'There's something in the trees!' The startled voice belonged to Iole, who stood at the edge of the group, peering into the thick greenery.

'Where?' said Medea, joining her, 'I see nothing.'

'There, high up,' said Iole, pointing to the thickest area of the wood. Medea looked hard. At first she saw nothing then, suddenly she found she could make out the shape of what seemed to be that of a young man, his physique nearly at one with the twisted branches of the aleppo pine trees.

'There is another!' It was Madeleine this time, pointing to another clump of trees close by. They heard laughter and the rustling of leaves, followed by the cracking of twigs as the intruders jumped from their precarious perches and vanished into the cover of the thick bushes.

The women listened, peering intently into the under-growth for some time, but all was quiet, save for the incessant chirruping of the cicadas. 'Animals?' queried Iole, in a frightened whisper.

Medea shook her head. 'I don't think so. The one I glimpsed looked human, although I couldn't be certain.'

'They've gone now,' said Madeleine. Hardly had these words left her lips, and the air was filled with high-pitched shrieks and cries from behind them. The women turned quickly, to be faced by a sudden rush of creatures from within the undergrowth: small, human-like, less than five feet tall, their faces and bodies those of young men, their ears and lower legs like those of horses, as were the fine, thick tails that cascaded from their muscular rumps.

'Satyrs!' hissed Electra, 'beware, they can be vicious little beasts!'

The strange visitors began to dance mockingly around the huddled group of women, their expressions filled with mischief, their voices chattering unintelligibly. Each was naked, sporting a fine, if small erection sprouting from his thickly haired groin and most carried a spear or gnarled wooden stave.

'I pray to Zeus that they are not going to rape us,' whispered Iole, 'they are revolting creatures.'

Medea watched the throng of imps cautiously, the same thought very much to the fore in her mind. Occasionally, one of the satyrs would stumble drunkenly, others would laugh as though equally intoxicated. On they danced, goading the terrified women into some sort of response, though what they wanted was unclear.

Medea began to get irritated with the game and sat deliberately on a small rock, her arms folded arrogantly. Madeleine saw her purpose and followed suit, squatting cross-legged on the grass, and soon all the Phallician crew were seated about the clearing, looking defiantly at their tormentors.

One of the imps walked over to Medea and glared at her, his lips curling back to reveal sharp and badly discoloured teeth. He prodded her gently with the tip of his spear, but

138

she merely turned her head and looked the other way, making her impatience obvious. Angrily, the Satyr uttered what could only have been an oath and stamped his hooves heavily on the ground. Medea turned her face to him and matched his glare with her own, a look so fierce that he recoiled in fear.

'What do you want of us?' she demanded, loudly. 'This place is reputed to be a land of ultimate pleasure, and yet all we find is you! Begone from here, unless you want to feel the wrath of the Phallicians!'

'Do not be angry with them, they merely do my bidding.' The voice was deep and full of authority, coming from the shadow of the nearby trees.

'Who are you?' demanded Medea, standing to face the figure that slowly appeared into the sunlight. He was tall, bearded with sandy-coloured hair, a man in his mid-thirties wearing a simple, light coloured robe tied across his shoulder and flowing to reach his feet. His face was handsome, strong, the beard trimmed thinly and his hair held back from his forehead by a narrow band of leather. His expression seemed kind, and yet full of mischief.

'My name is Dionysus, son of Zeus and leader of the people of Naxos. You are welcome as my guests.'

Medea walked over to the statuesque figure and stared into his princely features, her heart beating quickly. 'If you are truly a son of Zeus,' she said, 'then you must be an immortal.'

Dionysus smiled, resting his hand lightly on her shoulder. 'Not so, fair queen, my mother was mortal, and it was decided by the Fates that I too should be of that state. I am not sorry.'

'I am Medea, of Colchis, and these fine women are the crew of the ship *Phallicis*. We are on a quest to seek out many fine athletes to attend a great games in my new home, to celebrate the crowning of my husband, Jason, as king of Iolcus.'

'There are many healthy and virile men upon this island,' said Dionysus, proudly. 'I will arrange for those who wish it to journey to your land and, with your permission,

139

perhaps I will accompany them. In the meantime, the pleasures of Naxos are yours to enjoy. You will find yourself relaxed and uninhibited here. There is a freshness in the air, an atmosphere of freedom. Indulge your every whim!'

Dionysus held out his arm and Medea grasped it as he led her into the woods from whence he had come, the Satyrs busily ushering the other women to follow. The path led deep into the forest, the thickness of the canopy of leaves over their heads once more cooling the tired women despite the fierceness of the sun. Throughout their short journey the Satyrs chattered excitedly, playfully pinching and nipping the flesh of the women, their little cocks permanently erect.

Medea felt that she should be irritated, but instead found the attentions of the happy little imps extremely arousing, despite their ugliness. Dionysus was right. There was a magical ambience about the place, a feeling of total ease, far more so than they had experienced on Arcadia; less hypnotic, more real.

Presently the trees thinned out and they entered the bright sunlight again, to be faced by the splendid entrance to a magnificent palace. Great, stone steps rose between tall, solid pillars supporting an ornately carved plinth, beneath which were two large doors in heavy oak, both of them quickly flung open by the ever attentive Satyrs. Medea allowed Dionysus to lead her into a great hall, the marble floor feeling instantly cold to her feet. The others followed, looking around the palatial interior in wonder and admiration.

'This is truly a great palace,' said Medea, with genuine awe at her surroundings. 'You must be a favourite son of Zeus.'

Dionysus' expression changed to one of sadness. 'This place was dedicated by my father to the memory of my mother, Semele. She was tricked by her family and died as a result of seeing Zeus in his true state for, as is well known, no mortal can gaze upon a deiform and live.'

'I'm sorry,' said Medea, weakly, looking into his eyes,

noting their glassy appearance. Suddenly his face changed, a broad grin returning to his countenance.

'Enough! Naxos is a place of pleasure, not sorrow! We will eat and drink until you are all fully refreshed and then, my dear Queen of Iolcus, you and your companions will indulge in the wild bacchanalia for which this island is renowned!'

Medea lay back on the soft rug, her head cradled in Madeleine's lap, her stomach full and her head swimming with the effect of the copious quantity of wine she had happily consumed. Dionysus had acted the perfect host, treating the Phallician women to their every desire, the Satyrs rushing around them, feeding them and replenishing their goblets with a seemingly never ending supply of strong, sweet liquor. The only thing missing from this idyllic scene was the men, the fine athletes promised to them. The combination of the alcohol and the stimulating atmosphere was having a profound effect on all the women present, and the desire for the caress of strong arms and the feel of sturdy, muscular bodies was obviously foremost in everyone's mind.

Twice Medea had allowed her hand to trail nonchalantly between her legs, caressing the warm wetness of her pussy through the thin linen of her dress, impervious to the opinions of her host. Now she needed more than the fluttering touch of her own fingers; now she needed much more. She looked up into the face of their host, who was watching the sensuous action of her fingers between her legs most attentively.

Dionysus clapped his hands loudly. 'I feel the time is right to introduce you to the true pleasures of the Bacchants!' he cried, getting to his feet. A large door at the furthest end of the hall swung open noisily, the sounds of male laughter coming from the corridor beyond. Medea looked in the direction of the clamour, seeing to her utmost happiness a long line of near-naked men begin to walk into the hall, their faces bearing broad grins, their eyes shining with anticipation. The Phallician women sat up and watched in delight as the new guests entered, their eyes filled with lust as they gazed upon the superb physiques of the strapping figures that surrounded them.

'By Zeus,' whispered Madeleine, 'I'm going to be well fucked today!' She stood and walked over to a robust, heavily muscled character and reached beneath the linen of his tiny loin-cloth, quickly exposing a fine and vigorous erection to Medea's gaze. Immediately, Madeleine bent forward and took the monster's plum-sized end into her mouth, her free hand deftly unhooking her own garment and casting it away from her body.

Medea stripped off her own simple clothing and looked around excitedly, spoilt for choice, the room filled with men of all shapes, sizes and creeds. Ahead of her stood a tall, ruggedly-built man, his skin as black as night, his features seemingly chiselled from the deepest ebony, his body shining with sweat. Medea gazed lustfully into his eyes, memories of the strange dream Pan had given her, that of her fine stallion, flooding back to her.

She walked over to the man and unhooked the cloth from around his waist, her stare fixed on his. Reaching down, she took hold of his already stiffening cock and rubbed it gently, feeling it harden under her expert touch. She forced herself submissively against his nakedness, his heavy balls crushed to the warm cushion of her cunt, the thick stem of his shaft pressed against her flat stomach.

'What name have you?' she said, quietly.

'Dius,' the man replied, his big hands clutching the peach-like smoothness of her bottom.

'Well, Dius, you will be the first to fuck me. Make it good.'

Dius reached down and took Medea's calf in his strong grasp, raising her leg high, her foot almost to the height of his shoulder. Bending his own knees slightly and still gripping her ankle, he aimed his superb stiffness at her eager slit, the puffiness and redness of her sex-lips a clear sign that she was more than ready. She looked down and watched in awe and lustful joy as the black stalk slid effortlessly inside her cunt, seven or eight inches at first, then the rest, inch by inch, slipping into her hot sheath with each determined thrust of her lover's powerful hips.

She groaned as she took the full length inside her, the feeling of total fullness devouring her senses. Dius let her ankle go free and she curled her leg around his waist, lifting her other foot from the floor and wrapping this leg also around his body, her arms tightly holding on to his broad shoulders as he stood firmly, his hands gripping her soft buttocks.

Steadily, Medea began to dictate the rhythm of the fuck, slowly at first, raising herself up against his chest until just the very end of his cock was held within the soaked sheath of her pussy, and then letting herself slip sensuously down, absorbing the huge, thick length to the hilt. She felt his nails digging into the tender flesh of her bottom, one rogue fingertip finding her anus and slipping inside, moving in a circular fashion, opening her up in preparation for pleasures possibly to come.

Her movements became rapidly more urgent, her needs strong. Gradually she quickened her pace, using the strength of her arms to raise and lower her body impaled on his magnificent weapon, thrilling to each deep thrust. She looked around her; the sight that met her eyes was of an endless sea of copulation, heaving bottoms and bouncing breasts, legs and arms flailing as weeks of abstinence were sated.

Dius mischievously took his grip from her bottom and rested his hands on his hips, grinning broadly as Medea shagged herself mercilessly on his stiff pole. Suspended by her arms from his neck with her heels digging into his buttocks she rammed her crotch against his furiously, the wet sounds of their love-making filling her ears. Faster and faster she thrust at him, the speed and her strength surprising her, her orgasm quickly approaching.

With a squeal she felt her come tearing at her, filling her very soul with total joy as she pounded herself against this sturdy, solid man-flesh. She felt that his massive cock could almost split her in two. She cried out again as the release hit her, raising herself until just the large, spurting knob was held between her pussy-lips then letting herself fall against him, absorbing every magnificent inch of his throbbing prick, their pubic hairs meshing wetly together.

Medea held herself still in this divine position momentarily, then slowly let her legs slide down to the floor, her body slipping from his as his phallus became gradually flaccid. She fell slowly to her knees, kissing his firm stomach and taking his drooping cock in her mouth, suckling voraciously, swallowing her own juices.

Finally she let him go free and lay back on the cool marble tiles, sated for the moment but knowing that this was only the beginning. She looked around her at the scene of revelry, enjoying the sight of her splendid crew exhausting themselves and their many lovers. Close by, she saw Iole, no longer virginally innocent, happily accommodating two superb cocks within her once tight pussy, her young mouth eagerly sucking on a third. She looked for Madeleine and found her, standing straight-legged with her body bent almost double, her perfect bottom being penetrated by the stiff manhood of their host, Dionysus himself.

Two hands grabbed her arm, and Medea was pulled like a doll onto the reclining body of a golden-haired youth of little more than sixteen, a delightfully angelic-faced young man with eyes that shone with happiness as he helped her squat over his groin, directing his prick towards the heavenly target of her ravaged cunt. She sat down on him quickly, her insides already well-stretched as a result of her recent encounter, the hot sheath encompassing his full length in one movement. She began to move up and down on her new conquest until he curled his arm around her neck and pulled her face towards his, causing her to crouch on her knees, his penis still working steadily inside her, her bottom presented to the gaze of any who cared to look.

She kissed his beautiful, young face passionately, his sheer good looks filling her with enchantment. He gripped her buttocks and moved her bottom slowly up and down in time with his upward thrusts, a constant, easy

144

rhythm that she felt she could endure for the rest of her life.

For a moment he slowed, almost stopped, and she imagined that another hand was touching her engorged sex lips. Then, uttering a cry of pure exhilaration she felt a second, hard cock slide alongside the other in her soaked pussy, the two stiff erections filling her completely. She held herself still as the two men pumped in and out of her in unison, each withdrawal causing her sex-lips to pout widely with the sheer girth of the intrusion.

The thrusting became harder, more ardent and Medea raised her head, her eyes meeting those of another youth of about the same age as her golden-haired cherub and smiled at him, meaningfully. Taking the hint, he knelt beside her and pointed his long, slim erection to her open mouth. Greedily she took as much of his length between her lips as she could, rapidly moving her head in time with the pace of her double-fuck, her tongue licking round and round the superbly stiff stalk in her mouth.

All around her the sounds of women crying in orgasm and men groaning as they emptied their seed in intensely voracious orifices filled the air, the unadulterated atmosphere of pure eroticism completely taking control of Medea's mind, her only thoughts being of continued sexual satisfaction. The two young men inside her were coming, the thought of their sperm shooting in unison deep within her body and mixing with that of her huge-cocked black lover of only moments previously driving her into a frenzy of lust.

Suddenly, the cock in her mouth began to throb heavily and she tasted the salty delights of sperm as it spurted to the back of her throat. Swallowing greedily, she sucked on the sweet shaft until he had no more to give, finally letting his drooping stalk leave her hungry mouth.

Medea disentangled herself from her three lovers and clambered over the rutting bodies towards Madeleine, who was sitting exhaustedly on a pile of cushions, her hair dishevelled, her skin covered in sweat. Dionysus knelt before her, his tongue paying homage to her pussy.

'If I didn't know better,' said Madeleine, wearily, 'I'd swear I was home, in my beloved Tipos. There is such freedom here, not just for sex but for any indulgence. These people are pure hedonists; pleasure is their only aim in life, as it is in mine.'

'You may stay with us as long as it pleases you,' said Dionysus, taking his face from the warmth of her crotch, 'even for ever, should you wish it.'

'I must accompany Medea on the quest,' replied Madeleine, stoically but with more than an element of uncertainty in her voice. Medea knelt at Dionysus' side, taking his stiff erection in her hand and moving her face towards his groin, quickly detecting Madeleine's scent on his engorged flesh.

Suddenly, a loud crashing sound came from the far wall of the hall as the great doors were flung open to reveal the figures of a large group of women, tall, dark-skinned with long, jet-black hair, each dressed in the clothing of a huntress. The men broke off from their various couplings and cheered as the newcomers marched into the room, waving their spears in triumph as the accompanying Satyrs carried in the carcasses of many slain beasts and dumped them unceremoniously at the feet of Dionysus.

'These are the Maenads,' he breathed to Medea and Madeleine, 'the women of Naxos. Like you and your fellow travellers they are insatiable lovers and great warriors. They use the Bacchant men as their playthings, and enjoy each other's delights with similar gusto!'

Madeleine looked horrified. 'I can't believe this is happening again,' she wailed, 'my fair homeland was invaded by the vicious women of Lesbos, killing all the men of the island and ravaging the women. Now, just when I think I have rediscovered paradise you tell me that I will lose it again?'

'Not so,' said Dionysus, pulling himself to his feet and taking up his thyros, a long stick entwined with ivy leaves, in one hand and brandishing it in welcome, 'the Maenads enjoy the touch of both male and female with equal voracity. You are safe in your new-found heaven, although I fear your bodies will ache on the morrow! Now that the Maenads are here the Bacchanalia can really commence!'

'Greetings, Dionysus!' The voice was that of an extremely tall Maenad, her air of authority and the way she marched towards their host with her arms outstretched in welcome clearly indicating that she was someone of importance.

'Greetings, Niobe,' cried Dionysus in reply, entwining his arms about hers, 'the hunt was plainly very successful!'

Niobe grinned proudly and waved her arm towards the huge pile of animal carcasses. 'Enough for months! The Gods were with us this day!'

'This is Medea of Colchis,' he said, motioning the two girls forward, 'and her friend Madeleine, Queen of Tipos.'

Niobe's eyes widened in pleasurable wonder. 'Tipos!' she exclaimed, staring at Madeleine hungrily. 'Such stories have we heard of the exploits of the women of Tipos! And you, you are none other than their Queen?'

'Indeed I am,' said Madeleine, a trace of sadness in her voice, 'but the nation once known as Tipos is no more.'

'So I hear. Never mind, the Gods have brought you to Naxos! This will be your home!'

'Madeleine travels with the Phallicians, on a great quest,' ventured Medea, realising from the haunted look on her friend's face that she had lost her.

'No, Medea,' said Niobe, taking Madeleine's arm firmly and beginning to lead her away. 'Tales of the exploits of the women of Tipos fill many a winter's night here on Naxos. Madeleine will stay with us, where she knows in her heart that she belongs. Her days and nights will be filled with endless pleasure once more. She will become a Maenad!' Niobe led Madeleine away, one hand gripping her forearm, the other playfully stroking her naked bottom.

Medea watched, her emotions torn between sorrow at the extreme likelihood of losing her dearest friend and a tearing lust within her loins to enjoy the pleasures that she knew Madeleine was about to savour. Dionysus took her arm.

147

'Come,' he said, gently, 'we will leave the others. I have need of your fair body. I will teach you more of the secrets of the Bacchants.' He led her out of the room, away down a long corridor, away from the groans of passion and the cries and sobs of happy release, to the silence of his bed-chamber.

The room, like all the rooms in the palace was a temple to opulence. The walls were decked with tapestries woven by the feet of nymphs; the giant bed that formed the centrepiece of the room was surrounded by the most exquisitely carved of statues representing every immortal inhabitant of Olympus, the likenesses sculpted from life.

Medea gasped in awe at the sheer resplendence of the setting, the wetness returning to her sex-lips as she realised she was about to be the conquest of the most fabled lover since Adonis. Without waiting for Dionysus to speak she walked over to the bed and clambered across its soft magnificence, lying naked on her back, her body offered to him in total submission. Dionysus knelt at her side, his long stalk jutting from his crotch, the end wet as testimony of his desire for this stunning young woman. He knelt forward and kissed her lightly on the lips.

'I am going to taste every part of your divine body, lick every pore, every hair, drink from your sweet chalice of love until you quiver and beg for me to impale you. Still I will tease and torment you; I will make you come without feeling the touch of my skin upon yours, and this will be the first of many releases. Your juices will flood from your young body, soaking my flesh, my groin, my face. Close your eyes, fair Queen, the first delight will be all the better for it.'

Medea did as he bade, shutting her eyes tightly and waiting for his next move. She sensed a trickle of warm wetness slip from her pussy and trail slowly between her buttocks to dampen the silk cushion beneath her. Her breathing became stilted, her heart pounding, her nipples hardening. She felt the warmth of her lover's breath blowing gently over the erect buds, arching her back slightly in the hope of pushing her breast against his mouth, but he must have pulled back, teasing her as he had promised.

She sensed that he moved his head downwards, the delicate caress of his unrelenting breath moving tantalisingly close to her yearning pussy. Carefully he blew lightly around her, so close that she could feel the short hairs between her legs move like soft grass in a gentle, summer breeze, but not so close as to tease the erect bud of her clitoris or sooth the pouting lips that ached for him with an impossible lust she had never experienced before.

She wanted to grab his head, to force his face between her legs, ram his mouth against her cunt, make him lick and suckle at her prize, but she knew that this would break the spell, that she must lie in full submission. The need was tearing her apart inside, the wetness now soaking the cushion beneath her stiffening bottom as her hips made involuntary movements towards the unseen,

Medea dug her fingers into the softness of the bed, gritting her teeth and raising her hips from the cushion, arching herself painfully as the orgasm ripped through her lovely body with a suddenness that shattered her. She screamed; far louder than she intended, her voice as out of control as her emotions. She pumped her crotch up and down as though absorbing the length of some invisible lover, her eyes snapping open in a desperate desire to gaze at Dionysus as he blew gently at the engorged lips of her cunt.

She was alone on the bed. Dionysus stood some twenty feet away, watching her in mock amusement, spooning sweet goats' cream into his mouth from a silver chalice.

'Where ... how did you ...' Medea stopped, her body still shaking from the force and abruptness of her orgasm. Dionysus walked impassively to her, kneeling again at her side.

'Taste the food of the Gods,' he said, offering her the spoon loaded with the lemon-white emulsion. Medea opened her mouth and took it in, licking the sweet paste, relishing the delicate, scented flavour, a sudden warmth pervading through her body as she swallowed. 'The taste is that of the seed of Zeus,' he said, filling the spoon again from the deep cup and offering it again to her lips. She

149

suckled the cream slowly, savouring the strong essence, her vision glazing as though she were drunk on wine.

A third spoonful was offered to her mouth but, before she could take it in, Dionysus moved the spoon away, slowly towards her stomach, and then lower, closer to the excited, wet warmth of her cunt. Deliberately he turned the utensil until the cream oozed torpidly from it, a thick, glutinous stream of cool liquid running sensuously onto the tortured sex-lips, soaking the hair, flowing like a stream of sperm between her labia.

Dionysus put the spoon to one side and leant forward, pushing his tongue out until the tip touched the creamy lips, his mouth instantly suckling and sucking at the delicate meal. Medea shuddered, the cool paste against her hot cunt and the warm, wet tongue lapping at her lips causing her to groan in total ecstasy. As he suckled, more cream was poured from the seemingly bottomless chalice, coating her groin with sublime sensation, her mind drunk with euphoria.

Presently, he lay across her, his crotch matted wetly against hers, their lower bodies sliding together, oiled by their mutual feast. Medea opened her legs and drew them back, clutching the backs of her knees and pulling them to her breasts, the intrusion of his fine stalk inevitable. His movements began with a measured, easy pace, each forward motion allowing her to discern every thick inch of his long cock, the wide, bulbous end touching her cervix every time, causing waves of intoxicated bliss to undulate through her brain.

He gripped her heels and took over the control of their tender fuck, pushing her legs straight behind her head, his body now directly above hers, his weight supported by his grip and his toes. Medea had forgotten the bacchanalia outside, the memory of the four young cocks that had pleased her only moments before was gone from her mind. This was a lovers' fuck, pure and supremely exciting, the shared emotions theirs alone.

Pulling from her, Dionysus lay on his back, holding his huge cock at the root, the savage, wet length presented vertically for her pleasure. Medea clambered across his body, guiding the stiff stalk back into her hot sheath, sinking her hips down slowly onto his as she absorbed him within her. Now it was her turn; she controlled the pace, the rhythm of their copulation. Her movements quickly became urgent, lifting herself high on his superb length before crashing down hard on his groin, both lovers gasping for breath with the force of her efforts. The speed increased, faster and faster, her needs now clear. Dionysus matched her thrusts with his own, his hips pushing upwards, causing her to impale herself brutally on his fine weapon.

Medea slowed her movements somewhat, breathing deeply, her heart pounding inside her sweat-soaked body. Carefully, without letting him free from her tight sheath she turned her back to him, squatting on the balls of her feet, her wonderful bottom presented to his gaze. Clutching his ankles with her hands she resumed her erotic dance, knowing that his eyes would be filled with the sight of her stretched pussy and perfect arse.

In this position her clitoris rubbed constantly along the slithering length inside her, her arousal total. Once again she experienced the powerful, gut-wrenching feeling as the command of her very nerve-endings was taken into the control of Aphrodite, the pounding of her hips fast and furious as her come threatened to tear her from life itself.

Her buttocks slapped loudly against her lover's groin, her cries of elation echoing around the room, her joy complete as she sensed the familiar throbbing inside her tender flesh, the warm wetness of Dionysus' release entering her sated womb.

Medea stood at the beach holding Madeleine tightly around the waist, her friend hugging her shoulders with equal passion. Tears soaked the faces of the two friends, two lovers who knew the time had come to part. There was nothing more to be said. Madeleine had found true happiness, for her the quest was over. They would meet again, maybe love once more as they had done during the long

Aegean nights but, for now, Medea would lead the Phallicians alone.

CHAPTER EIGHT

Jason trod the hot sand of the deserted beach moodily, his gaze distant, his thoughts as ever with Glaucis. Many weeks had passed since the Argonauts had enjoyed the pleasures of the Sphyledes, the sounds and scents of their erotic encounters now distant memories.

The sweet virgin-child had soothed his aching frustrations occasionally with the delicate touch of her hand, although she never again dared to bring the pouting lips of her soft mouth too close to his raging stalk, perhaps fearful that her will would abandon her. These stolen moments of relief were always a joy, but the desire, nay craving he held within his soul to impale this sensuously innocent creature was fast becoming in danger of taking hold of his reason. Sometimes, in moments of dark fantasy he even considered that he might lose control and rape her, an act for which he knew he would never be able to forgive himself.

Of late, he had taken to seeking solace in the powerful but calming arms of Atalanta who, although maddeningly unwilling to allow him entry to her most precious of treasures, expertly sucked and suckled him to desperately needed orgasm. Jason felt safer, more in command of his libido when he lay with Atalanta, not because she wasn't beautiful; far from it. Her strong, athletic body was moulded and curved to perfection, the firmness of her sensuous flesh and suppleness of her long limbs ever a delight.

He simply knew that if he attempted to fuck her without her invitation she had more than enough strength, and probably the will to tear his manhood from his body and cast it into the sea.

153

The beach was on the mainland of Greece, and was to be the last contact with his homeland before the *Argo* was to head south, stopping briefly at the island of Icaria to deliver Glaucis to her betrothed. From there they were to sail for Cyprus, and complete the quest to find the cloak of Aphrodite.

The area around appeared deserted, the vegetation sparse and the soil unlikely to support the most able of farmers. Amidst this barren wasteland Jason found the peace and solitude he needed, time to think, space to breath.

The Argonauts had come to search for food and water, their last chance before at least three more weeks at sea. Their disappointment at finding little in the way of fruit and vegetables was compounded by the almost total lack of fresh water, and the men had split into a number of small hunting groups and gone off into the nearby mountains, leaving two crew-members to guard Glaucis and their precious vessel.

Jason sat wearily on a small clump of scrub-like grass and gazed out to sea. Why was this lust for Glaucis tearing him apart? Why was it so strong, so all-consuming? He clenched his fists and shut his eyes tightly, praying to the Gods that she would allow him to take her, to release his pent-up frustrations. Then, perhaps, once her virginal portal had been assailed he would lose this insane need for her.

Deep within his heart, however, he knew that it could never be.

'Jason, why so sad, my love?'

He swung around in abject shock, the voice as familiar to him as his own. His eyes met a sight that he could not believe. There, resplendent in perfect nakedness stood Medea, his wife, her long, red hair billowing in the rising breeze, her lovely face smiling, her arms outstretched in warm greeting.

He jumped to his feet and walked quickly towards her. 'How do you come to be here?' he said, taking her soft body in his strong embrace. 'Your quest should take you many miles from this point.'

154

'I could not bear to be away from you any longer,' said Medea, kissing his face rapidly between each word, her hands stroking his broad back passionately. 'I ordered my crew to head this way, praying to Zeus that we would meet.'

'Where are you beached? I had no sight of your craft.'

'We are hidden around the point, just to the south. The crew are all aboard, awaiting my orders.'

'And your quest? What of that?'

Medea tugged furiously at his loin-cloth, ripping it from his body, grabbing his quickly rising erection with an eager hand. 'Forget the quest,' she breathed, 'I want you to fuck me, now, on this beach! I yearn to feel your massive stalk deep inside me; come, fuck me, fuck me now!'

She pulled hard at his hardening cock, dragging him to the ground, lying on the hot sand with her legs splayed wide apart. Jason fell to his knees and reached out to touch her pussy, oddly feeling somewhat nervous. The shock of meeting his lovely wife on this distant beach hadn't left him, and her apparently intense desire for him seemed somewhat overstated and out of character. Medea enjoyed sex, but had never been so demonstrative before. He wondered what had befallen her during her travels, to throw her into such fervent desperation.

His fingers reached the pouting lips of her cunt, all four slipping easily inside the hot, wet sheath. She groaned, her eyes closed. Jason allowed his thumb to join his probing fingers as she raised her bottom from the sand, then slipped more and more of his hand inside her until the inner lips closed about his wrist. Never had Medea been so accommodating!

Clenching his fist within her soaked cunt he began to gently move his forearm backwards and forwards, wondering in astonished delight just how much of it she could take. Medea appeared unconcerned by the massive intrusion, wriggling her hips as though inviting further, deeper penetration. His arm slipped inside her almost to the elbow, the wet lips of her sex stretched around his muscular limb, her expression one of abject delight. Clearly, Jason

155

mused, she had accommodated a stalk of monstrous proportions at some time on her quest.

He began to feel a little jealous, his ego badly affected. It was true that they had agreed to dispense with their oaths of fidelity for the duration of their quests but now, with Medea lying in his arms so very obviously well fucked by someone of magnificent endowment, it was almost too much to bear.

He slipped his hand slowly from the tightly-gripping sheath of hot woman-flesh and brought his arm to his mouth, licking the sheen of juice from his skin. Medea looked at him lovingly. 'You look sad again, my husband. Do I not please you?'

'Have there been many lovers on your travels?' Jason wasn't sure he wanted to hear the answer, but the question had to be asked.

'Many, my love,' Medea replied, totally unconcerned, 'but none could touch you for the way you pleasure me.'

'How many? How many huge stalks have gained entry to this eager pussy?'

'What does it matter?' she said, gripping his stiff cock with both hands. 'All that matters to me is that I am to be fucked by this fine monster!'

Her words and her urgent, grasping palms against the aching flesh of his penis calmed his anger and aroused him to a sudden frenzy of lust. He rolled over the supine body of his beautiful wife, allowing her to guide the thick, bulbous end of his prick to her gaping slit. He slid into her easily, the silky walls of her hot sheath moulding themselves around his long shaft, the movements of her vaginal muscles emulating the sucking of a mouth, drawing him ever deeper to the hilt.

'Fuck me, Jason,' she cried, gripping his hair, her hips thrusting upwards to meet the heavy pumping of his groin against hers, 'fuck me like you've never fucked anyone before!'

Jason responded by driving himself harder and harder into her, his eyes tightly closed as he sated himself on the writhing body beneath his. His lover slid one hand down to his buttocks, a finger quickly finding his anus and pushing inside, wriggling through the resisting sphincter to the knuckle.

Jason felt his time near and stopped his movements instantly, anxious that Medea should have her pleasure before he emptied his seed within her lovely body. He allowed himself to rest his full weight upon her, his cock firmly embedded inside her throbbing cunt.

Somehow she felt different. Her flesh was harder, the muscles more defined, the breasts fuller, firmer even than their previous magnificence. He opened his eyes to gaze in hers; the sight that met him caused him to recoil in terror, leaping to his feet, his erection bobbing in front of him ludicrously.

There, lying prostrate at his feet was Atalanta, her legs open, the lips of her pussy splayed in evidence that her virginity was no more.

'What trickery is this? What evil work?' Jason shook with anger and bemusement, the sight of the warrior huntress lying so submissively both frightening and immensely arousing.

'What is it, my love?' cried Atalanta, opening her legs even wider. 'Is this not what you want? Enter me again. Fuck me until I come with you!'

Jason shook his head. 'This is magic! I am bewitched! Get away from me, spirit, have done with this!'

Atalanta struggled to her feet, her face covered with tears. 'But Jason,' she wailed, 'this was my first time. You cannot be so cruel!'

'You are no more Atalanta than I,' he said, angrily, 'begone!'

The lovely woman in front of him let her arms fall to her sides and bowed her head sadly. She reached out and took hold of his flaccid penis, clutching it gently. 'You droop, my lover,' she said, quietly, 'perhaps this will make you rise.'

With that she stood back, flinging her arms wide. A flash of lightning seared before Jason's eyes, causing him to close them against the intense brightness. Opening them quickly he blinked; Atalanta no longer stood before him.

157

'Jason, this is what you want.' The voice was sweet and melodious, gentle and innocent. It was the voice of Glaucis. Jason swung round. Glaucis stood close to him, naked, the fingers of both hands pulling apart her prominent, wet sex-lips. 'Fuck me, Jason, fuck your lovely Glaucis. Your dream will be fulfilled.'

She slipped the fingers of one hand into her pussy, her hips moving against their intrusion, her expression one of total lust. Jason felt his cock rising at the sight, seeing her smile as she watched it thicken before her. He clamped his hands over his eyes. 'No, no!' turning away. 'This is not Glaucis! She would not behave so!'

'Jason,' tempted the voice of Glaucis. 'My cunt, my mouth, my arse, all wait eagerly for you to impale them.'

Jason roared out, a long, gut-wrenching wail as though to block out the sound of her words and ran towards the sea, his hands now clasped over his ears. Falling headlong into the waves he began to swim furiously towards the *Argo*, still imagining that he could hear the cries of Glaucis begging him to return to the beach.

Then she was at his side, swimming faster than he could ever have managed, slipping her body along his, the feel of soft, wet skin against his tearing at his every emotion. Harder and harder he swam, his eyes closed to the sight of the naked nymph gliding through the water with the ease of a serpent.

'Jason, Jason, look again.' The voice was different, one he did not know. He opened his eyes cautiously, letting his stroke ease. His companion had allowed yet another metamorphosis to occur; this time she was a stranger, and a beautiful one.

'Come back to the beach, Jason,' she purred as they drifted slowly together in the warm swell, 'I will explain everything.'

'Is this you as you really are?' he asked, nervously trying to avoid the hypnotic gaze in her almond eyes.

'Come to the beach,' she said, her tone even more seductive, 'come lay with me again and you will learn much that will please you. '

Before Jason could answer she turned from him and swam powerfully towards the shore. He followed slowly, unsure that he was doing the right thing but desperately curious.

As he waded from the relative coolness of the waves he saw the girl lying again on the hot sand, resting back on her elbows, a broad smile on her face. Her features were oriental, the large eyes slanted, the nose tiny, the mouth full. Her skin was olive, coated in a delicate sheen of sea-water, fast drying in the scorching sun. Her breasts were small but perfectly rounded with long, dark nipples that stood proudly erect, proclaiming her arousal. Her long, shapely legs were parted slightly, the puffy lips of her hairless pussy clearly visible, the red gash distinctly damp.

Jason could hardly avoid his long cock rising as though in worship to this devastating beauty as he walked towards her, his lust quickly overtaking his good sense. She looked at his superb length and licked her lips.

'I want you inside me again, Jason. I will play no more tricks.'

He sat at her side, running his hand softly over the undulating curves of her delectable body. 'Tell me first,' he said, his heartbeat still racing from the effort of the swim, 'who are you? What magic is it?'

The girl sat up, taking hold of the now fully stiff erection in her hand and gently rubbing it up and down. 'My name is Thetis. I am mortal but was raised by Hera and endowed with the ability to change shape at will. My home is the sea.'

'Has the Goddess Hera told you of the quest I and my crew are embarked upon?'

'Indeed she has, and much more about you, brave Jason. I also know that you intend to steal from Aphrodite and caution you, for she is also aware of your plans, and will do everything to frustrate them.'

Jason decided to ignore her counsel. They had come too far and endured too much to be thwarted by a mere Goddess. 'Why did you appear as my wife, Medea?' he said.

'Fun, just fun. I had great difficulty holding back my laughter; you were so easily fooled.'

159

He grinned to conceal his embarrassment. 'Why then take the forms of Atalanta and Glaucis?'

'I took the shape of Atalanta because I know you desire her, and that of Glaucis because I know that you love her.'

Jason looked shocked. 'Love? I love only Medea, my wife. I merely *lust* for Glaucis like any man would.'

'Whatever you say, Jason, whatever you say. Now, what shape would you have me take? I can be anyone . . . anything you desire to copulate with. I can even grow a strong penis and impale your splendid backside. What is your desire?'

'Not that, I can assure you,' he replied, laughing, 'just be yourself, as you are now. You are very lovely; you need not change one iota to please me.'

His words plainly charmed Thetis, who leant forward and kissed him lightly on the lips before bending her body and taking the thick end of his cock in her soft mouth. Slowly, she moved her head down, her lips suckling at his stiff shaft, her throat swallowing until her face touched his hairy groin, the full length of his stalk held inside her silky, moist mouth. He felt her sliding her tongue around his thick stem, her throat undulating as she continued her swallowing, her head moving slightly back and forth.

Thetis carried on in this manner until he could stand it no more. 'Take care, Thetis,' he groaned through gritted teeth. 'I am near to filling your throat with my seed and will be unable to satisfy your hungry pussy if you drain me.'

He watched in awe as Thetis pulled her head from him, the long, stiff length slowly exposed. Finally the peach-like knob appeared from the suckling lips and she kissed it lightly. His cock throbbed involuntarily, sending a short jet of white fluid over the beautiful creature's smooth cheek. She scooped the juice with her fingers and put them to her mouth, licking the ends. 'You were certainly very near,' she said, grinning.

'That's quite a talent you have,' he said, steadily quelling his need to orgasm.

'I transformed my throat into that of a snake,' she said, almost matter-of-factly.

Jason breathed deeply. 'Lust with you would know no boundaries, no fantasy would be unfulfilled.'

'Anything, Jason, anything.'

'Turn your perfect bottom to me, my love. I want to fuck you as the beautiful woman you are. Fuck your cunt, fuck your arse, for as long as we both can stand it.'

She turned, kneeling on all fours, her bottom presented to him for his pleasure. 'Enter my bottom first, Jason, ravage my tight hole for, when you slide again within the folds of my cunt, I promise that you will not be able to endure the pleasure for long before I drain you of all the fluids of Eros.'

Jason leant forward and wetly licked between the glorious globes of her buttocks, allowing his spittle to run over her anus, using first one then two fingers to gradually ease the tightness of the tiny sphincter. She pushed her bottom against his face as he lapped at her hole, clearly enjoying the sensation.

When he felt she was ready he leant back and knelt between her calves, gripping the base of his big cock with one hand and using the thumb and forefinger of the other to open up her anus, the wetness of his spittle on the dark, puckered orifice glistening in the bright sunshine.

He pressed the thick knob of his tool against the hole and pushed forward. Thetis groaned, not with pain but with pleasure as the stiff intruder entered her backside, the muscles of her anus quickly relaxing and accepting the intrusion. Spitting onto his fingers he lubricated his thick shaft and eased it steadily inside the tight sheath until every inch was held within her superb bottom, his belly pressed against her rounded buttocks, his balls cushioned by the wetness of her hairless cunt.

Slowly but surely Jason began to pump his iron-hard cock in and out of the welcoming warmth, the tightness easing with every stroke. Leaning slightly forward he ran his hands under her acquiescent form, one palm cupping a small, firm breast, the fingers of the other quickly finding her clitoris, rubbing resolutely at the erect bud in time with the rhythm of his powerful pelvic thrusts.

161

Thetis groaned again, her head resting on the cushion of her arms which were folded on the sand in front of her, wriggling her sumptuous bottom provocatively. Jason let both of his hands grip her breasts, lifting her back to sit on his lap, until she was squatting across his kneeling thighs. Gripping her upper torso firmly, he raised her up and down on his stiffness, as though masturbating with her entire body.

'By Zeus, Jason,' Thetis breathed, her voice stilted with desire, 'you are almost too big to take me in this way. I fear you may split me apart with your fine weapon!'

Jason responded by forcing her to move up and down on him at a faster pace, the sounds of her buttocks slapping against his groin filling the still air of the afternoon. 'I am close to coming,' he grunted, 'let me enter your sweet cunt once more so that I might fill your womb with my seed, my balls ache so for release.'

Thetis raised herself up from his thighs, allowing the long, thick cock to slip from her bottom. Lying on her back she raised her legs and gripped her ankles, spreading her limbs wide apart, the pouting lips of her pussy seeming to pulsate with eager, wet excitement. 'Fuck me, Jason,' she commanded, 'fuck my cunt with your massive cock; fill my body with its glorious length and make me come with you, and I promise you will never forget the sensation for the rest of your life!'

Jason threw himself upon the sublimely submissive form of the beautiful woman, his cock blindly finding its way between the silky, yielding lips and into the hot, wet tightness of her sheath. Sinking deep within her pliant warmth he held himself still for a moment, a single throb of his hard stem allowing the urgency of his need to relax slightly, his buttocks clenched, his eyes closed against the beauty of her features.

Suddenly, he experienced a new sensation, a feeling so erotically exquisite that he cried out. The glove-tight sheath of wet tissue within her body transformed, the sensation now one of a multitude of tongues licking every part of his cock from hilt to tip, lapping, rasping, suckling against the tortured flesh. Jason snapped his eyes open, gazing in lustful joy into the face of his lover, her expression one of insane carnality.

'Come with me, Jason,' she panted, wrapping her legs around his body, her heels digging into his back, drawing him further into her. 'Come with me as you feel the tongues of a thousand wood-nymphs licking you into oblivion!'

Jason needed no further encouragement. With an animal-like bellow he felt his orgasm tear at his groin, the copious fluids of his lust flooding into her, the tickling, lapping sensation of this unearthly oral stimulation gradually fading until his throbbing stem was once again held within the slippery tightness of her cunt.

Jason lay exhausted, gazing at the cloudless, blue sky whilst absently sifting the grains of sand through the fingers of one hand. Thetis licked casually at the tip of his flaccid, spent penis, her head on his stomach, her long, black hair spread over his groin.

For a while the quest was forgotten, the entrancement of the moment mesmerising him, the memory of the exquisite sensations he had just experienced filling his mind.

He felt a stirring in his cock, the stalk stiffening once more, the head thickening, Thetis took it at once into her mouth. He sat up quickly, pulling himself reluctantly from the heavenly caress of her soft, wet lips.

'I must return to my craft,' he said, cradling her head in his hands. 'The crew will have returned by now, the *Argo* will be ready to sail.'

'Stay with me here, Jason,' Thetis implored, her eyes pleading. 'I will thrill you in ways that you cannot imagine.'

He shook his head with genuine regret. 'I must honour my quest; I have given my word. Besides, I have a wife, as you well know.'

Thetis stood up, brushing the sand from her olive-coloured skin. 'It is not your fine quest that calls you, nor your love for your wife. You fool yourself, Jason.'

'What do you mean?'

'It is Glaucis, that gentle nymphet that you love, and to whom you yearn to return.'

'How can you say this, when I have just lain with you?' Jason stood up, his face showing anger, his soul knowing that she spoke the truth.

'Your wonderful cock will rise for any willing female, but Glaucis has your heart.'

'She is betrothed to another. I am honour-bound to deliver her to Icaria.'

Thetis put her hand on the back of his neck, drawing his head towards hers and kissing him lightly on the lips. 'Fuck her, Jason, sink that massive cock between her slender thighs. You will never forgive yourself if you don't.'

'I couldn't rape her,' said Jason, weakening, 'she would have to be willing.'

'She *is*, believe me, I know. Don't call at Icaria; sail on to the land of Aphrodite with Glaucis at your side.'

'I have given my word . . .

Thetis sighed in exasperation. 'I don't give a fig for your word. You love her and she loves you, of that I am sure.'

'How can you know this?'

She looked into Jason's eyes and smiled, gripping his partly stiff cock. 'How can I transform the walls of my sex into the lapping tongues of a thousand wood-nymphs? How can I take the form of anything I choose? I am mortal, but I have many gifts. Do not doubt my words, Jason.' She rubbed gently at his stiffness, watching in admiration as it rose to full erection. 'Take this splendid monster and stretch those virgin pussy-lips that are waiting for you on board your vessel. Even now, she touches herself, thinking of you, craving for you. Fuck her, Jason. You will never sleep soundly again if you leave her on Icaria. The thought of another man's stalk breaking her hymen, filling her sweet cunt with his seed will haunt you for the rest of your days.'

Jason broke from her grip, these last words having the desired effect on him. 'You are very wise, Thetis,' he said, tying his loin-cloth around his body, 'and I thank you for your counsel. I swear I will impale no other woman until I have taken her virginity; you have my solemn word!'

With that, Jason dived into the waves, swimming towards the *Argo* with a strength of purpose he had never felt before. On the beach, Thetis the woman was no more, the entity now transformed into the form of the seabird that flew swiftly over him to land on the mast of his craft.

Jason stood on the deck of the *Argo*, his body quickly drying under the heat of the sun. His initial resolve had deserted him a little when he saw Glaucis appear from the cabin, her expression one of delight at his return, and he cursed his nerves. He hadn't felt this way since attempting to make his first sexual conquest many years ago, and his discomfort angered him.

He smiled weakly at her and strode over to Atalanta, who stood at her post on the prow. Glaucis returned to the cabin.

'We were becoming concerned,' said Atalanta, 'you were a long time on the beach.'

'I met with a strange entity; a woman of infinite beauty and wisdom. We spoke of many things.'

Atalanta grinned, knowingly. 'You will not have need of my mouth this night, I assume?'

Jason laughed and walked back towards the cabin door. Taking a deep breath he stooped and entered the relative darkness of the small room, finding Glaucis busily studying her charts. She looked up and smiled as he entered, her expression one of delicate innocence.

'It is two days to Icaria,' she said, quietly.

'Two days. Then you will be in the arms of your future husband.'

'Yes, I will. Just two short days away.' Glaucis stood and faced him, her small frame trembling. Jason touched her arm tenderly.

'You seem nervous,' he said.

'I have never even met the man to whom I must give the rest of my life. I don't know what he will be like; he may be ugly, he may be handsome; I just know he won't be . . .'

165

She stopped short, turning her head away. Jason reached up and took her chin, making her face him again. Glaucis caught hold of his hand and held it to her cheek, kissing it lightly, tears falling from her wide, blue eyes.

'You know he won't be what?' said Jason, knowing the answer.

'He won't be you,' she spluttered, gripping his hand hard, 'he won't be you!'

Jason took hold of her tiny body and hugged her to him, her sobbing loud, the tears soaking his bare chest. 'You must honour the wishes of your father,' he whispered, not meaning a word. 'He is a good man.'

Glaucis pulled herself from his embrace and walked over to the small window, peering out at nothing. 'He is a fool!' she retorted. 'A drunken gambler who settled the future of his own daughter to clear his debts.'

Jason looked at her, the light from the window shining through the thin fabric of her dress, clearly outlining the perfection of her body. He had never wanted anyone as much as he craved for this delicate woman-child. 'If this is true,' he said, firmly, 'then you have no obligation to honour your father's word. Creon must make other arrangements!'

'He will be furious if I don't go to Icaria,' said Glaucis, turning. 'I am his daughter; I *must* obey.'

Jason walked over to her and caught her shoulders, staring determinedly into her eyes. 'Your father has sold his only daughter as a slave to the lusts of a stranger. You owe him no allegiance, nothing. From this day the only thing you will obey is your own desire, your own needs.' He fought a sudden desire to press his mouth against hers, relaxing his grip on her trembling body. 'We sail for Cyprus!' he announced, walking towards the cabin door. 'Prepare the charts accordingly; I will inform Atalanta of the change of course.'

He flung the door open with a flourish and looked back at the tearful waif, the desire within his heart making him ache.

'We sail for Cyprus!'

* * *

166

Atalanta was in no way surprised when Jason told her of the change in plan. 'We have taken enough provisions for the journey,' she said, smiling broadly. 'I never felt that I would see the shores of Icaria.'

'You know me so well?'

'I have seen the look in your eyes, and the one in hers. My only sorrow is that I may have to wait a while before I can persuade you to race with me.'

She ran her tongue provocatively over her upper lip. Jason grinned. 'Go to her now,' she continued, 'she may need help with her charts.'

Jason leaned over and kissed Atalanta on the cheek. 'One day I *will* race with you, I promise.'

'And I will pray that you win,' she said, as he walked towards the cabin door.

Jason peered into the dimness of the cabin, at first not seeing Glaucis, expecting her to be seated as usual at the map table. Then he saw her. She lay naked on his bed, her long, blonde hair played across the pillow, her face a picture of anxious innocence. He stood stock-still, drinking in the vision of her beauty, her slim, lithe body, her small, perfectly formed breasts with pink, erect nipples, her flat stomach gently sloping to the soft, downy hair between her legs, her thighs pressed together as though protecting her prize from his lustful gaze.

He walked over and sat on the bed next to her, stroking her head. 'You are truly beautiful, Glaucis,' he whispered.

'Bar the door, Jason,' she breathed, 'and return to me.'

'Are you sure you want to do this, my love?'

'I have never been more certain of anything, Jason. This day is my last as a virgin.'

He did as he was bid, slipping the iron bolt firmly into its clasp. He turned and looked at her again, slowly unfastening his loin-cloth and letting it slip to the floor. Glaucis stared at his rising erection, licking her lips nervously. He walked back and sat at her side again, leaning over and kissing her mouth softly, her full lips parting to admit his probing tongue. He licked around her mouth, over her teeth and between, their tongues meeting and playfully darting around each other as their embrace became more tender, more passionate. He felt her reach down and grip his massive cock, rubbing it expertly as she had done so many times before. This time he knew, however, that his sperm would not be sent wastefully across the room; this time would be different.

He lay at her side, kissing her neck and face as she continued her soothing caress of his stiffness, looking at it in apprehension and awe. 'It is very big, Jason,' she said, clearly worried, 'will it hurt?'

'I will not allow it to,' he said, running his tongue around her ear. 'I will kiss, lick and caress you until you are more than ready for me, then I will allow you to control what happens.'

He began to suckle at one of her pink nipples, his hand caressing her other breast, arousing the erect bud by pinching it between his thumb and forefinger. 'I am ready for you now, Jason,' she whispered, 'I have been ready for weeks. I have thought of nothing but this moment.'

'Nor I,' he said, taking his mouth from her succulent breast and biting the hard nipple, 'nor I.'

'Even when you were being sucked by Atalanta?'

'Even then.'

Glaucis sat up, still gripping his iron-hard erection. 'I want to do that,' she announced, 'I want to taste your scent.'

Jason lay back, his head raised slightly from the pillow in order to watch the yearned for scene enfold before him. Glaucis moved her body to kneel at his side, her head bent over his groin, the tip of his prick inches from her pouting mouth. She gripped the base of his stalk and held it rigid, her other hand fluttering lightly over his balls, occasionally cupping and squeezing them gently.

Jason reached over and brushed her long hair from her face, tucking it behind her ear so that he could watch as her mouth moved cautiously nearer and nearer to its final goal. He bit his lip, determined that this time he would not lose control, even though the sight of the young virgin's mouth opening to admit his ludicrously swollen, plum-sized knob made it throb with anticipation.

A small, white drop of pre-come appeared from his slit. Glaucis dipped the tip of her finger into it and put it to her mouth, then stuck out her tongue and licked the remainder from his flesh. She looked up at him and smiled. 'It tastes of the sea,' she said, with a childish giggle. Jason gazed at her with a look of total adoration as she turned her face again to his cock, opening her mouth and moving her head down, taking the thick, wet end within her suckling lips.

She rubbed the stalk sensuously up and down, moving her head in the same way, running her tongue round and round the stem, her mouth accommodating as much of him as she could. He groaned in ecstasy and felt it throb again, knowing that she was swallowing more of his juice. Her sucking became steadily more urgent until she seemed to be devouring him, relishing the taste of his sex, her excitement increasing by the second.

Jason ran his hand over her bottom and between her legs until he touched her wet pussy. He heard her muffled moan of delight as he slid his finger back and forth along the full length of the slippery slit, the lips becoming fuller, opening to his incessant touch. He tugged at her leg and lifted her over his body so that her perfect bottom was inches above his face, her knees on either side of his head, his cock still firmly gripped within her suckling mouth.

He raised his head and licked the smooth globes of her buttocks, lapping over the soft skin, the scent of her arousal filling his nostrils. He drew his tongue wetly between her cheeks, running it over her tiny, puckered anus and onto her soaked sex-lips, tasting at last the sweet juices of her virginity. Lapping hungrily, he drew her labia into his mouth, sucking noisily on the warm flesh, before raising her slightly and slipping his tongue upwards to her erect clitoris.

Her bud was hard and long, much more pronounced than any he had seen before, and the touch of his tongue seemed to send shivers throughout her entire body. She groaned, her sigh muffled by his cock, raising her hips so that his lapping could concentrate on this one place, her groin moving sensuously, rubbing herself against his loving mouth. Then she pressed herself down on him, her pubic mound crushed against his jaw, his tongue suckling at the warm sex-lips that he knew would very soon enfold his stiff prick. She pushed harder and harder against him, her entire body shuddering, forcing herself to her first orgasm with a man.

Suddenly, she sat bolt upright, her bottom smothering Jason's face, his tongue embedded in the silky purse of her cunt. 'Oh, sweet Zeus!' she cried. 'What is happening? What is this feeling?' She gave another, short cry, wriggling her hips, her pussy rubbing hard against his mouth, the taste of her juices changing slightly, becoming somehow sweeter as she came, her whole frame shaking, her breathing sharp and stilted.

Gradually, her trembling subsided and she relaxed, raising her leg and clambering off Jason's body to lie at his side, her small breasts heaving, her heart thumping, an almost startled expression on her face. 'I knew sex to be a pleasure,' she said, after a few moments, 'but I didn't know that such a wonderful, tearing release was possible.'

'You knew nothing of orgasm? You've never pleasured yourself as you've pleased me all these long nights?'

Glaucis shook her head. 'I knew, of course of men's climaxes, and how to make them happen. Nobody spoke of the pleasures of women; such things were never said.'

Jason took her frail body in his arms tenderly. 'That was the first tonight,' he said, proudly, 'there will be more before the morning comes.'

'Take me now, Jason,' said Glaucis, nervously, 'I will never be more ready, never more eager.'

Jason kissed his love on the mouth lightly, moving his body to kneel between her legs. He looked down warmly at her perfect innocence, her eyes wide with wonder as she stared at his stiff cock, now so close to her virgin sheath.

'It is so big, so huge. Please take care, Jason. Please don't hurt me'

He leant forward and kissed her again on the mouth, the thick, bulbous end of his penis now touching the wet entrance to her heavenly treasure. Holding the base with his hand he moved the stem in a slow, circular motion, stirring the end against her sex-lips, opening them by stealth. Gradually he eased a little inside her, then a little more, until he felt her downy-haired lips enclose the knob and sensed the tender barrier of her hymen touching against it.

Kissing her hard and forcing his tongue deep into her mouth he moved suddenly, a quick thrust of his hips causing the delicate restraint to give, a slight moan from her throat indicating that there had been little pain.

'Relax now, my sweet,' he whispered, moving his cock slowly in and out, barely three or four inches entering her each time, 'your virginity is gone, the prize is mine. Now we can fuck!'

Taking care not to feed too much of his stalk into her too soon he eased more and more inside her, the soaked tightness of her delightful sheath gripping every part of his hard flesh. Four, five, six more inches slipped inside, more with each careful thrust until, at last he felt his pubic bone touch hers, his cock now fully accepted by the most perfect cunt he had ever fucked. Somehow she felt different to other women, the wetness of her juices, the grip of the soft folds of hot flesh around his raging stalk drawing him deeper inside her, absorbing him.

He held still for a full minute, letting the young nymphet become used to the intrusion, allowing it to become a part of her own body. He kissed her face and neck lovingly, licking her soft, flawless skin, nibbling the lobes of her ears, stroking her long, blonde hair. Then he ran his hand down, over her small, firm breasts, tracing the shape of her narrow waist to her thigh. Moving himself to one side, he raised her leg, holding it almost vertical by the ankle and began to pump into her with more determination, the wet sounds of their lovemaking filling his ears along with the pleasurable sighs of his precious conquest.

Glaucis stared into his eyes, her whole body moving with the rhythm of her first fucking, her breathing shallow. 'It feels incredible,' she sighed, 'why have I waited so long? I should have let you do this on our first night together, instead of teasing you with my hand.'

171

'Your teasing was delightful,' he said, his pumping becoming harder, more urgent, 'but this is better.'

Glaucis grinned, happily. 'There is no pain, only a feeling of wonderful fullness and a strange, rising sensation within my sex. Do it as hard as you like, Jason. Fill me with your fabulous cock.'

'I like to hear you speak in that way, my love. Tell me more.'

Glaucis closed her eyes and sighed loudly. 'Zeus! It touches me right at the back! It is so magnificent; I couldn't take another inch!'

Jason started to move his hips in a circular motion again, the effect this time being to probe every part of her silky insides, the heavy thrusting adding to her pleasure. 'Tell me more,' he said, pinching one of her nipples as he increased the pace of his pumping, 'tell me of all that you are feeling.'

'Oh, Jason my love,' Glaucis sobbed, 'that feeling is there again, deep within me. I'm coming! I'm coming!'

The youngster began to thrust back at him, her hips rising rapidly from the bed, her cunt accommodating everything he could offer with each, wild movement. Jason responded by fucking her as hard as he knew how, gripping her buttocks tight, allowing her to wrap her legs around his powerful body, the heels pressed against his shoulder-blades.

'Fuck me, fuck me, fuck me!' she squealed, her fingernails digging into the flesh of his back, her entire body humping against his, shaking with the force of the orgasm building up within her tiny frame. 'Yes, yes! I can feel it! I can feel it! My cunt's on fire! Oh, sweet Zeus, oh, yes, yes!'

She groaned; a long, guttural cry of total ecstasy, arching her back, her pubic mound held against his, the long, thick cock embedded deep within her shuddering form. Her words echoed around Jason's brain; the incongruousness of their obscenity, the sheer delight of such language falling from her delicate lips.

She remained, locked around her lover for a full minute until the sensation of her second orgasm subsided and she

172

fell back, exhausted and sweating profusely onto the hot bed of their love.

Jason eased himself from within the smooth grip of her tight sex-lips, his cock as big and hard as ever. 'That's two,' he said, proudly, grinning broadly. He would not come, certainly not until the morning. He wondered if she could take more, or whether the ecstasy of her first fuck had satisfied her needs. If not, he would totally sate this lovely woman-child, teach her everything, every pleasure known to mortals and gods alike. He gazed at her as she lay, breathing heavily, her eyes closed in happy release and knew that he loved her, that he must make her his own.

After a moment or two Glaucis sat up and took his cock in her delicate grip, bending forward to take it once more into her mouth. She ran her tongue lightly over the wet end, licking him clean of her love-fluids. 'I am ready for more, Jason,' she said, pausing from her oral caress. 'Fuck me again.'

CHAPTER NINE

The *Phallicis* moved cautiously through the smooth, early morning swell close to the jagged promontory and savage, half-submerged rocks that had to be expertly negotiated in order to approach the harbour-mouth of Rhodes. Nana held the tiller, the women-rowers hardly dipping their oars for fear of forcing the vessel to its doom. Medea and Iole stood at the prow, eyes squinting in the piercing sunlight which reflected from the glassy surface of the water, blinding them to the possible hidden dangers below.

'Once we've rounded this headland you'll see the town of Rhodes,' said Iole, 'and a sight that you will never forget.'

'The Colossus?' queried Medea, remembering hearing merchants' tales in Colchis of a giant statue that straddled the harbour entrance.

'You've heard of it, then, but I wonder if you know the true story of its creation.'

'Only that it is in the image of the sun-god Helios.'

'Not so. Many would have you believe that, the people of Rhodes in particular. Behind this deception is a tragic tale of unrequited love.'

'Tell me more,' said Medea, eager for another of her friend's fables.

'Many years ago, there lived on Rhodes a giant, a beautiful woman named Colus. She had been abandoned on the island by her mother who came to be banished by Zeus for her many blasphemous infidelities. The child grew up to become a giant as a result of drinking from an accursed fountain deep in the hills.

174

'As she grew from a child to a woman, so her loneliness and sexual desires increased. Many say she took solace from an oak tree, stripped of its limbs with the wood smoothed and shaped like a giant penis. Whether this is true or not, her need for male company became an obsession.

'One day, she came upon a youth bathing in a small, secluded lake, a delightfully handsome young man by the name of Tonis, with whom she immediately fell in love. Colus sacrificed ten goats to Helios and prayed that Tonis be made immortal, as she was, and for him to fall in love with her. Zeus heard her prayers and tricked her, giving Tonis the gift of eternal youth but cursing him with the spell of Narcissus, making him love nobody but himself.

'When Colus realised what had happened she became overcome with grief and decided to drown herself, the only way that an immortal can end her existence. As she tried to enter the waters near the town Zeus flung down a terrifying shard of lightning which pierced her heart, petrifying her body where it stood, straddled across the entrance to the harbour, and where it stands today.'

'Is she dead?'

'Neither dead nor alive. Frozen, ossified, cursed.'

'Can the curse be lifted?'

'It is said that she will be released from her torment only if Tonis gives himself to a woman and, sadly that can never be, his love for his own reflection being so all-consuming.'

'But why do the people of Rhodes hide the truth, saying the Colossus is a statue of Helios?'

'The whole population is cursed with a weakness of will, an inability to resist temptation. Their many indulgences saps their strength, leaving them vulnerable to attack. Whilst the Colossus stands, however the town is protected. The people don't wish to lose their precious guardian.'

Medea was quiet, her mind racing. Iole looked at her, knowingly. 'If anybody could seduce Tonis it would be you, Medea,' she said, grinning, 'but you would need strong magic to help you.'

'And do you know of such magic?'

'It is said that in a cave just north of the town, there lives a hag who possesses an item of the strongest erotic enchantment, the girdle of Aphrodite herself. Wear this girdle and you may defeat the spell.'

'How do you come to know all this? You are not even from these parts.'

'I know many things,' said Iole, dreamily, 'like I know my future lies with Heracles, though I have yet to meet him.'

'You are a strange, wistful creature,' said Medea, stroking the beautiful youngster's face with the back of her hand, 'will you lie with me sometime?'

'This is also in my fate.' Iole looked back out to sea, her gently spoken words drifting out into the warm air. Medea looked fondly at the form of the lovely girl, her near white-blonde hair billowing slightly in the rising breeze. She had seemed pre-occupied of late, agitated even. There was more to this child than met the eye.

Despite being prepared for the sight of the Colossus by Iole's tale, Medea was nevertheless astounded by the sheer size and magnificence of the creature, its bronze form, though heavily tarnished, still glistening like a beacon of welcome to the harbour. The closer the *Phallicis* drew to the monster the more superb it appeared.

Iole had spoken the truth. The features were clearly those of a female, a beautiful but sad-faced woman who gazed longingly at the distant horizon. The body stood naked, save for a strip of metallic gauze pulled between the powerful legs to preserve the modesty of the entity. Medea could see that, were she human sized and of warm flesh, she would indeed be a most beautiful woman, someone whose looks could rival even those of her own.

'She looks so sad,' said Iole, quietly as the *Phallicis* drifted closer towards the figure. 'I pray that we can help her.'

'If this Tonis is as handsome as she was lovely I will find it hard to resist him!' said Medea, her eyes glazing at the thought.

'First you will need the girdle, and even with its powers you will have to use all your seductive wiles to break the spell of Narcissus.'

176

Medea wasn't listening. She glanced upwards as their vessel slid quietly between the straddling legs of Colus, the sight of the firm, muscular thighs and perfectly turned bottom reminding her of Madeleine, her erstwhile night-time companion and lover. She felt a tear come to her eye and looked away, anxious that Iole should not be a witness to her weakness.

The crew of the *Phallicis* set foot at last on the welcoming firmness of the dusty Rhodes ground, the heat of the mid-morning sending shimmers of hazy mirages into the air. Sudden swirls of unaccountable breeze caused patches of dust to rise as though possessed by hidden spirits, the movement of air limited to these phenomena, the atmosphere otherwise stifling.

A small party of local people stood in greeting as the travel-weary women trudged up the steep slope from the water's edge. A tall, elderly man seemed to be in charge of their welcome, his manner and attitude one of importance.

Medea glanced towards Iole. She seemed overly nervous, even frightened, her whole frame trembling despite the intense heat.

'Are you feeling all right?' she asked, touching the young girl's arm.

Iole's gaze remained fixed on the group as they slowly approached. 'I will be,' she said, 'I will be.'

Medea decided to leave her friend to recover, assuming that she felt ill because of the extreme temperature. She walked over to face the old man, smiling and holding out her hand in greeting.

'Welcome to Rhodes, welcome to the island of infidelity,' he said holding his arms open in response to Medea's approach.

'A strange description of a homeland,' said Medea, clasping his hand and arm firmly and shaking them. 'Why do you call it so?'

'Ah, there is a great deal to tell you. This island has changed much since the Colossus was presented to us.'

'You mean, since Colus suffered her unearthly fate,' said Medea, by way of a statement. Their host looked troubled.

'You know of the legend? How can that be?'

'*I* told her.' It was Iole who stepped forward, her head held high, her expression strangely contemptuous. The old man looked at her curiously at first, then his face froze in shocked recognition.

'Iole!' he exclaimed, stepping back, 'you have returned!'

'Yes, father, I have returned.' Medea looked at her young companion, her eyes wide in amazement.

'Father?' she said, 'what do you mean?'

Iole turned to face Medea, her face a mixture of many strong emotions. 'This man is Pallor, son of Aphrodite. Once he was a favourite in the gardens of Olympus until cast out for stealing the sacred girdle and using its powers to seduce my mother. Now his looks are gone, and he ages like any other mortal. Is this not so, father?'

The last word was uttered with utmost contempt. The old man looked down at the ground, shame-facedly.

'This is true; I never . . .'

'You never thought I'd return from the cold, barren land to which you sent my mother when she told you she was with child?' The group of townspeople were moving slowly away, muttering with embarrassment. Pallor shook his head, sadly.

'How did he recognise you if he never saw you as a child?' said Medea, still shocked from this sudden turn of events.

'I have my mother's face. I look the same as she did on the day he deflowered her, impregnated her thanks to his trickery. She sent word to him when I was born, begging him to let her return to Rhodes, but he ignored her pleas. She died less than a year later. I swore that one day I would return, to face him, to punish him.'

'How did you know him?' Medea looked at the old man, his head still bowed, his gnarled hands shaking. Iole looked at her and smiled.

'I knew,' she said, 'I knew.'

'What will you do with me? How can you punish me on my own island?'

'The long journey here has mellowed my anger, caused

me to think hard. I have experienced the joys of sex, the wonders of release. I can forgive anyone who desires such pleasure. Yet I can never forget that you abandoned my mother. You have now seen your daughter, your own flesh standing before you, but you will never again hear the word 'father' fall from my lips.'

'That is punishment enough,' sighed Pallor. 'I have long thought to seek you out, to beg for forgiveness, but I am weak in body. I am ageing rapidly and will shortly die. I thank Zeus that I have lived long enough to see your lovely face.'

Iole suddenly burst into a flood of tears and rushed to hug the frail figure before her. 'So many wasted years,' she sobbed, 'years of pointless hatred and anger.' She kissed the old man on the cheek, her teardrops mixing with his own.

Medea breathed hard, happy that this unexpectedly traumatic meeting appeared to be reaching a civilised conclusion. 'The girdle!' she exclaimed selfishly, the thought suddenly entering her head, 'do you still have it?'

'It is guarded by a witch,' said Pallor, 'hidden in a cave not far from here. I will point you towards it and pray that you take the accursed thing from this island and so release the people from their endless faithlessness.'

'The island of infidelity,' said Medea, beginning to realise the truth, 'this is why you called it that. You are cursed by your own crime!'

'Only the women of Rhodes,' said Iole, walking slowly away from her father and looking out to sea, 'the men fall hopelessly in love and swear undying faithfulness to their spouses. The women find this impossible. This land is one of endless angers and jealousies.'

'Then we shall release the people from the curse, and save Colus also!' Medea was clearly warming to her task.

Pallor rushed up and caught her arm, the dawn of realisation in his eyes. 'You mean to seduce Tonis! You cannot! Colus, the Colossus . . . she will abandon us!'

'If you wish the people of Rhodes to be released from their curse they must also learn to become strong again,

179

once more a proud race.' Iole spoke grandly, brushing an errant tear from her face. 'Without the influence of the girdle's magic they shouldn't have need for protection.'

'It will not be easy,' said the old man, quietly, realising that his daughter spoke with great perception. 'You will need more than the enchanted girdle to deflower the youth.'

Medea smiled to herself. She would enjoy the challenge.

The room provided by Pallor for Medea and Iole's rest was small, but nevertheless comfortable, despite the heat. Medea lay naked on one of the two beds, lazily caressing her pussy lips to wet arousal, her thoughts filled with memories of her many conquests. Iole slept silently on the other bed, her skin soaked in sweat, bathed to an erotic sheen by the whiteness of the moonlight.

Medea slipped from her couch and crept over to kneel at Iole's side, her hand resting lightly on the young woman's thigh. The blonde stirred in her sleep, moving to lie on her stomach. Medea's hand now rested on the perfect curve of her bottom, the near-athletic firmness feeling sensuous to her touch. She stroked the warm flesh gingerly, her fingertips playing against the soft skin, the action raising goose-pimples.

The smooth globes of her buttocks were perfection in their pertness, the treasure between them as yet, as far as Medea knew, un-invaded. She leant forward and kissed one erotic orb wetly, her tongue tasting the saltiness of her skin. She began to lick more meaningfully, her tongue rasping over Iole's bottom, tracing the shape of each buttock.

The blonde groaned in her sleep and Medea pulled back, her heart beating rapidly. She watched with rising delight as Iole arched her back and began to raise her bottom, the buttocks parting to present the vision of her puffily-aroused sex-lips and tiny, sweet sphincter. Whether the girl was asleep or not, Medea decided that she would taste the fresh scent of Iole's excitement.

She bent forward again and licked gently around the

outer lips of her pussy, her nose pressed firmly between her buttocks. Running her tongue up and down, Medea suckled the increasing wetness of Iole's hypnotic enthusiasm, the heavy breathing of the young blonde a testament to her arousal. The pussy-lips opened like the petals of a rose welcoming the kiss of the morning dew, the incessant probing of Medea's expert tongue causing the juices of Eros to flow.

Iole's hips began to buck up and down, Medea clinging to her thighs tightly as she endeavoured to keep her mouth firmly pressed against the sleeping girl's bottom. Her groans of passion grew ever louder, the wetness of her cunt-juices smeared over Medea's face as she lapped hungrily at the enlarged bud of Iole's clitoris.

Suddenly, the blonde stiffened, trembling. A low, deep moan came from within her throat, followed by an abrupt, sharp squeal, then she moved her hips quickly up and down as though impaling some well-endowed stud. In her dreams she was being fucked, fucked hard by an unseen man. In reality she was the conquest of her queen, who would keep the secrets of her pleasure to herself, at least for the time being.

Medea set off to seek out the abode of the witch at first light, taking Electra along with her, more for protection than company. Iole had stayed with her father, clutching to the precious few hours that they would have together before the *Phallicis* must set off once more on its long quest.

The road into the thickly wooded hills was poorly marked and often hardly visible, but after close on two hours trek they found themselves outside the cave, just as Pallor had promised.

Peering into the dank, dark interior, Electra sniffed. 'It smells as though there's something dead inside,' she said, drawing back, 'are you sure this is the right cave?'

Medea looked around her. 'It's the only one to be seen, and is exactly where Pallor said it would be. It must be the right place.' She squinted into the darkness. 'Hello? Is there

181

anybody here?' Her voice echoed around the damp walls of the cavern, the only other sound being the steady drip of water onto the rocky floor. 'The hag must be elsewhere,' she whispered, 'come on.'

'What if she comes back and finds us here?' said Electra, nervously.

'She's only an old woman,' hissed Medea, 'besides, we may find the girdle and be off with it before she returns.'

Medea crept slowly into the dreary interior, followed, with marked reluctance, by Electra. As their eyes became more accustomed to the lack of light they began to make out the shapes of roughly-made furniture and other belongings. Electra somehow managed to find a partly-burned torch and, striking the flint against a dry stone ignited it, the welcome glow of the flames making them feel less uneasy.

'How can anyone live in such squalor?' asked Medea, looking with unconcealed disgust at the scene before them.

'It suits me fine! Why are you here in my home?'

The owner of the cracked, harsh voice stood behind them, her sudden appearance startling them both. Medea swung around. Iole's description of the woman as a hag was indeed very apt. She was old, very old, her face haggard with care and age, her features extraordinarily ugly. Her long, grey hair was matted and filthy, as dirty as the tattered rags which served as her clothing.

'I'm sorry,' began Medea, trying to hide her tenseness.

'So you are sorry,' the hag said, pushing her aside and lighting another torch from the flames of the first. 'You enter my home without invitation, make yourself comfortable and then say you're sorry!'

'We were sent here by Pallor to seek you out.' Medea spoke with a little more authority, the extra illumination helping to calm the atmosphere.

'That old fool. What is it that you want of me?'

'The girdle. The girdle of Aphrodite.'

The old woman sat on a low chair, rearranging her clothing to cover her vein-ravaged legs. 'I see,' she said, slowly, 'the girdle. What would two such delightful creatures as you want with it? Surely you have little difficulty in attracting many a well-endowed stud to satisfy your carnal needs.'

'I mean to use its power to conquer the will of Tonis, and thereby release the people of Rhodes from their curse.'

'Ah, I see. Another beauty vain enough to think she can seduce the lovely Tonis. Many have tried before; all have failed.'

'I will not fail.'

The old hag struggled to her feet again and walked over to a darker corner of the cave, reaching inside a large chest and pulling out a garment, the material of which shimmered in the half-light. 'You can take it,' she said, gruffly. 'I will collect it from your dead body when you have slain yourself.'

Medea took hold of the item, feeling the incredible softness of the silken material against her fingers. 'Why should I slay myself?' she queried.

'You will fall in love with Tonis. They all do. He is a most beautiful youth.'

'I have encountered many beautiful young men in my life,' said Medea, truthfully.

The witch ran a bony hand across her cheek, making her shiver with revulsion. 'I am sure you have,' she said, with marked sarcasm, 'and I wish you well. But Tonis loves none other than himself and, when you see him you will understand why.'

'Where can I see this vision?' said Medea, matching the hag's scornful tone.

'In the glade, near the bottom of the hill. You will have passed close to it on your way here.'

'Is there anything else I should know?' Medea was anxious to leave this dreadfully pungent cavern and breathe the fresh air outside, but she needed all the knowledge the hag could provide.

'Wear the girdle only; you must otherwise be naked. Its power is in the way it excites the wearer; your passion for whosoever you are in company with will devour you, and in doing that, should equally arouse your intended conquest. Your beauty will be even more pronounced, any flaw diminished or completely lost. But beware; should you fail in your quest to fuck with Tonis your desires will be so intense they will devour your soul.'

'I thank you,' said Medea, making to leave. 'When I have deflowered the virgin youth I will take the girdle as my prize.'

The hag grinned, evily. 'As I said, I will collect it from your corpse.'

The two women walked quickly down the hill in the direction indicated by the old witch. Straying off the rough path they forced their way through some bushes and, as promised, found themselves in the glade, as beautiful a setting for lovemaking as could be imagined in the heart of the most inspired poet. In the centre of the clearing was a small circle of water, more a pond than a lake, the surrounding trees reflected in its glassy surface. At its edge, on the far side of the glade they could see a figure, bowed over the surface of the water, the face shrouded by long, black hair, the body hidden by a screen of long grass.

'That must be him,' said Electra, excitedly tugging at Medea's arm.

'I see him,' she said, her heart pounding like a virgin on her marriage-bed, 'quickly, I must prepare.' She pulled her simple dress over her head in one, swift movement, and stood naked save for her sandals. Electra handed her the precious garment of glittering silk which she slipped around her slim waist, securing it with a golden clasp. Immediately, she sensed a warmth emanating from the girdle, a flowing sensuality that seemed to ooze within her body, filling her entire being with arousal. Her nerve-endings tingled, her nipples hardened, the lips of her pussy opened in wet submission as though being caressed by an unseen tongue.

Electra stood back, her eyes wide in shock. 'What's the matter?' said Medea, 'do I look as alive as I feel?'

'You are *beautiful*,' she cried, 'I must have you! Forget Tonis; fuck with me!' The young girl fell to her knees and grabbed Medea around the thighs, ramming her mouth against the saturated lips of her cunt. Medea felt her tongue lapping, suckling on her, drawing the fluids of love from her body. She couldn't resist the onslaught, raising one of her legs to allow Electra more access to her burning hole. The young girl licked ferociously at her, digging her fingernails into Medea's buttocks. She moaned with the sheer pleasure of the sensation, the feeling heightened beyond belief by the magic within the girdle. She pushed her pussy into Electra's face, groaning as she felt her orgasm building up within her loins, knowing that it would rip through her body with an intensity that would be hard to bear.

Resting one hand on Electra's head for support, she grasped hold of her own ankle, holding her leg straight with the calf pressed against her face, her obscenely stretched pussy still being attacked by the wildly fluttering tongue below her. The come was violent, the sensation of sudden release causing her to cry out loudly as the feelings coursed throughout her trembling body. Electra refused to stop licking, her tongue rasping heavily against her queen's clitoris, until Medea was forced to push her away and collapsed onto the grass.

Electra wriggled over to her and tried to plant her mouth back on her throbbing pussy, but Medea managed to hold her back, despite her near exhaustion. 'Stop, Electra, please!' she laughed, pushing the lust-crazed girl over with a shove of her feet, 'I have a task to perform! You can have more later, I promise.'

The timely reminder caused both women to look across at the figure, still crouched over the pond, seemingly oblivious to their presence. Medea stood and walked shakily over to him, brushing the loose grass from her glistening skin. Never had she been more consumed with lust; she knew she *had* to succeed.

As she approached the crouching figure she saw that he was naked, his golden-brown skin flawless, his physique superb. She could feel the juices of her arousal slipping from the pulsating lips of her pussy as she gazed at the perfection of his long back and small, rounded buttocks. Her breasts felt even larger than usual, aching to be fondled, her cunt and anus desperately yearning for male intrusion.

'Tonis,' she breathed, standing less than a foot from him. The figure barely moved. 'Tonis, look at me.' Still no response. He seemed to be spellbound, gazing at something in the water. Medea looked over his shoulder and caught her breath. There, reflected on the glassy surface was the object of his entrancement, the image of his own face.

Medea visibly trembled as she stared at the reflection, the sheer perfection of his features causing her mouth to become dry. Her hand moved automatically to between her legs, the fingers pulling at the already well-lubricated lips. Realising that Tonis was totally captivated she reached down and picked up a small stone, dropping it quickly into the water, the ripples temporarily breaking up the sublime vision.

Tonis glanced up, his handsome face still delightful in its anger. Medea held her ground, smiling uncertainly as she awaited his reaction to her own perfection. The youth's expression changed to one of calm interest and he stood, naked before her, his eyes darting from her face to her breasts and her downy covered sex. She looked at his crotch, delighted to see that he sported a fine, large erection, caused no doubt by his intense self-love. Her eyes feasted on his wonderful body, completely devoid of hair, in stark contrast to the long, flowing and curled locks that cascaded over his shoulders. His physique was youthfully muscular, slim but athletic, his long legs similarly powerful.

Medea gazed again at his superb cock, thick and gnarled with veins, the head angrily pointing directly at her. She reached out and gripped this fine weapon, pulling him closer to her.

'You are very handsome, Tonis,' she breathed, rubbing the hard flesh in her hand gently but persuasively.

'Yes, I am,' he said, turning his head to look once more into the water. Medea pulled his face back towards hers.

'Do you want me, Tonis? Do you want to sink this splendid prick into my soaking wet cunt?'

'I . . . I . . .' was all he could say before he pulled himself from her entrancing gaze and knelt beside the pond, staring lovingly at his reflection whilst casually masturbating. Medea glared at the crouching youth angrily, the ache between her legs building up to a crescendo of lust. She grabbed his shoulders and pulled at him, vainly trying to drag him away from the water's edge. Tonis shrugged her off, levering her away with a thrust of his powerful arm. Medea fell back on the grass, her legs splayed wide open.

'Look at me, Tonis! Look at the way my cunt weeps with desire for you! Fuck me, fuck me until I scream!'

The youth hardly stirred, his face turned towards the water, his hand happily rubbing his engorged member. Medea closed her eyes and gritted her teeth, the pain of unsated lust tearing into her like a knife. This was what the old hag had meant; the intense craving was too much for anyone to bear.

She tugged at the clasp holding the girdle about her waist but it would not break. She realised then that she had become a prisoner of her own hunger; she must have Tonis or die a quivering, lust-racked shell of her former self.

She thought of throwing another stone into the water but knew that once the ripples had settled he would return to gaze at himself. She had to break the spell.

As if to mirror her mood the sky suddenly began to darken. Thick, heavy clouds began to cover the sharply blue sky, its colour fading quickly to dull grey. A breeze started, swift gusts that made Medea shiver in her near-nakedness. She looked up at the sky angrily. 'Zeus, don't mock me,' she muttered, 'I will not be defeated!'

A single raindrop splashed heavily on her forehead, followed by another, then more. There was a flash of lightning and an immediate crack of thunder overhead and the storm broke, rain hammering down on the once idyllic scene. Medea looked at Tonis, seeing him desperately peering into the pond, trying to find his image in the churning water. She realised that, far from mocking her Zeus had come to her aid.

Quickly, she crawled over to the youth and pulled him

to her, wriggling her body under his and grasping his still hard erection. 'The image is gone, Tonis,' she shouted over the noise of the storm, 'you are free, just whilst the storm rages. Take this opportunity, Tonis, impale me with that massive prick of yours. Fuck a woman for the first time in your life!'

Tonis struggled to pull himself from Medea's vice-like grip but his will was gone with his lost reflection. She pulled hard at his cock, so hard that she knew it must be hurting him but with an urgent desperation that would not be ignored. She felt the thick end touching the puffy lips that yearned to devour him. Forcing her hips forward she felt the knob enter her, her extreme wetness making it difficult for her to grip him with her vaginal muscles. He struggled again and slipped out of her.

With a strength she had never known before, Medea forced the young man onto his back in the soaking grass and leapt astride him, grasping his thick stalk once more and guiding it to her aching hole. With a sudden lunge she sat down on his groin, his entire length buried deep within the silken sheath of her cunt. Tonis shouted out with the shock of her attack and tried to push her off but she held her position, squeezing his impressive length with her inner muscles, feeling him throb inside her.

He lay back, his eyes wide open in wonderment. She had him. She had won. Another flash of lightning and a loud crack of thunder sent the rain down on the scene of copulation in torrents, the recently warm grass turning quickly into a quagmire, the pond-waters overflowing and soaking their oozing bed. Medea smiled and looked into Tonis' eyes, moving her hips easily up and down, absorbing and re-absorbing his superb length. The youth stared at her, the sheer beauty of his features filling her mind with joy and then, to her utmost elation, a broad grin appeared on his face and he began to respond to her movements with cautious, upward thrusts of his own.

The spell was broken.

'That's it, Tonis,' said Medea, increasing the pace of her erotic ride. 'That's it, fuck me, fuck me.'

He gripped her bottom and raised her so that just the tip of his cock remained inside her. She worried he might escape and was about to force herself down on him when he began to thrust quickly upwards, the speed of his movements shaking her, her large breasts bouncing up and down heavily. She leant forward and grabbed his soaked hair and pulled his face to hers, clamping her mouth against his, her tongue forcing its way between his teeth. She did her best to match the speed of his upward thrusts, her bottom humping up and down rapidly, her breathing short and stilted.

Still the rain hammered down on her back; still the thunder roared as though the very heavens were engaged in copulation. The couple rolled over; now Tonis was on top and he wasn't going to run away. Medea looked at his beautiful face, his expression one of lustful desire and, without warning, she came, a sudden, crotch-tearing orgasm. She bit into his arm, whimpering as the sensations ran through her body, tears streaming from her eyes over her rain-soaked face.

Tonis fell back from her, obviously thinking he may have hurt his exquisite first lover. He looked startled, his big prick standing incongruously erect. Medea crawled over to him, smiling to reassure him and taking his cock in her hand. She kissed the end softly, then opening her mouth she took it between her luscious lips, her tongue rasping around the thick stem greedily. The youth groaned and she felt his cock throb against her cheek, tasting his salty pre-come at the back of her throat.

She pulled her face away from him, happily noting his look of disappointment and knelt with her bottom in the air, presented to him like a mare to a stallion.

'Fuck me again, Tonis,' she commanded, 'fuck me from behind.'

Tonis moved quickly to her rear, prodding his cock inexpertly at her nether-regions. Medea reached between her legs and caught his hard length, guiding it to her target. Once more it slid into her in one delightful movement and again he began to pump rapidly into her, fucking her as hard as any time she could remember. The ground beneath her was now sodden and she felt herself sliding through the mud on her knees and forearms with each hard thrust, the slithering, oozing bed exciting her with its clammy caress.

Allowing herself to fall forwards, she lay flat on her stomach in the mud, Tonis lying on her back, his cock firmly embedded in her cunt. He lay still, allowing her to savour the contours of his hard flesh against hers, his firm stomach pressed against her bottom. She moved her hips slightly, feeling the cool, wet mud sliding against her pussy, the sensation of this combined with the feel of his fat cock inside her driving her wild.

She began to press her crotch rhythmically into the ooze, Tonis matching her steady movements with his own, pumping his stiffness in and out, fucking her beautifully. Again, her orgasm was as sudden as the crash of thunder that accompanied it, and as wonderful as the feeling of her young conquest pumping his seed deep inside her, his big cock throbbing heavily as the sperm filled her sated sheath.

The couple lay still for some minutes, Tonis' prick still held within the wet warmth of Medea's pussy, the rain easing off at last. Soon, it stopped entirely, the clouds disappearing as fast as they had appeared, Apollo once more returning to fill the azure skies with his presence. Tonis eased his flaccid manhood from his lover and knelt at her side, gazing into her smiling face. Medea struggled to her feet and looked at the youth, his beauty still astounding despite his matted hair and mud-covered skin.

'How do you feel, now that you have known real sex?' Medea spoke quietly, her heart still thumping from her exertions.

'It is as though a great weight has been lifted from my shoulders. Never again will I be possessed by desire for myself. I know I am now mortal, that I will live, grow old and die, and it is wonderful.'

Medea smiled and kissed him lightly on the cheek before slipping into the pond, bathing herself in its soothing waters. Tonis joined her, wallowing in the shallow water, helping her to remove the mud from her lovely body. 'Will you stay with me?' he said, his expression showing that he already knew her answer.

'I cannot. I am married to another.'

'But this is the isle of infidelity. It is quite normal to lay with many men here.'

Medea was about to speak when there was a sudden and ear-piercing roar. She jumped out of the pond, tearing the soaked girdle from her body and running to join Electra. 'What is it,' she said, 'what was that sound?'

'I don't know,' said Electra, 'it must be a monster! It came from the direction of the town!'

The two women dressed quickly and ran back to the track leading to the town, Tonis following in his splendid nakedness. As they reached the dock they saw their crew hurriedly boarding the *Phallicis* whilst Iole stood on the harbour-side, looking frantically about her. Medea and Electra ran towards her.

'What is it, what has happened?' said Medea.

'Oh, Medea, I thought you were lost. It's horrible!'

'What is? Tell me!'

'The Colossus! It is alive!'

'Then the legend is true,' laughed Medea, 'I have broken the enchantment and released Colus from her fate!'

'That is clear,' panted Iole, ushering the two women onto the vessel, 'but to do so you had sex with the object of her desires, Tonis, and she is furious!'

'But surely she must be grateful?'

'I don't think it would be wise to try and reason with her. She is on the rampage, stalking about the island, determined to find the one who took her lover's virginity. We must flee!'

Medea couldn't help but agree with Iole's logic. It would be most unwise to stay and argue with a hundred foot enraged monster. The crew were quickly at their oars and the ship began to slide smoothly from the harbour, rapidly past the two stone plinths which had been the resting place of the Colossus, and out into the open sea.

It was well over two hours before Medea allowed the oars-women to ease their furious pace. Panting, they rested for a moment, Iole looking back in the direction of Rhodes, now long disappeared over the horizon.

'I think we are safe,' she said, 'the creature doesn't seem to be following us.'

'Perhaps your father explained that we meant no harm, that what I did was out of concern for Colus and the people of the island.'

'Let us pray that you are right. We were . . . wait, what is that?' Iole pointed to a pile of sacking, clearly covering something that moved. Picking up a spear, Medea approached the heap gingerly, prodding at it with the blade.

Suddenly there was a cry of pain and the sacking was flung back to reveal the naked form of her erstwhile lover, the beautiful Tonis. Iole regarded him in horror.

'What are you doing here?' she demanded. 'Don't you know what you've done?'

'I had to be with your queen,' he wailed. 'I need more of this wonderful sex.'

'He's here now,' said Medea, warming to the idea of spending the remaining days and nights of the journey to Crete in the arms of this delightful youth, 'don't take on so.'

'You don't understand,' said Iole, angrily. 'Whilst he is with us Colus will never abandon her search for him and will surely take her revenge on us. He must dive into the sea and swim back to Rhodes!'

Medea looked at the trembling young man, his long cock drooping hugely as a reminder of her earlier delight. 'It is too far,' she said, with little conviction in her tone, 'we have outrun the Colossus, we are safe. We will take Tonis to Crete. Come Iole, come with us to my cabin; and you Electra, we have much to teach him.'

The three women led the grinning young man to the rear of the vessel, his big cock rising in anticipation of the many pleasures to come.

In the distance, a giant figure swam clumsily but steadily towards them through the calm, Aegean waters.

CHAPTER TEN

Glaucis stood with Jason at the prow of the *Argo*, her frail arm wrapped proudly about his waist as they surveyed the nearing coastline. The hills were darkening quickly, silhouetted against the broad redness of the evening sky.

'It seems so quiet, so peaceful,' she said, gripping her lover tightly. Jason looked into her eyes, seeing them shining with new love, her perfect features framed by her gently billowing hair. He kissed her lightly on the forehead.

'Paphos is a fine city,' he said, stroking the softness of her blonde tresses, 'built many years ago by the ancient Cypriots in honour of Aphrodite. The temple to the goddess is reputed to be one of the most splendid in all the world.'

'And that is where we'll find the cloak, the magical cloak of Aphrodite?'

'According to King Pelias it lies in a golden casket, deep within the catacombs beneath the temple, guarded by many traps and entities. Our quest may be nearly over, but the most testing time lies ahead of us.' Jason looked again at the coast, the lights of the city becoming more evident as the sun disappeared behind the hills.

'It appears that we are to be welcomed,' said Glaucis, pointing into the half-light. Jason peered into the gloom, seeing a bright, pilot's light high on what appeared to be the mast of a small, harbour vessel. As the boat came closer to the *Argo* its shape became clearer, the mast-light casting illumination on its three occupants. Suddenly, a broad grin spread across Jason's face as his expression changed to one of delight.

'I know this man!' he exclaimed, startling Glaucis as he rushed forward to the edge of the deck. 'Yes, yes, it is he!'

Glaucis joined her lover and caught hold of his arm, happily sharing his excitement. 'Who? Who is it that the mere sight of him causes you so much joy?'

Jason said nothing, clambering precariously astride the deck-rail and catching the pilot's rope. Glaucis stood in bemusement, watching as the three figures climbed aboard.

The first was the pilot, a tall, reed-thin character with a hollow-faced expression, a greying, wispy beard emphasising his gaunt appearance. Next aboard was a woman, heavily cloaked and hooded against the coolness of the evening sea-breeze, her face all but covered with a thick, netted veil.

It was the last newcomer for whom Jason saved his most ardent welcome. 'Apollonius!' he cried, flinging his arms around the figure of a man of similar age and stature to his own. 'Apollonius, my dear friend! How do you come to be in Cyprus? I heard that you had made your home in Rhodes, to continue your great works!' The sarcasm in Jason's tone was marked. The other merely laughed uproariously, matching Jason's warm greeting with an equally firm embrace of his own.

'Jason, you rogue,' said Apollonius, his voice deep and warm. 'How could I stay in Rhodes when I learned that you were headed here? There is so much I wish to hear of your great quest to Colchis and your taking of the Golden Fleece. I plan to honour your adventure with a great epic poem!'

He spoke these last words with the pride of an artist confident that they would be much welcomed. He was right. Jason was delighted. 'You will undertake a work on the tales of the Argonauts?' he said, his voice filled with emotion.

Apollonius nodded. 'I would be proud,' he said.

Jason stood on the deck, facing the seated oarsmen who had been watching the scene with curiosity and bewilderment, feelings shared by Glaucis. 'This is the great Apollonius Rhodius, a fine poet and a man who will make the Argonauts legendary!' The men cheered, more in deference to their leader's pleasure than the thought of literary immortality. Jason turned to look again at the poet. 'He is also a good friend,' he said, quietly, holding out his hand.

As the two men clasped arms Glaucis walked forward, anxiously waiting to be introduced to her new lover's old friend. Jason seemed preoccupied with his continued greeting, chattering to Apollonius like an excited child. It was the latter that noticed the small figure of the beautiful, fair-haired girl standing before them.

He pushed Jason to the side, walking slowly towards Glaucis, his heavily bearded face beaming. 'Who is this delightful creature?' he said, taking her tiny hand in his massive grip.

'My friend, I am sorry,' said Jason, hurriedly, 'this is Glaucis. She is . . .' He paused. Glaucis looked hard at him, waiting to hear his words apprehensively. 'She is my companion,' continued Jason, nervously, 'and, and my love.'

Apollonius looked hard at Jason, eyeing him suspiciously. 'But I heard you had taken Medea of Colchis as your wife. Is this not so?'

Jason nodded. 'What you have heard is the truth, and now you know a new truth,' he said, proudly.

Apollonius rested his hand on Jason's shoulder, still clutching Glaucis' hand in his other, a look of deep concern on his face. 'Medea has a reputation for a sharp temper and a penchant for revenge. I hope you are prepared.'

Jason shrugged him away, anxious to make light of the situation. 'There is no problem,' he said loudly, 'Medea and I have relinquished our vows of fidelity.'

Apollonius seemed relieved. 'If you say there is no problem for you then there is none for me.' He bent forward and kissed Glaucis on the fingers, then looked into her face and winked. 'A delicate and sensual creature,' he laughed. 'You have done well, you old dog!'

Jason shared his laughter, glancing over to the others and noticing the hooded woman once more. 'Forgive me,' he said, walking over to her, 'I was so concerned with welcoming my old friend that I neglected to allow him to introduce you. You must be Apollonius' wife?'

'Were it so,' said Apollonius, 'then I would indeed be a contented man. No, this is Paphia, one of the temple nymphs of Aphrodite. She begged to be allowed to meet you before you landed at Paphos.'

Jason held out his hand in greeting. The woman bowed, taking his fingers lightly between hers and looking into his eyes through the thick veil that shielded her image from his curious gaze. 'How can I be of service, my lady?'

'I come to plead with you, to beg you to abandon your quest, before it is too late.' The woman spoke with a husky, sensuous tone, the words spoken only loud enough for Jason's ears to catch their meaning.

'Can I see the face of one who implores so delicately?'

'I suffer from an allergy to even the dimmest of exterior light,' whispered Paphia, the quietness of her voice causing him to lean close enough to her to catch the scent of her intoxicating perfume.

'Come,' he said, taking her arm, 'come to my cabin. We will discuss your business there whilst the pilot does his work.'

Glaucis stepped forward. 'May I join you?' she said, awkwardly.

Jason looked at her and smiled. 'Of course, my love, of course. And you, Apollonius, there is wine below, and we have much to talk about!'

Jason led the way to the cabin, cautioning Paphia to bow her head as she walked in. Once inside, Jason and Apollonius sat on cushions scattered on the wooden floor whilst Glaucis poured wine from one of many bottles stored under the map-table. Paphia remained standing, close to the small oil-lamp that was the only illumination.

Glaucis handed glasses to the men, Paphia refusing the offer of refreshment. 'Your reason for travelling to Cyprus is well known,' she began, 'the Cloak of Aphrodite is the prize you seek. It is precious to the worshippers of the goddess. I beg you, please respect the sanctity of the temple and leave without it.'

196

'I need its powers to rescue my kingdom from the hands of a pathetic old tyrant,' said Jason, standing to face her. 'Once this is done I will return the garment; you have my word.'

'The goddess will be angry,' said Paphia, her voice raised a little, 'and she may wreak terrible revenge.'

'I have incurred the wrath of many entities in the past and survived to tell.'

'Is there nothing I can say . . .?

'Nothing,' said Jason, impatiently, 'the cloak will be returned when it has served its purpose.'

Paphia began to unfasten her hood and cloak. 'Perhaps,' she said, 'perhaps I can persuade you . . .' With that she threw back the hood and veil with one movement and dropped the cloak to the floor with a flourish, revealing herself to be totally naked beneath the heavy garment. Jason stepped back, open mouthed. Apollonius gasped, allowing his glass to slip from his fingers, the contents spilling on his lap. Glaucis stared in pure admiration and astonishment.

Paphia was, without doubt, the most beautiful young woman that any of them had seen or could have imagined. The flawless skin of her naked body seemed somehow to catch the flickering light of the lamp and give off a sheen of its own, highlighting every curve, every contour of her exquisite sensuousness. Her hair was golden and shining, falling in heavy curls over her shoulders, the ends just touching the curves of her large, full breasts, the dark nipples long and fully erect.

Her narrow waist accented the sumptuous lines of her hips, her flat stomach curving erotically towards her pussy; the hair sparse and wet, the pouting lips puffy and red, clearly aroused and ready for sex.

Jason felt his cock rising uncontrollably. He looked across at Glaucis nervously, but she remained transfixed by the sight of the woman's sheer sexuality, her eyes wide and filled with lust.

Apollonius was the first to speak. 'If I had known the secrets that lay beneath my travelling companion's cloak the pilot's vessel would be heading for some distant beach. I must have her!' He stood and tore at his clothing, revealing his naked form to the others, his erection firm and threatening.

Paphia stood impassively. Jason avoided having to take in the sight of his friend's arousal by returning his gaze to the vision of her perfect nakedness. Apollonius moved forward, reaching out to grab her, but before he could catch hold of the sumptuous body before him, Glaucis let out a moan of delight and pushed him aside, falling to her knees and burying her head between the soft thighs of the beautiful woman, the wet sounds and swift movements of her head confirming to the astounded men that she was suckling Paphia's cunt for all she was worth.

The urge to possess this devastatingly gorgeous young woman was tearing at Jason's very soul. Seeing his new lover taking her with her mouth only served to increase his desire. He flung aside his simple clothing, approaching Paphia cautiously, his cock jutting forward as stiff and large as it could ever be. Apollonius stood at her other side, the tip of his own erection wet with the juice of his arousal, his body shaking with lust and desire.

Paphia reached out her hands and took a hard cock in each, raising her leg slightly from the floor to allow Glaucis closer access to her pussy. The latter was totally absorbed in her task, completely oblivious to the two naked men at her sides. Jason felt Paphia's fingers delicately circle his engorged prick and closed his eyes, his will slipping from him as his body responded to her expert caress.

Never, in all his life had he experienced such absolute stimulation, her steadily pumping grip coaxing him to the brink of orgasm then stopping, her fingertips stroking across the swollen head of his cock, causing the urgency to subside immediately, before once again rubbing with an ethereal, airy touch on his tortured flesh.

He opened his eyes to meet the image of Apollonius kneading and pawing at her superb breasts, pinching the nipples between the thumb and forefinger of each hand, his cock also held in her unrelenting clasp. With Glaucis continuing to pay oral homage to Paphia's cunt Jason slipped his hand over her pert, round bottom, his finger quickly finding its way between her firm buttocks to nestle against the tight sphincter of her anus.

He looked with genuine affection down at Glaucis, who was now running her tongue in long, upward strokes, rasping its surface against the wide-open lips, her face wet with the juices of Paphia's excitement. There was no pang of jealousy, no concern at her infidelity, and she clearly held no such concerns for him as he gave himself totally to the pure sexuality of this woman.

'Lie on your back on the bed, Jason.' Paphia's voice was even more husky than before, her face slightly flushed, her eyes shining with emotion. Jason obeyed, meekly, lying on the cot and holding his stiff prick erect by clutching it at the root, the purple head swelling to plum-like proportions as he waited for this beautiful creature to impale herself on his eager stalk.

Paphia let go her hold of Apollonius and stepped over the kneeling form of Glaucis who simply watched with adoration as the woman straddled the supine body of her lover and guided his stiff cock to her soaked pussy. Jason felt his shaft throb involuntarily as his tormented flesh touched the hot outer lips, a short stream of sperm jetting within the folds of her softness. Slowly, she sank down on him, easing his splendid length inch by inch into the deep warmth of her sheath, the flesh of her vagina gripping him with velvety wetness. She leant forward on her hands, her large breasts brushing against his chest as she began the rhythmic movements of love.

After a moment of this, Glaucis walked over and stood at Jason's side. Then, as though it was the most natural thing to do, she climbed onto the bed, her back to Paphia, her legs straddling Jason's head and her wide-open pussy an inch from his mouth.

Raising his head from the pillow, Jason dipped his tongue into her sweet chalice, tasting the scent of total arousal. Her extraordinary wetness soaked his face immediately as he drank from her, all the time feeling Paphia fucking herself on his long, stiff stalk.

He gripped Glaucis' thighs and raised her slightly so that he could run his tongue along the full length of her outer lips, the tip sliding from her anus to her clitoris. Her fluids ran copiously, her arousal total.

Paphia stopped her movements and raised her body so that just his thick knob remained inside her succulent grip. Jason started to thrust upwards, thinking that this was what she wanted, until he felt the unmistakeable pressure and realised that Apollonius was forcing his not inconsiderable length into her bottom. Presently, the two fine cocks rested together within their respective sheaths, separated by the thinnest of tissue, Paphia moaning lustfully for the first time, thoroughly enjoying the sensations of the double intrusion.

She began to move steadily up and down on Jason's upward thrusting tool, Apollonius matching her motion with long, deep strokes as he fucked her superb arse. Jason resumed licking Glaucis who knelt happily across his face, groaning with the pleasure of his oral stimulation. He flicked his tongue rapidly over her clitoris then prodded it as far as it would allow into the warmth of his young lover's pussy, then slid it down again to her anus. This time the tip of his tongue touched the full mouth of Paphia, finding her lips pressed against Glaucis' bottom, clearly and expertly tongue-fucking the younger girl.

The knowledge was too much for Jason. With a muffled roar he shot his sperm deep into Paphia's welcoming sheath, his hips rising and falling over the bed with remarkable speed. His cock seemed to throb endlessly, the excruciating joy of his orgasm tearing at every nerveending in his cock, balls and groin. He roared again, almost sobbing against the cushion of Glaucis' downy-covered cunt until at last the feelings subsided and he was able to slip from the warmth of Paphia's heavenly trap.

After taking a moment to recover from the intensity of his orgasm, Jason managed to free himself from the tangle of bodies and sat on the floor by the side of the bed, content now to watch and savour the erotic scene before him. Apollonius seemed satisfied to continue his steady assault on Paphia's bottom, Glaucis receiving similar treatment from the older woman's tongue. He couldn't resist staring at Paphia, her utter beauty captivating him entirely. His wife, Medea, and his new lover, Glaucis, were both ravishing in their own way, but this woman was stunning, completely perfect. The sight of her kneeling on the bed, her face pressed hard against the pert buttocks of the elfin Glaucis, whilst at the same time the long, thick cock of his friend slipped in and out of her bottom, was so incredibly erotic that Jason felt his own stalk quickly rising in response, once more ready for a continuation of the bacchanalia.

Almost pushing Glaucis from her heavenly perch he knelt in front of Paphia, presenting his thick erection to her face. He watched with delight as she parted her lips and swallowed much of his length, the tip touching the back of her throat. Jason grinned as he caught the glance of the exhausted Apollonius, still pumping furiously at the lovely girl's rear. 'Welcome to Cyprus, Jason,' he panted, 'welcome to Cyprus.'

He was unable to answer. Paphia was drawing the very seed from deep within his groin with her expert suckling whilst Glaucis had wriggled her head under his bottom and was hungrily lapping her tongue over his anus and balls. The sensation of having two girls of infinite beauty sucking and licking him was too much, his second orgasm within minutes coming like an explosion, his juices spurting deep into Paphia's willing mouth.

Apollonius could hold back no longer, pulling his throbbing prick from her tight sheath and falling on the prone body of Glaucis, her head still buried between Jason's legs. Jason watched as his friend's cock entered the place that, until then had been impaled only by his own shaft. Glaucis moaned and raised her legs high to accept the full length. At first Jason wanted to stop it happening, but he soon realised the nonsense of his jealousy, his own penis, albeit quickly becoming flaccid, still held between the succulent lips of Paphia's mouth.

He pulled himself from her and settled to watch his lover

and his friend enjoy each other. Glaucis opened her eyes and caught his stare and smiled, nervously. He returned her smile with one of encouragement, feeling an incongruous excitement within his sated body as Apollonius hammered his cock into the frail body of his love.

Paphia moved to the head of the bed, sitting on the pillow with her legs bent and splayed wide apart. Glaucis wriggled from Apollonius' grip, his long cock slipping from her tiny pussy, and knelt before the other woman, burying her face once more against the soaked lips of her cunt. Apollonius saw his chance and slid a powerful arm under Glaucis' slim body, raising her hips in preparation for an assault from behind. Jason prayed that he wasn't going to take her in the same way that he had used Paphia, the tiny sphincter still virginal and, somehow, a prize he valued for himself. Whether it was in his friend's mind or not was of no consequence for, no sooner had the tip of his long cock touched the wet lips that guarded the hot sheath before him he roared and stiffened his body, rubbing his cock furiously, his seed shooting over her lovely back, soaking her sweat-covered skin with the white streaks of his release.

Paphia reached over and smoothed the cream into Glaucis' pale skin, massaging the flesh as the young girl continued to suckle between her legs. Jason reached under Glaucis' hips and fingered her clitoris, rubbing furiously, whilst Apollonius slipped three of his fingers deep into her pussy, pumping them in and out steadily.

Gradually it became clear that Glaucis was building up to her inevitable orgasm, arching her back and raising her knees from the bed, her moans and sobs muffled within Paphia's sex. Suddenly, her body jerked once, then again, and she raised her head and cried out, 'Oh, Zeus, oh Zeus, my cunt's on fire!' Jason frigged even faster against her hard bud, Apollonius plunging his fingers wetly in and out of the shuddering nymphet's cunt, until she fell back trembling, her head once more resting on Paphia's thighs.

The four lovers lay quietly on the cushions, their exhaustion gradually easing. Paphia began to dress.

'Have I convinced you that the Cloak of Aphrodite should remain here?' she said, standing.

'Your beauty is unquestionable, your love-making divine, but my quest must continue.' Jason felt a twinge of regret at having to say these words, but they had come too far, endured too much to be thwarted now.

'I am sorry. There are many dangers in the temple. The cloak is well protected. I had hoped to save you from certain death. Goodbye, Jason.'

There was a sudden lurch as the *Argo* seemed to hit something substantial. Jason staggered to his feet and peered out of the small window. There was nothing; the sea remained dead calm as the vessel continued to move steadily towards the harbour of Paphos. He looked back into the cabin. Paphia was gone.

For the first time, he thought of the similarity of the names; Paphia . . . Paphos. Her incredible beauty and hypnotic charm; perhaps there was more to her than she had led them to believe.

The temple of Aphrodite looked beautiful in the bright, morning sunlight, its pillars of white stone and grey-streaked marble sharply defined against the background of the scorched hillside. Nevertheless, despite the aura of peace and tranquillity that pervaded the scene Jason felt distinctly nervous as he, Apollonius and four of the Argonauts approached the steep, stone steps leading to the ornate portal.

He had chosen Calais, Zetes and Castor, his strongest fighters to accompany him on this final stage of the quest, along with Acastus, son of Pelias, a veritable mountain of a man whose courage had been well proven in past adventures. He had thought of bringing more men but had decided in favour of this smaller band, considering that what would have appeared to be a blatant attack on the temple would greatly anger the goddess.

The group spread out, stepping gingerly up the cool steps, their swords drawn. All was quiet; not even the birds chattered. Acastus coughed, more out of a need to break

203

the silence than to clear his throat. The great doors were wide open, the priests and hand-maidens nowhere to be seen.

'Where is everybody?' hissed Castor, anxiously. Jason shook his head, his eyes darting from side to side as he surveyed the scene of opulence before them. They walked slowly into the great hall to be immediately confronted by the massive golden statue of Aphrodite standing before them, demanding their adulation. Apollonius, Calais and Zetes fell to their knees, Jason bowed his head in respect. Castor and Acastus ignored the spectacle, their thoughts clearly on more earthly matters as they looked cautiously around the room.

Jason rested his hands on Apollonius' shoulders. 'Come,' he said, 'we must seek out the golden chest that contains the cloak and be away quickly.' Apollonius led the way to the rear of the great statue, pointing to a small door set in the base.

'The way to the catacombs,' he said, darkly, 'and, with good fortune, to the end of your quest, Jason.'

Jason said nothing, cautiously opening the heavy, wooden door. Ahead of them stretched a flight of steps descending rapidly into the gloom. The only illumination was provided by the occasional flamed torch set in the damp, stone walls. He took a deep breath and moved forward, the others following closely. Their footsteps echoed loudly; Jason felt his heart racing. Not since his capture of the Golden Fleece had he sensed such fear. He was about to steal from a goddess; he, a mere mortal intended to desecrate the temple of Aphrodite.

They reached the foot of the steep flight with some relief, the descent having become more and more precarious with every step. They stood still for a moment, their eyes becoming accustomed to the dimness, then walked forward once more. Rounding a corner, they stopped.

Ahead of them stood what appeared to be a woman, tall, statuesque and naked, exquisitely desirable were it not for the fact that she had not one but three pairs of arms set in her otherwise perfectly formed body. She stood stock-still, her arms held open in incongruous welcome.

'Is she real?' whispered Apollonius.

'She must be the guardian of the treasures of the goddess,' answered Jason, his eyes transfixed by the eerie sight before him. 'We must pass her somehow.'

'She holds no weapons,' hissed Castor, 'and there are six of us. Come on!' He marched quickly forward, only to stop short when he stood no more than a couple of feet from the smiling entity. 'She is beautiful,' he sighed. 'I, I cannot resist, I must . . .'

The others watched in awe as the woman reached forward with one of her arms and slid her hand under his loin-cloth, drawing his rapidly rising penis into view. Castor groaned as she moved her grip up and down, throwing his head back in ecstasy.

'Quickly,' breathed Jason, 'whilst she is otherwise occupied; slip past her!' Apollonius and Zetes stepped forward, inching their way on either side of the being, their backs pressed hard against the wall of the narrow passageway. Suddenly the woman grabbed at them with two of her arms, grasping them by the crotch before deftly worming her hands under their clothing and clutching their cocks. The moment that she gripped them with her intimate grasp they stood passively, their erections stiffening under her expert caress.

Calais and Acastus were next, seemingly drawn towards her, their cocks already jutting from their clothing, presented to her for her delicate manipulation. The entity grasped both offered prizes willingly, immediately rubbing them with rapid, sensuous movements of her supple wrists.

Jason stood his ground, feeling his own stalk rising, her one free hand tempting him forward. His five colleagues moaned with pleasure as they were simultaneously masturbated, standing in a circle of delight around this strange being. Jason began to walk forward, desperate to savour the joys that the others were relishing.

Calais suddenly snapped his eyes open. 'Jason!' he shouted, 'Jason, we are bewitched! Save yourself!'

'What do you mean?' said Jason, stopping short. 'The hardness of your cocks suggests nothing but pleasure in your predicament.'

'He is right,' said Acastus through gritted teeth, his body shaking as his stiff prick was steadily pumped. 'I feel my very soul being drawn from within me. I know that if I come I am lost to this devil; we all are!'

'Use your swords!' shouted Jason, 'put an end to it!'

'We cannot!' groaned Calais, 'we cannot resist. I, I'm going to come, I'm going to come!'

Jason watched in horror as the woman pumped ever more rapidly on the five cocks in her grip. Calais shot his seed first, the sperm trailing across her stomach and breasts. Apollonius was next, his fluids spurting high from his big tool, soaking her face. The others quickly followed suit, their juices mixing on the flawless skin of their captor.

One by one the men slipped to the floor, apparently unconscious. Jason regarded them closely, his eyes filled with terror. Even in the half-light he could clearly see that each man was now without genitals, their once proud erections somehow spirited away by this vicious entity. Paphia had spoken truly when she had warned of the dangers in the temple.

'Come, Jason,' hissed the creature, beckoning to him with her six hands, 'come, let me take your fine prick within my heavenly grasp.'

Jason gripped his sword, his hands shaking as he walked forward. She was beautiful; her eyes shining with lust and evil, her tongue licking over her lips in eager anticipation. Jason averted his gaze.

'Look at me!' she commanded. Jason ignored her, his grip on his sword tightening whilst his cock maddeningly began to rise. 'Look at me,' she said again. Jason glanced at her face. Her eyes had turned flame-red, burning with evil intent. He felt his hold on his sword weakening.

Suddenly she reached out and grabbed his now fully erect penis, clutching and rubbing it with four of her hands, the fingers of the other two pinching his nipples painfully. The sword clattered to the floor. 'Such a prize, Jason,' the creature cackled, 'so huge; a wondrous trophy!'

The threat to his precious manhood momentarily snapped Jason out of his trance and he forced himself from her grip, grabbing his sword from the stone floor and stepping back against the wall. The entity howled in anger, her face changing rapidly, her beauty rapidly dissolving into the image of a monster. Her previously silken hair began to stiffen and curl, writhing about on her head like hundreds of snakes. Her mouth became twisted, her teeth rotten and sharp. Jason avoided looking directly into her eyes, concentrating instead on her hair which, to his horror he perceived to have transformed into hundreds of writhing, wriggling penises, the flaccid prizes representing the souls of many long-lost adventurers who had dared to seek to steal from the temple of Aphrodite.

Jason knew her now; this final metamorphosis made it all clear. This was a Gorgon, a sister of Medusa, and a terrifying evil. She walked towards him, her six hands reaching out, her face grinning with diabolic lust. He knew he must kill her now or he would be lost, as would the souls of his friends who lay around them.

'No!' he shouted, raising his sword, 'die, fiend, die!' With monumental effort he plunged the weapon deep into the breast of the creature, her ear-piercing scream telling him that he had pierced her heart. She fell slowly to the ground to lie harmlessly at his feet, her face crushed against the stone floor. Gradually the hideous tresses of living flesh on her head resumed the appearance of hair, the air about him rushing noisily as the captured souls of the past were finally released from their hellish imprisonment.

Jason looked across at the prone figures of his men. Each once again sported a fine erection, Apollonius gently rubbing his in his trance. Jason smiled with relief; the terror was past.

Once all the men had recovered from their ordeal they resumed their search for the treasure-room, their senses sharpened by the recent adventure. One by one rooms were examined, passageways explored.

At last they came upon a large, high-domed and well-lit hall filled with many fabulous and magical prizes. The temptation to the Argonauts to loot the hoards was great but they all knew, especially after their encounter with the Gorgon, that it would not be wise to enrage the goddess any more than was necessary to complete their quest.

Jason eventually found the cloak, hidden, as he had been told, in a small, golden casket. The garment was quite unremarkable; a dull, brown colour with cloth of simple design but, even as his fingers touched it, he sensed that it had great power.

'I have it, men!' he cried, gripping the casket with excited fingers. 'Come, let us not tarry here a moment longer!'

He turned to leave the room, to be faced by what appeared to him to be yet another vision of loveliness. At the far end of the chamber, standing on a raised dais was a tall, shapely young girl, her naked, shining skin as jet black as that of the wondrous Sphyledian nymphomaniacs. Her gorgeous face shone with desire, the thick, dark lips pouting, the large eyes filled with lust. Her breasts were huge, mountainous, brown globes supporting thick, coal-black nipples. Her waist tapered narrowly, emphasising the wideness of her welcoming hips, her hairless cunt clearly visible between her slightly parted legs, the red gash between her darkly-pouting sex-lips wetly inviting. Jason took a step forward. Apollonius caught his shoulder.

'Take care, Jason,' he said, 'it is another trick.'

Jason stood still, mesmerised by the animal-like beauty of the creature. The girl smiled sensuously, putting a finger to her mouth and tilting her head coyly before turning her back to the men and bending, straight-legged until she rested a hand flat on the floor, her breasts hanging heavily, the nipples all but touching the cool marble.

Acastus groaned. 'Look at that arse,' he said, hoarsely, 'did you ever see one so perfect?'

The girl looked back at them, licking her lips and smiling appealingly. Again she put her forefinger to her mouth, wetting it liberally with her tongue then, with deliberate slowness moved her hand round to her superb bottom and deftly wriggled the long finger deep into her anus, all the time holding Acastus' stare with her own.

'Oh, by all the Gods, I must bugger this one!' he cried,

208

stepping forward quickly, his hard cock already in his hand. It was Apollonius who saw the danger. Rushing forward, he shoved the huge man with all his strength, the surprise of his attack knocking Acastus back onto the floor. 'What are you doing?' said Acastus, angrily, 'she will have us all! Let me free!'

'Look, you fool,' bellowed Jason, 'look at your feet!'

Acastus glanced down. Less than two feet in front of him, exactly where he would have trodden, the floor had opened up revealing a deep, black shaft. The big man gulped and looked up at Jason stupidly. 'I think it's time we left this place,' he said, simply.

Jason sat on the harbour wall watching the Argonauts loading his vessel with supplies, the heat of the midday sun bearing down on their bronzed bodies unmercifully. Glaucis lay in the shade of a large olive-tree, her eyes closed. After the events of the past hours the bustle of the labouring men seemed somehow reassuring and pleasantly normal.

The main part of the quest completed, there now lay ahead a long journey back to Iolcus to present the Cloak of Aphrodite to Pelias, and to claim his kingdom. But then there was Medea. She would not take kindly to Glaucis, and yet he loved them both. He glanced across at the lovely young girl, savouring her delicate sexuality, her slim, lithe body, her innocent features. He thought of his wife, her flame-red hair, her massive breasts and plump, round bottom, and her wild, insatiable lust for erotic encounters. They were so very different; perhaps he could somehow have them both?

His thoughts were broken by the arrival of Apollonius. 'Jason,' he called, 'my dear friend. Before you leave, I have a gift for you and your lovely lady.'

'A gift?'

'A treat. Come, bring Glaucis and follow me.'

Jason did as he was told, taking Glaucis by the hand and leading her in the direction Apollonius was quickly taking. They followed him around the back of a tall building and into what appeared to be a stable.

'There,' said Apollonius, proudly, 'mount these steeds

209

and let them take you to a special place I have furnished for your pleasure. You will know what to do when you get there.' He winked at Jason wickedly.

'I have never seen the like,' said Glaucis, looking in wide-eyed amazement across the paddock. Tethered against the rail were their mounts, two fine built centaurs, both male, their lower bodies those of strong stallions, their torsos and heads handsomely human.

'They are the centaurs of Thessaly,' said Apollonius walking over and patting the rump of the smaller of the two. 'They are mute. Ride them carefully, they can be quite excitable.'

Jason grinned and cautiously mounted the larger centaur, feeling it rear up as he sat astride the broad back. Apollonius helped Glaucis to climb onto the other steed, guiding her hand to clutch the beast's hair for support. He then untethered the creatures and slapped Jason's mount broadly on the rump, causing it to rear and gallop out of the paddock, Jason gripping the broad shoulders for all he was worth, glancing back with a glare at his friend. Glaucis' centaur followed at a gentler pace, catching up with Jason as he managed to coax his beast into an easier gait.

Soon they were riding slowly through a sweet-smelling lemon-grove, the trees casting a carpet of blossom at the feet of their mounts. A slight breeze wafted against their skin, cool in the fierce assault of the sun, the occasional shade of the trees a welcome relief.

Presently they arrived at a small clearing, surrounded by thicker bushes and trees. In the centre a bed of fruits had been laid on the ground, peaches, plums and lush berries, over-ripe and succulent. Jason looked at Glaucis and grinned. Sensing his intent she coloured slightly, then smiled.

Jason leapt from his steed and helped Glaucis to her feet. The two centaurs ambled quietly to the edge of the clearing, as if in deference to the lovers' need for privacy. Jason took her frail body into his strong arms and pressed his mouth to hers, his tongue searching between her teeth, tracing the shape of her small mouth. With one hand he unhooked her thin dress, standing back to let it slip to the ground, admiring her delicate nakedness. He stroked her small breasts, coaxing the nipples to stiffness, all the time kissing her lightly on the face and neck.

'Apollonius has created a bed of Demeter, Goddess of fruit,' he said. 'We must take advantage of his generosity.' He swept her up off her feet, carrying her to the carpet of glistening succulence and laid her gently on the cool flesh.

Glaucis shivered. 'Oooh, it feels strangely wonderful,' she purred, sliding her legs and her bottom in the ooze. Jason tugged at his loin-cloth and removed it, proudly displaying his fierce erection. Glaucis looked at it and smiled in happy anticipation. Kneeling between her legs he raised them by the ankles, lifting her bottom from the ground and bending his head to lap hungrily at her juice-covered buttocks. The mixture of the flavours of fruit and flesh and the scents of peach and aroused pussy invaded his senses, his tongue now licking purposefully at her wet sex, his need to possess his love as great as it had ever been.

Lowering her legs, Jason rolled her over onto her stomach, moving her deliberately about in the squelching fruit, scooping it up and rubbing it over her back and bottom. Taking a large, ripe peach he squeezed it hard between his fingers, letting the juice fall copiously over her pert buttocks and run between them. He took his forefinger and worked the sensuous fluid against her virginal anus, hearing her groan with pleasure.

Carefully, very carefully, he eased his finger inside, feeling her incredible tightness. Taking up a handful of dark plums he crushed them in his other hand, again allowing the juice to flow onto her bottom. He pushed his finger in further, as far as it could go and began to turn it slightly, feeling the muscles of her sphincter begin to relax as they became used to the intrusion.

Kissing her wet back he pulled his finger out of her a little, then eased two fingers inside her anus together. She raised her bottom slightly to accommodate him, the juices of the fruit lubricating her perfectly. A third finger now, then a fourth, turning, easing, preparing her for what was now inevitable. Glaucis continued to groan pleasurably, clearly aware that her final virginity was about to be lost.

211

Jason moved to kneel between her legs and eased his fingers from her anus, raising her hips with his other hand. She now crouched on her elbows and knees, her perfect bottom presented to him, the hole open and ready. Taking his stiff stalk in his grasp he moved forward towards her, the huge, bulbous end still looking far too large to penetrate her tiny orifice. He pressed it against the sphincter, expecting her to cry out in pain. Instead, it slid into her anus easily, the wetness of the juices and his earlier ministrations having prepared her perfectly.

Gradually he eased more and more of his superb length into his lover's beautiful bottom until, to his joy and elation his groin touched her buttocks, his cock penetrating her completely. He held himself still for over a minute, savouring the depth of his intrusion and the heat of her flesh clutching his engorged shaft like a suckling mouth.

He felt himself throb inside her and a little of his own juices slipped deep within her. He began to steadily fuck her, moving in and out of her bottom at an easy pace.

'Does that feel good?' he whispered, kissing the back of her head.

'Wonderful,' she said, 'wonderful.'

Jason leant forward on her, easing her body to lie in the mush, his prick still firmly embedded in her backside. As he fucked her they slid over the soft fruits, slithering about in the mush as his pace increased. His movements were rapid, now, his need urgent. Glaucis began to moan loudly, wriggling her hips as he plunged in and out of her tight anus.

'Oh, Jason, my love,' she cried, 'I'm coming, I'm coming! Fill my bottom with your seed; come with me, my love!'

Jason pumped harder and harder, bouncing his groin on the sweet cushion of her buttocks, her anus now easily accepting every inch of his intrusion. He felt the first warnings of impending bliss, the surge at the base of his penis, and thrust hard into Glaucis, pushing himself past the point of no return. Forcing his cock as deep as it would go he stiffened his buttocks and groaned as the sperm flooded

212

from him, his stem throbbing heavily against her gripping sheath. Glaucis shouted out, 'Yes! Yes!' and came with him, pushing her lovely bottom back at her lover's groin in the apparent hope of accepting more of his fine stalk.

Jason eased his still large weapon from within her tiny sphincter, marvelling at the way she had accommodated him. They both rolled onto their backs in the oozing mush and rested, their breathing short, their bodies sated.

At the edge of the clearing the centaurs watched and waited, their stallion erections fully hard.

CHAPTER ELEVEN

A thick sea-mist hung sullenly over the glassy waters as the *Phallicis* cautiously moved towards the narrow inlet. Medea held herself still, scarcely daring to breath, listening hard for the tell-tale sounds of waves lapping against the treacherous jagged edges of the rocks. Iole stood transfixed, her expression one of almost hypnotic enchantment.

Medea regarded her friend curiously. Throughout the journey Iole had maintained that her destiny lay in the arms of Heracles and now they were about to anchor at his island of self-imposed exile.

'Are you feeling ill, Iole?' ventured Medea, touching the young waif's arm lightly.

'I am nervous,' Iole whispered, her fixed stare held by the gloom, 'and yet, strangely aroused. He is there, waiting for me, hidden within the deathly shroud of this fog, waiting to possess me. I have dreamt of this moment for so many years, thought of nothing else, imagined his fabulously muscled body and his long, thick manhood that will soon impale me.' She turned to look at Medea and smiled. 'I thank Zeus and Hera that I have learned the pleasures and techniques of fucking, so that I may now gladden my lord Heracles in many ways.'

Medea gripped the young girl's arm tightly. 'From the day that you accommodated the massive stalk of Rapis you became a member of the sisterhood and I have watched you with envy and lust many times since.'

'With lust, Medea?' said Iole, coyly.

'With lust, sweet Iole. I have long yearned to run my tongue between the velvety lips of your honeyed pussy.

214

Whenever I have seen your delicate, upturned bottom as you thrust yourself down on some rampant cock I have longed to fling myself upon you, to taste your juices for myself. You are not angry, I hope?'

Iole rested her hand lightly on Medea's shoulder, her softness of expression making the older woman's heart melt. 'How can I be angry? We spoke of this in Rhodes when I told you that I was fated to lie with you, just as my destiny hails me from within this eerie mist. When you, Electra and I made love with Tonis I remember wanting you desperately then. When I saw his thick cock slide into your sweet cunt it was your sex that I wanted to taste at that moment, not his.'

Medea caught hold of the lovely girl and hugged her tightly pressing their bodies hard together, their naked flesh separated by the thinnest of cotton. Their mouths met, their tongues darting forward, searching, licking and tasting, their hands caressing each other's bottom, crotches pressed firmly together, rubbing gently from side to side.

'Fuck with me now,' implored Medea, kissing Iole's face wetly, 'before we land and it becomes too late. See, the anchor-stone slips into the water already. We have arrived in Crete to meet your destiny; come, before the mists clear; I must taste the fresh scent of your pussy and feel your delicate tongue lapping at my aching cunt!'

Medea was virtually dragging the slim blonde towards her cabin. 'What of Tonis?' said Iole, feigning resistance to her advances, 'he sleeps within the cabin.'

'Should he be awakened by our cries of release he will learn how two women can please each other. He has much to discover of the secrets of Eros.'

Iole giggled like a child and allowed Medea to take her hand and lead her into the near-darkness of the cabin. Once inside, Medea closed the door to her lips. 'Ssh,' she whispered. 'He is still sleeping heavily. When his eyes open they will be met by quite a vision, of that I am certain.'

Iole smiled broadly and reached for the hem of her diaphanous garment, drawing it quickly over her head to reveal her slim, pert nakedness. Medea followed suit, revelling in the way the young girl's eyes widened at the sight of her voluptuous body, despite having seen it many times before. The difference was, of course, that this time it was displayed solely for her pleasure; no wonder Iole was clearly taking such joy in the spectacle.

The two women hugged each other tightly again, the wetness of their arousal merging as they pressed their mounds together, their tongues once more licking around the shapes of their mouths. Silently and gradually they allowed themselves to slip to the floor, lying side by side on the bare wooden boards covered in thick goats' fleeces. They fondled each other with the passion of new lovers, Medea squeezing the small, firm breasts of the lovely blonde, Iole lying on her back submissively. Medea lay on top of her, still kissing her mouth heavily, grinding her crotch against the prominent pubic mound, feeling the hardness of the young girl's bud against her own.

Iole groaned and pushed her hips upward, moving her bottom from side to side. Medea responded by quickening her movements, the slight roughness of the lithe blonde's downy pubic hair exciting her button-hard clitoris. Iole clawed at her back, running her hands down to her buttocks, gripping them tightly and forcing her own bottom from the floor, moaning noisily as she orgasmed. Medea thrust her hand between them and found Iole's bud and fingered it rapidly, her own need for release close. Iole's hips bucked and writhed, her cries of blissful torment uncontrollable. Medea clamped her free hand over her trembling lover's mouth. 'Ssh!' she hissed, 'you'll wake Tonis!'

The two girls pulled themselves apart and sat up guiltily, silently looking at the reclining figure on the bed. The youth was naked, his cock half-erect and lying heavily on his stomach.

'I might not mind if he wakes,' said Iole, with girlish coyness, 'he looks more than ready to serve us.'

'Perhaps later,' said Medea, turning herself to bury her head between Iole's thighs and squatting across her face. The young girl lost no time, her long tongue quickly snaking out to meet Medea's pouting sex-lips; the sensation of the conquest, the exquisite feeling of Iole's fluttering oral contact with her aching cunt filling her with delight.

Medea pressed her mouth firmly against the nymphet's warm, soft pussy, drawing the wet lips into her mouth, running the tip of her tongue between them, tasting the honeyed juices for the first time other than on the stiff erection of one of Iole's lovers. Parting the outer lips with her fingers, she delved her tongue deep between them, slipping it in and out of the puffy folds of sex-flesh, feeling Iole treating her in the same, enthralling way. Wetting her finger with spittle and the copious juices glistening in the half-light on the young girl's matted pubic hair she deftly wriggled it inside Iole's anus, moving it purposely forward until the full length was accommodated. At the same time she slipped two fingers of her other hand inside the open lips of her pussy, concentrating the flicking of her tongue on the hard bud of her clitoris.

To her joy she felt Iole perform the same delights to her nether regions, one then two fingers slipping inside her bottom, followed by three, maybe four of the other hand inside her pussy. She responded by moving her hips so that her pubic mound ground against Iole's chin as she licked furiously at her love-bud.

Finally, Medea could take no more. With a cry that would have woken Pluto in the Underworld she came, the juices of her orgasm soaking the face of the young girl beneath her. Iole's hips began to move rapidly up and down and Medea resumed her oral homage to this delightful creature, rasping her tongue wetly over her mound until, quickly, she squealed with her own pleasurable release.

The two lovers lay still for a moment or two, breathing heavily from their labours, their faces resting gently between each other's thighs. Eventually, Medea reluctantly raised herself, sitting cross-legged by the side of the lovely girl she had desired for so long, and whom she had now possessed. She gazed lovingly at the slim, lithe body and beautiful features, stroking her hand soothingly over the warm, sweating flesh. Iole's breathing eased under the delicate massage and she closed her eyes to savour it.

Medea glanced up at the bed seeing with little surprise the grinning face of Tonis, his body propped up on his elbow, his other hand casually fondling an impressive erection. Without a word, Medea crawled over to him and pushed him onto his back, taking over the manipulation of his stiffness with her expert touch. Iole joined her, slipping onto the bed between Tonis' outstretched legs, putting her mouth to his thick knob and taking it within her pouting lips. Medea bent her head forward and allowed her tongue to trace the length of his cock, Iole soon copying her actions, the two tongues meeting occasionally at the tip of his stalk.

Their mouths met over his plum-sized knob, their tongues lapping it and each other's lips as they kissed, both girls rubbing the long stem of his cock with their firm grips. The sight and sensation was clearly too much for Tonis, who groaned and shuddered, his fluids shooting into their mouths as they simultaneously pumped and suckled him through the oblivion of perfect orgasm.

As he fell back from their erotic clasp the two women kissed fully on the mouth, the juices of their mutual lover shared and swallowed, knowing that for the first time in both of their lives they had experienced the delights of the kiss of Aphrodite.

The mists were clearing quickly when the two women resumed their place on the deck, the shoreline of Crete now sharply visible less than a stone's throw from the *Phallicis*. The cliffs were high and potted with caves, the rock-face bleached nearly white by the harsh sun, the vegetation sparse.

The morning sun was now rising rapidly behind the cliffs. Most of the crew were already disembarking on their customary search for provisions and water, Tonis and Electra remaining behind to guard the vessel. Medea and Iole clambered into a small boat and rowed for the beach.

'I wonder when we will meet the great Heracles,' said Iole nervously, 'or even *if* we shall meet him. This is a large island; he may not even know we are here!' Her voice bore traces of panic. Medea felt a pang of jealousy.

'He will know,' she said, reassuringly. 'Hera will make certain of that.'

As if to confirm her words there came a sudden cry from behind them. They swung around, letting their oars loose in the water, the boat drifting the final few feet to the sand. Peering towards the very top of the cliff they saw a figure waving to them. They returned the gesture and clambered out of the boat, pulling it safely from the reach of the lapping waves.

'Is that him?' said Iole, excitedly. 'Is that Heracles?'

Medea nodded. Even at this distance she knew the form and physique of the most powerful man in the known world. Iole turned and looked again at the figure of her future spouse, watching in awed disbelief as he skilfully began to scale the cliff-face, descending rapidly over the jagged rocks, his bronzed nakedness sharply defined against the chalk-white surface.

'What strength, what bravery,' said Iole, her eyes glazed. Medea couldn't help but agree. She had witnessed Heracles perform many seemingly impossible tasks in the past; nothing he did surprised her.

The great man allowed himself to fall the last fifteen or so feet to the ground, landing heavily onto the soft sand but springing up to stand before them, his face grinning broadly. Medea smiled happily in greeting, Iole merely stared, open mouthed.

'Welcome, Queen Medea of Iolcus! Welcome to Crete, and to my home!'

'Not Queen of Iolcus yet, Heracles,' said Medea, clutching the arm of the naked man before her tightly, the desire to touch every other part of him already welling up inside her. 'That is why I am here.'

'How so? Did not Pelias deliver the kingdom to Jason on receiving the prize of the Golden Fleece?'

'Jason had to agree to undertake another quest, just one more, or so he says.'

Heracles laughed. 'Jason will never cease his wanderings, not even for you, Medea.'

'I fear you are right. Nevertheless, I must complete my

219

side of the bargain. I am to return to Iolcus having des-
patched many fine athletes to take part in the celebratory
games to mark Jason's taking of Pelias' crown. You are to
be part of the team.'

Heracles stepped back. 'I?' he said, his grin disappearing,
'I cannot. I have sworn never to leave this island.'

Medea clutched his arm again. 'Just for the games, Heracles, I beg you. Then you may return and live here as long
as you please.' She ran her free hand over his back, allowing her fingertips to stroke gently across his buttocks. He
shivered noticeably.

'Have a care, Medea,' he said, quietly enough for only
her to hear. 'I have been celibate these past three years. I
fear I would kill any woman whom I impaled now, my
needs are so great.'

'Then I have a prize for you,' she said, indicating the
mute figure of Iole standing by the boat. 'She has travelled
many miles and suffered many dangers to be with you, for
she believes this to be her fate.'

Iole stepped forward, as though expecting him to take
her in his arms and carry her off into the distance. Heracles
merely shook his head. 'It cannot be,' he said, sadly, 'see,
she is too small, too delicate.'

He indicated her slim frame with a wave of his arm, his
other hand taking his stiffening penis within its grasp.
Rapidly it rose, the length and thickness causing the two
women to stare in disbelief. Iole fell to her knees and
buried her head in her arms, sobbing loudly. Medea licked
her lips, gazing at the proffered monster with increasing
desire. She reached out and gripped the stalk, her hand
barely circling its massiveness. 'This would certainly kill
the child,' she whispered in Heracles' ear, 'but I would
welcome the challenge, provided you agree to return to
Iolcus with us and compete in the games.' She ran her free
hand over his bottom and squeezed the base of his cock.
Heracles gritted his teeth and nodded acquiescently.

'You are a hard mistress to defy,' he groaned.

'Then you will come to Iolcus?'

Heracles pulled himself from Medea's heavenly grip and

walked towards the edge of the sea. 'I need time to consider,' he said, carefully. 'I have sworn never to leave this island, to atone for the death of Hylas, my squire. The temptation to possess your fine body tears at my very crotch, but I must have more reason than the mere ending of three years of celibacy to break my oath.'

'Jason needs you,' implored Medea, standing at the great man's side, resting her hand nonchalantly on his strong back. 'Pelias has reneged on his promise to hand over the kingdom on receiving the gift of the Golden Fleece and these two further quests were set. Jason is at this very moment seeking out the Cloak of Aphrodite in order to restore the old lecher's libido whilst I am charged to return to Iolcus with the greatest athlete in the modern world, the noble Heracles himself. We cannot give Pelias reason to cling to the throne any longer; it is Jason's by right.'

The powerful man looked down into the pleading eyes of his queen, his resolve disappearing fast. Medea felt that she was winning; she would have her athlete.

'Before I give you my decision,' said Heracles, grandly, 'we will feast and celebrate your safe arrival at my island. Then we will sleep, and I will inform you tomorrow whether I journey with you. First, however, I have something to show you.'

He held out his arm and Medea gripped his muscular flesh, allowing him to lead her towards the mouth of one of the many caves set in the rock-face. She was about to follow him into the darkness of the cavern when she remembered Iole, who remained prostrate on the sand, sobbing quietly, her head buried in her arms. Medea walked over to her and hugged her tightly around the shoulders, her sympathetic action merely causing the lovely waif to cry loudly. Heracles took Medea's arm.

'Come,' he said, 'leave her with her sorrow.'

Medea realised the wisdom of his words and followed him into the cave, her thoughts divided between sadness for the gentle Iole and whatever mysteries lay ahead.

Heracles guided her through the passage that tunnelled through the sheer cliffs, helping her to step gingerly over

221

the sharp, wet rocks until they were once more in the open, the brightness of the sun causing her to shield her eyes for a moment.

'There!' announced Heracles, proudly, 'is he not magnificent?'

Medea took an instant to focus her eyes, then recoiled in horror. There, kneeling massively on a high, stone plinth was the unmistakeable figure of Talos, the bronze giant they had destroyed on their last quest.

'Talos!' she exclaimed, 'he is re-built . . . he will kill us all!'

She made to scurry back to the relative safety of the cave, the image of the crouching statue of the warrior Titan filling her with terror. The giant had tried to crush the Argonauts and their vessel as they returned with the Golden Fleece and had only been thwarted by the bravery of Heracles who had distracted him whilst Medea had managed to remove the pin which kept his life-force within his great, bronze body.

She remembered the sight of him crumbling to the sand, shattering into a thousand pieces. Now he crouched on his plinth as before, incongruously silent, waiting to awaken and destroy again.

Heracles laughed and caught her arm, pulling her to his side. 'Fear not, my queen,' he said, forcing her to look again at the monster's fearsome form. 'I recast the monster using the bronze of his original form, his life-force now granted by Zeus, my father. He serves me now, as you will see. Talos! Awake!'

Medea heard the words of her strong companion but nevertheless felt anxious as the great statue creaked and groaned into life, stepping from the high plinth and standing before them obediently.

'Talos! Bow to the Queen Medea!'

The creature turned its head and faced her, its blind eyes expressionless, and bowed its great head slowly, the metal within his neck-joints screeching through under-use. Talos was unused to subservience.

'Talos, step to the highest point of the island and guard

our guests whilst we feast!' The order was barked and immediately obeyed, the monster lumbering off towards the nearby hills. Medea breathed a sigh of relief.

'Can you trust him?' she asked, returning with Heracles to the coolness of the cave.

'With my life,' said Heracles, casually stroking her firm buttocks as he once more guided her over the slippery rocks. Medea stopped and allowed his fingers to roam over the pert globes of her bottom, his breathing becoming heavy with desire. She reached out and gripped his huge stalk, her hand unable to completely circle the iron-hard flesh.

'Let me ease your pain,' she said, turning and squatting before him. She took hold of his cock in both of her hands and rubbed it vigorously, occasionally slowing her movements and licking the juices of his excitement which wept from the purple tip. The depth of his breathing became even more pronounced. Medea looked up at his face, his eyes closed in ecstatic agony. 'Come, Heracles,' she panted, rubbing him furiously, 'I want you to come into my mouth.' She clamped her lips over his massive knob and sucked at the flesh. Heracles gave out a long, slow groan that echoed all around the cavern and she felt the thick stem of his cock pump within her grasp, tasting the salty fluid as it shot to the back of her throat. She swallowed hard, the juices filling her mouth, her tongue lapping hungrily around the throbbing, spurting knob, the flow seemingly endless.

At last he eased himself from her and sat back on a small rock. Medea smiled and wiped the back of her hand across her mouth suggestively. Heracles grinned. 'It has been a long time,' he said, exhaustedly.

Heracles had built himself a small, but well-furnished shelter, the larger of its three rooms more than adequately accommodating the crew of the *Phallicis* who happily sat on the cool tiles of the floor consuming the abundant fare provided by their host. Iole had decided to stay away, declaring that her heart was broken and that she must

223

consider her future. Medea sat with Heracles, her hands rarely ceasing to touch the magnificence of his naked flesh, the yearnings within her groin becoming ever more intense.

His cock lay flaccid throughout the banquet, its size, even in this state, hardly smaller than Jason's when fully erect. The taste of him still filled her senses, the memory of his throbbing stalk within her mouth serving to increase her desire.

Heracles caught her looking at his fine weapon and she blushed. He grinned, turning his body slightly towards her so that the monster appendage flopped against her thigh. Medea reached out and clasped the slowly thickening shaft, rubbing it up and down steadily.

'Even if you decide not to return with us to Iolcus,' she said, her voice husky with lust, 'I mean to savour the delights of holding this monster within my loins.'

Heracles grinned and reached under Medea's thin dress, his hand quickly finding the wetness of her pussy. She breathed hard as the rough-skinned fingers forced themselves against her tender sex-flesh, the outer lips opening to welcome his intrusion.

'Father! At least wait until you are alone in your bedchamber!'

Heracles pulled his hand away in surprise. Medea looked up, guiltily. The voice belonged to a young man who stood at the doorway, his face all but hidden in the shadows.

'Hyllus! Welcome, my son!' Heracles stood up, apparently unconcerned that his stalk now stretched close to the level of his knee thanks to Medea's delicate attentions. 'Come, meet Medea, soon to be the queen of Iolcus!'

The young man stepped into the light, revealing that he had inherited none of his father's powerful muscles, his body slim and almost poetically delicate, his face fresh, beautiful, and above all, sensuously appealing to Medea's eyes. As seemed to be the custom of the island he was naked, save for the bow and quiver of arrows slung around his narrow shoulders.

Although no match for Heracles his penis hung heavily from the thick, blonde curls of his groin. Medea licked her lips; perhaps there was more sport to be had here. She looked at the others of her crew, all of whom were gazing in more than friendly welcome at the handsome youth who now walked towards her. No, she shouldn't be greedy, she thought, Heracles would more than satisfy her needs this night.

Hyllus held out his hand in welcome, taking Medea's fingers in his grasp and bending forward to kiss them lightly. She felt a slight shiver run across her as his lips touched her fingertips, the feathery contact exciting her as much as the sight of his sylph-like physique. 'Greetings, Hyllus,' she said, her voice trembling. 'I didn't know Heracles had such a handsome son.'

The youth stood erect and smiled. 'I have heard tell of the beauty of Medea, wife of Jason,' he said, 'but until now I have never believed the legend. Now I know it to be true.'

Medea smiled graciously and was about to speak when she noticed the figure of Iole, standing close to the doorway, naked and shivering, her body soaking wet, her hair plastered to her face and neck. Letting go her grip of Hyllus' hand she rushed over to her friend and hugged her tightly.

'Iole, my love, what has happened to you?'

'I felt I must die,' sobbed the lovely blonde, 'knowing that I can never fulfil my destiny. I threw myself into the arms of Poseidon, hoping to drown in the warmth of his embrace but he cast me to the shores. I don't know what is to become of me.' Iole began to sob, burying her head in Medea's flame-red tresses.

'What is this destiny that holds you so fearsomely?' It was Hyllus who spoke, stepping forward to take Iole's arm. She stood obediently in front of him, Medea continuing to stroke her head lovingly.

'My dreams have always shown me to be here, in Crete,' she said, her head bowed, 'destined to be in the arms of Herac ...' She stopped short as she raised her head and looked into the handsome face before her. Medea noticed the sudden shock in the young girl's expression as her eyes met his.

'The arms of Heracles?' said Hyllus, tenderly, 'or perhaps the *son* of Heracles?'

Iole said nothing, her mouth opening, her eyes wide. Hyllus drew her to him, their naked bodies touching and lifted her chin, pressing his mouth against hers in the gentlest of kisses. 'I, too have had dreams,' he said, drawing his face back and gazing into her eyes, 'dreams of meeting my future lover at a great festival, and she was to have risen from the depths of the sea to be with me, a gift of the Gods.' He stepped back, revealing to all that his cock was now firmly erect. 'Come, sweet child, let us fulfil our destinies now, before this worthy assembly.'

The Phallician women cheered as one as Hyllus swept the food and dishes from one of the tables and gently laid the enchantedly submissive figure of Iole across it, her bottom resting against the edge, her legs splayed apart with her feet remaining on the floor. He knelt before her and pressed his mouth to her prominently displayed pussy, this first, sudden sexual contact making her groan softly.

The assembled throng watched in quiet respect as he lapped and suckled hungrily at the puffy, down-covered lips, the sounds of his oral affection filling Medea's ears, the twinges of lust within her body once again dampening her own yearning cunt. Heracles stood at the back of the room, probably fearing that his son may become inhibited if he made his presence too obvious. She looked at him and smiled, running her tongue across her lips slowly, her meaning clear. The big man grinned and looked back at the naked couple, watching as Hyllus stood before the lovely, prone nymphet, his long stalk gripped firmly in his hand, the thick head less than an inch from its ultimate target.

Iole simply lay back, her eyes closed, waiting to be fucked. The silent witnesses held their breath as the young man pressed the bulbous head to the wet slit, the pouting lips of her pussy opening to welcome his intrusion, and sighed in unison as his cock slid slowly into her body, her legs raising from the floor and wrapping themselves around his slim waist.

Medea could feel her juices dampening her upper thighs as she watched the youth plunder Iole's delicate treasures, the sight of his small, firm buttocks clenching as he thrust forward becoming almost too much for her to bear. She turned her head and looked across at Heracles, finding him gazing at her. The expression on his face said all that she needed to know. She pushed her way through the women and stood at his side, taking his arm in hers.

'The Gods play tricks on us mere mortals sometimes,' she said, gripping his muscular flesh tightly.

'They make a fine couple,' said Heracles, taking her other hand and putting it to his half-erect penis, 'but now I grow impatient to end my self-imposed celibacy. Come, Medea, ease my pain once more.'

Heracles led the compliant Medea quickly from the room, her hand still gripping his rising stalk, the groans of Iole in the throes of her first orgasm filling her ears. They entered a second room which was clearly the bed-chamber, a giant, fleece-covered bed being the only furniture. She glanced at his cock, now fully erect, the oozing tip level with his firmly defined pectoral muscles. She felt an ache within her groin, not of fear of his size but of lust for him; her need to be impaled upon his massive length tearing at her very soul.

Heracles gripped her under the arms, his face still grinning, his eyes filled with animal-like craving. He lifted her bodily from the floor and threw her onto the bed, leaping upon her and tearing her flimsy dress from her body in one, fearsome movement, throwing the ruined garment to the ground. Medea laughed almost insanely and flung her legs wide apart as she lay on her back, pulling the lips of her cunt apart, displaying her prize to her lover obscenely.

'Fuck me, Heracles,' she commanded, 'fuck me now! This is not a time for caress and coaxing. I am ready for that long, thick pole to enter my soaked cunt to the hilt. Fuck me!'

She grabbed at his cock and pulled it to her pussy, the other hand holding the thick lips apart. She groaned with delight as the spongy, peach-sized end entered her, making her pull her legs further back as it filled her with its very immensity.

'Yes, Heracles, yes, I feel the monster within me! Ram it home! Spare me nothing; I will have every inch!'

'Take care, my lady, I may split you apart!'

Medea grabbed hold of his buttocks and dug her fingernails into the sinewy flesh, pulling his hips towards hers with all her strength. 'Just fuck me, fuck me hard!' she cried, gasping for breath as his thick shaft plundered deeper and deeper into her tight, wet sheath. She felt the tip touching the entrance to her womb and ran her hand down to clutch the root of his cock, finding at least four inches still to be accommodated. She shifted her position slightly, holding her legs erect, coaxing him forward with her hand until, to her joy, she felt the heavy sack of his balls press against her bottom, the full length of his amazing prick now held deep within her shuddering body.

They held still for some moments, Medea content to feel his superb size inside her, getting herself used to the intrusion. Presently, however, the needs of the great man took over his will and he began to pump his mammoth stalk gently in and out of her pussy, the expression on his profusely sweating face making it clear that he was having much difficulty in controlling himself. The sight of him desperately trying not to come filled her mind with delight. He held still again, gritting his teeth, swallowing hard as she felt him throb heavily within her. The crisis past he moved in and out of her again, raising himself on his hands and toes, the only physical contact between them being their genitals.

Medea gazed into his eyes and smiled. 'Come,' she ordered in a whisper, 'come all over me. Soak me with your sperm!'

Heracles didn't need telling twice. With a roar he pulled his massive cock from her, grasping it in both of his hands and rubbing it furiously. Medea gripped it with him, matching the speed of his pumping, watching as the huge knob swelled, the colour near-purple, her free hand clutching his balls.

The first jet of his seed shot over her head, splashing on

228

the tiled floor behind the bed. The second sent a stream of hot come over her face, the third soaking her breasts and stomach. Still he groaned, still he rubbed as more and more of his agonising frustrations became relieved with spurt after spurt of white fluid, soaking the flesh of Medea who ran her hands over her skin, massaging herself with the erotic oils of Heracles' lust.

He slowed and finally stopped his self-caress, his cock hanging hugely, the final emissions of his seed trailing down slowly to meet Medea's flesh. She raised herself and leant forward, taking his tool in her grasp and putting it to her mouth, sucking the remains of his lust from him until he pushed her head away and fell back, panting. She lay again on her back and, lifting her head slightly licked a trail of sticky come from her breast.

'Forgive me for ravaging you so,' he said, quietly, 'my need was great.'

Medea sat up, her body glistening with sweat and come. 'My need was the same,' she said, truthfully, 'and the night will not be over for many hours. That fine stalk of yours will rise many more times before I allow you to leave this bed.'

There was a sudden, loud cheer from the other room and they knew that Hyllus had soaked Iole in the same way, and that their bond was complete.

The morning came too quickly for Medea. The sun rose behind the house, shafts of searingly bright light tearing like shards of glass through the narrow windows, the heat of the early sun already unbearable. She lay across the bed, gazing at the plainness of the ceiling, Heracles at last asleep beside her, his head nestled against her groin.

There had been little rest for either of them that night; the needs of the powerful athlete's return from sexual abstinence had been great, greater even than the previously insatiable desires of Medea herself.

Now she ached; her jaw pained her from seemingly endlessly sucking his huge cock, her pussy from accommodating the monster time after wonderful time.

His head felt heavy, and she needed to relieve herself. Carefully lifting his head so as not to wake him she wriggled from under him and padded across the cool tiles to squat over the pot in the corner. Her flow was immediate and copious.

Heracles raised himself up onto the bed, his eyes open. Medea groaned inwardly; he would surely wish to possess her again, and she wasn't so certain that her ravaged pussy could take more pummelling from his splendid weapon.

'I would gladly bathe in that golden shower,' he said, staring pointedly between her legs as she pissed.

The flow became a trickle. 'Too late,' mocked Medea, standing, 'perhaps another time.'

'There will be many opportunities during the long voyage to Iolcus.'

Medea's eyes lit up. 'You mean you will come to the games?' she said, excitedly.

'How can I refuse, after a night such as we have just enjoyed? Hyllus will remain here with his new-found love and care for my island until I return.'

Medea was about to fling her arms gratefully around his neck when there came the sound of cries of alarm from outside. Heracles leapt off the bed and ran to the window. 'By Zeus,' he gasped as he looked out, 'what in Hades is that?' Medea hurried to his side.

'Oh no,' she sighed, 'it cannot be so.' In the distance, possibly a mile from the shore but nevertheless clearly distinct she could see the wading, malevolent figure of Colus, the Colossus of Rhodes.

'You know of this creature?' said Heracles, looking back in panic at the terrifying sight.

'It is Colus. She has followed us from Rhodes to seek vengeance.'

'Why should such a monster seek revenge? What terrible deed could you have performed to cause it to follow for so many miles?'

Medea was about to answer his question when there was an ear-splitting screech of metal on metal from outside. The two ran into the sun-baked quadrangle, just in time to see the awesome figure of Talos crashing through the sparse undergrowth, heading for the cliff-edge. He stood facing the sea, held up his great arms and roared menacingly, then leapt from the cliff, disappearing from their view.

Heracles and Medea ran towards the cave which gave access to the beach, quickly stumbling over the slippery rocks and out onto the sand. 'Talos means to protect us,' shouted Heracles as they ran towards the water's edge, 'but I fear he has quite a fight on his hands!'

They stood still, watching fearfully as the gigantic form of Colus closed in on them. Talos was nowhere to be seen.

'Where is he? Where is the Titan?' Medea looked around anxiously; there was no sign of the bronze warrior. 'Has he drowned? Can he swim?'

Heracles said nothing, staring instead at the fearsome spectacle before them. The face of the Colossus could now be clearly seen, the tarnished features twisted by anger. Now less than half a mile away from the shore, the waves caused by her wide strides thrashed against nearby rocks and over the sand.

Suddenly she stopped. There was an eerie silence as she stood stock-still, her face turned towards Medea and Heracles, her dead eyes clearly seeing them.

'If Talos is drowned then we are lost,' whispered Medea.

'Head back for the cave,' shouted Heracles, 'we'll be safe in there.'

'What of the others, my crew? They will fight and, just as surely they will die.'

Before Heracles could speak the surface of the water in front of Colus started to bubble and boil, then with a sudden surge the waters erupted into the air, the gargantuan figure of Talos bursting from the depths to stand face to face with the Colossus. He roared in defiance, raising his arm high as if to strike the other. Colus roared with equal ferocity and defended herself against his crashing blow by holding her arm before her face. The sound of metal striking metal echoed around the hills, gulls screeching in terror as they flew from their cliff-face perches into the air, circling wildly around the scene of conflict.

231

Talos suddenly grasped the arms of Colus, pinning them to her side. Moving closer, he pushed his face close to hers, then stood still.

'What's he doing, what's going on?' said Medea.

'I don't know, I don't understand,' said Heracles, walking once more to the water's edge. They watched in awe as Talos relaxed his grip with one hand and gently ran his fingers over the mammoth breasts of the Colossus. Colus groaned, a loud, deep but clearly pleasurable sound that echoed against the cliffs. Talos let go of her other arm and reached down to grasp the thin, metallic gauze that covered her loins, ripping it from her with the ease of a mortal man tearing thin fabric from his lover. He flung the meshed bronze into the air and grasped Colus between her legs, rubbing his fingers rapidly against the hard surface, the rasping, squealing noise of metal on metal becoming deafening.

The Titan turned to face Heracles, his face, for the first time in his existence showing distinct pleasure. Medea gasped in awe and amusement at the sight of a penis of immense proportions which now miraculously grew from the erstwhile barren crotch of the creature. The life-fluids of Zeus were certainly powerful!

'He's asking to be released,' she said, realising that Talos needed Heracles' blessing before he could leave the island. Heracles nodded and waved to his guardian, then turned his back in respect as the gigantic lovers walked quickly towards the horizon.

The people of Rhodes erected a mock Colossus in memory of their lost immortal. Nothing was ever seen again of Colus and Talos although, legend has it the sounds of their lovemaking can be heard throughout the known world, accompanied by bright flashes of light reflecting the sparks caused by their many copulations, the phenomenon often confused with thunder and lightning.

CHAPTER TWELVE

The Argonauts pulled heavily on their oars, the craft cutting a swathe through the swell as the quest for the Cloak of Aphrodite drew rapidly to a close. Despite the heat of the afternoon the men laboured cheerfully, their sun-bronzed bodies glistening with sweat, their spirits high.

Iolcus could be seen in the distance, the varied hues of the vineyards and groves cloaking the gradual slopes of the hills, the red-roofed buildings nestling by the shore.

Jason regarded the tranquil scene with mixed emotions. Glaucis had been quiet these past few days, and he understood clearly what was going through her mind. The *Phallicis* would have returned already, Medea's journey being much shorter, and his wife would be waiting to welcome her loving husband. Difficult, nay impossible decisions would have to be taken.

He had toyed with the idea of asking Medea if she would be willing to share their marriage-bed with Glaucis but, for all his bravery in battle, he knew he would never summon up sufficient courage to ask her.

He knew also that he loved Glaucis, and that the very idea of being without her was tearing at his heart.

Castor stood at Jason's side. 'Pelias will still try to hold onto his kingdom, Jason,' he said, staring intently at the nearing shoreline, 'you need to have your wits about you.'

'I am well prepared,' he replied, purposely sounding unconcerned. Somehow, the thought of taking the throne of Iolcus, the very reason for undertaking the quests seemed unimportant now. Too much had happened over the previous months.

'You know that the Argonauts are with you to a man,' said Castor, resting his hand on Jason's shoulder, 'and that we will protect you with our very lives.'

Jason looked warmly at the big man and clasped his hand tightly. 'I know, my friend,' he said, gratefully, 'and I am honoured by your words.'

Castor grinned and patted him on the shoulder heavily before returning to his station at the stern of the vessel. Jason looked back at the nearing coastline, now clearly making out the shape of the *Phallicis*, its dark form silhouetted against the white of the harbour wall. Medea would be aboard, waiting to possess him, eager to make up for months of abstinence.

Medea knew that her husband had returned when the *Argo* was merely a speck on the horizon. She watched the slow progress of the vessel from the window of her cabin, resting her arms against the ledge, her naked body bent forward, her bottom being gently licked by the ever attentive Tonis. She thought of Jason's fine, muscular body, the smoothness of his skin and, above all his superb cock which would soon impale her, ravage her with the urgency of a man too long without sexual relief.

She closed her eyes as she felt Tonis prodding his long tongue into her tight anus, arching her back to afford him easier access. He licked her wetly, coating her sweet orifice with spittle, his fingers playfully working in and out of her soaked pussy. She shivered, her nipples hardening as she felt him work two fingers deep inside her bottom, readying her for a much larger intrusion.

The *Argo* would be alongside in less than an hour. This could possibly be the last time that she would be able to allow Tonis to enter her, to feel his youthful, gorgeous body against hers. She sensed a tear straying from the corner of her eye and became angry with herself. Surely she felt no more than lust for this delightful adonis, barely yet a man, his body perfect but his soul still that of a carefree, adventurous child.

Tonis pulled his fingers slowly from the relaxing sheath

of her anus, quickly replacing them with the thick, insistent hardness of his cock, forcing it forwards until it became totally swathed in the tight, welcoming warmth of her bottom. Medea groaned loudly as he began to pump in and out of her, her fingers grasping for her clitoris, her buttocks stiffening rhythmically, clenching his stiff intrusion.

Tonis plunged ever harder, ever deeper, forcing her feet from the floor with each forward thrust. His breathing became heavy, stilted, a clear sign that he was nearing his climax. Medea pulled herself from him, throwing herself to her knees before the trembling youth, taking his iron-hard cock in her hand and rubbing it quickly. Holding it erect against his stomach she licked his tight scrotum, tracing the shapes of his balls, then ran her tongue sensuously along the full length of his cock to the tip, tasting her own scent on his tortured flesh.

She looked up at him, her eyes filled with manic lust and opened her mouth widely, ready to engulf his plum-coloured stalk. Tonis groaned as her lips closed wetly around his thick knob, her hand delicately but unrelentingly pumping his long shaft until, with more a whimper than a cry she felt him throb within the warmth of her oral caress, his sperm rushing to the back of her throat. She sucked and suckled him expertly until his throbbing ceased and he withdrew from her, kneeling before her and kissing her lightly on the mouth. Medea pressed her lips hard against his, pushing her tongue forward into his mouth, sharing the salty texture of his seed with him, a kiss of true love.

The stadium at Iolcus had been completed; a grand, expansive arena fitting for a royal games. Jason surveyed the scene proudly, Medea at his side.

'The athletes have laboured well,' she said, 'this is truly a great monument to the new ruler of Iolcus.'

Jason smiled happily, curling his arm around his wife's small waist. Their meeting had been a little awkward, Medea quizzing him as to why Glaucis had not remained in Icaria, his carefully rehearsed explanations sounding unconvincing in the harsh light of reality. For his part he had found it difficult not to observe the devastatingly hand-some youth who stood shyly in the background, the stranger's eyes never leaving Medea for an instant.

The night, however, had been one of endless fucking; Medea's new desire for anal pleasures the source of surprised delight. He had at first been wary of penetrating her in this way, fearful of injuring her with his huge cock but she had encouraged him and accommodated him happily, with seemingly little discomfort.

As they stood on the hill-top overlooking the stadium watching athletes preparing themselves for the games, Jason's thoughts strayed to his forthcoming audience with Pelias. He had fulfilled the old man's bidding and the Cloak of Aphrodite would be presented. The kingdom was rightfully his.

He was also well aware that Pelias was a wily character, capable of any trickery or deceit. Somehow, Jason felt better knowing that Medea would be at his side. He needed her strength, her self-will. He hugged her tightly, kissing her head with genuine affection, her scent clouding his senses.

'We must go to Pelias,' he said, 'I am anxious to have this business dealt with. Come, we will return to the *Argo* and collect the cloak.'

They walked slowly down the hill-path towards the harbour, their arms entwined. Above them, the sun burned fiercely in a cloudless sky, Apollo's chariot riding high, the Gods at peace.

The *Argo* was virtually deserted when Jason and Medea boarded her, the crew long since departed to savour the delights of the city's bars and brothels. Only Castor remained, sleeping drunkenly against a pile of ropes on the sun-baked deck, snoring like a bull.

They stepped quietly past his huge form and headed for the cabin. Jason was about to open the door when he froze, cautioning Medea with a wave of his hand to be silent. From within the cabin came the unmistakeable sounds of lovers in the full throes of joyous copulation, their moans and cries of shared ecstasy muffled by the thick, wooden door.

236

Jason grinned and lifted the latch quietly. Then, with a sudden movement he pushed the door wide, rushing into his cabin to surprise the errant couple. Light from the doorway filled the small room, Medea and Jason standing before the bed, viewing the startled expressions of Tonis and Glaucis, their youthful nakedness entwined in the embrace of Eros.

Jason was the first to speak as the young couple disentangled themselves, Tonis still sporting a fine, wet erection. 'Glaucis!' he cried, unable to conceal his anger, 'I ... I don't understand, I ...' He suddenly caught the eye of Medea. Fearing her fury he looked furtively around the cabin, as though seeking escape. Medea *was* upset, but not with him.

'Tonis,' she said, sadly, 'I thought your love was for me.'

Jason regarded her quizzically. 'Tonis is your lover?' he said, quietly.

'As Glaucis is yours,' she replied, reaching out and grasping his hand, 'and now they mock us both.'

Glaucis jumped to her feet, angrily. 'Not so!' she said, in a tone whose firmness shocked Jason. 'We cried in each other's arms last night as we were forced to listen to the sounds of your lovemaking throughout the long hours of darkness.'

'The cries we heard just now were not those of sadness,' said Jason, the sight of the beautiful waif filling his thoughts with desire.

'In our hearts we both love you; we needed to share our pain, quell our jealousies.' Glaucis took hold of Jason's and Medea's clasping hands and put them to the puffy, wet lips of her aroused pussy. 'Come,' she said in a whisper, 'come and join us and savour our new unison.'

Jason looked hard at Medea, the wetness of Glaucis' sex-lips running over his trembling fingers. For an agonising few seconds there was no expression in her face, then she smiled and nodded gently. Glaucis grinned broadly and lay back on the bed with her young conquest, the two watching eagerly as Jason and Medea stripped themselves of their garments.

Still a little anxious, Jason stood naked in front of Glaucis, his long cock thickening noticeably under her excited gaze. Medea reached out and took hold of his shaft, rubbing it gently. 'Come, husband,' she breathed, 'let me see you sink your wonderful stalk inside this nymphet's tight little pussy.' She pressed her hand lightly on the small of his back, guiding him towards the impatient girl, holding his now fully hard erection and pointing it directly towards Glaucis' face. The young girl parted her lips, allowing Medea to ease Jason's cock into her soft, wet mouth, the sensuous touch of her tongue fluttering around his stalk causing it to throb with anticipation.

Glaucis sat on the edge of the bed orally serving Jason whilst Medea knelt on the floor between the splayed legs of Tonis who leant back on the mattress, his eyes closed as he savoured the pleasure of her mouth suckling his rock-hard penis.

Jason watched as his wife sucked the youth steadily, feeling no jealousy, no possessiveness, only enjoyment in her delight. He began to move his hips involuntarily as he fucked the beautiful face of Glaucis, her much practised fellatio techniques thrilling him beyond measure. Next to him Medea sucked loudly, before taking Tonis' cock from her mouth and licking his balls and the long, thick stem, worming a finger between his legs to tickle his anus.

Glaucis pulled from Jason and leant over to kiss Tonis fully on the mouth, turning to present her lovely bottom to Jason as she knelt on the soft bed. Jason crouched and gripped the smooth globes of her buttocks, running his tongue wetly between them, savouring the delicate taste of her sweat, prodding the end of his tongue into the tiny, puckered sphincter before licking further down, lapping hungrily over the puffy lips of her open cunt.

He sensed Glaucis move her position and drew his face away from her bottom to be met by the sight of her sharing the taste of Tonis' fine cock with his wife, the two women sucking and licking at the young man's rampant erection for all they were worth. Jason stood and took hold of his own stalk, pointing it to the offered prize of Glaucis' open sex-lips and pressed the thick end to the wet, receptive hole, sinking his shaft deep within her welcoming sheath in one long, slow movement. She groaned as she became used to his size, the sound muffled as she sucked heavily on Tonis' cock.

Medea lifted her face from Tonis' groin and wriggled her head under Glaucis' kneeling form, positioning herself so that she could lick her husband's long stalk as he pumped in and out of her pussy. Jason watched in fascinated awe as Medea lapped at his cock, her tongue occasionally flicking over Glaucis' cunt, the action causing the latter to groan ever louder. The feelings of having a beautiful woman licking his balls and penis whilst he steadily thrust into the warm, wet cunt of another gorgeous conquest drove Jason to distraction. He began to hump rapidly, Medea's tongue still rasping over his exposed length, licking the copious juices from his stem.

Tonis clambered over the supine body of Medea, his not inconsiderable length slipping easily into her soaked pussy, the sight of the handsome youth thrusting quickly into his wife's body bringing Jason to the point of no return. With a loud moan he felt his seed rushing from his body into the tightness of Glaucis' sweet cunt, her vaginal muscles relaxing and contracting, easing every drop into her as he held himself still, allowing his orgasm to take control of his very soul.

After a moment his heavily drooping penis fell from the warmth of Glaucis' sheath, to be taken immediately into Medea's wet mouth. She suckled him until he could take no more, and he fell back onto the floor, happy to watch as Tonis fucked his wife with the force of a wild stallion serving a mare on heat. Glaucis knelt behind the rutting couple and pressed her mouth to Tonis' bottom, licking between his small buttocks as they thrust rapidly up and down, her own backside once more presented for attention.

Despite his sated state, Jason couldn't resist the tempting offer. He crouched behind Glaucis and licked the wide-open lips of her pussy, tasting his own seed, lapping greedily and hearing her groan with pleasure. Quickly, his erection rose again and he plunged its massiveness once more into the nymphet's ever-eager depths, fucking her rapidly, the power of his thrusts forcing her to lie on the back of Tonis, the two men humping in unison. Medea suddenly squealed, the loud, familiar cry that heralded her orgasm. Her body bucked violently despite the weight of three bodies lying over her and, with a resounding crash Tonis, Glaucis and Jason were thrown to the floor, Medea carrying herself through the final throes of her come by rapid use of her fingers.

Jason looked at the tangle of bodies and grinned broadly. 'This is just the beginning!' he announced, proudly, 'there will be much more between us all!'

Medea stood up, shakily. 'Come,' she said, taking Tonis and Jason by the hand, 'let me savour both fine cocks inside my body together. I need to be stretched.'

Jason sat on the edge of the bed, happy to oblige, holding his big tool erect. Medea faced him and squatted over his legs, lowering her body until his stalk slid effortlessly into her saturated pussy. She pushed her hips up and down on him for a few moments, her large breasts swaying heavily with the rhythm of her movements then raised herself so that just the tip of his erection remained inside her. 'Come, Tonis,' she commanded, 'join Jason inside the warmth of my cunt. Fuck me!'

Tonis stood behind her and bent his legs so that his stiff cock pointed directly at her waiting opening, the entrance blocked by Jason's massive tool. Medea caught hold of Tonis' weapon and pressed it against Jason's, lowering her body quickly so that both cocks slid into her sheath in one movement. Jason sensed the strangeness of having another hard erection pressed against his own but, within the confines of Medea's hot pussy the feeling was anything but unpleasant.

Medea began to move up and down on Jason's lap, absorbing the full length of both stalks each time. From his seated position, Jason was able to see every erotic detail of the magnificent copulation, the sight tearing at his groin, causing him to throb against the hard, plunging erection that slid effortlessly against his own.

240

Glaucis reached over and stroked Medea's stretched sex-lips, wetting her finger with the juices of love before pushing it deftly into Medea's anus, the action causing the latter to moan. This was the last straw for Jason who threw his head back and roared, his cock pumping deep within his beautiful wife's body. Almost immediately Tonis pulled his well-soaked cock from Medea's pussy and, pulling Glaucis' finger from her anus plunged his prick in its place, the force of his thrusts pushing the quickly flaccid member of Jason out of its wet sheath. Jason lay beneath the couple, watching adoringly as Medea was humped mercilessly until she squealed once more in violent orgasm, falling heavily on Jason's body, sobbing loudly with pure elation.

Tonis pulled from within her, his erection still stiff. Glaucis knelt before him and took it deep within her mouth, sucking noisily as she pumped his raging stalk with both of her small hands. He came almost immediately, Glaucis swallowing hard as she drained his body of its seed. Exhausted, he fell back onto the bed, his cock lying wet and flaccid on his stomach. Glaucis caught Jason's glance and grinned broadly, running her tongue suggestively across her teeth. Jason closed his eyes to the temptation; perhaps in a little while . . .

The four lovers lay quietly for a time, each with their own thoughts. Jason had never felt happier; the shared love of two lovely women . . . surely the gods must be smiling on him this day!

Pelias lay on his couch in the grim throne-room looking, if anything, even more wizened than before. The scowl on his face betrayed his true emotions as Jason and Medea entered.

'Do you have it?' he barked, without uttering a word of greeting, 'do you have the cloak?'

Jason stepped forward, holding out the folded garment. 'I have it, Pelias, now it is your turn to fulfil our bargain.'

The old man struggled to his feet and grasped the cloak. 'Let me have it, let me have it,' he cried, pulling at the cloth roughly. Jason held it firmly within his grip.

'You will have it when I have the crown, and your oath that you will leave this kingdom forever.'

Pelias looked at him evilly. 'You fool,' he cackled, 'I can have you killed at a single command and take the cloak from your slaughtered body!' He wrenched the garment with a force that shocked Jason and wrapped it around his thin, stooped frame. 'I feel it!' he cried, his face breaking into a manic grin, 'I feel the strength returning to my loins!' He wrapped the cloak tightly around himself, his expression one of sheer joy as the garment worked its magic. Then, with a flourish he threw open the cloak, revealing that he now sported a magnificent erection, a thick, gnarled stem and plum-sized end, the large slit weeping with desire. Jason turned his head in disgust at the sight.

His eyes darted around the room. 'Who will savour my new-found strength first,' he said, rubbing his hands like a miser. The small group of naked young girls that permanently graced the throne-room cringed back in terror at the sight of his monster stalk. Pelias leapt at one hapless girl, a delicate beauty of flawless complexion who squealed in fear as he threw her onto the couch. With a triumphant cry he launched himself upon her, impaling her immediately, thrusting furiously as the cloak slipped from his body to the floor.

Jason reached down and picked up the garment, carefully folding it again. 'Come,' he said to Medea, his voice barely concealing his revulsion, 'the cloak has done its work. Let us leave this place before we are made sick by the sights inflicted upon us.'

The two left the room, the cries of the young virgin echoing in their ears.

The eve of the great games came quickly, just two days after Jason's arrival. There was to be a great feast to honour the new king of Iolcus, arranged by Medea without, of course, the permission of Pelias, who still refused to hand over the crown.

Pelias himself had not been seen since the sudden transformation of his spent libido, remaining locked in his bed-chamber, constantly demanding a supply of young maidens to satisfy his carnal urges, his needs seemingly insatiable. One by one the girls staggered from the room, their bodies ravaged and exhausted, speaking in awe of the old man's amazing staying power.

Jason had spent the days watching the athletes training, marvelling in particular at the prowess of his friend Heracles, who threatened to win every contest with little effort. His nights, however were spent in the company of Medea, Glaucis and Tonis, their relationship becoming firmer with every ecstatic moment. Every conceivable sexual game was played by the four lovers, their variety bounded only by the imaginations of the participants.

Medea and Jason were readying themselves for the feast, Glaucis and Tonis having already set off for the great hall in the palace of Iolcus. The evening was warm, allowing Medea to dress in a sheer silken dress, the diaphanous material accentuating rather than concealing her superb figure. Jason was dressed in satin pantaloons and a fine, silk shirt. He felt uncomfortably over-dressed, his normal garb at any occasion being a simple loin-cloth. Nevertheless, as Medea had stressed, he was to be *king*, and appearances mattered.

There was a sudden cacophony from outside their room, shouts and cries followed by the clash of metal upon stone. Jason grabbed his knife as the door burst open and a young girl rushed in to fall at his feet, sobbing hysterically. Castor followed, making to grab the wretched girl from the floor.

'She forced her way through four of us to get to you!' he shouted, 'she must be possessed!' He tugged at the intruder's hair. Jason put his hand out to stop him.

'Leave her, she is clearly distressed. Leave her be.' Jason knelt before the young girl, holding her chin in his hand, gently raising her tear-stained face. 'What is it, child? What ails you so?'

'Oh, my lord,' sobbed the girl, her tears falling wetly onto his hand, 'it is the king, Pelias. He's gone insane!'

'Insane?' asked Medea, kneeling at the girl's side, 'what do you mean?'

The youngster was managing to take control of herself. Breathing deeply, she continued, 'My lord Pelias has impaled every available maiden in Iolcus with his fearsome stalk, never letting up for a moment. He rushes from body to body, ramming it in as hard as he can, caring nothing for the wishes or desires of his women, babbling all the time dementedly. I tell you he has gone mad! I fear for the lives of the girls in his bed-chamber; he becomes crueller by the hour in his insatiable demands!'

Jason raised the girl to her feet. 'Stay here with Medea,' he said, 'and I will pay a call on Pelias. The time has come to deal with the old lecher once and for all!' Tucking his knife into the belt of his pantaloons he walked quickly from the room and headed towards the king's quarters.

Outside the bed-chamber two girls lay on the stone floor sobbing, their eyes staring vacantly into the distance. Jason stepped over their prone bodies and pushed open the heavy door, nervously clutching the hilt of his dagger.

The room was in near darkness, the only light emanating from a solitary torch set in the wall above the large bed. As his eyes became accustomed to the half-light, Jason saw the figure on the bed, a crouched, shaking form that had to be the king.

'Pelias?' said Jason, cautiously walking towards the bed, 'are you feeling unwell?'

The old man raised his head slowly, his features haggard and weary. He opened his mouth as if to speak, even finding this simple act onerous. 'Help me, Jason,' he said, his voice barely audible, 'I am cursed.'

Jason moved forward. Pelias was trembling because he was rapidly rubbing his firm erection that rose incongruously from his withered groin. Jason tried not to look at the unpleasant sight. 'I cannot stop,' said Pelias, realising his distaste, 'I keep fucking and fucking and, when there is no wench to serve me I must do this. But I cannot come! I cannot come! I fear I am dying of exhaustion!'

'He *is* dying, Jason.' The voice belonged to a young woman who stood in the shadows behind the bed. She walked forward into the light, her face instantly recognisable.

244

'Paphia!' exclaimed Jason, 'how do you come to be in Iolcus?'

'You are a great warrior and even greater lover, Jason, but your mind is not so sharp. You know me as Paphia, others know me better as Aphrodite.'

Jason's eyes widened as the beautiful woman opened her cloak to reveal the shimmering dress of a goddess, her face and body suddenly bathed in light that seemed to emanate from within her perfect form. 'But I, we . . .' stammered Jason, falling to his knees in submission.

'Yes, Jason, you have made love to a goddess. Few mortals have attempted such a thing and lived. But it was I who tricked you; I cannot punish you for that. I have retrieved my girdle and cloak and will return to Cyprus with them, and I must have retribution for their theft. You will never again adventure forth, Jason, you will remain here, as king of Iolcus. You will marry your Glaucis but Medea will become jealous and wreak a terrible revenge leaving you to wander the lonely beaches, dreaming of past glories until you will die, a hapless victim of one you love. This will be your punishment, although you will forget my words the instant I leave.' She looked across at the figure of the old man, his trembling hand stopped. 'See, Pelias is no more; Iolcus is yours.'

Jason watched in wide-eyed amazement as the figure of the goddess gradually faded, and with it his memory of her prophetic words.

The death of Pelias seemed to bring even more joy to the gathering at the great feast, his passing lamented by no-one, least of all the many deflowered virgins of the past two nights. Jason sat at the head of a mammoth table, eating and drinking his fill, Medea at one side and Glaucis at the other. All around them athletes and maidens laughed and cavorted, the scene gradually descending into one of bacchanalia. Sexual contests were arranged, wagers accepted. Men proudly measured their erect stalks, winning or losing bets lightheartedly. Soon, all clothing was removed, the room filled with heaving, sighing bodies, the scents and sounds of sexual ecstasy pervading the entire scene.

245

Medea suddenly announced that she would accommodate eight men simultaneously and, much to everyone's delight proceeded to demonstrate her skill. Causing one young man to lie on his back she impaled herself on his stiff stalk, her sheath already wet from the evening's absurdities. Beckoning to a second stud she guided his cock to her pert bottom, sighing as it sank deep into her anus.

As her lovers fucked her nether regions she took hold of two more firm erections and pulled them to her mouth, taking both plum-sized ends within her pouting lips. Bidding two more athletes to stand behind her she raised her feet to their groins, caressing their genitals with her toes whilst her hands gripped and rubbed the seventh and eighth stalk, to the rapturous applause of her audience.

Jason laughed uproariously, banging his hand on the table to signal his approval. Medea disentangled herself from the group of admiring lovers, a beaming smile on her face, looking directly at Glaucis, challenging her to go one better. Glaucis looked around herself nervously, then stood up slowly, her slender nakedness displayed for all to see. 'Enough of these childish games,' she said, awkwardly, 'let's just fuck!'

She threw herself on the reclining body of a young, black warrior and grasped for his rapidly rising erection, forcing it inside her quickly. Medea caught Jason's glance and grinned, a smile of victory.

Jason decided to leave the assembled throng to their indulgences, the surfeit of wine beginning to cloud his thoughts. Out in the fresh, cool air he felt better, glad of the peace and quiet of the garden. The full moon illuminated the trees and bushes in the palace groves in an eerie but beautiful way, the silvered branches coldly twisted, their leaves shimmering in the light breeze. He felt good to be alive.

'Jason.' The voice was husky, warm and very feminine. He peered in the direction of the sound to see the familiar shape of Atalanta moving from the shadows, the moonlight catching her naked flesh, highlighting her sturdy sensuality. Jason felt a stirring in his loins as he gazed in

246

admiration at her large, full breasts and the gently curving slope of her stomach to the downy-covered treasures between her muscular but shapely legs. 'Jason,' she breathed again, 'come, race with me now.'

He shook his head, wistfully. 'No, I have eaten and drunk too much. I would never catch you.'

Atalanta reached out and took hold of his thickening penis, rubbing it slowly as she stared meaningfully into his eyes. 'The road is rocky and pitted; I may stumble in the darkness and you would surely reach me. My loins have been too long unplundered; I need you to race with me now!'

The invitation was too much for Jason to resist, the sight of Atalanta's firm bottom as she turned to run in the direction of the hills enough to break any man's will. He began to run steadily, pacing himself, knowing that she had the stamina of a race-horse and that perseverance would be the only way to capture her.

The moon disappeared behind a large cloud, the consequent darkness total. Jason peered hard into the blackness, desperately attempting to stay on the treacherous road and avoid running headlong into the trees and sharp-spined bushes that lined the route. On and on he ran, his feet sore from the rough ground, his heart thumping, his long penis swinging from side to side, the urge to possess the lovely amazon driving him forward.

He stopped, exhausted. Holding his breath he listened hard. There was no sound, no thump of running feet or swish of bare thigh against the long grass. Atalanta must be far away by now; he had been foolish to attempt to race after such a grand feast. He began to walk slowly back in the direction he had run, his breathing short and heavy.

The moon broke free from its shroud of darkness and bathed the scene around him once more with its ghostly light. Jason stopped short, his heart pounding. Close to the side of the road, the very place where he had been running blindly just moments before the ground gave way in a sheer drop to the sea below. He closed his eyes and thanked Hera silently for her guidance, realising how close he had been to meeting his death.

'Jason!' The voice was Atalanta's, but the tone was harsh and fearful.

'Atalanta? Where are you?'

'Jason, I am trapped, help me.'

He stepped cautiously to the edge of the cliff and looked over, seeing the large moon's reflection broken in the surging waves below. 'Atalanta, I can't see you, where are you?'

'Here, Jason, by your feet, I dare not move.'

Jason knelt on the treacherous edge and peered under the overhanging rock. Atalanta stood on a tiny ledge, her hand clutching a small tuft of grass, her whole body trembling with fear.

'Jason, please help me. The grass is breaking free in my grip!'

Lying flat on his stomach, he reached over and managed to grasp her wrist, feeling her hand clasp his arm, the fingernails digging into his flesh. Summoning all the strength that Zeus had granted him he pulled for all he was worth, steadily dragging the terrified girl to safety.

Atalanta lay on the grass, panting heavily, her tanned skin soaked in sweat. 'Oh, Jason,' she sighed, gratefully, 'I thought I was dead. Thank you for saving me.'

Jason stroked her head with his hand, more to calm her than in affection. 'Come,' he said, getting to his feet, 'let me escort you back to the feast.'

Atalanta stood and faced him, her hand gripping his elbow. 'No, Jason. You have raced with me and caught me. I must give myself to you. I cannot refuse.'

'But you fell . . .'

'No matter. The Gods have decreed it; I must submit.' She spoke grandly, but a coy smile played across her lovely face. Jason grinned, his penis rising in response to her invitation.

'Then we must not disobey the Gods,' he said, leading her to a soft, grassy area further away from the cliff edge.

They lay together quietly for a moment, Atalanta still recovering from her ordeal. Jason stroked the firm flesh of her thighs and stomach, the muscles hardened from the labours of the quest, the skin taut and silky-smooth. She

248

sighed as his fingertips strayed onto her large breast, the nipple hardening immediately under his touch. He reached over and took the long, thick nipple in his mouth, sucking it in and out, his teeth rasping against the tender bud. With his hand he found her other breast, squeezing the nipple to hardness, pinching it playfully.

Slowly, he ran his other hand down, down over her flat stomach, down along the smooth curve to touch the coarse hair that signalled the prize was near. Teasingly, he circled her pussy with his fingertip, avoiding touching her sex flesh. Atalanta moved her hips in response, desperately trying to force him to touch her where she wanted him, but still he teased, all the time suckling her breast, the sound of her pounding heart echoing in his ear.

He moved his hand further between her legs and allowed his fingertip to touch her anus; then, with a slowness that must have felt agonising to the hapless virgin he slid his finger steadily upward, slicing through the creamy-wet lips of her cunt until it touched the erect bud of her clitoris.

Atalanta groaned and shuddered, this first intimate touch of any hand but her own clearly delighting her. Jason fingered her expertly, occasionally pressing his hand over her pussy, feeling the moistness increase and the lips begin to part in readiness.

He took his mouth from her nipple and ran his tongue slowly down her body, following the route taken by his fingers, tasting her fresh sweat and savouring her womanly scent. Moving round, he knelt between her legs and cupped her buttocks in his large hands, raising them from the ground. She lay still, her back arched, her shoulders resting on the soft grass, her pussy presented to him in sensuous submission.

He looked at her face. She was beautiful, nervous and very aroused. He ran his tongue provocatively over his lips and smiled then, gripping her bottom tightly he bent forward and pressed his mouth to her cunt, his tongue delving into her pouting sex-lips, pushing quickly in and out of her tight sheath. She shivered and moaned, her hand clutching the back of his head, the fingers gripping his hair.

He lapped hungrily, flicking the tip of his tongue incessantly over the hard bud, her thighs moving against his mouth in response. She was ready, ready to lose the virginity that she had prized for so long.

Jason leant back, still on his knees and holding Atalanta's bottom a few inches from the grass. His cock stood out hard and willing, the peach-shaped end almost touching the soaked, puffy-red lips it was about to defile. He moved forward slowly, the knob cleaving the warm petals of flesh, the gentle barrier of her hymen parting with the ease of a stone breaking the surface of the water. Steadily, he sank ever deeper, moving cautiously in and out, more and more of his massive cock becoming absorbed by her delightfully tight sheath.

'Oh, Jason,' she breathed, 'at last I am fucked, at last. Why have I waited so long?'

Their groins met, their pubic hair meshing together, his full length inside her. He held himself almost motionless, his cock throbbing inside its heavenly glove, juices of his excitement entering her warmth, easing his task. Gradually he began again to move in and out, drawing much of his long stalk from her then plunging back, the head of his monstrous erection touching her cervix with each forward thrust, her groans of pleasure ringing in his ears.

She raised her legs and held them vertically then drew them back, bending at the knee and pressing her thighs against her superb breasts, every inch of his cock now accepted within her shuddering body. She was coming; he could see it on her face. He raised himself on his hands and toes, his hips moving rapidly, the full length of his shaft sliding in and out of her ravaged flesh. Her eyes took on a wild, startled expression, a long, low moan uttering from deep within her throat. Then, with a howl she came, her fingers gripping his buttocks painfully, her crotch pressed hard against his.

Jason tensed his groin, forcing his orgasm, wanting to share her joy. Suddenly he was lost, the sperm gushing into her, his stiffness throbbing heavily against the hot, gripping flesh of her pussy. He shook visibly, his head held back, his expression twisted as though in pain, groaning and panting as each throb took more of his strength, the intenseness of his release tearing at every nerve of his body.

Jason and Atalanta sat quietly, their backs resting against an old olive-tree, staring into the moonlit distance. He mused over his good fortune; his future as the king of Iolcus, his life with Medea and Glaucis and now, even Atalanta had given her charms to him.

There would be other quests, other adventures. Medea would guard his kingdom, or perhaps he would marry Glaucis and she would rule in his absence. He turned and kissed Atalanta lightly on the cheek. She snuggled warmly against him, wrapping her arms around his waist.

Yes, truly the Gods were with him.

THE END ACCORDING TO CLASSICAL MYTHOLOGY

Sadly, Aphrodite's prophecy was nearer the truth. Jason married Glaucis, but Medea became jealous and gave her rival a lethal wedding present, a cloak which enveloped the bride in flames. Jason ended his days wandering the beaches, remembering past quests and adventures, but never again venturing into the unknown. He died when he was struck by a falling piece of timber from the wreck of his original vessel, the *Argo*.

NEW BOOKS

Coming up from Nexus and Black Lace

The Cloak of Aphrodite by Kendal Grahame
November 1994   Price: £4.99   ISBN: 0 352 32954 8
Having completed the quest for the Golden Fleece, Jason must
embark on an even more demanding mission: the recovery of
a mythical cloak with aphrodisiac powers. Medea has the task
of bringing back the world's most gifted athletes. Kept apart
on their respective missions, the lovers vent their desires on
the men, women and gods they meet en route.

His Mistress's Voice by G. C. Scott
November 1994   Price: £4.99   ISBN: 0 352 32961 0
Tom can't believe his luck when Beth picks him up and takes
him home. Her proclivities become clear when she ties the
young man up – but when her dominant friend Harriet ar-
rives, things get even kinkier.

Melinda and the Countess by Susanna Hughes
December 1994   Price: £4.99   ISBN: 0 352 32957 2
Everyone's favourite blonde submissive has arrived in Paris to
meet her new Master – or in this case, Mistress. Beautiful and
capricious, the Countess wastes no time in demonstrating just
how cruel, and how loving, she can be.

The House of Maldona by Yolanda Celbridge
December 1994   Price: £4.99   ISBN: 0 352 32962 9
Deep in Andalucia lies a world all its own: a world devoted to
discipline. A group of women calling themselves the House of
Maldona act out all kinds of bizarre erotic rituals. Interference
or disobedience earn severe punishment – as Jane, on holiday
in the area, finds out.

BLACK
lace

Wicked Work by Pamela Kyle
November 1994   Price: £4.99   ISBN: 0 352 32958 0
All her life, Suzie Carlton has been in control. Now, as a jour-
nalist on a major women's magazine, she holds as much power
as ever. But a meeting with the masterful Michael shows her
that by nature she is sexually submissive. Will her budding
masochistic impulses undermine her career?

Cassandra's Chateau by Fredrica Alleyn
November 1994   Price: £4.99   ISBN: 0 352 32955 6
Cassandra has been living happily and sinfully with the Baron
for eighteen months. Now a friend's daughter has come to
stay, and there is a familiar gleam in the Baron's eyes. The
dark, erotic games look set to begin again . . . This is the sequel
to the hugely popular *Cassandra's Conflict*.

Dream Lover by Katrina Vincenzi
December 1994   Price: £4.99   ISBN: 0 352 32956 4
Film producer Gemma de la Mare is holidaying in Brittany
when she feels a powerful presence nearby. While she is unable to identify the source of this overwhelming sexual aura,
her desires begin to boil within her. Can she find her dream
lover before she loses control?

Path of the Tiger by Cleo Cordell
December 1994   Price: £4.99   ISBN: 0 352 32959 9
India in the 1850s: Amy Spencer, a ravishing young English-
woman, is exploring this land of exotic pleasures. One of the
many exciting people she meets is Ravinder, handsome son of
the Maharaja, who shows her the great wisdom he has ac-
quired – chiefly from the Kama Sutra.

NEXUS BACKLIST

Where a month is marked on the right, this book will not be
published until that month in 1994. All books are priced £4.99
unless another price is given.

CONTEMPORARY EROTICA

CONTOURS OF DARKNESS	Marco Vassi		
THE DEVIL'S ADVOCATE	Anonymous		
THE DOMINO TATTOO	Cyrian Amberlake	£4.50	
THE DOMINO ENIGMA	Cyrian Amberlake		
THE DOMINO QUEEN	Cyrian Amberlake		
ELAINE	Stephen Ferris		
EMMA'S SECRET WORLD	Hilary James		
EMMA ENSLAVED	Hilary James		
FALLEN ANGELS	Kendal Grahame		
THE FANTASIES OF JOSEPHINE SCOTT	Josephine Scott		
THE GENTLE DEGENERATES	Marco Vassi		
HEART OF DESIRE	Maria del Rey		
HELEN – A MODERN ODALISQUE	Larry Stern		
HIS MISTRESS'S VOICE	G. C. Scott		Nov
THE HOUSE OF MALDONA	Yolanda Celbridge		Dec
THE INSTITUTE	Maria del Rey		
SISTERHOOD OF THE INSTITUTE	Maria del Rey		Sep
JENNIFER'S INSTRUCTION	Cyrian Amberlake		
MELINDA AND THE MASTER	Susanna Hughes		
MELINDA AND ESMERALDA	Susanna Hughes		
MELINDA AND THE COUNTESS	Susanna Hughes		Dec
MIND BLOWER	Marco Vassi		

MS DEEDES AT HOME	Carole Andrews	£4.50	
MS DEEDES ON PARADISE ISLAND	Carole Andrews		
THE NEW STORY OF O	Anonymous		
OBSESSION	Maria del Rey		
ONE WEEK IN THE PRIVATE HOUSE	Esme Ombreux		
THE PALACE OF FANTASIES	Delver Maddingley		
THE PALACE OF HONEYMOONS	Delver Maddingley		
THE PALACE OF EROS	Delver Maddingley		
PARADISE BAY	Maria del Rey		
THE PASSIVE VOICE	G. C. Scott		
THE SALINE SOLUTION	Marco Vassi		
STEPHANIE	Susanna Hughes		
STEPHANIE'S CASTLE	Susanna Hughes		
STEPHANIE'S REVENGE	Susanna Hughes		
STEPHANIE'S DOMAIN	Susanna Hughes		
STEPHANIE'S TRIAL	Susanna Hughes		
STEPHANIE'S PLEASURE	Susanna Hughes		Sep
THE TEACHING OF FAITH	Elizabeth Bruce		
THE TRAINING GROUNDS	Sarah Veitch		

EROTIC SCIENCE FICTION

ADVENTURES IN THE PLEASUREZONE	Delaney Silver		
RETURN TO THE PLEASUREZONE	Delaney Silver		
FANTASYWORLD	Larry Stern		Oct
WANTON	Andrea Arven		

ANCIENT & FANTASY SETTINGS

CHAMPIONS OF LOVE	Anonymous		
CHAMPIONS OF PLEASURE	Anonymous		
CHAMPIONS OF DESIRE	Anonymous		
THE CLOAK OF APHRODITE	Kendal Grahame		Nov
SLAVE OF LIDIR	Aran Ashe	£4.50	
DUNGEONS OF LIDIR	Aran Ashe		
THE FOREST OF BONDAGE	Aran Ashe	£4.50	
PLEASURE ISLAND	Aran Ashe		
WITCH QUEEN OF VIXANIA	Morgana Baron		

EDWARDIAN, VICTORIAN & OLDER EROTICA

ANNIE	Evelyn Culber	
ANNIE AND THE SOCIETY	Evelyn Culber	Oct
BEATRICE	Anonymous	
CHOOSING LOVERS FOR JUSTINE	Aran Ashe	
GARDENS OF DESIRE	Roger Rougiere	
THE LASCIVIOUS MONK	Anonymous	
LURE OF THE MANOR	Barbra Baron	
MAN WITH A MAID 1	Anonymous	
MAN WITH A MAID 2	Anonymous	
MAN WITH A MAID 3	Anonymous	
MEMOIRS OF A CORNISH GOVERNESS	Yolanda Celbridge	
TIME OF HER LIFE	Josephine Scott	
VIOLETTE	Anonymous	

THE JAZZ AGE

BLUE ANGEL DAYS	Margarete von Falkensee	
BLUE ANGEL NIGHTS	Margarete von Falkensee	
BLUE ANGEL SECRETS	Margarete von Falkensee	
CONFESSIONS OF AN ENGLISH MAID	Anonymous	
PLAISIR D'AMOUR	Anne-Marie Villefranche	
FOLIES D'AMOUR	Anne-Marie Villefranche	
JOIE D'AMOUR	Anne-Marie Villefranche	
MYSTERE D'AMOUR	Anne-Marie Villefranche	
SECRETS D'AMOUR	Anne-Marie Villefranche	
SOUVENIR D'AMOUR	Anne-Marie Villefranche	
WAR IN HIGH HEELS	Piers Falconer	

SAMPLERS & COLLECTIONS

EROTICON 1	ed. J-P Spencer		
EROTICON 2	ed. J-P Spencer		
EROTICON 3	ed. J-P Spencer		
EROTICON 4	ed. J-P Spencer		
NEW EROTICA 1	ed. Esme Ombreux		
NEW EROTICA 2	ed. Esme Ombreux		
THE FIESTA LETTERS	ed. Chris Lloyd	£4.50	

NON-FICTION

FEMALE SEXUAL AWARENESS	B & E McCarthy	£5.99	
HOW TO DRIVE YOUR MAN WILD IN BED	Graham Masterton		
HOW TO DRIVE YOUR WOMAN WILD IN BED	Graham Masterton		
LETTERS TO LINZI	Linzi Drew		
LINZI DREW'S PLEASURE GUIDE	Linzi Drew		

Please send me the books I have ticked above.

Name   . . . .

Address   . . . .

                . . . .

             . . . . Post code   . . . .

Send to: **Cash Sales, Nexus Books, 332 Ladbroke Grove, London W10 5AH**

Please enclose a cheque or postal order, made payable to **Nexus Books**, to the value of the books you have ordered plus postage and packing costs as follows:

   UK and BFPO – £1.00 for the first book, 50p for the second book, and 30p for each subsequent book to a maximum of £3.00;

   Overseas (including Republic of Ireland) – £2.00 for the first book, £1.00 for the second book, and 50p for each subsequent book.

If you would prefer to pay by VISA or ACCESS/MASTERCARD, please write your card number here:

Please allow up to 28 days for delivery

— — — —   — — — —   — — — —   — — — —

Signature: ——————————————————————————